D1112680

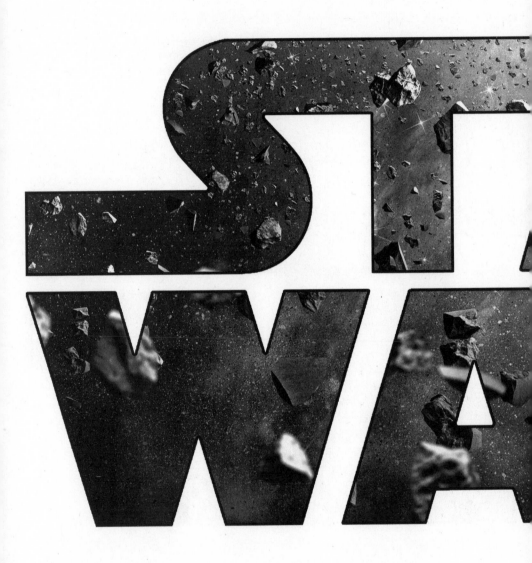

™

STAR WARS™
JEDI
BATTLE SCARS™

SAM MAGGS

RANDOM HOUSE

WORLDS
NEW YORK

Published in the United States by Random House Worlds, an imprint of Random House, a division of Penguin Random House LLC, New York.

RANDOM HOUSE is a registered trademark, and RANDOM HOUSE WORLDS and colophon are trademarks of Penguin Random House LLC.

Hardback ISBN 978-0-593-59860-3
International ISBN 978-0-593-72267-1
Ebook ISBN 978-0-593-59861-0

Printed in the United States of America on acid-free paper

randomhousebooks.com

2 4 6 8 9 7 5 3 1

First Edition

Book design by Elizabeth A. D. Eno

For everyone who has gone out in the world
and found their own family:
We're never hiding who we really are, ever again.

THE STAR WARS NOVELS TIMELINE

THE HIGH REPUBLIC

Convergence
The Battle of Jedha
Cataclysm

Light of the Jedi
The Rising Storm
Tempest Runner
The Fallen Star

Dooku: Jedi Lost
Master and Apprentice

I THE PHANTOM MENACE

II ATTACK OF THE CLONES

Brotherhood
The Thrawn Ascendancy Trilogy
Dark Disciple: A Clone Wars Novel

III REVENGE OF THE SITH

Inquisitor: Rise of the Red Blade
Catalyst: A Rogue One Novel
Lords of the Sith
Tarkin
Jedi: Battle Scars

SOLO

Thrawn
A New Dawn: A Rebels Novel
Thrawn: Alliances
Thrawn: Treason

ROGUE ONE

IV A NEW HOPE

Battlefront II: Inferno Squad
Heir to the Jedi
Doctor Aphra
Battlefront: Twilight Company

V THE EMPIRE STRIKES BACK

VI RETURN OF THE JEDI

The Princess and the Scoundrel
The Alphabet Squadron Trilogy
The Aftermath Trilogy
Last Shot

Shadow of the Sith
Bloodline
Phasma
Canto Bight

VII THE FORCE AWAKENS

VIII THE LAST JEDI

Resistance Reborn
Galaxy's Edge: Black Spire

IX THE RISE OF SKYWALKER

A long time ago in a galaxy far, far away. . . .

CHAPTER 1

Today was going to be a good day for the Jedi.

Jedi Knight Cal Kestis was going to make certain of that.

Sure, it was possible that he was one of maybe only two Jedi left.

But those Jedi? They were going to have a good day.

"Hey, buddy, things looking clear?" Cal asked, his voice reverberating in his ears inside his helmet. From his back, Cal heard two little taps from his droid, BD-1's way of communicating with him while on a stealth mission. Cal could hear BD-1's trills via comms, but sound was risky while sneaking and the droid often preferred to communicate by a more rapid and tactile method, knowing the rest of the crew couldn't understand him anyway. "Thanks, Beedee. Have I told you lately you're the best?"

A pause. Then:

Tap.

Cal laughed. "Well, this is me telling you. I won't slack off on it again."

Tap tap.

A damn good day.

Which wasn't usually the case, when a guy was crouched on a small, fast-moving space rock hurtling around a large asteroid in the middle of deep space, but Cal's life wasn't usual, and he preferred it that way. Kitted out in a full space suit, Cal took stock of his surroundings, breathing in recycled air slowly and steadily so as not to waste it. The orbital debris field circling the asteroid was dense; Cal had to make his way, leaping shard by rocky shard, each one a step closer to the main asteroid at its center, a massive excavated rock, home to a Haxion Brood base Cal and his crew were currently attempting to infiltrate. Ironic, considering the last time Cal had been around a Brood base he'd been trying to break *out* of it. That time, on Ordo Eris, he'd been captured. This time, the better move was to get someone on the rock first in order to disable the security systems so that nothing would pick up the *Stinger Mantis*, Cal's ship, entering from orbit.

And the best way to do *that* was for someone to hop, from tiny rock to tiny rock, all the way down to the surface of the big rock. From one moving asteroid to the next, flying through space without a tether.

No problem.

Taking a deep breath, squinting his eyes in concentration, Cal bent his knees before pushing off from the craggy rock beneath his boots.

It didn't take much out here. One jump, and Cal was—*airborne* wasn't the right word, without atmosphere or air to be found. It was more like floating. Different from flying, entirely; when Cal pushed himself into the air with the Force, he always felt that swoop in his stomach, the familiar lurch of his still-very-human body alerting him to the fact that he was far, far too high above land for good sense. But out here in space, this felt more like swimming, forward propulsion, his body with no concept of up or down, right or wrong, too high or too low. Forward, floating, only.

He missed the little swoop.

Cal aimed himself toward the next fragment asteroid, soaring straight for it with purpose. Slowly but surely.

The first time his master, Jaro Tapal, had taken Cal out into space, he'd told his Padawan: Once you set something to motion in space, it will continue to move in exactly that way—the same direction, and at the same speed—unless acted upon by an unbalanced force.

Today, for whatever it meant, Cal was that unbalanced force.

Arms straight out in front of him, Cal's hands scrabbled for purchase the second they made contact with the next floating fragment. Cal's impact sent the little asteroid, and him, spinning. He hung on for dear life until, after what felt like ten minutes but was surely just a few seconds, BD engaged Cal's gription boots and, magnetically driven, they came slamming forward into the rock, stabilizing the Jedi.

Cal had—in polite company, he would say "rescued"—these boots off a Haxion Brood bounty hunter, part of a kit the hunter would no longer be needing after Cal and Merrin had dealt with him. The boots were one of the best salvages Cal and his crew had made to date.

Shakily, Cal let go of the rock and slowly returned to a standing position. He was glad this was his second-to-last jump. He was used to swinging around from handhold to handhold, making giant leaps of faith first as he worked as a scrapper back on Bracca and then as he infiltrated one shady Imperial facility or another over the years, but for some contrarian reason, the pull of gravity was a comfort to Cal. Did it mean, if he missed a jump or his climbing claws failed him, that he'd go plummeting to the ground in almost certain death? Sure. A little bit, probably. But it also meant that he *wouldn't* be condemned to die floating away alone in the void until he became a dried-out but freakishly well-preserved Jedicicle.

That was way, way worse.

"Did you live?" Merrin's voice crackled to life over Cal's comms. Her accent and often wry way of speaking made the question come off glib, like she didn't really care about the answer one way or another.

"Did you hear something, Beedee?" Cal asked his droid rhetorically, knowing Merrin well enough to know that the sound of his voice over comms would be enough of an answer to satisfy Merrin's sarcastic but still genuine query. "Sounded almost like . . . someone who was worried about us?" he added in a sing-songy voice.

"Must have been your imagination," Merrin responded contemplatively. There was a beat of silence as though she were deep in thought. "Yes, next time we're hard up for credits we'll just drop you in a cantina. You'll survive."

"Hey," a voice interrupted—Greez. "If anybody's gonna be makin' tips for their looks around here, it's me. You bipeds don't appreciate what a catch I am to those with real taste out there."

A flurry of taps was the response from Cal's back. He made sure to momentarily turn off his comms before he let out his laughter.

"If we're done, crew"—Cere's more cere-ious (Cal's favorite way of thinking of his mentor and Jedi Master) voice commanded attention, even over the comms—"Cal, how long until you make landfall and can grant us access?"

Back to business, then. Always.

Now on the precipice of entering the Brood base, Cal took another moment to survey the situation in front of him. This wasn't a typical mission; none of the *Mantis* crew's exploits were, he supposed. But even for them, this was a bit of a reach.

He stood on a small, spinning rock in the middle of open space, surrounded by the debris of a ruined planet. What was once, Cal had been told, a verdant, bright home to millions had been chewed up and spit out at the hands of one Empire or corporation or another; it was hard to keep track, after a point. What remained were only the fragments of what once was, shards and dust and islands in the void, orbiting the former planet's solid-iron core.

It was the core Cal set his sights on now, directly above him—the core, and the Haxion Brood base dug directly into it, surrounded by a hastily assembled outer ring with an assortment of hastily assembled shacks and market stalls, and covered by a vacuum-proof bubble of shielding, with sensors to detect ships of any size.

But not, conveniently, to detect anything human-sized that happened to be equipped with a jetpack.

Or in Cal's case, equipped with enough foolhardy bravery to float in without one.

Greez had explained the mechanics of the base's sensor system during a pre-mission briefing. The shield's sensor field swept the asteroid just fast enough to detect anything bigger than a person, but just slow enough to allow bounty hunters individual access to their base without being monitored.

But the *Mantis* crew were the best at what they did. And they were doing it right now.

And that's why Cal was having such a damn good day.

"Eyes on the landing pad," Cal responded to Cere. "Launching in three—two—"

For the—blessedly—last time today, after what had felt like hours of leaping from rock to rock across the asteroid belt, Cal felt BD disengage his boots and he pushed off from the final rock, launching himself straight up. He experienced a brief moment of disorientation approaching the base headfirst: Up was down and down was up and did anything really matter in space? This was why Cal preferred gravity.

"Greez, you better be right about this," Cal muttered, mostly to himself, but without turning off his comms, as his head approached the magnetic shield at a rapid pace.

He felt his helmet make contact with the shield bubble and, for just a second, he felt resistance—like when you pushed on Greez's infamous Gelatin Surprise (the surprise was that it was *full* of salt) and it kind of, weirdly, pushed back. But it was only for a moment, and then Cal was through.

And suddenly there was his old friend, gravity, to meet him.

Cal took back everything he'd just thought about missing gravity. He would actually have preferred to be back in the void, thank you very much, because now he was plummeting headfirst toward the ground, which was approaching his face *very rapidly,* and—

Focus.

He heard the voices in his head—not voices, really, but more of a feeling, and a memory, and a ghost, all at once.

And himself.

Cal had no idea if the Force felt the same to everyone; he'd read and heard all sorts of descriptions since he was a kid. From his first teacher, Jaro Tapal. From his most recent master, Cere. From the other younglings he'd trained with, before—

Before.

But for Cal, it was always the same. It was like a deep pool, blackest in its deepest fathoms, swallowing him whole as he dived down, down into it, emerging into a void where color and sound became muted, distant. It was an expansion of his consciousness; a brief direct connection to the source of all things. Like stretching his arms forward into meditation, settling into and moving through the void that connected every living being, his ripples spreading out concentrically like interlocking circles affecting the world around him. This had been harder, once; he'd had to suppress his abilities for so long that the void had felt stagnant, empty. But now years later, with great practice and focus and peace with the present . . .

Now Cal reached out to the Force, and the Force reached back.

With speed and balance most beings wouldn't—shouldn't— normally have access to, Cal managed to land arms-first, tucking and rolling flawlessly. A move that would, under other circumstances, have snapped his neck.

He jumped back to his feet before he could consider it much further.

"Landfall," Cal reported quietly over his comms. He tucked himself into the shadows at the corner of the closest building.

He'd made it past the Haxion sensors, taking advantage of the Brood's built-in weaknesses: its members' impatience for reentry with their zippy little jetpacks and their reluctance to admit they could be found, even all the way out here, far from any populated systems.

The Brood sure did love their broken-up space rocks for bases. But, Cal supposed, they killed people for credits, so.

There really was no accounting for taste.

Cal had managed to land close to his ideal infiltration point. The Brood base here on the central asteroid was set up like a bull's-eye; the outer ring, where Cal had landed, was a makeshift way station that had popped up to facilitate trade and sleep for bounty hunters on their way to and from assignments. In the center of the bull's-eye was the Brood base itself—though *base* was really giving the thing too much credit. It was more like a glorified cantina on stilts, a way station offering a Bespin Fizz and a bed or charging port for the night to the worst kinds of people in the galaxy. A place to refuel and, Cal assumed, exchange stories about how much they loved their amazing bounty hunter leader, Sorc Tormo, blurrgstain extraordinaire and perpetual pain in Cal's ass.

Or whatever.

And in between the outer ring and the bull's-eye, directly in front of Cal: a void, nearly clear through to the other side of the asteroid, meant to be crossed only by those confident enough with a jetpack to hit the landing pad on the other side without falling to their death.

Unfortunately for the Brood, not falling to his death in situations where he probably (absolutely, even) should was Cal's specialty.

In a rush, Cal popped off his helmet and began to free himself from his constricting space suit. BD-1 hopped down from his back and shook himself out for a second, readjusting to gravity and solid ground. BD bounced from foot to foot watching Cal remove the rest of the space suit. Cal smiled at his friend, and then BD-1 took off around the corner toward the location where the sensor jammer needed to be installed, executing the next part of the plan without having to be reminded. He was such a good little droid.

Tucking the suit and helmet behind a crate, Cal tugged his tunic into place, patting his pockets and belt to make sure he had everything he needed—lightsaber, comlink, credits—before sidling around the corner to catch up with his droid. BD was halfway down the cliff face that made up one side of the chasm between the outer ring and inner ring in the middle of a slice, humming away to himself as he jammed his little scomp link into what appeared to be sheer cliff—but Cal knew it was actually just clever disguising via rock formation of the massive amounts of tech necessary to keep this place safe and running. The entire hollow ring housed the generators for the shield, the life-support systems— even the distillery buried in the rock under the cantina.

A Brood member they'd run into earlier that month—the one whose boots Cal was currently wearing—had divulged both the location of this base *and* the way that it functioned. It had been so kind of him to open up like that. And all it had taken was Merrin being particularly convincing with her equally scary and impressive space-witch magick for a moment or two.

He and Merrin made a damn good team.

The Brood had been relentless in pursuit of Cal and his crew for years. It was, if Cal was being completely honest with himself, a little annoying; they had bigger burra fish to fry than a mob of cybernetically enhanced Outer Rim gangsters. But Greez had owed them money, Cal had attempted to, uh, deter them, and he'd ended up escaping from their crime lord leader Sorc Tormo and his prisoner-fight pit plus gambling ring. Ever since then, the Brood had really had it out for Cal (and the rest of his crew by default, sadly). There had been a bounty on his head for years and he couldn't imagine the kind of credits he was worth, at this point.

It was kind of an ego boost.

BD-1 bee-beeped, signaling the completion of his slice, and Cal knelt down to meet the droid as he climbed back up the ledge and resituated himself on Cal's back. (It always felt like little claws on his back when BD was scrambling up there, but Cal didn't mind. The droid was too good a friend.)

And then the semi-opaque shield dome overhead flickered off for a moment, signaling the dropping of the base's sensors, just as they planned.

It was on again just as quickly, and Cal hoped desperately that no one but someone who knew to look for the disruption would have noticed, but they could never be too sure.

He would be prepared, either way.

"That's a go, *Mantis*—"

"All over it, kid," Greez interrupted before Cal got the words out. "Meet us at the drop."

BD was small, but he was a mighty little droid. The speed of the shield's sensor sweeps was typically set to be just slow enough for something small to burst through—like Cal himself. But thanks to all the technological wisdom stored in his tiny little processor, BD had managed to turn it off just long enough to allow for something much, much bigger to get through without notice.

Something as big as, say, an S-161 XL luxury yacht like the *Mantis*.

After BD scrambled back into his favorite position on the Jedi's back, Cal jogged to their previously agreed-upon meeting place—a tight squeeze between two tall-ish buildings in the outer ring that looked like a poor excuse for what might pass as "overnight accommodations" on this rock—and watched with a half smile as the *Mantis* came sliding quietly into position from above. Sure, it was Greez's ship, technically, but over the last couple of years it had become Cal's home, and a home for the people he loved most in this messy galaxy.

Long and sleek, the *Stinger Mantis* was shaped like a knife's blade, tapered in the front where the four-armed Latero pilot Greez Dritus sat in his specially made cockpit chair. The most striking feature of the *Mantis,* though, was the imposing fin that jutted out just prior to the ship's stern. The massive fin, taller than the ship was long and also jutting slightly out the keel, was set in a rotating segment of the ship's hull that also housed the main outrigger engine. The fin could spin completely around the ship, depending on where and how Greez wanted to take her. A dingy white with blue and yellow detailing, the ship had originally been created to spirit wealthy executives back and forth while they stripped the galaxy of everything good.

Cal liked to think of the *Mantis* as their final crewmember, rescued from a life of servitude to the worst of the worst and drafted into the service of those who were forced to rebel against those who would otherwise have used them and thrown them away.

She was built to be sleek, stealthy, and comfortable, and she slid right into place among the outer ring buildings without, as far as Cal could tell, anyone from the Brood being any the wiser.

"Look who finally decided to show up," Cal teased as the hydraulics wheezed, lowering the ship's ramp.

"This was the plan all along." Merrin stepped off the *Mantis* first, her deep voice in its unique accent turning the *was* into *vuz.* Cal stared with just a little bit of envy as Merrin descended the ramp; somehow she managed to look daunting and intimidating everywhere she went, whether she intended to or not. A Dathomirian, Merrin had skin so pale it was like chalk; it reflected the light from the shield above, the gray markings on her face sprawled out like a spider. She kept her long, equally white hair tucked back into a severe bun—except the one piece around her face that always seemed to escape, no matter how hard she tried to keep it in place. Cal had seen her touch it a million times. And even years after leaving Dathomir, she still wore the black and red her people loved so much (though far less in the traditional Nightsister style—she'd really been finding what clothing worked for her in the field and out of it), but Cal could swear he saw a tint of green in it all—the color of her Nightsister magick.

Which Cal definitely understood and wasn't at all unnerved by.

"Joke, Merrin," clarified Cere as she followed the younger woman off the *Mantis*. "He was making a joke." Cal nodded to her, his Jedi Master. It was a testament to her humility that Cere looked so . . . normal, despite being possibly the most powerful Force-user in the known galaxy. She kept her tightly coiled black hair in a no-nonsense halo, cropped short at the sides but left tall on the top. But Cal could see, too, the toll that the last few years on the run had taken on his master; the bags under her eyes were several shades darker than the rest of her russet-brown skin. She wore a utility vest over her tunic and leggings, similar to Cal's, and her boots made little sound on the ramp.

That was a skill Cal had yet to master. It was pretty great, though.

"It wasn't funny," Merrin responded. Cal was pretty sure that was her own idea of a joke.

At least, he hoped so.

"Stick with the plan, and we'll be able to run free without the Brood tracking our every move. We need that freedom, and we need this base eliminated. The Brood continues to launch devastating attacks against local systems from here. They're hurting innocent people, and they'll only get bolder if it's allowed to continue," Cere reminded them as she checked her gear. "Everybody out in one piece. Got it?"

"Got it," Cal affirmed.

"Yes," agreed Merrin.

Bwee doop, said BD.

"Good," Cere said, double-checking that her lightsaber was strapped down into place. "Then let's blow this heap to hell."

CHAPTER 2

Merrin could not wait for this day to be over.

They'd landed on this asteroid and gotten to work on their usual tasks: Cal infiltrating from below, Merrin from above, Cere working out the tech, Greez back on the ship, prepared for a quick getaway. She stood on the roof of the Brood base and gnashed her teeth.

The Brood was an annoyance, a pest that refused to politely die off or at the very least find more appealing prey. Missions like this were a necessary part of life on the *Mantis*; it was difficult to fight the bigger fights when droid bounty hunters called Blorp (Greez had said that was his name) kept trying to blow your head off at unexpected intervals.

But to Merrin, they were a distraction from her larger, more important goal: destroying those responsible for destroying Merrin's heart. At all costs.

Still, the Blorps of the galaxy had caught up with them yet again, so here they were, on some dead rock in the Outer Rim, attempting to claim their own bounty from the hunters who hunted them. It was fair game.

"Does no one else find it bizarre that the outer ring was deserted?" Merrin asked over comms.

"They're probably all drunk as skeezumps in the cantina." Greez's drawl was clear in her ear. Merrin could picture him back on the *Mantis*, his feet up on the dash, waiting for the rest of the team to finish their work.

"What in the galaxy is a skeezump?" Cal sounded out of breath; he was likely hanging by his arms at that very moment from some rocky handhold with nothing but empty air for kilometers beneath him.

"You know, a skeezump," said Greez, as if that should answer all their questions. "You guys don't have those where you're from?"

Cere huffed out an unimpressed breath from where they'd left her, bent over the mechanical guts of the Brood base, hanging down over the chasm wall next to where BD had initiated his slice. "We absolutely do not."

"They're all over Lateron," Greez explained with new enthusiasm. "Fuzzy-lookin' things. Somethin' about their digestion ferments everything they eat. Blitzed outta their minds all hours of the day and night. Not great pets."

While Merrin listened to the chatter of the crew, she walked across the base's roof, scanning the ground for anything that looked like an entrance. Not long after they landed and rendezvoused with Cal, he'd raced across the single, spindly bridge separating the outer ring from the central base, then launched himself headfirst down the sheer cliff face supporting the building. He was now scrambling around the lower exterior of the base, searching for another way inside that would cause the least amount of disruption and potential death to the *Mantis* crew. Using her Nightsister magick—as well as she could, these days—Merrin had made herself invisible and run, her powers augmenting her speed, to climb to the base's roof, searching for the same thing.

There was power in having more than one entrance and exit at any given moment; limiting yourself, on a stealth mission, to one escape route was a fool's game. Far too risky. Cere, brilliant with technology, kept an eye on the mechanisms that kept the base running. One ask, and she could have any turbolift running, any door open in a flash—

anything that BD-1 was too far away with Cal to handle, or was too complex. Greez kept the engine running, their getaway driver; and when all went to plan, they would be far, far away from this place before it surrendered to the vacuum.

They had settled into a rhythm, this strange crew, over the years. They didn't have the power of an army behind them; they were more of—what had Cere called them?—a strike team, able to get in and out of situations quickly and quietly, leaving as much destruction behind them as they possibly could. Greez, their weird little pilot, the best Merrin had ever known (though, admittedly, she hadn't met that many since leaving Dathomir), always ready to fly them in and out of danger with an unending string of complaints that never stopped him from doing his best work. BD-1, the little droid who was so nauseatingly cute it made Merrin want to hug him until she crushed him to death (she settled for sassing him with regularity). Cere, impressively aligned with the Force, the most even-keeled of the group, the one who saw the big picture. The closest thing to an elder sister that Merrin had left in the universe.

And of course Cal, the Jedi, a fellow survivor who made an alliance with a Nightsister. Together they were the light and the dark. Cal was the star that illuminated Merrin's shadow. His earnest face, pale for a human, dusted with darker spots. Scars crossing his nose and eyebrow that spoke of a hard life. Hair like burnished copper, always pushed up and back out of his green eyes in a way that seemed to defy gravity. His smiles came quick and easy, like his connection to the Force.

Must be nice.

Over the last few years, Merrin saw something different in Cal almost every time she looked at him. Sometimes he was the hardened warrior leader of their crew, bent on vengeance. Other times, though he tried his best to hide it, Cal was the scared and lonely Jedi on the run. He was dedicated, but equally dedicated to his cause and to his crew. He was so *sweet*.

It was kind of annoying.

Merrin had lived among only Dathomirians for most of her life; before her clan had been so brutally decimated during what Cal referred to as the Clone Wars, she had known mostly other Nightsisters and the occasional Nightbrother. In the years before Cal had found her, she'd first been alone, and then subjected to the rantings of the fallen Jedi Taron Malicos and his cult of Nightbrothers.

So after a largely homogeneous upbringing and a lifetime of living mostly with other Dathomirians, Merrin still felt the *Mantis* crew made up a motley ensemble. But their differences made them a nearly unstoppable force. United in their cause, each bringing their own strengths to the fight.

Well, mostly united, Merrin supposed. They didn't talk about it much. There was an assumption, really, that they were all after the same thing. They weren't exactly a heavy heart-to-heart kind of group. Merrin didn't even know what a *heart-to-heart* was until Cal explained it to her early on, awkwardly, when he tried to ask about her sisters in what Merrin thought was meant to be a bonding moment.

Merrin sighed as she scanned the rest of the roof; she was simply having no luck here, either.

"No entry from this zone," she reported, interrupting the chatter of her crew for a crucial mission update. On this section of the roof, she could see no vents or other access channels; she'd have to keep up the search elsewhere. "Repositioning."

Merrin peered over the roof of the base, down onto the level below. The base had clearly been built up over time, new additions at all different heights. The roof below her wasn't navigable by foot; too many hazards belching skin-meltingly hot steam, edges sharp as a knife, gaps too wide for even Cal to jump.

But Merrin had other ways of traveling.

Despite her . . . recent struggles, with her powers, over the last few years, the ability to disappear and rush her way around the battlefield unseen had stayed with Merrin no matter what. There was a part of her that wondered if it was because unmaking herself, disappearing the visible parts of herself, appearing to dissolve into the wind—was the only thing that truly came naturally to her. If that was what she was best at, and maybe the way she should stay.

But living in that thought was dangerous. And Merrin still had work to do. Too much work to ever give in to that kind of lie.

But accessing her magick was not as easy as it once was. The conjuring, the manipulation of things outside of herself, the *projection* of her power . . . It was difficult to call that fire into her palms like she once did. But disappearing, moving, that was the one thing that had never left her—when her physical body was engaged, Merrin found her connection easier.

And so she closed her eyes. She willed herself to become unseen. In the darkness, everything lit up green; the luminescent green of Dathomir's core, of the magick that ran through Merrin's veins.

She felt the visible parts of herself dissolve like parchment fed to a fire.

For a moment, she burned. It consumed her from the inside out. It was the only time, these days, that Merrin felt truly connected to herself. Every nerve alive with the feeling of being seared away into nothingness. She felt everything.

And then she felt nothing.

But it was never long enough to truly enjoy. And even if it were, she wouldn't have remembered it, anyway; Merrin always felt disappearing was comparable to falling asleep. When you're unconscious, you have no memory of not being conscious. Her powers allowed her to run faster, jump higher, react faster, but while she was unseen it all felt as though she weren't really experiencing any of it at all. When you have no visible physical form, even momentarily, there's less to record your experience of the world around you for your brain. You simply . . . are not.

And then you are.

Reality came rushing back to Merrin all at once as her body revealed itself in ash and flame. It was never not disorienting, no matter how many times Merrin disappeared and reappeared having propelled herself forward faster than she could otherwise. It took the brain a second to adjust. Even for a witch.

She was on the far end of the base roof now, surrounded by vents billowing steam. The edges of her long red tunic were immediately caught up in the air blasts, sending it flying upward toward her chest. Merrin threw an arm over her eyes to protect them from any debris that might also be flying up with it.

"Found the central heat distribution," reported Merrin. "Cere?"

"On it," came the response in seconds.

Cal breathed heavily into his comms. Merrin imagined him running sideways across a vertical surface, leaping for the next one, making it. "Wish you could teach me how to do that," he said in a tone Merrin recognized as only half joking.

"All your fire would come from your hair," Merrin answered as she waited for Cere to shut down one of the vents. "You would disappear from the top down, just consumed by—"

"Where the hell did you come from?" a voice behind her interrupted.

Merrin spun and found herself face-to-face with the dangerous end of a bounty hunter's flamethrower. She wore one of those hideous bucket helmets, with a heavy jetpack strapped to her back. Merrin couldn't tell how much of her was cells versus circuitry.

Deremo. Damn. Foolish mistake. *Cere*—

Thank the lords of Dathomir that Cere was so locked into the Force; it was like she knew exactly what Merrin wanted before she even got the words out of her mouth. A superheated jet of steam came exploding out of the vent immediately between Merrin and the mercenary, giving Merrin just enough time to burst into flame.

Out of sight and back in, running and revealing herself behind the hunter before she'd finished regaining her balance from the backward impact of the steam vent. Merrin quickly eyed the hunter's back; she had a fuel canister connected to both her jetpack and her weapon.

Speaking of foolish mistakes.

Moving quickly, Merrin lunged forward, yanking the connecting cable free from the fuel cell. Liquid accelerant splashed down across the hunter's legs and the ground at the same moment the hunter came roaring around, finger on her flamethrower's trigger. Merrin burned out of and into sight again, reappearing on a roof above just in time to see the flames ignite the accelerant by the hunter's feet.

Merrin didn't look away as the hunter was consumed by the very flames that were meant to protect her.

Once her screams had ceased, Merrin hopped back down from the ledge. The charred remains smelled . . . well. They reminded Merrin of home.

She smiled.

"Thank you," she said over comms, knowing Cere would be listening. "I'm heading in."

The metal of the heat distribution vents was still warm under Merrin's palms as she shimmied her way down the venting system toward the central core of the Brood's headquarters. This wasn't the worst pipe she'd ever had to crawl through in her time as part of the crew of the *Mantis,* but still. It didn't make the shuffling-through-vents part of the job any more fun.

But their goal was quick, quiet, and simple; there was no point in fighting through hordes of bounty hunters if they didn't have to. This base had been terrorizing nearby systems in the Outer Rim for cycles, not to mention serving as the launching point for countless Haxion Brood members who had hunted the *Mantis.* Cere had described it as "very virtuous" of them to be stopping, but Merrin would just be happy to be rid of the annoyance of the Brood constantly catching up to them.

There was meant to be a critical mass of Brood here today after finishing a raid. The sooner they returned this place to the hell it was before some fools decided to resettle a crushed planet, the better. And the easiest way to do that was to plant charges inside the base to ensure maximum destruction, set them, and run.

Efficient. Just the way Merrin liked it. Especially on days she wanted to end.

Finally, after what seemed like an eternity of yanking herself forward on her stomach—it was going to take her an age to get the grease stains out of her tunic, its red hung on to *everything*—she spotted the end of the vent system, right where Greez had predicted it would be in their pre-mission planning session. Perfect.

"I'm nearly in position," she reported.

"Same," Cal's voice came back just a moment later. "Coming in from below. Let's scope the best locations for the charges, and—"

Cal went silent.

Merrin frowned. Cal was almost never silent.

"And . . . ?" she prompted, hoping her comm had merely dropped the signal for a second.

There was another pause. Merrin kept pulling herself forward toward the slatted vent cover again.

Cal's voice came back, quieter this time. "I think I know why the outer ring was so deserted."

With a grunt, Merrin dragged herself forward the last of the way. "Oh?" She grabbed at the vent, pulling herself to peer through the slats. "And why is—"

She didn't have to finish her sentence.

The center circle of the Brood base—the bull's-eye, the most valuable location: the cantina—was full. Two groups, split down the middle by garb into dark and light, like two sides of a coin. Behind the bar, every Brood member currently on the base. Bounty hunters, commandos, bounty droids. Dark and oily and grimy and . . . Brood-y. Cautiously serving drinks.

And on the other side of the bar, gleaming like the karking sun in this forsaken place: a legion of bright, white, shiny stormtroopers. Just . . . standing there. Like they were having a nice little chat. One of them was drinking, doing so through a little induction port in the front of their helmet. Just sucking away on a little straw.

Stormtroopers. Right there in the Haxion Brood's bar.

"Oh," Merrin said again, sounding like an absolute genius. "That's new."

There wasn't a lot out there that surprised Cal Kestis anymore, really.

After so many years on the run from the Empire and the Brood and whoever Greez had managed to piss off in a bar that week, Cal felt like he was virtually *unable* to be surprised anymore. He was also so used to his Force sensitivity alerting him in advance when something was hinky—it was just hard to sneak up on a Jedi. When you're connected to the energy that connects to the energy of everything else, what? Were they going to tiptoe?

Didn't work like that.

So it was kind of nice, actually, on the rare occasion when Cal was actually caught off guard, like right now, with stormtroopers apparently littering this Brood base. He found it kind of charming.

It was the only way a stormtrooper could be charming, frankly.

Cal scanned the cantina quickly, feeling BD-1 craning over his shoulder for a better view. After a perilous and precarious journey clambering around the rocky spire holding the base aloft, Cal had found his way into the facility through a service entrance buried in the asteroid far below the base. After dispatching one Brood commando with a green helmet and a mouth that wouldn't shut up for two seconds until it had to, it was easy to sneak into the lower supply room with a ladder and hatch that led up to the bar.

Cal carefully pushed the hatch up slightly, just enough for him to peer through without drawing any unwanted attention. From his low vantage point, Cal could mostly just make out a lot of feet. On one side of the bar, the side with the bottles: a varied assortment of boots, cybernetic feet, and droid legs. On the other: a forest of sparkling white boot covers in that nice plastoid that smelled sugary sweet when it made contact with the burning tip of a lightsaber, a smell Cal wished he hadn't had to get to know so well. He did a quick count: maybe ten bounty hunters, as many as they'd expected, and at least double that many troopers. Not great odds against a Jedi and a witch.

For them.

While climbing his way toward the facility, Cal had felt a tickle at the edges of his senses, like there was something *wrong* in the air. Like the asteroid had taken on a kind of overwhelming atmosphere he couldn't quite deal with, like a migraine halo, a sensory overload that he'd learned early on to tuck into the back of his brain so he could still function, even when things weren't quite right in the galaxy.

It turned out that was most of the time.

So Cal hadn't thought anything of it when the Force had tried to tell him something was wrong; when his connection to the energy outside of him felt tinged with darkness. He was on a Haxion Brood base on a dead rock in the middle of nothing; it would be weird if everything felt *right* in the Force.

Anyway, there was a cavalry's worth of stormtroopers in the bar, so. That was Cal's mistake.

Still, it was nice to be surprised every once in a while.

"What are they *doing* here?" said Merrin.

"Did something happen?" Greez asked at the same time.

"Stormtroopers." Cal answered Greez first.

"This changes nothing, we *stick* to the plan," Cere quickly replied over comms.

Greez blew air out through his mouth, lips flapping in a sigh. "'Cause why not, right? Why the hell not."

"Are they . . . talking?" Merrin sounded more curious than concerned.

Cere was clearly uninterested. "It doesn't matter. Set the charges and get back to the *Mantis*."

"You really don't want to know what they're doing here?" Cal responded, while attempting to figure out the next best move. He was good at changing plans on the fly; it was one of his better skills. From necessity. "There weren't any Imperial ships in range; we'd have caught them on sensors."

"Ehhhh," Greez countered. "There're a lot of floating rocks to hide behind here. I'm just one guy."

"Of *course* I want to know." Cere's voice was calm, given the circumstances. "But what are we going to do, ask them? Set the charges and get out. Don't be fancy. We're not here for them."

Cal sighed. As usual, Cere was right. He *did* have a tendency to get carried away when he didn't need to. Why waste energy on a fight he didn't have to fight?

"All right," Cal agreed. "Let's—"

Just then the hatch was thrown wide open. One of the Haxion Brood stood over the opening, calling out to someone at the bar, "We got more Bantha Blasters in the deep freeze—"

The bounty hunter looked down and froze, staring straight at the Jedi and droid clinging tight to the ladder that led down into the supply rooms.

Cal stared up at the bounty hunter.

Necessity? Is that you?

Cal grinned. "Hi, there."

In a matter of seconds, the bar exploded. And not in the way Cal and the crew had originally planned.

The bounty hunter roared "*Jedi!*," followed by the sound of countless weapons being unholstered; a flurry of stomping feet at Cal's eye level; a shouting of orders through the stormtroopers' voice filtering units; the whirring of droid gears; glasses shattering on the ground.

And through his comms, louder than all the growing din above him, Merrin's voice:

"Perfect."

For once, it was devoid of sarcasm.

Pushing off the ladder, Cal launched into the air and, at the peak of his jump, reached out and *shoved* underneath him with the Force, propelling himself up and over the bewildered bounty hunter's head before the mercenary could even grab his weapon. With a flip, Cal landed behind the hunter, his lightsaber already in his hand.

When the blue blade flared to life, Cal could feel the heat of it radiating back onto his face. The only warmth this place had ever seen.

Cal slashed his blade across in front of him, swung it back, and used the momentum to spin, cutting across the hunter's back a second time in quick succession, his other hand hitting the ground in front of him to maintain his balance. The hunter fell forward down the open hatch like a sack of bricks—cybernetically enhanced bricks, but still—as Cal hopped back onto his feet, twirling his lightsaber back into a ready position to take on whoever was next.

The answer: a room full of awestruck stormtroopers who were decidedly *not* expecting to run into a Jedi in a Haxion Brood base on a dead rock floating through the Outer Rim, alongside a number of said Haxion Brood bounty hunters all eager to be the one who brought Cal's head in on a platter for the prize credits.

A fight against both the Brood *and* stormtroopers? At the same time? The chance to get some real action in, to do more than just sneak around and set charges? To put a dent in the Empire at the same time as doing literally anything else?

Okay, *now* this was a good day.

Cal wasted no time. He felt his brain unfurl, opening himself fully to the Force. With the energy flowing through and around and *with* him, Cal felt as unstoppable as ever. He tried not to be overly cocky, but hey, he'd yet to meet a stormtrooper he couldn't beat.

Ducking into a roll to avoid incoming blasterfire, Cal threw out one of his hands, establishing his focus on the Force just long enough for it to build up and then shoving the energy away from himself, sending a group of troopers flying backward and slamming into the wall behind them. A flash in his mind, a warning: Cal twisted up quickly to catch a bolt fired from a bounty hunter on the edge of his lightsaber. Enough of his senses remained on the wall of stormtroopers to notice that Merrin had dropped down from her vent above them to finish them off in her own special way.

If Cal was unnerved by Merrin at the best of times, he kind of loved thinking about how the stormtroopers must feel staring her down in their final moments.

The hunter who had shot at Cal reached back for the nozzle on their flamethrower, but Cal didn't give them the chance. He leapt to his feet and lunged forward with a powerful overhead slash, ending the hunter for good.

No time to celebrate; from Cal's right, one of the Brood's loadlifter droids came slamming into him, charging full speed with its blocky and incredibly heavy center bulk—it was basically just a massive brick with two arms and two legs. The hit sent Cal crashing through the cantina's wall out into the open air. He landed hard on his back—briefly hoping BD had managed to get free—and as Cal oriented himself he looked to his left.

To see nothing at all. He was on the edge of the sheer cliff face surrounding the base. The wind ruffled his hair out of place. Cal swallowed.

But the loadlifter was charging again. Cal rolled out of the way just in time, and watched the droid hit the brakes just before rushing themself off the cliff edge.

Well, nearly. Balancing on one knee, Cal threw out an arm and helped the droid the rest of the way off the cliff.

He was pretty sure he could hear a slowly fading "Kaaaaaaark . . . !" from the droid's vocoder as it fell to its doom.

Cal caught his breath for a second, looking back through the hole he'd created in the cantina wall. Merrin was holding her own against the troopers, as she always did, disappearing and reappearing around them so quickly that the troopers were just shooting at one another instead of her, taking themselves out methodically and foolishly.

Very few times had Cal ever seen stormtroopers have good aim, and even then it was when they were accidentally aiming at each other.

A beep and a trill from beside him—BD-1, who had indeed leapt off his back in the nick of time. The little droid flicked his head up, and a glowing green canister came flying out of one of his myriad compartments. Cal grabbed the stim canister from midair, jabbing it into his other arm without thinking about it too hard (nobody liked needles, but Cal hated them especially after a bad experience with a rabid dianoga). Cal felt the stim spread cool and soothing through his veins, like sinking into an ice bath after a hard workout. The bruises on his back begin to fade and his tired and injured muscles start to knit. His heart beats faster; the combination of stimulants and healing fluids was exactly what Cal needed to get back on his feet.

"What would I do without you, buddy?" Cal asked his droid.

Bwee beep, BD agreed. He clambered back onto Cal's shoulders, his little claw feet a familiar and comforting sensation as they scratched their way into place.

"I know you're having fun, but this is getting messy. Drop the charges and go." Cere's voice was loud over the comms, shouting over the sounds of battle. "Back to the *Mantis,* right now!"

Cal got back to his feet. He could do that.

But on his way out he could also take out a few more goons.

"The troopers are mine," Merrin responded. From where Cal stood, on the thin rock ledge just between the shattered outer cantina wall and the sheer cliff face down into the chasm, he could watch Merrin do her thing. She'd managed to take out a sizable chunk of troopers already. It was damn impressive.

But then so were most things Merrin did. It was kind of inspiring, actually.

Inspiring, and worrisome, at times. Cal knew that Merrin was displacing her rage at the Separatists who had destroyed Dathomir onto the troopers, and he understood the need to direct emotion in a useful manner. He understood, too—a little, anyway—that Merrin's magick was somehow connected to the dark side. But he knew the places a vengeful heart could take a person, and—impressive or not—he hoped Merrin would have been closer to healing by now.

As Cal let loose the charges from his belt, kicking them down the hatch from whence he came, Cal watched Merrin bolt through the now standing-sized gap that her vent entrance had become, cracked and shattered under the weight of the group of stormtroopers Cal had pushed, leading the remaining wave of troopers away behind her. She could take the rest of them out with ease. And Cal knew Cere could support Merrin should she get into a jam with the troopers just fine on her own; they weren't even Purge Troopers, the Empire's elite Inquisitor-support troops.

So it was just him and the Haxion Brood bounty hunters left.

Dusting himself off, Cal walked back into the cantina, where a mess of bounty hunters still stood: the Brood's hunter variety, augmented with droid parts, jetpacks, and flamethrowers; the Brood commandos, with their massive shields and flash-bang grenades; and the Brood's bounty droids, recklessly strong and built for charging. All just waiting for Cal to make it a fair fight.

He could do that, too.

Cal winked at the hunters.

He held his lightsaber out in front of him and ignited its second blade.

CHAPTER 3

The bounty hunters had been more difficult to handle than Cal would have liked to admit; not *hard,* exactly, but not *easy,* either. The Brood was no joke, which made destroying this base all the more important.

And they never came at you one at a time, either. There was no cleanly having a fight with one person trying to kill you before you got a chance to have a breather, then moving on to the next one. Of course not. There were always more bounty hunters than you had limbs coming at you all at once and having to kill or be killed in the moment.

Frankly, Cal found it impressive that anyone could fight without the Force. He didn't know how people did it.

When he'd walked back into the cantina, both ends of his lightsaber ignited, he'd barely had a chance to step over the threshold before one of the hunters dropped a flash-bang and a shielded commando charged him at the same time. Cal barely managed to dive and roll out of the way to avoid being barreled right back off the side of the cliff. He deflected two blaster bolts while leaping to his feet then rushing forward with his sword twirling overhead, cutting into the commando's armor with a whirlwind. At the perfect moment, he let go of his grip on the sword, sending the twirling blade flying in a circle around him, hitting every hunter in reach, kicking into place the one who wasn't quite at the right angle to hit the lightsaber's track. Catching the hilt on the rebound, Cal *yanked* with the Force, pulling the circle of hunters in close enough that another whirlwind from his blade was enough to take a couple of them down for good.

As they fought, Cal knew some of them were quipping at him; the Brood was famous for taunts and weapon-swinging braggary. They always expected Cal to answer, to bicker back, and to be distracted by the banter. But Cal found that his silence was a stronger weapon than insults. His quiet often distracted them; the lack of response to their jabs made them think Cal was either dull, nuts, or both.

Either way, better for him. He liked being underestimated.

He was used to it.

The Force had tickled, alerting him, and Cal knew he was about to be attacked by a large bounty droid, its long ovular body held aloft by two thin legs, one arm strapped with a rapid-fire missile launcher and its other made for massive, heavy punches. Cal took the bounty droid gearing up to launch its missiles at a run, leaping into the air and slashing downward, just managing to avoid the barrage. He dashed between hunters at lightning speed, quick flashes from his lightsaber cutting wide marks into their armor, keeping them off balance and guessing where he was going to turn next. Two of the hunters fired up their jet-packs and took to the air, putting distance between themselves and Cal, readying their flamethrowers.

"You're toast, Jedi," one of them called down from above.

Ugh, and a bad pun, too? That was *not* going to fly.

Leaning into a repulsor blast, Cal allowed himself to be pushed back toward the edge of the cliff. Spinning his blade to bounce back bolts with one hand, Cal used his other, focusing in on the Force, to aim for one of the airborne hunters. He pulled with the Force, dragging one of the hunters forward and directly into his hand against his will. Holding him by the shoulder, Cal flipped his lightsaber to sever the hunter's connection to his jetpack, turned just a little bit, and then used the Force to shove him outward.

His "Noooooo!" got quieter and quieter the farther he fell.

Cal eyed the other flying hunter. He wasn't sure if it was his training, or the Force, or both, but he saw his path illuminated for him, and he took it. Running forward toward one of the last two droids left in the cantina, Cal kicked out, using his foot as leverage to land on the droid's back. He stabbed downward with his staff, burning through the droid's brain circuitry while leaping up again on his way toward the hunter, who was flaring out with a flamethrower preemptively.

The distance was too much; Cal wouldn't make it off one jump alone. He used the energy beneath him to boost himself upward into a second midair leap, flipping forward and over the bounty hunter's head, nearly avoiding the stream of fire—he could feel BD frantically spraying some kind of flame suppressant over the back of his tunic where he'd obviously gotten caught in the spray.

Cal landed on the hunter's back like he was one of those terrifying Dathomirians who rode on the backs of chirodactyls. (Ugliest damn birds in the whole galaxy, if Cal had to vote on it.)

"Hey, not fair!" came the strangled voice of the hunter under Cal.

Cal wasn't typically afraid of heights—too much of his job depended on him swinging from vine to vine on jungle planets while avoiding situations just like this one—but he was usually more in control than he was in this current moment. Balancing on the shoulders of a jetpack-wearing flamethrowing bounty hunter was like riding an Oggdo Bogdo, but more unpredictable and also somehow more likely to break your neck.

Cal didn't have time to mess around, and something he'd learned early in his training was that sometimes, the simplest moves were the best. He holstered his lightsaber, just for a moment, then used both hands to yank off the hunter's helmet and end the fight.

Without someone alive to control it, her jetpack flared out of control, shooting straight up into the sky. It was now or never, and Cal had to take the chance. He grabbed his lightsaber and made a jump for it, swinging downward with his staff like death from above, hurtling down toward the other commando with the jetpack flying through the air beneath him.

The commando didn't have her shield above her head.

She should have.

Cal hit the ground hard, rolling to keep his balance, hearing the commando land with a thud next to him, not getting back up.

There were still too many of them. A blaster bolt pinged off BD's shell and he trilled; Cal would fix that later. With one hand and his willpower, Cal reached out to the Force and *pushed* on the hunters, sending those unwisely positioned in front of the hole in the wall flying backward into the open chasm.

Bye!

Cal was starting to tire; he had to rest soon, recharge, or he'd risk collapsing in the middle of the fight. Another flash-bang; Cal squinted, managing to get his lightsaber up in time to deflect another missile. This one boomeranged back to hit its launcher—

And the cantina went up in flames, the explosion rocking the entire building. Cal suddenly became worried that the rock spire holding the base wasn't meant for this kind of destabilization.

It was time to finish this up.

When the dust had cleared and the halos from the flash-bang had faded, there were only two bounty hunters left. With surprise, Cal realized he recognized them both—Killena and her ever-present droid, T1L-D4.

They'd been leaving him messages throughout the galaxy, constantly threatening that they were tracking him closely, and were one step away from catching up to him. But they never showed up. He guessed the messages were merely meant to throw him off his game.

As if that were the worst kind of thing anyone had ever sent to him.

"Kestis, has anyone ever told you you're the *worst*?" demanded Killena, brandishing her blaster with all the confidence of a person who hadn't just watched Cal decimate the entirety of her colleagues.

"The worst: calculating," said T1L-D4.

Cal shot the droid a sidelong glare.

"Confirmed," T1L-D4 added.

Jerks.

"Seriously, we were just minding our own business here, having a drink," Killena said, sighing. "Did you have to ruin it?"

He tried to be silent during a fight, he really did, it was just so *hard*, and Cal wasn't one to turn down an opportunity to gain some knowledge when the chance presented itself. "New friends, huh?"

"Very boring," T1L-D4 said. "Samey outfits."

"Tilda's a bit of a fashion snob, you have to understand," Killena said as she circled Cal slowly. He knew she was looking for an opening while she tried to distract him with banter. It wasn't working. "Wanna know what we were talking about?"

"Honestly?" Cal gritted his teeth. "Kinda, yeah. Besides footwear."

The droid scoffed. "Tilda would never take *their* advice on footwear."

"An interesting business opportunity." Killena dangled the non-answer in front of Cal like a carrot. "The Empire has credits. We aren't picky about who pays. Just that we get paid."

"Your parents must be so proud," muttered Cal.

"My father lives in a paid-off hilltop mansion on Alderaan thanks to me," Killena snapped.

"I do not have parents," confirmed T1L-D4. "I was created wholesale out of parts."

Jerks.

Cal held his lightsaber at the ready in front of him, both blades blazing. He was working out his best strategy—deflect one of T1L-D4's missiles back toward Killena, watch them both get annihilated—when the ground under Cal's feet shook again, the charges beginning to detonate, and then, through the Force, he felt the whole pillar on which the cantina stood start to crack off into the void below.

"Run!" Killena shouted. Cal knew he should make sure they couldn't follow him, but he wasn't about to die himself in a grisly fall because he was too fixated on finishing off two bounty hunters who would probably laugh over the color of Cal's tunic as his corpse went cold. He was getting *out*.

The hunters must have had the same plan, because they didn't give Cal any trouble as he took off toward the hole in the wall and the cliff face. No time to go back down the hatch to the supply room, if it was even still there. He'd have to really leg it back to the rock bridge.

"Cal!" came Cere's voice over his comms. "The rock bridge just collapsed into the abyss."

Okay, great. The place was shaking itself apart, and now he had lost his own path back to the *Mantis*.

Which meant Cal would have to make his own way across the chasm.

The walls on either side of the chasm were crumbling now, sending chunks of rock flying down into the gap between inner ring and outer. That was going to be his way across. It was the only way. He'd have to time it right, and it was going to be hard, maybe impossible, but—

BD-1 let out an encouraging trill from Cal's back—don't think about it, just *go!*—as the Jedi took a running jump off the edge of the cliff. He hit a falling rock hands-first, hoisting himself over it into another leap. He hit the next falling boulder to his left feetfirst, running forward on the horizontal until he could flip off it, hitting a rock on his right with his feet and running forward in the same way. He was almost there; just one more jump—

Cal's hands barely grabbed onto the edge of the wall on the other side of the chasm and he scrabbled to get better purchase, cursing himself for not thinking to bring the climbing claws he'd . . . liberated from a Nightbrother on Dathomir.

He'd need to remember to just keep those things on him, no matter how bulky they looked under his favorite poncho.

Cal had just managed to climb the rest of the way up over the wall at the edge of the outer ring. He lay on his back heaving to catch his breath—

And then he'd heard the telltale march of stormtrooper boots.

These must have been reinforcements from whatever ship had brought the original group to the cantina; he had full confidence that Merrin had taken out her cadre.

Cal dragged himself to his feet and took off running again. This really had started out as a good day.

With the exception of disappearing—which, thankfully, still came easily to her—Merrin didn't need to use her magick to destroy these Imperial soldiers.

They managed to do that job just fine on their own.

Even with the difficulties Merrin had been having with her powers as of late—her frustrating inability to access them, so frustrating Merrin could barely even think about it—killing Imperials was still satisfying. She wasn't picky; magicking them to their death was very funny, yes, but a blaster bolt to the helmet worked just as well, sometimes. Today, though, she kept them guessing: blinking in and out of sight the second they got a lock on her, sending them walking off cliffsides and shooting one another in the back. She knew Cal would eliminate the remaining bounty hunters; she'd seen him in action enough times to know that the man knew how to handle his lightsaber. But she was grateful he'd left the troopers to her.

Yes. Merrin was glad that she finally got to do something useful on this trip out to the middle of nowhere. Not that destroying this base wouldn't be useful to the *Mantis* crew in general, but Merrin generally found that these side trips felt like distractions from the main event. From bringing down the people who had brought down her people. Or as close as she could come to that, these days.

Still, she was grateful to be useful. She was also grateful that she didn't have to crawl on her stomach all the way back to the exit.

Every time in these last few years she had watched another stormtrooper's little helmet shatter, or be crushed under a rockslide, or explode, or—she was getting lost with it. But every time she took another one out, regardless of how, she imagined it lighting a spark inside her. And every spark was one more chance to ignite what had gone out.

Every death, another opportunity.

There were times when Merrin fought the Empire when all she saw, all she felt, was Dathomir. Its red skies and dark energy, sustaining and motivating and, more than anything, raw with potential. Her sisters; the witch clans united under Mother Talzin, before the woman turned to the Sith. The verdant marshlands covered in red mists where Merrin had grown up, always knowing the danger inherent in the loveliness. The chirodactyls, floating lazily on the hot winds overhead, their cries waking her in the morning when the red sun first crested over the mountaintops. The clear, rejuvenating Water of Life, created with her own hands with the world around her, with which all Nightsisters were initiated. A world so strong and so beautiful and so terrifying all at the same time.

The ichor that flowed through Dathomir's core had flowed through her veins, hot and molten. Their magick was more powerful than anything the Sith had to offer.

But it did not last.

And now, in each stormtrooper's pathetic little helmet, Merrin saw reflected the stark white face of another: golden eyes in a mechanical shell, too many arms, too many lightsabers. Leading far, far too many troops into battle for the soul of Dathomir.

General Grievous.

Air strikes. Assault tanks. The forests burned, Merrin's sisters fell. Not even an army of the dead could hold them back.

Merrin was lucky to have survived. Lucky, and very, very good.

Or she had been. Once.

And now she would not stop until the people responsible for Dathomir's destruction lay charred at her feet. She would trace the markings on her face with fingers coated in their ashes. She would avenge her beautiful, terrifying sisters, and her beautiful, terrifying planet.

It was the only thing in the galaxy that she was meant to do.

And so Merrin watched the stormtroopers fall one by one on her way out of the Brood base, and she smiled grimly.

She'd run in the opposite direction of the *Mantis,* not wanting to accidentally lead any straggling troops right back across the spindly bridge to their location, but now she had to find her way back. Fortunately, this damn rock was just built like one big circle; she couldn't get lost even if she tried. All roads led back to the *Mantis,* eventually. Greez usually kept the ship hidden well, but she hoped he'd perhaps be favoring expediency over stealth at this point and have the engines already running by the time she arrived. Disappearing, rushing, and reappearing in small bursts from one ramshackle alley to the next, Merrin moved slowly around the ring, checking for any remaining troopers who had escaped her wrath.

In and out. Feeling and unfeeling. Something, then nothing. Again and again, until—

There was someone behind her. Trailing her even as she disappeared. Following her.

Between bursts, Merrin smiled. Finally.

The next time she disappeared, instead of continuing forward, Merrin doubled back. When she reemerged, she revealed herself directly behind her pursuer.

Merrin stared into the back of the shiny white helmet, and gold eyes stared back.

She blinked.

They were gone. Merely a trick of the light.

Didn't make the trooper any less dead, though.

Merrin lifted her arm, *willing* herself to find the fire—*scraping* her insides, desperate for the spark, when she heard—

"Wait! Wait." The stormtrooper lifted her hands over her head. She was taller than Merrin, broader. Through her voice filtering unit, she sounded . . . different. Scared.

As she should be.

"I know about Dathomir," the trooper blurted. "And I'm sorry."

Merrin paused. She couldn't tell if the feeling in her was cold fury . . . or something else entirely.

"I don't like to play with my food," Merrin responded. Better the stormtrooper didn't know she was having . . . hard times, with her powers, anyway. "And I don't like when people speak about things they can't possibly understand."

"No, I'm—" the trooper stuttered as Merrin placed a hand on the back of the trooper's helmet. "You're Merrin. Witch of Dathomir. Part of the crew of the *Stinger Mantis*. You're working against the Empire."

Merrin rolled her eyes, even though there was no one to see her. "Are you reading my arrest warrant? I've heard it all before."

"No," the trooper said. "I need your help."

Now Merrin had *really* heard it all.

She dragged her fingers down the smooth white side of the helmet, felt for the latch on the right. *Click.*

"Please," begged the trooper. "Merrin—"

"You don't know me." Merrin traced her finger around the neck joint to the other side, slowly, methodically. "And you should refrain from speaking my name again." Her finger caught on the second catch. *Click.*

Maybe she did like to play, after all.

You learn something new about yourself every day.

One finger still on the helmet, Merrin walked around the stormtrooper until she was just beneath level with what passed for the white mask's eyes. There was hardly any distance between Merrin and the trooper, and she thought it was odd that the woman had left her weapon holstered. When Merrin exhaled, she could see her breath leave condensation on the plastoid. She let her smile return as she noticed the trooper shaking.

With both hands, Merrin carefully grabbed both sides of the trooper's helmet and lifted.

She wasn't certain what to expect, but it wasn't this.

A lavender neck. Jutting chin and full lips, several shades darker than the rest of her skin, violet like spilled ink, matched the hair cut short over her shoulders. Strong-featured soft face with freckles like crater orchid petals across her nose.

And eyes as red as the sky over Dathomir's Rift Valley.

Not a human. That was unusual for a stormtrooper, as far as Merrin had seen.

From a hair's breadth away, Merrin watched the woman swallow.

The helmet clattered to the ground. Merrin had forgotten she was holding it. But the noise was what Merrin needed to bring her back into the moment, and she shot her hand back up, wrapping it around the woman's throat.

Hard. Muscular. Stronger than the stormtroopers Merrin usually fought.

Interesting.

"Talk," Merrin demanded.

"Listen," the woman said in a strange, sharp accent, quickly, pushing her words out through Merrin's fingers. "I want out. I know you have no reason to trust me, or believe me, but I've read up on you. I know what the Separatists did to Dathomir."

Merrin moved her face closer. She was shorter than the other woman, but Merrin didn't need height. Her power made her fearsome. She would use that to her full, intimidating advantage.

She hoped the red-eyed woman could feel the fire radiating off her at the mention of something she had no right to be mentioning.

"War took my people from me, too," the woman said, looking down and meeting Merrin stare for stare. If it weren't so foolhardy, Merrin would almost be impressed. "I can't—do this anymore. We all know about the *Mantis* crew. You're my only chance at getting out."

Merrin stared up into the red embers of the woman's eyes. The dying coals left behind by the burning forests.

Had she been one of the people to send Separatist droids to Dathomir? No, she was far too young. But at the right time, she would have been, if asked. She worked for the people responsible for the same kind of crimes now.

She saw blood in the woman's eyes.

Merrin squeezed her fingers around the trooper's neck, just a little— just enough and in just the right place. The lavender of the woman's neck turned pale under the pressure, stark in comparison with the thick, dark-gray bands on Merrin's fingers. She watched the woman's red eyes widen, just for a moment, in fear.

And then, expectedly, the trooper gave the smallest smile, radiating out from her eyes.

Surrender. It was what Merrin wanted from her.

Wasn't it?

Merrin dropped her hand and took a step backward, putting as much space as she dared between her and the trooper while still remaining in control. The trooper lifted her eyes, rubbing her neck a few times while she caught her breath.

"You're a spy," countered Merrin. Why was she even considering this?

The trooper shook her head. "I'm not. But I have no proof."

"I can't endanger my crew for a stranger."

The trooper's indigo brows knit together. "I thought that was the whole point."

I thought that was the whole point.

As if no time had passed at all, Merrin was back on Dathomir. She had spent years answering to a strange invading Jedi on her planet, giving him all the firepower she had. She hadn't chosen where she was born, or the circumstances of her life. She had been working with what had been left to her, attempting to clean up the mess made by others.

She'd been trapped on Dathomir. Trapped by her past. Cal had told her—she could find her own way in the universe. Her own path.

She'd been trapped by Dathomir. She still was, in the ways that mattered. But now, at least, she had purpose. She had made a choice, and she'd stuck to it. And it had been *hers.*

Nightsisters and Jedi did not travel together.

Neither did Nightsisters and stormtroopers.

But . . .

The trooper's eyes bored holes into Merrin's.

Fire igniting parchment.

Merrin took a deep breath. "The base is collapsing—"

"No time for you to play with your food, Merrin." Greez's voice was too loud in her ear, as if it were from a different reality. Merrin started. "We have—"

"Company!" Cal finished Greez's sentence in a way Greez couldn't have been anticipating, as Merrin saw the Jedi come ripping around the corner of a nearby alleyway at top speed. "Time to go!"

Merrin spun; concentration broken, she could now hear the boots of what sounded like *very many* stormtroopers running her way, not that far behind Cal. She'd dealt with all the ones in the bar—there had been more, hiding out below the facility somewhere? *Deremo.*

When she turned back to take the stormtrooper by the scruffy hair at the base of her neck, fully intending to drag her back to the *Mantis* one-handed, if she had to, she was gone.

Merrin didn't like that. That was *her* trick.

And then Cal grabbed her by the wrist as he went racing past her, dragging Merrin along with him instead. She wondered if Cal had even seen the unmasked trooper.

Taking off to keep up with her Jedi and his little droid, Merrin shot one last look back, just to be sure. Seconds later, what seemed to Merrin a small army's worth of stormtroopers came rushing around the corner after them, weapons drawn.

She felt a squeeze on her wrist and turned back to look at Cal, running just slightly ahead of her. "Go," he urged. "I'll meet you there."

Merrin dipped her head once in acknowledgment. She focused her magick and felt herself rush forward as she disappeared once more.

Despite Cal's best efforts to keep the blast doors to his past sealed tight—nothing behind there but pain he didn't have the time to deal with, not until his crew was safe and the Empire had fallen for good—as he listened to Merrin's conversation with the rogue stormtrooper, he found himself in places he never wanted to be again: with his youngling friends on Ilum, receiving his first kyber crystal; with his master and mentor Jaro Tapal, the commander to Tapal's general during the Clone Wars; with Prauf, his closest companion while in hiding from the Empire as a scrapper on Bracca. Prauf, who never knew Cal's true history but never asked questions and loved him like a brother all the same.

All dead.

And all at the hands of an Empire that claimed to have the best interest of its galactic citizens in mind.

But that's what the *Mantis* was here for. That's what Cal and its crew were going to put an end to. And it started right here, with people like that stormtrooper. He'd heard Merrin's conversation with her through their open comms; hadn't wanted to interrupt. But he had wanted to believe her. He wished that they could have helped her—but that wasn't what they were here for.

Now was not the time to get lost in thoughts like that. Cal had told Merrin to go on ahead with her witch powers and leave him to run from the stormtroopers on his own. This, in theory, was what Cal thought of as his most important job on the crew: to be the shiny object, the distraction. The one at the front lines, holding back the darkness so the rest of his family could make a clean escape. The one who always put himself on the line, so no one else he loved would risk hurt.

That was the idea, in theory. In practice, however, it meant almost getting singed by blaster bolts every four seconds and barely keeping a bunch of white-armored goons at arm's length as he sprinted at full speed through the outer ring alleys, toward where they'd parked the *Mantis*.

Please let Greez have the damn engine running, *please*.

CHAPTER 4

"Do you see a trooper with their helmet off?" Merrin shouted through her comms as everything started to fall apart around her. The entire asteroid was collapsing, shattering itself into space, and this was not where she planned to die.

"Helmet off?" Cal's voice huffed over the speaker. "What are they, suicidal?"

Maybe, thought Merrin.

She didn't have time to follow up, just grabbed the side of a hastily made stall for leverage and used it to swing herself around the last corner. Finally the *Mantis* came into glorious view, ramp down—engines, miraculously, running.

"Let's go, let's go!" Greez shouted. "We got Imperial and Brood ships all over my scopes! We are out of time!"

Merrin took the ramp at full speed, sparing only a glance toward the cockpit. Greez's arms were a blur, two of them flying over the *Mantis*'s controls while the other two buckled himself into his pilot's chair.

"Everybody strap in!" Cal launched himself up the boarding ramp, BD-1 trilling at top volume from his back. Blasterfire, from closer than

Merrin would have liked, followed right behind Cal; he ducked just in time, and the bolts hit the ship's overhead, sending sparks flying down around them both. Cal threw his arm out in front of him as he turned back toward the opening, the little frown he always wore when he was concentrating on the Force flashing across his face. One of the stormtroopers who had been on Cal's tail made it half a step onto the ramp before being ripped away from gravity itself, sent flying by Cal's powerful energy push into a nearby wall with a satisfying crack.

The deck of the ship shook beneath Merrin's feet, and she grabbed hold of the entryway doorframe, watching the stormtrooper blown into the wall. Merrin assumed their shiny white armor was the opposite of cushioned.

Good.

"Cere!" she yelled in warning over the roar of the ship's engine. "We're missing Cere!"

Either Greez couldn't hear her, or he had infinite faith in Cere's ability to defy the laws of physics—or, possibly, both at once—because Merrin held on to the doorway for her life as the *Mantis* lifted off from the ground. She watched as the ramp, still lowered, screeched and bent, its hydraulics not meant to hold it deployed while aloft. The *Mantis* wasn't designed to fly in such cramped quarters as between these buildings in the outer ring; Merrin felt as though the ship was about to shake itself apart. She stared at the corner of the drab stall around which she'd virtually thrown herself in order to make it to the ship and willed Cere to appear.

She had to make it. Cere *always* made it.

"Hey." Cal's hand landed on Merrin's shoulder. She looked at it in surprise, then up to his face as his other arm fitted itself securely around her waist to steady her. "She was right behind me. She'll be right behind me."

Merrin stared hard at Cal's face. He wasn't looking back at her; he was already fixated on that same corner of the stall. Merrin couldn't tell which Cal was trying harder to do: convince her that what he said was true, or convince himself.

She flicked her eyes slightly to the left of Cal's head and made eye contact—if one could call it that, really—with the little droid strapped to her friend's back. BD-1 twitched his antennas. She didn't understand many of the droid's words yet, but this she knew to mean: *Yes. I'm worried, too.*

"We're outta time, here, kids!" Greez's voice was loud over the ship's comms, and Merrin snapped her eyes back to Cal with a frown. "Cere, what's the holdup . . . ?" Greez was attempting to sound calm in the most Greez way possible, which was to say—not at all, especially since Cere wasn't responding.

Merrin turned, prying one of her hands off the door, and reached for the comms console next to the door, using Cal's weight as a counterbalance. She hit the button that would connect her with Greez at the exact moment blasterfire exploded off the doorframe just over Merrin's head, and she ducked away from the sparks at the same moment she heard Cal yell, "There!"

By the time Merrin turned back toward the ramp, Cal was already halfway down it, the machinery groaning under the added weight. They weren't high off the ground, but high enough that the troopers would have trouble getting on board. Merrin squinted away from the bright spark of his lightsaber ignition, her eyes adjusting in time to watch him deflect one, then another, blaster shot.

And there, careening around the corner of the stall, was Cere—followed seconds behind by a small army of rushing stormtroopers.

"Taxi!" Cere shouted, throwing up a hand as she made a bolt for the *Mantis.*

Cal laughed—a relieved kind of half laugh, strained by his one-handed death grip on his lightsaber and the tightness of the expression Cal always got on his face when he used the Force, shoving any trooper who attempted to enter Cere's space away from her.

Merrin took a deep breath—Cal could keep the blasterfire away from the ship, but he was only one person, and there was only so long he could maintain his concentration both on his lightsaber *and* on pushing enemies away from Cere with the Force when they got too close. Merrin's eyes flicked quickly around the little square, and she immediately knew what she had to do.

Now she just had to do it.

On Dathomir, using her powers had always come easily to Merrin. It was, after all, her birthright. She'd watched some of her other sisters struggle, fight to connect to the fire that lived deep within each of them, that made up their cores. Merrin had never had that problem. Merrin came into her power early and fierce.

From the moment she knew to reach for the fire, it was always right there, waiting and eager, licking at the inside of her soul, desperate to be freed, to be put to good use. To consume.

When they came and took her sisters from her, Merrin's fire consumed everything. Burned the way she saw her world and its enemies down around her like an inferno. It spared no one.

Merrin suspected, in the quiet moments—of which there had been many, since—that her soul, her core, had been no exception.

But she'd left Dathomir. Her world, her sisters, everything she had ever known . . . she couldn't even point in the direction of Dathomir, wherever it might be from where she stood, on shaking metal in mortal danger on some strange planet she would likely never see or smell or feel again. She felt as unmoored as the *Mantis,* her feet off the ground, her head in the void of space.

And when she closed her eyes and looked within herself, reached for the fire that made her who she was, she found . . . nothing. She grasped and searched and grabbed—she knew it was there, or how would she still draw breath? It *was* her—but she'd lost her way toward it.

What was a Nightsister of Dathomir with no sisters, and no Dathomir?

She felt the weight of the necklace she wore every day—beaded chain, heavy golden triangles in a crescent, like the bared teeth of a smiling predator that knows it has cornered a meal—felt it bounce against her chest with the jerky movement of the *Mantis.* It was a memory that came up all at once and was gone before she had time to consider it, more like a feeling than a vid, a fingerprint pressed into the folds of her mind: chalky-white skin like hers, piercing ice-blue eyes, silver hair cropped short, freshly grown. Light and agile fingers stringing it together one tooth at a time, sometimes shaky and weak. Face all angles, except dark plush lips, soft against Merrin's own, pressing the necklace into her hands, an unspoken thank-you, a gift to the one who cared for her when she needed it most. To Merrin.

It was moments like this when Merrin felt her homesickness most keenly—and when she knew she would be letting down the only people she had left in this galaxy if she couldn't get herself under control.

Greez was having trouble holding the ship steady as he maneuvered to avoid both blasterfire and buildings; the *Mantis* wasn't made for this kind of flight. The ship jerked up a few meters, then down; drifted right, then swerved left. It was difficult enough for Merrin to make her blind grabs for her power without such distractions; with them, it was nearly impossible.

Nearly.

It took Cere nearly dropping to a blaster bolt that did it. A spark of fear, true fear, and Merrin finally, finally felt it—an itch in the palm of her hands, not the racing fire she'd once known but just enough—and she threw her hand out.

Surrounded by the green fire of Merrin's magick, down below, a stall blew itself apart. High-velocity shards of wood and metal turned into deadly projectiles, slamming into the stormtroopers chasing Cere, cutting them dead short in their tracks. Merrin watched them fall with a small smile as the itch receded from her palm.

They all fell.

All, save one.

The last of the Empire's soldiers was hot on Cere's tail, mere steps behind her. Cal had thrown himself onto his stomach, arms and upper torso hanging off the edge of the struggling ramp, reaching for Cere. Cere went to make her final running leap for the *Mantis*—just as the ship jerked itself upward, meters out of reach.

Merrin heard herself shouting—she wasn't sure what—as Cere's feet left the ground, her arms stretched above her, reaching for Cal as Cal shifted himself as far forward as he could without toppling off the edge of the ramp. Behind Cere, Merrin watched the stormtrooper raise their arms—well within reach of Cere, close enough to grab—

And *shoved* her into the air, right into Cal's waiting arms.

Merrin didn't have the time to consider what she'd just seen; momentarily forgetting her fear of the ship shaking itself to death around her, she rushed forward to grasp at Cal's ankles, yanking him back as hard as she could until both Cere and Cal were back over the ramp's edge.

"Move!" Cal shouted to Greez via comms, at the exact same time Cere yelled "Hold!"

And then their fearless leader was launching her torso out over the edge of the ramp all over again.

"Pull!" Cere demanded from somewhere below the ramp. Merrin, eyes wide, resumed her grip on Cal's ankles, as he held on to his mentor by the waist.

Cal held fast. "On three! One—two—"

"Out of time!" Greez's voice came over the comms.

The *Mantis* shot up into the air in a steep ascent as Merrin pulled on Cal with all her might. She heard Cere's battle cry from below get louder and louder as the ramp tilted back and Cal came tumbling back into the entrance of the ship with Cere safely wrapped in his grip.

And beside both of them came the last stormtrooper, rolling into the *Mantis*'s hold as the ramp started to rise, its hydraulics finally relieved of the unwelcome pressure. Before Cal could turn his lightsaber on them, the stormtrooper rolled onto their knees, throwing one hand in the air in a gesture of surrender as the other popped the seal on their intimidatingly familiar helmet. With a flick of their hand, the helmet hit the ground with a *clang*—revealing the red-eyed, purple-haired trooper.

"We brought *her*?" Greez was incredulous, and twisted around in his chair for a moment to take in what was happening. "We almost lost my ship for a *stormtrooper*?"

"We'll discuss later!" Cere snapped, rushing for her copilot's seat next to Greez in the cockpit. The *Mantis* was blasting through the collapsing asteroid's shield bubble as the base was torn apart by the exploding charges—still shaky, but at least now in a way that felt familiar to Merrin.

Merrin watched Cal regard the unmasked stormtrooper, still kneeling in the middle of the room. Cal blinked before holstering his lightsaber in one smooth movement. Without a word, he wedged himself into the curved bench behind the common area's only table, gesturing between the stormtrooper and the seat next to him with what Merrin imagined passed for a welcoming smile, under the circumstances.

The stormtrooper—a Keshiri, Merrin noted, unusual for an Imperial—slowly brought both her hands down to the common room's metal floor, levering herself up. She maneuvered her way into the bench seat next to Cal, her plastoid armor making a grating sound as it rubbed up against the table. The table where they sat and played games; where they ate their meals; where they discussed Empire-breaking strategy.

Now, sitting there, calmly and like this was something she did every day, was a red-eyed purple-haired woman with shaggy hair. A stormtrooper.

As Cal busied himself getting BD-1 settled in to charge via the scomp link beneath the seating bench, directly under Cal's feet, Merrin cautiously slid into an open space on the bench. The stormtooper sat squeezed between the Jedi on her right and the Nightsister on her left, shoved into them by the tilting motion of the ship. Merrin thought the woman looked equal parts relieved and hysterical.

Maybe that getaway wasn't quite as routine as the stormtrooper was trying to play off.

"Once again, I am asking you all to strap in." Greez sounded annoyed over the comms now. "Because this is about to get exciting."

The red-eyed stormtrooper cocked an eyebrow and looked at Merrin with a lopsided smirk. "About to?" she asked, her voice lilting in a very unusual manner. "I like this place already."

Merrin's palms started to itch.

Oh, she thought. *There's the fire.*

BD-1 secure, crew strapped in, Greez behind the wheel . . . Cal finally let himself turn his attention to the stormtrooper-shaped issue next to him, settled into the squeaky potolli-weave cushions of what passed for the *Mantis*'s couch and caf table. From between his feet, Cal felt BD bump his head into his ankles with a quiet trill of support. The little guy always did know when Cal needed a little boost. Most empathetic droid in the galaxy, Cal would swear.

"Merrin," Cal began, "you have to know this is a dangerous idea—"

"Cute droid," the stormtrooper squashed onto the bench next to Merrin cut in. All Cal knew about her, from the conversation with Merrin he'd overheard via comms, was that she had turned her back on the Empire—but that and good taste in droids was enough to make Cal feel like they'd made the right decision, for the moment. He didn't trust her, of course; hard to trust a buckethead at all, no matter the circumstance. But he knew how hard it could be to leave everything you knew behind, once you knew it was wrong; he had Merrin sitting right on the trooper's other side to account for that. He wanted to trust her, even if he didn't, quite yet. And he didn't want her to feel pressured to give her life story the second she got on the ship. Cal imagined she'd just been through something incredibly stressful and traumatic. Not exactly conducive to eloquence.

And not that it took him much to imagine the woman's state of mind. Not after he'd been there himself, again and again, at the hands of a greedy Empire powered by consumption and conformity that spit out anything and anyone that didn't align with its goals.

Cal gave the newcomer, who was both wider and taller than Merrin, what he hoped was a welcoming smile. "That's Beedee-Wun," Cal explained, pausing for a moment while Greez apparently hit some bad turbulence on the way out of the asteroid's collapse, pelted by rocks and debris. "Beedee units are some of the best explorers in the galaxy, and you won't find a better example than this little guy right here. Beeps in the face of danger."

"Yes, the droid is just as foolhardy as his human," Cal heard Merrin mutter next to him, bright and cheerful as the Nightsister ever was. Under the chalky-white skin of her face, Cal swore he could see a bit of a green undertone, her eyes glued to the table in front of her. Greez wasn't driving *that* badly, even if things had stayed pretty bumpy.

Cal reached behind the trooper, clapping his hand onto Merrin's shoulder, giving her a friendly shake. "Right, so, this is Merrin. She's a Nightsister of Dathomir, and exactly as scary as she sounds. But it's part of her charm. Okay, all of her charm." Cal gave Merrin a smile and squeezed her shoulder lightly, just until he caught her rolling her eyes.

"And I'm Cal," he continued, turning back to the woman. "Rigger. Swoopdueling enthusiast." Cal paused as the *Mantis* made some questionable noises while Greez went careening away from the asteroid belt at full speed. "And Jedi. One of . . ." Saying it never got easier. No matter how many times he did it. "One of the last of my kind."

"Yes," Merrin said softly. "We have that in common." Cal looked back at the Nightsister, to find her staring right at him. She looked like . . . it wasn't pity in her eyes. It wasn't even sympathy. It was just—acceptance. Acceptance, and . . . something else.

Caring?

As the stormtrooper opened her mouth to introduce herself in return, Cal suddenly realized he was still reaching behind the stormtrooper with his hand on Merrin's shoulder.

And then, just as suddenly, Cal—and everything else—was upside down.

He registered the hit to the *Mantis* in the split second before the plasma bolt actually connected with the hull, the Force sending the blast splitting through his brain like the worst kind of headache just before he found himself hanging by the waist from his seatbelt strap. Cal wasn't upside down, technically—the *Mantis* was. And the antigrav was malfunctioning, and all the lights in the *Mantis* had taken on a red hue, a clear sign that hull integrity had been compromised or something else was very, very wrong with the ship. For a wild second, the only thought in Cal's head was that he was super grateful he'd thought to install an independent gravcore in the ship's terrariums, or else all of their plants—so carefully tended by Greez—would be mulch right now.

Cal wondered hysterically why he was thinking about plants as reality came roaring back to Cal with BD-1's panicked trills from below— above?—his seat.

Next to him, the stormtrooper was yelling obscenities, the shiny plates of her white armor sliding through the belt. In the instant she came loose from her strap, Merrin's arm shot out, grabbing the woman by the wrist—just quickly enough to send them both careening down headfirst toward what was, typically, the *Mantis*'s overhead. A carpet of green fire cushioned both women's fall just before impact, but it disappeared as quickly as it came. Cal noticed the stormtrooper's eyes go wide, and realized she'd likely never seen Nightsister magick before.

This was about to be a real adventure for her.

Suddenly Cal's attention was caught by a screech. Their ship's resident stowaway, a little fuzzy bogling from Bogano, came tumbling out of her home vent, clutching desperately onto the first thing she came in contact with to stop herself from hitting the floor: the front of Cal's shirt. The bogling's tiny claws latching into the skin on Cal's chest was enough to push Cal out of his momentary shock and into action.

"Greez!" Cal yelled, fumbling with the buckle at his lap around the screeching bogling and over the sounds of BD's trills. "What's—"

"Exiting the asteroid belt, but it looks like we've got incoming—!" Greez's yell interrupted Cal in the middle of his ask. Just as quickly as the ship had gone belly-up, Cal felt the ship rock with impact, and he felt gravity's pull on his head disappear, the weight tethering him to his seatbelt gone in a flash. In a shock of silence, the only sounds left inside the *Mantis* were the shrieks of the klaxons and the crew, the stormtrooper, BD, and the bogling's shock echoing through the small ship.

"TIE Brute on our tail!" Greez's voice crackled over the *Mantis* intercom this time, to be sure he was heard over the racket. "They hit our gravcore. Cal—"

He knew what he had to do before Greez even said it. "On it!" Cal confirmed, finally giving up on his jammed buckle and squinting at it with the Force until it came undone.

Pushing off from the seat above him, and dislodging the bogling in the process, it took Cal a moment to reorient himself; his gravity-addled brain was still thinking of the *Mantis* as upside down, even though now, without gravity, there was no up or down—whichever direction Cal faced, there he was. He turned 180 degrees until he was face-to-face with a vocally disgruntled BD-1, still safe and braced on the console.

"You okay, buddy?" Cal confirmed with his droid, who beeped in the affirmative—though Cal could tell it was tinged with the obvious grumpiness of someone who had just been through a deeply uncomfortable situation against their will. Cal tried to hide his smile so his droid didn't see it.

"Okay, moving to the secondary breaker panel," Cal called out, hoping Greez could hear him. He pushed off and spun, shoving forward toward the panel near the holoprojector table where Cal knew the backup grav generator could be activated, and almost collided with a lightsaber, lit up and in Cere's hands. He'd been so caught up he hadn't even noticed her ignite it.

With a gasp, Cal jerked his head to the side, sending himself careening into a zero-gravity backspin. He bumped into the wall behind him and grabbed hold of the edge of the vent that the bogling had come tumbling out of, taking in the scene in front of him.

On Cal's left, Greez was holding on to the *Mantis*'s controls for dear life, executing a series of evasive maneuvers so complex that only someone with as many eyes as Greez had arms could have accomplished it. The bogling had ended up wedged underneath Greez's seat, holding on to his pant legs with an iron grip.

And in front of him, floating over the galaxy map, were Merrin, Cere, and the stormtrooper, locked in a standoff that had happened in the seconds that Cal was checking on BD. It shouldn't have surprised Cal as much as it did, but he was always a little bit shocked at just how unflappable Cere was—nothing sent her into shock.

Not even Darth Vader himself.

This, in comparison? This was nothing.

The loudest sound in the *Mantis* now, besides Greez's grunts over the control console, was the hot, heavy flare of Cere's lightsaber. Well, Cal corrected himself as he watched the stare-down, patting at his side: the lightsaber Cere was currently in possession of, which at this moment happened to be Cal's, knocked out of his holster during the antigrav shift.

Cere had the tip of Cal's lightsaber right up against the stormtrooper's purple throat, steadying herself in the antigrav with her other hand on the edge of the holoprojector. The trooper herself was held in place by Merrin, who was grasping the woman's hand so hard her already white knuckles had turned somehow even whiter.

"Wait—" Cal started, but he'd barely had a chance to get the word out before he was overtaken by Cere herself.

"Convince me you're not here to sabotage us," Cere said calmly over the buzz of her borrowed lightsaber. "We all heard your conversation with Merrin. I want to believe you're a deserter, but the Empire is on our tail and I can't have a liability on board." The blade moved, by just a centimeter, closer to the woman's neck.

The stormtrooper shook her head violently. The blue of Cal's lightsaber reflected brightly in her red eyes, her pupils blown wide with fear. Red embers glowing in the lightsaber's heat turned suddenly violet. Bright, vivid violet.

Blue light mixed with red.

Merrin's magick formed a thin but still-visible wall directly between the woman and Cere's weapon. Cere's head snapped toward her crewmate, but Merrin lifted her other hand in a gesture of good faith.

"She should have the chance to explain herself," said Merrin. "Before she dies by a weapon that she's likely only seen used in the hands of the Empire."

At the mention of such a lightsaber—bled red like her former Padawan's—Cere's lips pressed together in a seam so tight Cal thought she might implode. There was a moment when the tension among the three women was so thick he would have been hard-pressed to cut through it even with a laser sword.

"Why are you threatening her after pulling her aboard?" Cal demanded. He hadn't seen that kind of behavior out of Cere in years.

"Why aren't you?" Cere shot back. "I need to know what she knows about us. Plus, only humans serve as stormtroopers, which means she must have done something to prove her loyalty to the Empire. We may have just let an Imperial agent in stormtrooper gear onto this ship— a *wanted* ship, mind you, and one that survives only because we take *great pains* never to be tracked or followed. The safety of my crew is paramount. She is not my crew."

"Cere," Cal said incredulously. "Neither was Greez, when you pulled him out of that gambling den. Neither was Merrin, when we flew her off Dathomir. And neither was I, when you reached out a hand to me and saved me from Trilla's blade at the last possible moment."

Cal knew mentioning Trilla would be a blow Cere wouldn't be able to recover from easily, so he did it softly, to be sure she didn't wince away from them. He only wanted her to consider all possible options here. It worked; Cal saw the shadow of doubt cross her face, just for a moment. He wasn't trying to be manipulative; he just needed Cere to keep her focus, so they could talk this out.

"Merrin sees something in her," Cal said after a beat. "She's vouching for her. We've all had moments where we've had to trust each other, even when we're making seemingly bad calls.

"You trusted your gut about us," he continued. "I trust Merrin's gut. If she wants to give this stormtrooper a chance, we give her a chance. But at the first sign of funny business—"

"We dump her." Cere nodded. "Fine. I hear you. And . . ." She took a deep, steadying breath, and added: "Good advice, Cal." Then she turned her attention back to the faux-trooper.

"Talk," Cere demanded. She moved the lightsaber away but kept it ignited. "And talk fast. Like your life depends on it."

"Chellwinark Frethylrin." Words came tumbling out of the woman's mouth as quickly as she could force them out. She was pointing at herself. "Fret." She lifted both her arms to match Merrin's raised hand, mirroring the nonthreatening gesture. "You're right; I'm not a stormtrooper. Also not an agent. I'm just an analyst. I stole the outfit. It was my best shot to escape unnoticed. I know this looks bad. But I *am* a deserter. And you, the crew of the *Mantis* . . ." Her voice lilted in a way that Cal thought was charming. "You're my only hope of getting out."

Cere's expression didn't change, but Cal could tell she was not yet convinced. "Twenty seconds," she said tightly.

"Less," Cal heard Greez mutter from the cockpit. "I'm good but I don't know if anyone's good enough to shake this damn ship off our tail—"

"Okay. Right." The wheels in Fret's head appeared to be turning so fast Cal could feel things clicking together behind the eerie red of her irises. "Okay. Let's try something else." She paused for just a moment before turning toward the cockpit.

"Arms!" Fret shouted, clearly taking on a new tactic. "If I get some space between you and the TIE Brute, can you hit hyperspace? You're that good, right?"

"Is she talking to me?" came Greez's incredulous response. "I know she isn't talking to me right now, because—"

"Okay, good," Fret cut in. "Distract them and then do some fancy flying—loud static on all channels and then put the ship in a full flip. Input your nav coordinates right before you make your move. Cal—" She flashed a look over at him. "Same time, activate the secondary grav generator. The Imperial systems will be confused, and the operator should be disoriented enough by the noise through their comms that we can immediately jump to hyperspace without anyone accurately capturing our trajectory. After a quick count of three, we'll make it happen. Got it?"

Both Cal and Greez just stared at Fret. She shrugged. "I used to be close with a really, really good engineer."

Cal looked at Cere. He knew time was up, and a choice had to be made.

Cere tilted her head. She was leaving the decision up to Cal.

There was no other option at this point. Greez was the best pilot this side of the galaxy, but he wasn't making any headway—the Imperial ship was too close, and they weren't going to be able to shake it without a miracle.

But Cal had been known to attract a miracle or two around here lately.

He was ripping the panel out of the *Mantis*'s wall before Fret had even finished her ask. "One!" Cal started the countdown.

"Cal, what are you—?" Greez protested.

"Two!" Cal reached into the guts of the *Mantis*, searching for the breaker port he'd need to hit.

"Argh!" He heard Greez's frustration echo from the cockpit.

"Three . . ."

"Now!" Fret cried.

Cal yanked on the grav breaker in the *Mantis*'s wall with everything he had, activating the secondary drive at the right moment and reestablishing gravity aboard the ship. Simultaneously, he watched Greez hit two buttons at once with his lower arms while his upper two arms yanked so hard on the *Mantis*'s joysticks, he thought they might snap off. Cal could feel the *Mantis* do a full turn on the vertical—"upright," again—at the same moment Greez fired off broadcast static.

The Imperial ship's sensors, momentarily confused by Greez's haphazard flight path and his overloading the comms channels, were unable to react to the sudden maneuver—giving the *Mantis* just enough distance that—

"Lightspeed, here we come!" Greez yelled, and one of his arms slammed back the lever that would send the *Mantis* into hyperspace. Cal felt the kick of the hyperdrive just as he felt the pull of the secondary grav generator come back online, and as he tumbled to the *Mantis*'s floor, he heard the rest of the crew do the same.

And he heard the unmistakable sound of a lightsaber retracting into its hilt.

With a grunt, Cal got back to his feet, hoisting himself up using the holotable. His first instinct, as always, was to ensure the well-being of his crew. BD-1 was still braced beneath the table; Greez was muttering about totally being able to do that himself, without help; Merrin had dropped her magick, and she had fallen to the floor in a sprawl, arms and legs wide open to support herself. Fret had landed right between Merrin's legs, back-to-front, Merrin's chest supporting Fret's wide, obviously strong back. Cal noticed himself frowning; he didn't trust Fret *that* much, not yet.

Cere was on the ground, too, her back against the holotable, starring at Fret. "Tell me, Frethylrin. What other inside knowledge do you have that we might be able to use against the Empire?"

Cal looked over at the sound of a soft chirp. The bogling had taken a tumble from under the cockpit, and had scuttled over to what she perceived was safety—in Fret's lap, with a weird little bogling smile that, somehow, matched Fret's grin at Cere.

"Where do you want me to start?"

CHAPTER 5

There was a stormtrooper in the kitchen.

A stormtrooper—okay, not actually a stormtrooper, but an *Imperial* nonetheless—with a bit of a twangy accent and mesmerizing eyes, right there in the *Mantis*'s kitchen. Where Merrin ate her breakfast bar every morning; where Greez ambidextrously fried four desserts at once, when he was feeling particularly chef-y; where Cere insisted that dessert—however abundant—wasn't enough for dinner, and made Greez choke down a protein bar first.

Helmet, gloves, and plastoid shell discarded, the stormtrooper was leaning up against the food prep counter in just her black bodysuit and boots, the suit clinging to every sturdy, strong curve of her body. Fret was tall and broad, imposing, with wide strong shoulders sloping down to a flat chest to a surprisingly soft and sweet waist that blossomed out into full, curved hips that mirrored her plush lips and strong—had Merrin thought strong already?—thighs that looked like they could crush Merrin's head clean off between them and she had to remind herself that she was staring. *Merrin, spirits, don't be such a complete and immediate embarrassment.* She couldn't look at Fret's face; there was too much there that made Merrin nervous: her round cheeks, the way her nose scrunched up when she smiled, those *lips,* the way her hair curled thin at the base of her neck but flared out thick and long on top, begging to be pushed into and out of place.

Instead Merrin shifted her focus to a surely more innocuous location: the woman's hands, wrapped around a steaming mug of caf, thick, strong fingers and short nails, more dexterous than they were long, surely very capable—

Merrin swallowed.

Regardless, it all came back to: There was a very hot stormtrooper in Merrin's kitchen, and the rest of the *Mantis*'s crew was all standing around to interrogate her. This is just what happened on the *Mantis.* Things that made Merrin feel somewhat outside of reality.

Merrin had been virtually alone on Dathomir for years with only her own thoughts for diversion, but she'd never felt really, truly like she might have lost control of her mental faculties until she'd joined the crew of the *Mantis.* There was something about this ship—this crew— that attracted trouble on a galactic scale.

Sure, it was part of what Merrin loved so much about being aboard the repurposed luxury yacht. But it also made her question whether or not she had any sense of self-preservation left in her, or if it had been killed off for good alongside her sisters.

Was that too dark? Merrin suspected that was a joke she should keep to herself, unless she wanted her crewmates to really start worrying about her.

The stormtrooper—Frethylrin—took a sip of her caf. Those red eyes Merrin couldn't pull herself away from closed as a satisfied smile— a smirk, really—stretched over Fret's lips. Merrin found herself blushing, heat rushing up to her cheeks. She ducked her head before anyone else could notice the green. What was going *on* with her?

The elders always did say foolishness ran in her family.

"Thank you," said Fret, in her light accent. "For the caf, mostly. But also for the rescue."

Greez leaned against the doorframe out of the kitchen, both sets of arms crossed over his chest, watching Fret's every move with a skeptical glare. He was maybe a third of Fret's height, and looked like he always looked; Merrin had never seen Greez without his bomber jacket, gold necklace, and silver pants. She assumed he owned several sets of the same outfit. "Yeah, well," Greez grunted. "It's expensive out here, and I only get the good stuff, so don't drink too much."

From his seat at the kitchen table, Cal awkwardly tried to cover up a laugh with a cough. It didn't work. The bogling peeked out from behind his legs for just a second, just until she noticed Fret's eyes on her, and then she scurried away to one of her many hideaways on the ship.

Merrin wanted to follow her.

"All right." Cere entered the kitchen from where she'd been examining the map projected on the holotable, giving Fret a glance. She straddled the chair next to Cal's, facing Fret. "We're safe, for the moment. No one's followed us. Before we set our next course, now would be the moment for explanations."

Fret took another sip and nodded. "You know, we heard a lot about the *Stinger Mantis* on the Imperial side. They make it sound like a dangerous warship full of terrible rebels." She looked around for a moment. "Obviously it's that. But it's also pretty cute."

Merrin heard Greez scoff at "cute," but she didn't necessarily disagree with Fret's assessment. She tried to remember how the *Mantis* looked the first time she boarded the ship with Cal—the first time she'd ever been on a ship at all—fresh off Dathomir: the three-seater cockpit in the bow with its floor-to-ceiling viewport and Greez's specialty chair; the cozy common room with its curved benches framing the circular holotable always glowing with the light of possibility. The living area, with its fuzzy L-shaped couch, nearly every centimeter of spare space taken up by terrariums encased in Umbaran glass, growing plants Cal helped Greez collect from across the galaxy; a few steps up to the raised kitchen, where you could sit at the table and see straight down through to the cockpit viewports when all the blast doors were open, a perfect morning view to fill you with the awe of the vastness of space (or the existential dread of the unending vacuum mere centimeters from where you sat with your breakfast bar, depending on what side of the cot you woke up on that day).

And behind all that, the corridor with crew cabins that led to the noisy engine room—what Merrin thought of as "Cal's room," because it was where he spent most of his time. Meditating, fixing up his lightsaber or his little droid, sleeping; the engine room was indistinguishable from Cal's space because they were one and the same. Always on, always moving forward, propelled through space by self-generated momentum alone.

And below it all, the escape pods and more crew quarters. Merrin sometimes thought of her room as a third escape pod. After so long planetside on her own, these close quarters with her crewmates could be both a blessing and a curse.

It was good, in her darkest moments, not to be alone. But it was equally hard not to be alone.

"I want out. *Need* out." Fret's voice brought Merrin back to the present moment, where she sat between Cal and Cere, still staring at the kitchen table.

"How'd you end up *in* in the first place?" Greez cocked a fuzzy eyebrow. "Bit weird to see a purple stormtrooper, is all I'm sayin'."

Fret looked down into her caf cup. "I'm Keshiri. From a planet out in Wild Space not many people have heard of. Kesh never saw the appeal of joining the Republic, and we moved when I was young—came up during the Clone Wars. My folks were inspired by the Separatist cause, for a while there . . ." She looked up at Cal and Cere with a shrug. "And eventually the Empire needed bodies for their dirty work. Analysts, coders. Clones weren't cutting it anymore, I guess. Never even bothered giving us much training before they set us to our jobs, supporting the Imperials. I had to leave my family. I never saw them again."

"I'm sorry," Cal said softly. BD-1 beeped in what Merrin assumed to be agreement.

"The Empire doesn't value life." Merrin stared down at the table in front of her as she spoke. Merrin knew that her feeling of rage toward Imperials wasn't entirely transference; it was clear to her, after many long conversations with Cal and Cere over the years, that the Separatist leaders had always been pawns of the now-Emperor. He was responsible for Dathomir, and his current followers would pay. The faces of her sisters swam at the edges of her vision, threatening to overtake her.

She would not let them; this was not the moment for selfishness like that.

"No," Fret agreed. "They don't. But I was young, and it was all the life I ever knew. It's not like you show up and they tell you you're the bad guy; they tell you all the good you're doing for the galaxy, how brutal it is out there for planets outside Imperial control. I had an itch about it, but—"

Fret sighed. "It took seeing the Empire from an outside perspective for me to start to get it, start to question things. Start to ask the *right* questions, anyway. To get that we weren't helping people, we were—we were harming them. And in some really, really dark cases . . . we were *hunting* them. And I was a part of that. I might have just been an analyst, a surveyor, a people-watcher, really. But I was propping up the fear they were spreading. I was a victim, but I was also a perpetrator. And once I knew, the *second* I knew—I couldn't, anymore. I wouldn't."

Merrin saw Cal's head drop out of the corner of her eye, but she couldn't take her gaze off Fret.

"I never asked for that life," Fret continued, "but I couldn't see a way out, either. Out to where? The Empire is . . . everything. Until I heard about the *Stinger Mantis*," she added. "Until I heard about you."

Merrin's palms itched. When she raised her eyes up from the table, leaving her ghosts behind, she expected to find Fret looking at Cal. Obviously she was talking about Cal.

So why was Fret staring right at her?

Merrin felt herself going green again, the heat rushing from her palms up her arms and through her neck to her cheeks and into her hairline, fire blooming under her skin faster than light. She stared back at Fret at a loss for words.

Next to her, Cal cleared his throat, tearing Merrin's attention away from the stormtrooper for just long enough to free her from her momentary . . . what? Daze? *Crush?*

"And what, exactly," Cere asked Fret with narrowed eyes, "had you heard about the *Stinger Mantis*?"

Fret paused for a moment, long enough for Merrin to silently reprimand herself. Heart racing at the first sign of a woman with a blaster and a beguiling voice. Had she forgotten this Keshiri was an *Imperial*? That she very well could have been one of the minions responsible for the downfall of Dathomir? Or if not her, soldiers exactly like her?

Not that Merrin exactly had the best taste in crushes, generally. She'd never fixated on beings of a single gender as some of her friends did; Merrin fell freely and with few limitations for people of all genders, especially those with exceptional personalities, and with whom she felt a strong connection. In her years on the *Mantis,* there had been a few brief flings in the moments where they stayed in one spot long enough for them to happen; one who was more in love with her power than anything else, one who ran so hot-then-cold that Merrin could never quite find her footing with him.

Back on Dathomir, when she was younger, there had been only one that had mattered. The one Merrin had cared for through a difficult convalescence after injury. The girl who had pressed a gold-toothed necklace into Merrin's hands, telling her to keep it with her, always, to remember her by. The girl who Merrin had loved, she thought, despite everything, but who Merrin hadn't seen since the destruction of the Nightsisters.

So, not an amazing track record overall.

And here on the *Mantis,* Merrin's body and heart were betraying her mind in ways she didn't want to think about right now. First the connection to her magick, lost and unclear in a way it had never been before. Now drawn to a shaggy-haired Imperial whom Merrin was willing to bet could give her almost a fair fight in head-to-head battle.

That was appealing to Merrin, for reasons she felt better left unexamined at the moment.

"Merrin?" she heard Cere ask from next to her, bringing the witch back into the present moment. "Your thoughts?"

Merrin had decidedly not been paying attention to anything but her own traitorous heartbeat. "Apologies, Cere. Could you go over it one more time?"

"Distracted?" asked Fret. She had one purple eyebrow raised, opposite the corner of her mouth that lifted in a self-assured smirk.

That was appealing to Merrin, too.

"Ah." Merrin cleared her throat, trying very hard to ignore Cere's attempt to hide a smile and Cal's furrowed-brow confusion on either side of her. "Yes. Lots to consider."

"I bet." Now it was Fret smiling, but she wasn't bothered to try to hide it. The self-confidence that poured off this woman was intense.

Merrin could tell that the rest of her crewmates were still not entirely sold on the idea of Fret aboard the *Mantis*. But, besides the obvious effect she had on her, Merrin had heard the way Fret had begged for help. The desperation in her voice, and the bravery it had taken for her to even ask. Had seen in her eyes everything she knew she was leaving behind, and the knowledge that she could never, ever go back.

Merrin knew how that felt. Intimately. She wanted the rest of the crew to see that in Fret, too. To understand, as she did.

"You've lost everything." Merrin forced herself to look into Fret's red eyes. "Your life, everything you've ever known, has been taken from you by the Empire. I can see the pain, still so fresh on your face. And I want you to know I understand it."

Fret's face softened, for a moment, as the rest of the crew stayed silent. They'd all lost things—lives, people—to the Empire. Merrin knew that. But by the time she had joined the crew, Cere and Cal had already come to terms with that. It was all part of a greater commitment to their Jedi order. As much as Merrin had wanted to talk about how she felt about losing her life on Dathomir, she had never quite been able to feel entirely *heard* about it by Cere and Cal.

They felt the anguish of it, but they were at peace with their choice.

Merrin had never known peace about Dathomir, not for a single moment.

And Fret was still there, too, tumultuous and torn up. Merrin knew, in that moment, Fret would be someone who would commiserate and understand.

"Thank you," Fret said, less softly than Merrin had expected. With an edge. "Once I'd seen . . . Once I knew what was really happening in the galaxy, there was no going back. There's nothing for me to go back to.

And . . ." She took a deep breath. "And I'm furious about it. I'm so, so mad. And I hate it."

Merrin watched Cal look at Fret as she spoke, knew talk of strong emotions like fury and hate made him and Cere uncomfortable. But was Fret wrong to feel that way?

Was Merrin?

"All that is behind you is loss," Merrin said. "And all that is in front of you are questions. It is not fair. And I am here to talk. Should you need to."

Fret smiled, small and appreciative. "I'm going to take you up on that." She turned back to Cere. "And to the rest of you: I owe you all a great debt. And I don't like accruing interest. So let me pay you back right now."

"We're waitin'." Greez gestured impatiently. Despite his penchant for grump—actually, no, *because* of it—Merrin liked Greez. The gray-skinned, four-armed Latero was like the greasy uncle Merrin never had on Dathomir; his squat, wide face made wider by his bushy gray side-burns, his little ears like antennas sticking out from his balding head, his long mouth and wide-set eyes set in a perpetual grin, like Greez always knew the punch line to a joke nobody else was privy to.

Frustrating, how much Merrin liked Greez, frankly. Not as frustrating as what was happening between her and Fret. But still.

"There's a job," said Fret, putting her empty mug down on the counter next to her. "Something your crew can take. Something that could put a real dent in the Empire. And I have the information you need to pull it off. I know it's a big thing, to request your trust in this. But if you can, and you're willing to give me a shot—it could change the galaxy as we know it."

There was a pause as the *Mantis* crew absorbed Fret's words. Then they all spoke at once.

"Done—"

"Absolutely not—"

"Damn right—"

"We'll take it under advisement—"

"Breeeeep beep—"

The crew stopped. Everyone looked at one another.

Merrin swallowed. This was about to become more complicated than even she had thought.

The day that had started out so well was suddenly not going at all how Cal had expected it to when he woke up this morning in his little cot in the engine room.

Everyone was staring one another down in a way that just didn't happen on the *Mantis*. Greez was shut off entirely, arms crossed, face turned up to the ceiling, unwilling to engage. Cere looked as impatient as Cal had ever seen her, trying to keep the situation under control, frustrated that people weren't listening. BD was hopping from foot to foot, the way he did when he was particularly stressed.

And worst of all, Merrin couldn't seem to look away from Fret. And Fret was looking right back at her. Cal was intrigued by it, and he couldn't put his finger on why; was puzzled by the way he could feel a connection between the women, radiating through the Force, like a tether connecting the two of them that he just—hadn't felt before, not very often. Felt that the two of them were drawn to each other in a way he couldn't quite explain.

And that was dangerous. For someone they barely knew. Of course.

It's not that Cal didn't do well in moments of conflict. His entire life had been a series of conflict moments, tied together through threads of the Force.

It was more that he didn't like it when his crew disagreed. They were family, or as close to family as Cal was going to get. And his family didn't fight. Not if he could help it.

"Beedee, can you show our guest to the crew quarters, please?" Cal asked his buddy, lifting the droid off his perch on the galley table and setting him down in front of Fret. "We're gonna need a second to talk this over. Fret, make yourself at home in—uh—"

"She can use my cabin," Merrin interrupted quickly. Cal shot her a look.

"Sure," he said. "Merrin's cabin, then." That made sense, after all. They were both around the same age, both women. That made the most sense. Obviously. Why wouldn't they share space, if Fret was going to be staying here for a bit?

Or maybe Fret shouldn't stay on board, after all.

"Take your time," said Fret, pushing off from the counter to follow BD back to the engine room. "Just, you know. Not too long. We have an Empire to crush."

When Fret had cleared the room, Cal was left with just his *Mantis* crew. The people he had come to think of as his family. Sure, an unusual, multispecies family, with varying numbers of limbs, different types of magical powers, alternately organic or mechanical guts, and always on the run from unknowable evil, but. What was a "normal" family in the galaxy these days, anyway? Who was to say the *Mantis* crew weren't a perfectly normal family?

And when families fight, the next thing they do is they talk things through, and they work it out. No matter what.

With a tilt of his head, Cal directed the crew toward the circular benches surrounding the holotable in the common room near the prow of the ship. He found it easier to think strategically there, in a space designed for it; plus, from a leadership perspective, he hoped it would remind his crew that they were here to do a job. To do whatever it took to oppose the Empire. To grasp at any opportunity they were given, no matter how small, on the off chance that it might be the first rung on a ladder that led to a galaxy where the Empire no longer controlled people with an iron fist.

Since their escape from the Fortress Inquisitorius—by the skin of their teeth, if Cal was being completely honest with himself—their lives hadn't exactly been easy, or simple. But they were doing good work. Pockets of rebellion were disparate, but the *Mantis* had been making contact with as many as they could, taking on jobs whenever and wherever it seemed that they could hit the Empire hardest.

But ultimately, Cal still thought of himself and the *Mantis* as the advance scouts, the forward team out in front of the anti-Empire movement. They were fast, stealthy, powerful—and they were *good*. With a

Jedi Knight, a Jedi Master, and a witch of Dathomir aboard, alongside the best pilot Cal had ever known and a genius droid, he felt like they were virtually unstoppable. And they'd proved it time and again. Together, they were capable of anything. A well-oiled machine, honed over years of strikes against the Empire. Sure, the work was slow—sometimes even demoralizing, on the worst days—but it was meaningful work. It was important work. And they were the best people to do it.

The *only* people to do it, really. How many other Jedi were left out there? How many other Nightsisters? War had taken so much from them all. BD-1 had lost his first master. So had Cal. Cere, her Padawan. Merrin, her family. Even Greez, though he liked to complain, had his heart in the right place. There was no one else out there. No one more likely to fight the Empire than their little strike team. And it was imperative that they make it happen.

Cal thought everyone understood that.

"What's the problem here, team?" he asked once they were all settled in their typical spots around the planetary display projected on the holotable. This was far from the first crew discussion they'd had over strategy since facing down—and, against all odds, surviving—Darth Vader, but Cal still felt as though, typically, he knew what was best for his crew and for the mission. Hearing them out was important, but he wasn't concerned about being able to convince them of the best move.

The Force had yet to steer him wrong. And the crew was always willing to listen to him.

Almost always, anyway.

"Is that a serious question you're asking?" Greez leaned back on the bench. "We just picked up Stormtrooper Surprise over here and now we're gonna, what—make her part of the crew?"

"Yes, what a terrible idea, to pick up a woman who typically opposes the Jedi but now wants to fight for the same cause," said Merrin drily.

"Okay, c'mon." Greez put his arms up in defense. "You were a totally different circumstance."

"Was I?"

Greez started pacing around the galley. "Yeah! You were, you know—there was—with the magick, and—"

He stopped, suddenly, stubbing his toe with a curse on a large pile of—junk?—in the corner of the galley that Cal hadn't even noticed amid all the chaos.

"The heck is that?" Cal asked. He tilted his head; it looked, for all of space, like a pile of ship scrap.

"It's ship scrap," Greez snapped defensively, bending down to rub his offending toe. "What? I thought I'd actually make us some money while you guys were running around setting off bombs on the Brood base. You know how much good cybernetic junk they had just lyin' around on that rock? We can make some real credits offa this. You're welcome, by the way."

"So now I'm back to scrapping?" Cal shook his head. "You were off the ship, wandering around the alleys, stealing stuff, when we could have needed you back on board for a quick getaway?" He could hardly believe what he was hearing.

"Yeah!" said Greez, slapping at the pile. It went collapsing to the floor with a crash, scattering all over the galley. "Okay, I'll clean that up. I'm just sayin', your thing was risky, my thing was certain. And I'll tell you what else—"

This was getting off track. "Fine. Whatever. We can talk about this later. And we aren't even here to talk about Fret joining the *Mantis,*" Cal clarified. "We just need to decide if we want to get details on her job. Sounds like it could have real potential in our fight against the Empire."

The crew all took a beat. Cal appreciated that.

"Merrin's right," he added, after a second. "Look at us all. We might as well call this crew the Second Chances. If Fret wants to change—if she specifically sought *us* out so she could make that change—are we really going to deny her before she even has the chance to prove herself to us?"

"Do we even owe her that?" asked Greez.

"And I do have to say," Cal pushed on and said, thoughtfully and deliberately, "I think it's important we take into consideration what Fret said about the *Mantis.* How it's proliferating through the Imperial ranks as a symbol of hope, of possible escape. If that's true, wouldn't helping Fret run from the Empire just further cement our status among Imperial troops as the potential for freedom? If there are other people like Fret out there—don't we want to encourage that? Nurture that kind of reputation?"

"I don't trust her," Merrin said, surprising Cal. "But I don't *not* trust her. Or—" She exhaled in obvious frustration. "You know what I'm trying to say. It's worth the risk."

"Not to be that guy but—is it?" Greez always said he didn't want to be "that guy," but he was awfully good at it, Cal thought. "What's the goal here? The long-term plan? Do we just keep throwing ourselves at random chances to put a ding in the Empire's gigantic, impenetrable hull?"

Cal shook his head. Greez was missing the mark entirely. "The plan is what it's always been. Bring the fight to the Empire. Or we'll never stop being hunted by the Inquisitors."

"Lofty." Merrin was shaking her head. "As long as I've been here, the plan has been to *fight back* against the Empire. I want revenge for my sisters. I can't kill the Separatists, so I'll settle for as many warmongers as I can. *Bringing the fight to* the Empire is a very different thing. A suicidal thing."

Greez sighed. "I'm just sayin', why are we acting like the fate of the galaxy is on *our* shoulders? Isn't there a point where we get to count our wins and go?" Cal opened his mouth to protest, but Greez cut him off. "Yeah, we're good. We've been lucky for a few years, sure. But we should really ask ourselves what the endgame is for us here, before we lose too much of ourselves to a fight we can't win."

Cal couldn't believe what he was hearing. "What, so you want to just—give up? Spend the rest of our lives in hiding?"

"At least we'll *have* lives to *spend*," Greez shot back. "This is a *gamble*, Cal. You're gambling on this stuff, all the time. You're chasin' that high, the win, and I get it—trust me, I get it—but you gotta know, you could always sink a lot lower. It's always waitin' for ya. Is this gonna be the gamble that doesn't pay off?"

There was silence for a second. Cal hated that Greez had a point.

"Enough." Cere's voice cut through the ringing quiet of the argument, clear and calm like a flat stone being skipped across a cool lake,

disrupting but not escalating. Up until now, she'd been quietly survey-
ing the discussion as she often did when she was still formulating her
thoughts. Cal admired her ability to think before speaking, something
he was self-aware enough to realize he often lacked. "You're all right,"
continued Cere. "And you're all wrong."

Useful. "Cere—" Cal started.

"Cal." Cere gave him a look that clearly said *let me finish* as much
through her eyes as through the history Cal and Cere had together. Cal
knew her looks as well as he knew BD's machinery at this point. So he
decided that letting Cere finish was the best course of action here, if he
didn't want a lecture on an important life lesson afterward.

"There is a middle ground here. I understand Greez's concerns. I also
feel that we have a responsibility to the galaxy. I *also* would prefer to not
die in the process of any of this. I've spent much of my own time meditating on the best way to move forward, the best way to preserve what's
left of the Jedi and our teachings . . ." She sighed. "There are no easy
answers."

"Sure there are," said Greez. "Right now, there definitely is. Drop the
stormtrooper on Batuu and send her off with a fruitcake. Bing bang
boom."

"And leave her to die?" Merrin asked incredulously.

At the same time, Cere said: "And abandon our best—and, might I
add, *only*—current lead against the Empire?"

"I don't trust her," added Greez.

"We don't *have* to," Cal interjected.

"It's too risky!" Greez shot back.

"We are *better* than this—" started Merrin.

Screeeeeeee!

BD-1's screech rang out through the circular room. Cal's little droid,
back from his duties with Fret, had returned to a shouting match. Cal
always suspected that BD had an extra empathy chip installed, and he
obviously knew that Cal was upset by the fighting. He put a stop to that,
and all that remained in the wake of his trill was a ringing silence.

This is why they never made family decisions without the *entire* family present.

"Beedee is right." Cal took the opportunity to regain control over the situation. "This is getting us nowhere. We need a new mission, and we're not turning our backs on this opportunity any more than we're going to turn our backs on someone in need. Get the details from Fret and set a course. And everybody—have something to eat. We'll all feel better after. Okay?"

Cal looked around the holotable at each of his crewmembers as they all sat still for a moment, digesting his words. Cere looked pleased; Merrin, more relieved. Greez broke the silence first, shrugging both sets of shoulders and making his way back to the cockpit with an "All we need is somebody to say *What could possibly go wrong*" under his breath.

CHAPTER 6

There was no reality in which Greez wanted to be on Hosnian Prime, and yet here he was, landing his ship on a Core planet like that wasn't the last place a bunch of wanted damn fugitives should be landing their *ostentatious, eye-catchingly beautiful space yacht.* Oh, yeah, and they were there on the ask of a stormtrooper they'd decided to adopt in a fit of, whatever, niceness or something equally getting-you-killed-worthy. An airtight plan. Just, generally, a great idea. Real big-brained stuff.

But what did he know, right? He was just the pilot.

So after a couple of days of making false hyperspace jumps to make sure they weren't followed by the Imperials from the Brood base—and so, at Cere's request, she could watch Fret to make sure for herself that there wasn't anything shady going on—Greez set his baby down just outside Chikua City, far enough that he felt *reasonably* certain no one looking for a quick credit was going to find the *Mantis* and call it in. Far enough that their new little stormtrooper friend had the audacity to complain about the distance of the walk, when apparently there had been a landing pad *right there* blah blah blah.

Greez had the shortest legs of the bunch. If anyone was gonna complain about the walk, it shoulda been him. But as he reminded them all,
getting arrested and sent to an Imperial prison to be tortured was probably a lot less comfortable than a few hours' walk through the hanging
gardens into the city center, so.

The stormtrooper shut up after that.

Nice.

"Pretty fancy place," said the stormtrooper. She and Merrin were
walking right in front of Greez, making googly eyes at each other like a
couple of Lateros in love. It was sickening, frankly, to see two people so
into each other when Greez himself hadn't seen so much as a Latero
lady's eyebrow hair in months. Merrin was holding on to the stormtrooper's offered arm, and the two of them were so deep into conversation it was like everybody else ceased to exist. Had been like that on the
Mantis, too, the whole way here.

"You're gonna like my contact. You're gonna like this job. He'll help
us. I know it."

"It *is* a pretty city," agreed Merrin. "But . . . not really my kind of
place."

Understatement, thought Greez. Chikua City itself was a Core night-
mare, more pavement than plants. Buildings tall enough to reach into
the clouds, the air between them clogged with traffic all hours of the day
and night. How was a guy supposed to live with no plants except in one
plant-specific space? Imagine living in a city that was so much building,
you had to carve out a specific space just for plants, or people would
forget about them entirely?

Greez wasn't saying that nobody but Lateros knew how to live, but
the more of the galaxy he saw, the more he was convinced that might be
true.

Anyway, the one good thing about a planet like Hosnian Prime was
that, like most Core planets, it was so full of people of all different species and races that it was easy for the *Mantis* crew to blend in with the
crowds once they got past the city outskirts. Other places, a Latero, a
Jedi, some purple lady, a pale Nightsister, and a somehow even paler

other Jedi might have drawn some attention to themselves. Greez had at least convinced Cere and Cal to leave their so-called in-genius hooded robe disguises on the ship. He got that the hoods were good for covering faces, but seriously, had they never looked in a mirror? Hooded robes screamed, *I'm a Jedi in hiding, please don't look too closely!*

Amateur hour.

They were lucky they had Greez around all the time, honestly. They all meant well, but he knew they'd have gotten themselves scooped up by some dimwit Inquisitor years ago without him.

Greez felt an elbow nudge his shoulder: Cal, bringing up the rear of the party behind him. "You okay, Greez?"

Greez looked up as Cal strode up alongside him, BD on his back as ever, beeping what he could only assume was the same question. Or maybe it was the most vile curseword known to the galaxy. None of them knew for sure, but Cal seemed to usually have some understanding of what the droid was trying to communicate.

"Eh." Greez shrugged noncommittally. "I mean, I think this is a horrible idea, and I think these two"—he jerked one of his thumbs in the direction of the couple in front of him—"are gonna make me scream if they don't just cut the tension and kiss already. A bunch of stuff I hate. You?"

Cal winced. "Yeah. Glad we're checking this out, but . . ." He faded off, and Greez watched his attention float back to Merrin and Fret.

Sheesh. *Kids.*

Greez wouldn't be here at all, frankly, if he hadn't been overruled by their eternal-optimist team leader. Greez loved Cal, he really did, like he was family; he felt like the kid's own flesh-and-blood, devastatingly handsome uncle in a lot of ways. But if Cal wasn't careful, his all-in attitude was gonna get them all captured or killed sooner rather than later. Greez had been serious when he said they needed to think about the future and gamble on it less. Greez himself had some pretty well-thought-out retirement plans involving a nice little restaurant where he served regulars and everyone had to listen to his stories whether they wanted to or not, because he was the one providing them with drinks.

Being imprisoned or dead was going to get in the way of that, so he wasn't trying to catch a blaster bolt between now and then with any particular urgency.

But Greez loved Cal, so here he was to protect the kid from whatever shenanigans he managed to get himself into this time. Where Cal went, shenanigans followed.

And only *sometimes* the shenanigans were Greez's fault. Like, one time out of ten. Max.

Okay, there was the whole Haxion Brood thing. Greez hadn't even thought his gambling debts were *that* bad, really, but the Brood had disagreed. They'd tracked him through the galaxy with the relentlessness of a cute Latero gal pursuing Greez on a late night at the bar. (He couldn't help that he was a lady-killer back home; it was the sideburns and more than a few well-traveled rumors about his quad-armed dexterity.)

But his debts had been that bad. They were worse than that bad, actually. They were, objectively, worth more than his life. But it was a big, empty galaxy out there, and Greez had always felt like he was looking into a mirror when he stared out through the viewports of his cockpit: just a big, empty void inside of him, searching for the thing that would make him feel something, just for a second. Girls, games, fast times and faster ships—none of it made an impact for long. The thrill would come and go, and then he'd be back to himself. Back to feeling . . . nothing, really.

Gambling was next. The other stuff hurt people, might have hurt him one day, but the gambling—that had consequences Greez hadn't bothered to consider at the time. Higher and higher stakes meant Greez could keep feeling, keep upping the ante, over and over again . . .

And then it came crashing down around him. He'd been working for Cere as her pilot and part-time cook for a while at that point, but Greez figured he'd be outta luck. Nobody had ever cared enough to stop him from screwing up his life before; why would that have changed now?

But Cere cared. Cere gave a damn. Cere, currently walking the party up to the entrance of a massive crystal skytower, who gave a damn *so much* that she sold her own kyber crystal to pay off Greez's debt. Her *kyber crystal*. The thing that made her a Jedi Master, as far as Greez understood it. The heart of her laser sword. The shiny green soul of her powers. She *sold* it.

For *Greez.*

And that hadn't even been enough for the Brood, so they'd captured Cal to call things even, and then Cal had escaped, and now the Brood chased them all over the galaxy, but honestly what was one more group of dillweeds chasing them all over the galaxy when they already were on the run all the time anyway?

So now Greez chased a different kind of high: keeping his foolish friends alive. And getting them out of all this, before it was too late.

All while trying not to drown in the guilt of knowing that Cere had been without a lightsaber for so long because of him. And even though she had a new blade now, it would never truly replace her first light-saber if he wasn't able to get it back for her.

But, whatever. Not a good idea to get caught up in all that while traipsing through a Core planet on their way to meet some stranger at the behest of a stormtrooper.

So Greez kept his eyes and ears open, and one hand on his blaster, the whole walk through the plantless city, all the way into their skytower of choice, up to the doors of an endless elevator, listening to his friends chatter away their nerves. Cal trying to get Cere to laugh (not that it worked that often, everybody knew Greez was the funny one), and the stormtrooper flirting with Merrin so hard Greez thought it would be kind of gross, if it wasn't also kind of hilarious. Obviously she was a babe, for a quadruped. Stocky, like she could take a hit and give back better; a real cocky smirk; and a sort of short-hair-in-the-front, long-hair-in-the-back situation that would have looked good on any Latero gal. But still, only two arms *and* a stormtrooper?

That was gonna be a dealbreaker for Greez.

And just as well, since Merrin was blushing so hard around her that she was basically green in the gills every time Greez saw her these past couple of days. Totally embarrassing.

Kids. Honestly.

"Take us through it one more time," Cere said to Fret as the group of them boarded the elevator.

"Right," said Fret. "Qeris Lar. One of the galaxy's wealthiest men. You've definitely heard of him. Born into it, obviously; got into politics first but didn't have the patience for it. Hated the bureaucracy. Used his money and his connections to accumulate more money and connections, and shockingly weaponizes it all for good."

"If that's true," Greez said and frowned, "why doesn't the Empire just take him down?"

Fret shrugged. "I don't know. But he's far from being the only rich guy in the galaxy that the Empire has left alone. He's just hiding under his piles of money in plain sight while funding anti-Imperial operations under the glass table. We heard about him on the inside for ages; he's kind of a legend." She grinned. "I risked it all to connect with him about getting out. He's the one who passed me the info about the location of the *Mantis;* the reason I knew you were going to be on that Brood rock. He told me to bring you by after—that he had a big job for you."

"Rich people," Greez sighed. They were all the same, like it or not.

When the elevator dinged open on the building's top floor, Greez made to step out, clocking the security agents flanking the doors—when he did a double take and froze. If those were Hosnian Prime security forces, he was going to eat his own shoe.

Greez swung a glance back at his crew and saw Cal, Cere, and Merrin come to the same conclusion almost simultaneously. But the stormtrooper just frowned at their hesitation and stomped out of the elevator, pushing ahead of them all.

Not willing to let her out of his sight, Greez took a deep breath and a step forward—and to his shock, nobody shot at him. The guards just kinda stood there, lookin' . . . normal. Unbothered.

All right. Maybe he was wrong. Just this once.

Greez walked double time to catch up with the stormtrooper, keeping up with Merrin as they entered into one of the most dang beautiful spaces Greez had ever seen.

Here was the thing about rich people, Greez figured. They were all awful. But they sure knew how to make a nice-lookin' space with all that money that coulda gone to feeding orphan kids or saving destitute planets. He'd walked straight out of the elevator into a room the size of a grav-ball field, all bright luminescent blue and reflective like he'd just stepped out into open air and not into the highest floor of a supra-atmo skytower, ceilings so high he couldn't even see 'em. It was incredibly disconcerting, and Greez didn't like it one bit. Where'd inside end, and outside start? It was basically impossible to tell. People lived like this?

The *Mantis* crew stepped out under what felt like the Hosnian Prime sky, hushed both in awe and probably also from nerves, if they were feeling anything like Greez, when from behind them they heard a voice that sounded like some kind of weird, high-pitched flute:

"Welcome, friends. As we are one with the air, so too you are one with me."

Greez whipped around fast as he could without losing his balance and found himself watching someone else exit the same elevator he and the crew had just used (how fast did that thing go?). He was an Omwati, a species Greez could comfortably say he'd never seen in person before, but he was immediately into the vibe. He looked like a big skinny blue bird crossed with a real tall human, with two arms instead of wings. Definitely had a good half a meter in height on Cal, but also looked so fragile Greez was pretty sure the wrong gust of wind up here could crack the guy in half. His head was topped off with, what—hair? Feathers? Cobwebs?—all translucent and iridescent floating around his delicate head.

Big ol' bug eyes were pretty weird, though. Took up way too much space on his face. Made him look so earnest he could be taken advantage of real easy.

Greez tucked that away in the back of his mind as the guy toddled on over on his spindly little bird legs.

"Qeris," the stormtrooper breathed out in relief, rushing over to the birdman to envelop him in a hug that Greez thought might just break him. "Thank you for seeing us on such short notice."

Qeris nodded, stepping back from the stormtrooper to eye the rest of their motley little gang. "Crew of the *Mantis*," he breathed, his subvocals making Greez think he was hearing birds in the sky. "I am *honored* to meet you. Your exploits are *legendary*. I am Qeris Lar, and I have a job for you. Something that will benefit everyone in this room."

"How?" Cal spoke for the first time since stepping out into the open air. BD-1 beeped in support. Qeris seemed to hear the rest of the question without Cal having to say it; he knew exactly what answer to give.

"Oh," Qeris Lar added with a whistle, "by bringing down the Empire as we know it."

If the Omwati, Qeris Lar, wanted to give them a job, thought Cere, they'd be foolish to turn it down. Fret was right: His reputation preceded him. He'd funded a successful operation years ago that Cere *had* heard about, one that had saved a system from Imperial gutting. This would be no different.

She knew that. She knew there were benefits here. She saw the way Cal's face lit up at Qeris Lar's words; the way Merrin wanted so badly to believe in Fret. There was potential here. The same kind of *real* potential they'd been chasing for years, over and over again, without any real big payoff.

Fighting the Empire was the task, if you asked Cal.

If you asked Cere? She wasn't so sure what her answer would be anymore.

Not that she'd ever admit it to his face, but Greez made some points. There were four and a half of them on the *Mantis,* trying to crush the Galactic Empire. There was something to be said for strike teams, sure, but there was a difference between a strike team and a suicide mission. She was getting older; she'd started to think about what might happen after her, who would be left to rebel against the Imperials once Jedi Cere Junda was no more than a memory. What was she leaving for Cal? For Merrin?

What was she leaving behind for the galaxy, when she was no longer around to shepherd it forward?

"I share your team's sentiment with regard to the way the galaxy is handling the Empire." Qeris interrupted Cere's thoughts as he guided the party to an area with a small table and soft, cloudlike chairs that Cere was certain hadn't been there just a minute ago. "Though you likely know me now as a prolific entrepreneur and job creator—finally able to do some *good* for the system—I was once a member of the Alderaanian government. I fled once I realized that Republic senator Bail Organa was all too willing to become Imperial senator Bail Organa. The royal family was never going to take a strong enough stand."

Cere squinted up at the Omwati as she took a seat on the surprisingly dense cloud. "You have history with the Empire?"

"I have a . . ." Qeris paused. "Strong difference of opinion when it comes to their politics. Competition is invaluable in the free market. Are we supposed to live entirely under the rule of one? Seems like a bad idea for me, personally." His whistlelike voice pitched downward.

"Completely okay with the murdering and the magic-choking people, though, huh?" Greez grunted as he settled himself into a cloud-chair.

Cere saw Qeris stop himself mid-eye-roll, his irises pointed straight to the skies visible above them. "We're on the same team, Greez Dritus." Using Greez's full name caught Cere's attention. Had Fret sent information on the crew ahead of their arrival? Or was this information Qeris somehow had already known?

"Motives are one thing," Qeris continued. "Results are what matter."

"Which is why I brought you here," interjected Fret. "When I was on the inside, Qeris was one of the prickliest and most immovable thorns in the Empire's side. He acts like he loves them, but everybody who looks close enough knows it's an act. It's why I reached out to him for help, and it's why I knew he could get you access to something that could repay you, in part, for getting me out and helping me start a new life, to get off the grid and drop off Imperial sensors forever."

Cere paused at that. Earlier, Fret had framed this as repaying a debt. Then it was a job, or mission. Now it was being presented to them as a gift.

There was too much going on here, and she didn't like it. Or she didn't understand it.

Both.

But Qeris was nodding his long head. "It's called the Shroud. Personal shielding that makes the wearer invisible to most technology and sensors. Difficult to build—requires access to mirkanite, a notoriously difficult ore to get one's hands on, very touchy in the presence of heat of any kind—but buildable."

Cal frowned. "What makes this different from other shielding? We've seen similar tech before."

Fret shook her head. "Not like this, you haven't. *Nothing* can find you. It's unbeatable. No sensors, no mapping, not even *cams*. It's as invisible as a person can get without actually becoming invisible. It makes you unstoppable. A hidden thing that stays hidden, period. It's . . ." She had a look on her face almost like pride. "It's the best there is. And that's what makes it so dangerous."

Cere felt her eyes widen like saucers as she quickly did the mental calculations on what the Shroud could mean for the galaxy. In the hands of those on the run from the Empire: invaluable. Jedi in hiding could be kept in hiding. If they managed to collect, one day, any important artifacts or historical documents pertinent to the Jedi, it could keep them hidden. It would be just the kind of thing Cere could leave behind for those who came after her, to make things better.

But in the hands of the Empire: devastating. Jedi on the run wouldn't know they were being chased. Any potential cells of guerilla fighters could be quickly and destructively infiltrated. The Empire, which already operated so much in the shadows, would become that much more potent and frightening.

And that would not do.

They'd chased a lot of missions over the last few years, a lot of big leads that hadn't panned out, or had fallen through. It had been tough on morale, Cere knew. Tough on her, too, as a leader. It was hard to feel like she was letting her crew down, over and over, even if she knew they didn't necessarily feel that way themselves.

But if this worked out . . .

This could be the thing they'd been waiting for.

"Its inventor—" Fret started, and then stopped just as suddenly. Cere watched Merrin's brow crease, however minimally. After clearing her throat, Fret continued: "The Shroud's inventor was tracked and killed by the Empire, but they weren't foolish: Their only schematics for the Shroud existed on a datacard, and they were hidden."

"How did you know them?" Cal prodded, carefully, but still firm.

Fret turned to look Cal in the eyes. "I worked with them," she said, and Cere could see the strength it took to answer. "I've seen their other builds. I'm telling you, they're the best." She paused and took a breath. "They were the one who wanted to get me out, initially. That . . . didn't end well for them."

Cere looked down; she knew how that story went, and she felt for Fret because of it. She wasn't entirely certain she could trust Fret, not yet, but she heard a real hurt in the woman's voice when she spoke about the people she cared about in her past. She heard that same note in Cal's voice, sometimes, too.

"Unfortunately," Qeris continued gently, after a moment, "the Shroud itself not having been built to prototype yet, the schematics have been recovered by the Empire. They're currently under heavy guard in an Imperial garrison, awaiting shipment to the Empire's theoretical applications testing facility on Eadu for decryption and eventual fabrication."

Cal was nodding, and Cere could see the wheels already turning behind his eyes. She was always so proud of her Padawan's ability to think three steps ahead; it was the reason, she was certain, that the *Mantis* had managed to avoid capture for so long.

"So you want us to retrieve them," Merrin extrapolated. Her eyes were still on Fret, who was studiously looking at Qeris Lar.

"Yes," Qeris breathed. "I have heard much of the *Mantis* crew, and I believe if there is any team that can liberate the datacard that holds the schematics, it would be you. All I ask is that you bring the schematics back to me. Once you have the plans, my vast resources will allow us to produce the Shroud en masse for those who would rebel against Imperial tyranny."

"And what's in it for you, feathers?" Greez was always more forward than Cere would have preferred in situations like this, but it was often for the best. His candor had a way of getting people to give their most radical honesty in return, purely out of a sense of shock more than anything.

It was fun to watch.

"If the Empire were to gain hold of the Shroud," Qeris said slowly, as if speaking to a very small child, "they would be able to track and infiltrate my location before I became aware of their presence. I fund and direct many operations like this one, though the Empire has, for the most part, no idea. Fret just said that. Just a moment ago, she . . . just said that."

Greez blinked once. Twice.

"'Kay."

Cere had to hide her smile behind a hand.

"All right," she said, standing. "We'll have to discuss, but we're interested; and Fret, we appreciate the tip. Where is the prison located?"

"Ah," whistled Qeris. "Yes. The Tion Cluster, but I trust you're familiar with the Outer Rim. A planet called Murkhana."

Cere was halfway out of her chair as the memories engulfed her like a great wave.

Murkhana.

Murkhana.

She wasn't in the bizarre skybox on Hosnian Prime anymore; she was a Padawan herself, watching with wide-eyed awe as her master Eno Cordova told her stories of Jedi artifacts, preserved and passed down to maintain the teachings and the mythology of the Jedi Order, crucial to its inheritance by future generations. Then she was a teenager, pressing her fingers into the glass of the case that held the one she always felt the most connected to, the Circlet of Saresh. A crown that radiated power so strong Cere could feel it pressing into the front of her brain no matter where she stood in the Jedi Archives. Then she was on the run, watching the Archives burn, grieving for the Order and for the artifacts that symbolized it.

Finally, she was with a black-market art dealer on Wells, three months ago, following a lead on a beautiful crown that people were just drawn to, with no real explanation.

She heard that it was being held by its current owner on Murkhana.

Cere spent a lot of time wondering about her legacy, and, by extension, the legacy of the Jedi. What she was leaving behind, when she was no longer able to fight. What the purpose of the *Mantis* crew was, or should be. It seemed to her that, maybe, establishing the potential of freedom in any way she could—or leaving the guidebook on how to do so, should she be unable—would be the best possible move.

The Shroud could help her do that, yes. But it was an idea, a thought. It was still just a hope, printed on a datacard. As of right now, it didn't exist.

But the Circlet of Saresh: That was real. That was tangible. That was a link to the Jedi of the past, the ones who stood for order and balance and light. The ones who would stand in front of the Empire and refuse to move, or perish. The ones who would place the lives of those they were sworn to protect above their own.

The Circlet was on Murkhana, and it could be the first piece in Cere's puzzle, in her very own archives. The archives that would become the coals on which the Empire would burn.

"Discuss, and decide fast." Qeris's piercing whistle brought Cere's eyes back to his. "The Imperials will be picking up the schematics from Murkhana in a matter of days. This is extremely time-sensitive, and I fear that, should we not move quickly, we will be on the back foot for the rest of the days of the Empire. We will never be able to regain our footing."

"We can move fast," said Cal. "That's not a problem."

"It *is* a problem, Cal Kestis," Qeris snapped. "Because it's not just any Imperials that are on their way to collect them."

Cere knew what was coming next without having to hear it.

"It's the Inquisitors."

CHAPTER 7

The Fifth Brother hadn't been expecting such an interesting mission. There were no Jedi involved; that usually displeased him.

"This technology holds infinite potential." The Grand Inquisitor was imperious even as a hologram. The Fifth Brother knelt in front of the projection in the room aboard his ship specifically designed for that purpose. He liked the pomp of it, the way it made him feel like he, too, had purpose.

"Including helping us to eradicate the remaining Jedi forever," the Fifth Brother added, completing the Grand Inquisitor's thought.

And that was what mattered to the Fifth Brother. Whatever other assignments he was given, *that* was his true purpose. The day he killed his first Jedi was the day the Fifth Brother truly knew he had made the right decision. The Grand Inquisitor had trusted him then with a mission of the utmost importance, killing a Jedi, and he had, of course, executed it flawlessly and without complaint. The Inquisitorius had already showed him so many things about the Jedi that he'd never considered; had branded the Jedi's misdeeds into his skin and pulled them out of his nail beds over and over again until he couldn't look away from them anymore.

The Jedi had taken him from his family on Artemesium with promises of a better life. Of a grand spirituality. A meaningful life in service to the greatest power in the known universe. The great equalizer. The Force.

He saw, now, that they had lied.

Instead, over time the Jedi had made him a servant to politicians, conveniently ignoring the fallibility of people easily corrupted by power and prestige. Upholding and reinforcing even the most heinous decisions, refusing to see that, in the process, they failed to bring balance to the Force, much less truly understand it.

"Yes." The Grand Inquisitor's voice was booming, echoing around the room and drawing the Fifth Brother's attention back to the hologram. The Fifth Brother's knees hurt; he was pleased about that. He liked the reminder that he was real, and the pain was part of it. "The remaining straggling Jedi in the galaxy will fall, once the Shroud is in our hands. Are you capable of this task, Fifth Brother?"

The Fifth Brother took a deep breath and tried to ignore what he perceived to be the Inquisitor's patronizing tone. The Inquisitors had helped him to see the Jedi's failings in the Jedi's opposition to critical thought, to dissent; in the way they hadn't stepped in when he was young, when the Senate decided Artemesium was made to be stripped for resources. Practicing the brutal calculus that determined the lives to be saved using the component parts of his home were more valuable than those lost in the exploitation of it. Now the planet was so ruined that it was merely a fact.

That fact had become a scar that he dug his fingers into often so he would not forget.

He bowed deeper and kissed the ground at the Grand Inquisitor's holographic feet. "I am capable," said the Fifth Brother. "I will find the Shroud, and put an end to the last, pathetic vestiges of the Jedi once and for all. I rededicate myself to the only path on which I see true balance. True enlightenment. I know my own truth, and the Force speaks it to me through the stars above and the gravity beneath my feet."

"Then go. I shall await your triumph," the Inquisitor said with finality. His hologram disappeared, and the Fifth Brother rose, moving back toward the cockpit to enter the coordinates that would take him to Murkhana.

He saw the stars streak by through the viewport as he moved toward his next mission. But mostly, the Fifth Brother saw hypocrisy. The Jedi had sworn a sacred oath to be the brightest stars in a universe that was otherwise an empty vacuum, trending toward darkness and a blank nothingness into which all beings risked falling.

That is what the Jedi were meant to be. What he was promised. A billion suns in a dark and hungry void.

Instead they chose to become a black hole. Sucking in the light and the lightest among them, using that light to feed their own egos. The center of destruction; a promise of beauty, but in reality only greed. Not even a reflection of the darkness around it; somehow, impossibly, something even darker.

The Jedi ate the darkness around them, and they became it.

As the ship carried him toward his next mission, the Fifth Brother imagined his next encounter with a Jedi. His next opportunity to walk on the path that the Force had destined for him and *truly* triumph.

He imagined, and he hungered.

Cal watched Greez flop onto one of the benches around the *Mantis* holotable the second they reboarded their ship. "Inquisitors. We're really considering taking this on, even though he just said 'Inquisitors'?"

"It's that big," Cal said from his vantage point, leaning against the wall that backed up against the cockpit. "If the Shroud is that important, it's worth the risk. And don't we have the best pilot in the galaxy? We can be in and out before they even get there."

Greez stared at Cal in disbelief. "Cal," he said slowly. "*Inquisitors.*" He dragged the word out like Cal wasn't fully understanding it.

"In and out," Cal repeated. "We're small, fast, and agile. We can do that."

Greez sighed. "I don't trust Qeris as far as I could throw him," the pilot grumped, crossing all four of his arms.

"You don't have to," Fret said cheerfully, sidling onto the cushion next to him. Cal saw Greez shift over, just a little, so there was no chance that the two of them would touch. "If his information is good, we grab the plans for the Shroud; we can discuss if we want to return them to him then. If his information is bad, we do a little shooting and a little scooting. But his information isn't bad."

"Awful lot of 'we' coming out of your mouth right now," Greez grumbled. "Since when are you even coming with us beyond, like, right now? Actually, what are you even doing back on the ship? Why didn't you just stay in your buddy's cloud palace? Who let her back on?"

"Fret has access to codes that will help us infiltrate the facility on Murkhana without setting off alarm bells," said Merrin, leaning her palms onto the holotable and staring at Greez. "Plus, she's in danger. She's a fugitive, like us. You just said you don't trust Qeris as far as you can throw him—"

"Probably pretty far—"

"—so why would we leave Fret with him?" Merrin finished. "She's safest here, on the *Mantis*. We've managed to avoid capture for years."

Cal shook his head. "Greez makes a good point. We're missing a key component here."

Fret tilted her head. "And what's that?"

"Qeris." Cal swiped at the holotable, replacing the image of Murkhana with a floating and semi-transparent spinning replica of the birdlike man from Hosnian Prime.

"What about him?" asked Fret.

"It's all about him," Cal said with a frown. "He said it himself; he's one of the galaxy's richest opportunists. Or 'job creators,' whatever. He's got the resources to help us against the Empire, to put the first real dent in their hull we've been able to since we started. We have to figure out how we get it out of him."

Cere had a skeptical look on her face where she'd settled into a seat on the other side of the circular room, taking everything in as it happened. "Cal, you're right about Qeris, but we're never going to be able to match the Empire in strength, and he can't come out against them directly. Not without bringing the Jedi Order back in full force."

She was a good leader, Cal thought. He'd learned a lot from her about how to lead this crew.

"Cere is right," Merrin said, quieter than usual. "If we're going to get any help from Qeris, it should be for something more specific. A targeted strike."

But Cere was shaking her head. "That's not what I meant. Lar has the connections to find us the kind of pieces of Jedi history we might not be able to get anywhere else. We need to—"

"There won't be anyone to show artifacts *to* if we don't create a real opposition. To stop people like Vader in his tracks," Cal interrupted. Why were they having this same argument again?

"The Shroud *is* the reward," Fret threw in. "That's the whole point. That's the aid; that's the targeted strike."

"'Kay, so she can help us do the job," Greez continued, like Fret wasn't right next to him. "I'm still not convinced why we're even doing the job in the first place?"

"Oh, do you have something else lined up?" Merrin snapped.

"I'm just sayin' "—Greez shrugged—"we could simply not do this. Qeris is rich and connected, like you've all said; I'm sure he could find somebody else to liberate some schematics. Let's drop Fret on a nice little moon in the middle of nowhere and go back to doin' what we were doin'."

"And what was that?" Cere asked, her sudden, commanding voice drawing everyone's eyes to her. "What were we doing before this? Putting dents in the Haxion Brood's seemingly endless supply of bounty hunters? Were we doing anything for the cause?"

"Cere's right," Cal agreed. Cere was making sense; he was relieved that, in this instance at least, they were in agreement. There had been too many moments otherwise lately. "You heard what Qeris said. Even if he's exaggerating, if the Shroud has half the potential he said it does, we owe it to the galaxy to check it out, and to get it away from the Empire. We owe it to ourselves. After that, we can decide exactly what to do with the plans and what comes next."

"Thank you," said Fret and Merrin at the same time. Cal noticed the two of them looked at each other with barely suppressed grins.

"And there may be more on Murkhana that could be helpful for us," Cere said enigmatically. Cal waited, but Cere did not elaborate. He would have to follow up with her later about what, exactly, she meant by that.

"Sure, okay." Greez sighed the most dramatic sigh Cal had ever heard him make—and that was saying something. "But Cal." Greez's eyes were right on him. "You see how this has a high probability of being absolutely, totally messed up, right?"

Cal swallowed.

He really, really did. And he really, really wished he didn't have to.

"Guess I'm sticking around, Nightsister."

Merrin looked up from studying her palms to see Fret leaning in the doorframe to the engine room, arms crossed over her chest, the perpetual half smile that seemed to be an intrinsic part of her face fixed into place. She'd changed out of her stolen armor into some of Merrin's borrowed clothes: stretchy black shorts and a long-sleeved shirt, short-cropped on Merrin and *far* too short on Fret, hitting just below her waist, her soft violet stomach visible between hem and waistband. Merrin tried not to note that her shirt, in Merrin's favorite shade of Dathomirian red, offset Fret's eyes in a way that made them glow like hot coals, and seeing it on Fret was certainly having an effect. She was so tall, so self-assured; despite her casual pose, Merrin could tell that Fret was completely in control of herself and the way in which she presented herself to the world. Fret was confidence personified, and it made Merrin flush at the very sight of her. Her fingers, quiet just a moment ago, now itched with the need to bury themselves in the long little curls at the base of Fret's neck.

Rude.

And beyond all that, there was something in Fret's eyes: a glint, a tease. A challenge.

Turning her traitorous palms away from her, Merrin leaned back on them, shifting her weight back on Cal's bunk. She'd come in here ostensibly to practice, but she wasn't getting anywhere by this point, and that typically meant she wouldn't at all. It was no use trying to force the magick; she knew that well enough by now. Merrin might as well enjoy Fret's company, instead. She could bash her head against the brick wall blocking her access to the fire again later, when she felt like torturing herself further.

"We do okay," Merrin answered, hearing the Cal in her voice. She'd been spending too much time around him in the past couple of years; he was starting to rub off.

"That was some fight out there."

"It wasn't a fight," Merrin disagreed. It wasn't. Though they'd been having disagreements like that more than usual lately, which she didn't want to think about too closely. "It was just . . . a temporary disagreement."

"Right." Fret pushed up off the doorframe, wandering around the engine room, her eyes raking over everything but Merrin: the engine, the workbench, the little cot. Everywhere but Merrin. "Homey," she said, trailing her finger across one of the discarded lightsaber parts on Cal's workbench. "A gal could get used to a place like this."

Merrin watched the other woman like a hawk, noticing the way Fret's fingers played over the mechanism.

Because she didn't want anything to get damaged. Obviously.

Not because they were sure and thick and capable and moved so smoothly over the complex and delicate mechanical parts of the laser sword.

Obviously.

"You're welcome here as long as you need." Merrin focused on keeping her voice steady, even. "There are no tests to pass. The *Mantis* is home for those without one."

Fret, still not looking at Merrin, which wasn't driving her up the wall at all, picked up the small part, examining it. "So trusting," Fret said, just the hint of a scold in her voice. She spun the piece around between her fingers, brought it up to the light of the engine, illuminating her strong hand. "How do you know I'm not going to betray you?"

A surprised laugh burst out of Merrin; she couldn't help it. Something about the tension in the room and the absurdity of the question; it was a balance she couldn't handle without a release.

"Because this isn't one of Greez's favorite poorly written holodramas," Merrin answered. "Real life rarely works like that. Contrived plots and dramatic, overwrought backstabs are few and far between. People simply make choices, and you're stuck with the outcome."

Merrin paused, considering her next words carefully. There was a feeling in the air like her next words would determine something big, something world shattering; she didn't want to trip over them and be left wondering what, for the rest of time, would have been.

"You'll do what you'll do," she landed on. "Your decision. I can't predict it."

Merrin couldn't see Fret's face, turned away toward the workbench as it was, but she could see her fingers tighten around the mechanism.

"But if you *do* betray us," Merrin added, a sudden burst of confidence overtaking her when talking about her family, her crew, "I will not hesitate to put you in the ground."

Fret's head swung around in an instant, eyebrows almost to her hairline, her eyes finally meeting Merrin's. Her hands had stilled on the lightsaber part.

"Really." Fret drew the word out deliberately, slowly, her half smile ticking up with every lengthened syllable. Merrin caught herself staring at Fret's mouth as she said it, forced herself to pull her eyes back to her own lap for a second. She heard the sound of Fret dropping the spare part onto the table. By the time she looked back up, Fret had crossed the room. She was standing right in front of Merrin now, looking down at her. Fret's expression had a heat that Merrin hadn't seen on her before.

A heat that reminded Merrin of her own fire, the core of Dathomir, writhing and uncompromising and hotter than any sun. Able to bring whole planets to their knees. Feared by the galaxy, and with good reason.

Dangerous and deadly.

As she looked up into the hot red coals of her eyes, Merrin's heart was beating so fast she swore she would be light-headed if she stood.

"I like a good threat." The sear in Fret's eyes came out through her voice, burning through Merrin to her own core, setting the pit of her stomach pulsing. Fret's eyebrow quirked, just the smallest bit; Merrin knew, in that instant, that *Fret* knew. Knew what effect she was having on her.

Had had on her since the moment they met, somehow.

"*Love* a good threat actually," Fret corrected herself, drawing Merrin's attention out of her body and back to Fret. "But yours lacks *specificity.*"

The taller woman bent forward, placing each of her hands down just outside of Merrin's where they rested on either side of her on the cot, Fret's thumbs brushing Merrin's pinkies. She was leaning right into Merrin's personal space now, boxing her in on the cot. Everywhere Merrin could see, could feel, could *smell*, there was Fret: outsides of her hands touching the insides of Fret's, vision full of her face and her *throat*, her exquisite dusky-lilac throat where Merrin could swear she could see Fret's pulse beating faster and faster despite her aura of self-control; despite how contained she kept herself.

"Having a hard time imagining it for myself," Fret continued, her voice quieter by steps in a way Merrin found inexplicably infuriating. She smelled like spiced ahrisa and wax on grave thorn wood. Merrin's head swam with it. She was surrounded.

"So tell me, Nightsister." Fret's voice was lower still, cracking; Merrin swore she heard a hint of a growl beneath the words. Merrin felt feather-light, Fret's nose ghosting across her cheekbone, breath hot on her face. She had to fight the sound that threatened to escape her throat. "Tell me how you'd take me out."

Merrin swallowed so loudly she was sure the whole ship heard it. She was taking too long to answer. What was the question?

"Use your words," Fret breathed, teasing. Her lips were down by Merrin's neck now, a hair's width away from the divot between her shoulder and her throat, threatening. Promising. She knew exactly what she was doing, and it made Merrin absolutely furious.

Furious. And nothing else.

But she was a Dathomirian. And she could hold her own.

Merrin narrowed her eyes, forcing herself to stare directly forward instead of turning to look at Fret's mouth or the slight purple flush on her cheeks or her damn neck. "It would be easy," Merrin answered, pausing when she noticed her own voice cracking. "Easy enough."

"Mmm?" Fret encouraged. Nose tracking up her neck now. She hadn't retreated at all, hadn't given Merrin any breathing room. *Infuriating.*

Merrin had to even the score here or she was going to find herself in even more desperate trouble than she was already in.

Pushing herself forward off her palms, Merrin turned her head and grabbed Fret by the chin, pulling her face up and away to meet Merrin's gaze, but not widening the distance between them, their lips now just a breath apart. "Yes," Merrin said, dropping Fret's chin, trying to keep her wavering voice casual. Her heart felt like it was about to hammer out of her chest; she felt her hands trembling the second she pulled them off the cot. "When you let yourself get this close to the enemy, you open yourself up to attack. You make yourself vulnerable."

Fret's devastating smirk was back. She inhaled slowly, and it reverberated like a snarl. "And that's a bad thing."

"You never want to give your opponent an opening." Merrin kept her gaze focused, purposeful, antithetical to her labored breathing. This close to her, Merrin could see Fret's black pupils blown wide open, the fiery ring around them just a narrow band. "Or they might be able to exploit your weakness."

Before Fret could register what was happening, before she could pull away and prevent it, Merrin had snaked her other arm up between them and struck out in a flash. Her hand shot forward, her fingers wrapping around Fret's neck, holding the other girl still and steady. Merrin didn't use any real pressure; she wasn't trying to actually *hurt* Fret.

She was simply trying to illustrate a point. A reminder of the first time they had met.

"So," Merrin finished, willing a fresh hardness into her eyes, "you better not let us down."

Fret's own eyes responded to the change in Merrin's, a flash of want and—was that triumph?—all at the same time. Before Merrin could process what was happening, Fret had one of her hands up and had wrapped it around Merrin's wrist, pushing the Nightsister's chalky-white hand harder around her own lilac neck. Pressure. Merrin could feel Fret's blood rushing through her throat; her fingers left white marks in Fret's skin.

Fret's smirk was suddenly gone, replaced with a dead seriousness at a speed that made Merrin dizzy. "Then I hope I'm the right girl for the job." Fret's voice was strained, raspy, and Merrin could barely handle that. Fret's stare was too much, all black and filled with an intent Merrin was desperate for and desperate to run away from. She dropped her eyes to Fret's mouth, watched with stunned awe as Fret's dark-purple tongue ran its way across her bottom lip, slowly, deliberately.

"The right girl . . ." Merrin repeated, half dazed. For a moment, they remained frozen like that. Grasping, staring, holding on to each other.

It wasn't entirely clear to Merrin who moved forward first, who crested the wave of their words and crashed into whose mouth first. All Merrin knew was that one second she was just her, and the next second she was her and Fret and there was no more space between them and she was falling headfirst into the way the other woman was making her feel.

Merrin believed in no gods. There were some on Dathomir who had treated their magick like a religion, creating a kind of shamanistic tradition out of it, but by and large she was not part of a religious order. Merrin hadn't been cloistered; she dedicated herself to no higher power.

She *was* the higher power. And the galaxy bowed in service to her and her sisters.

But there were times, Merrin found, when she felt like she understood the draw, the urge to believe in something greater than oneself. When Merrin kissed Fret—or Fret kissed Merrin, or—it didn't matter—when their lips finally met and the rest of the room fell away, the sounds of the engine replaced by the roar of her blood in her own ears, Merrin thought she might just fall to her knees at Fret's feet. Whatever this was—when Merrin kissed a person she had this kind of connection to, well . . .

These moments felt like they could be holy.

On her way to ruin, Merrin flung out a hand, and without even having to think about it, the door to the engine room swung shut, ensuring they wouldn't be disturbed.

It was sealed by a line of green fire.

He couldn't put his finger on why, but something about Fret didn't sit right with Cal. Posted up in the *Mantis*'s cockpit with Greez, he told his friend as much.

"Uh, well, not to be the stater-of-the-obvious here, but she's a stormtrooper," Greez said helpfully. Greez was manning the controls as usual, and Cal absentmindedly fiddled with buttons from the copilot's chair. It would be a couple of days between here and Murkhana, the fastest they could possibly get there safely and without being followed, and hopefully well within the time line before the Inquisitors arrived, and it was going to be a long trip. Merrin had been periodically commandeering the engine room as of late for some peace while she tried to get a handle on whatever was going on with her powers; Cal hadn't wanted to pry about it, but she said the white-noise roar of the engine helped her think, reminded her of the winds on Dathomir or something equally poetic, like the rest of the brilliance that tended to come out of Merrin's dusky lips.

"I mean, I know she's a changed woman or whatnot," the Latero continued with a shrug, dragging Cal's attention back to his butt in the chair, the stars outside the viewport. "I know we have a whole Nightsister on board. But . . . *stormtrooper*, man. Some things are kind of unforgivable. And we're trusting her."

"She wasn't an actual stormtrooper, Greez." Cal's focus shifted from the stars outside to his reflection in the reinforced glass. "And we've all done some pretty unforgivable things because of the Empire."

Greez let out the longest sigh Cal had ever heard him make, a drawn-out raggedy thing, like it was the last of his puffed-up energy about this and he didn't have the strength to keep it up anymore. "Yeah. Yeah, I know that's true." He paused. "Even more garbage when you're born into it."

His reflection was too bright in the starfield; Cal had to drop his gaze to his lap, concentrate on the dirt under his bitten fingernails, the edges raw. The skin around his cuticles was red, angry; a habit he'd had since childhood that was hard to kick. "If you'd had a choice," Cal asked, "would you have wanted to be born somewhere other than Lateron?"

Greez turned to grin at Cal, baring his pointy teeth in a way that would have been predatory to anyone who didn't know him as well as Cal did. "Nah. The ladies would never dig me as hard anywhere else."

With a laugh, Cal had to agree. "You're a real acquired taste, Greez."

"Don't blame me just 'cause you have no game." Greez flipped one of the *Mantis*'s switches to punctuate his point.

"Kind of hard to find the right gal when you're the galaxy's most wanted fugitive," Cal said. "And Jedi don't really do that. It's not something I've ever even really considered I might get to have; I've just been focused on surviving, you know?"

"And yet," Greez said enigmatically.

Cal waited, but Greez just busied himself with flying the ship and didn't choose to elaborate further.

And Cal wasn't going to ask.

"Still, you gotta see how weird this is, right?" asked Greez. "And now the *Inquisitors* are involved, and we're walking right into that? Really? Somethin' weird's goin' on. I can't put my forehead on it, but I know it's there."

"I know," agreed Cal. "Don't worry. It's my job to figure it out."

There was a brief, comfortable silence. Cal had always felt like he could be himself with Greez, could relax without pretense or put-on. Cere was working on BD-1 in the common room, fixing one of the little droid's servos; it was just the two of them, and the bogling under Greez's feet, her new favorite spot. Greez was already worried he was about to step on the little bogling whenever he got up; the creature seemed to like to live on the edge.

Cal understood that. She was too much like him. Like father, like daughter.

"Would you, uh—" Greez paused, his eyes ahead, fiddling with some dials. He took a breath, steadying himself, preparing to say something that he was clearly nervous to ask, and started over. "Would you have wanted to be born a Jedi, Cal? If you had the choice?"

Cal had already known what Greez was going to ask anyway. As if that was the first time someone had asked him that. As if it weren't the question Cal asked himself most, many, many times over the years, alone in his cot, on the run, scared and moments away from capture and death.

At one time, Cal thought that being a Jedi was the worst thing that had ever happened to him. It had felt less like an opinion and more like a fact. It had ruined his life, set him on the run as a child, denied him a home, stability, safety. Taken from him everyone that he'd ever cared about. It made him a fugitive, a criminal; he lived his life in half measures, in the shadows, always sleeping with one eye open. He should say no. He should tell Greez that all he had ever wanted was to be something else, anything else. To be normal.

But the real truth, the raw truth of it, at Cal's very core—the thing he knew in his gut, when everything else fell away, when nothing else, none of the material things or the fear or the discomfort mattered—was this: Being a Jedi was the best thing that had ever happened to Cal. He loved it, even when the galaxy told him he shouldn't, told him he should hide. There was more to Cal than his connection to the Force; it wasn't the most interesting thing about him, nor should it have been. But it was Cal's favorite thing about himself, this connection to something greater than his own soul, his own spirit. It gave him purpose. For all the pain, and all the fear, mostly—mostly, it brought him joy. It brought Cal his family, these people he had found whom he loved better than anyone else he had ever known. It brought him the ability to help others who needed it. Gave his life meaning. And it felt really, really good.

But it tended to be hard to explain all that. So instead Cal just said: "Well, it led me to Greez Dritus, didn't it? So how could I not?"

And Greez laughed, and, at least for a few moments, everything was going to be fine. No need to complicate things unnecessarily; that was how the *Mantis* crew had lived over the years, keeping the peace, and that was how they'd continue, if Cal had anything to say about it. They kept their course for Murkhana, and Cal left Greez to pilot in peace.

Still, though, no matter what he said to Greez, there was still a nagging pull in the back of Cal's mind, something he had learned better than to ignore.

So he decided to take a quick wander over to Merrin's cabin. Just in case.

As Cal left the cockpit, he passed Cere on her way in, asking Greez about the last time he'd been to Murkhana. Good; he would let the two of them keep busy with planning while he did what he needed to do.

The door to the engine room was sealed shut, as Cal had assumed it would be, as it usually was when Merrin was practicing using her powers again. With a spark of pride, he noted that it was lined with green fire; Merrin must be having luck with her magick. Of course she was; she was the strongest person Cal knew.

Still, even the strongest people needed someone to look out for them. And Cal would always be the one to project the strength that they needed, that might not always be there.

Merrin's cabin looked as it always did; neat—severe, almost— everything exactly in its place as much as it could be in a bunk this size. He expected Fret to be here, and if she had been he could have just spoken to her directly; but she wasn't, so it had to be Plan B. And indeed, there was a new addition to Merrin's quarters: a pile of white plastoid composite and black bodysuit mesh that made up Fret's stolen stormtrooper equipment. The helmet sat on top of the pile; Cal was grateful that it faced the wall, and he didn't have to stare into its cruel, unseeing eyes.

It probably had better aim empty and facing a wall than it ever did when it was occupied by an actual stormtrooper.

Cal had always had the ability to feel some objects' sense echoes, something his first master had called psychometry. It was rare, in Jedi, and it was something Cal had found difficult to handle for many years, especially as a youngling. Touching an object, focusing on it, opened him up to the object's past. He would be hit with feelings, sights, sounds—whatever the Force felt was important to impart to him. It was like being transported into some*one* else, via some*thing* else.

It had taken a very, very long time to get a handle on. Not every object could be read, but he'd gotten better at sensing which ones had something to say. And still, he only tried to use it on objects of people he didn't know. It was too close to snooping, otherwise. Plus, a lot of the time, he simply couldn't help it—the flashes just *happened*.

And he wasn't trying to *snoop*, really; it wasn't coming from a place of pettiness. He wasn't trying to gain information for any nefarious purpose. But it was becoming clear to Cal that Fret and Merrin had a connection, something deeper and more immediate than Fret had with the rest of the crew—something that reminded Cal very much of the connection he and Merrin had right off the bat, the chemistry in the air between them sparking off the light side of the Force and the dark, traveling between them through the liminal space in which the energy of the universe flowed perpetually. He felt it in the cord that connected their spirits to this day.

And he felt it when he reached for the tether between Fret and Merrin, too.

And that worried him. Because he knew he could trust himself.

But could he trust Fret? He wanted to. He very much did. But . . . he had to admit that Greez made some good points. And he couldn't be sure, not really. She wasn't Merrin.

Cal was just trying to find out the truth. That was all. No need for Merrin to know what he was doing. No need for her to think that he was sneaking around behind her back. Because he wasn't. He was just . . . looking out.

And it wasn't like he could control his psychometry. The ability wasn't predictable; it wasn't something Cal could turn on and off at will, reading the history of any object he touched at his whim. It also wasn't frequent—and thank the Force for that—or he'd be walking around in a constant daze, every object in close proximity a vid just waiting to play its story out on the back of Cal's eyelids. Nor was it a typical Jedi power; it was something else Cal had been born with, an unusual but not unheard-of ability to connect with a thing or a place through the Force, reading what it had seen and heard and felt throughout its lifetime.

If walls could talk, indeed.

So there was every chance that this wouldn't work. *Probably won't work!* Cal thought as he stepped quietly toward the pile of discarded armor. Once it failed, then he would never have to admit to anyone that he had been down here, snooping through Fret's things, such as they were—and, by extension, Merrin's.

Cal picked up a piece of the armor and underneath it noticed two leather strips—the wrist and forearm wraps he'd seen Fret wearing since she'd come on board. Setting down the plastoid, Cal picked up the wrap, focusing on it. Willing himself to see into it, while also half hoping he would see nothing.

Not that he was snooping. This was his ship! Well, it was Greez's ship. But it was his crew! And they were his responsibility. And—

And then Cal was hit with a blinding flash of white light, and he thought: *Oh, no. It worked* just as he fell into the clutches of the sense echo, retrocognition overtaking his consciousness.

It was always the same, and somehow it was always different: first, that white-out overtaking all of his senses. Then a sort of sense-memory haze, like the halos Cal got after a bad migraine when he pushed his Force abilities too hard: visuals, sounds, even emotions, all distorted. They were his, but they weren't his; a memory he shouldn't be holding, one that didn't belong to him, overlaid onto his own thoughts, using his own synapses, finding their own shape through the pathways in his brain, entirely different from the ones that had created the impression in the first place.

The echo was the manuscript; Cal's mind, the palimpsest.

And then he wasn't himself much at all, anymore. He was in a market square, it was a blistering-hot day, he was wandering into the shade of an awning—a droid repair shop. He felt his actions were casual but carefully so; he was trying not to appear as eager as he was, as nervous, trying to keep his breath steady so it wouldn't betray his beating heart. He walked around the counter inside the shop, otherwise deserted, straight into the back rooms, and heard himself breathe "Irei"—his voice soft and feminine—embarrassed at the neediness he heard.

And in front of him, towering over even his tall frame, was an alien—

a Kadas'sa'Nikto, far from home—slender and graceful, her coarse scaly skin a deep green, her nose and mouth jutted slightly forward, all framed by a crown of bone-pale horns and spikes that jutted out from her lovely face. And she was lovely, for something that the part of Cal who was still Cal would say looked more like a lizard than a person; the memory wrote her as a celestial beauty, someone who dragged the sun out of space and made it shine, someone he would pick up a sword and slay great beasts for. He wanted to write poems to her long, willowy neck and lie down at her clawed feet.

"Chell." The Nikto, Irei, dropped whatever droid part was in her hands and rushed over to Cal, swept him up in her arms, and Cal learned what it felt like to kiss the ghost of a lizard and a woman that he loved all at the same time: a rough tongue, sharp teeth, the smell of the sun reflecting off hot sand, a tightening in his stomach, and an expansion of his heart.

It was over as soon as it started and then Irei had him by the arms, her talons digging into the backs of his biceps, her voice suddenly very serious and her eyes narrow with fear and care, and she was saying, "Come with me, you know I can't stay, they'll kill me here, come with me, Chell—"

And then Cal was back in Merrin's cabin and back in his own body and all that was left of the Force echo was a ringing in his ears, a brightness on the edge of his vision, and an imbalance in his core that he knew would fade within minutes, if he just concentrated on getting over it. He was here, and Irei was gone, and he wouldn't be responding to her pleas.

But he knew what his answer—Chell's answer—was going to have been, as surely as he'd been about to say it himself.

No.

"Find what you were looking for?"

Cal's head snapped up as he walked into the galley. Cere was already there, her legs propped up on the table, hands folded around a steaming teacup.

She frowned, and Cal realized he must have been telegraphing his guilt all over his face. "I assume you were looking for Fret?" Cere clarified. "I haven't seen her in a while, either."

"Oh!" Cal felt it burble out of his throat, strained and relieved. "Yes. I mean, no. I didn't find anything. Done talking with Greez? How's the plan coming together?"

Cere squinted at the rapid change in subject as Cal slid into one of the chairs across from her. "Yes. I think we're ready for whatever is waiting for us on Murkhana. Or as ready as we can be. He's plotting out a series of escape routes in case of the worst."

"But when have we ever had to deal with the worst-case scenario?" Cal joked. Neither he nor Cere laughed. The best they both could manage was a strong exhale that passed for a wry chuckle.

They sat in companionable silence for a few moments; it was one of the things Cal loved most about spending time on the *Mantis,* and especially about spending time with Cere. Cal had lived in solitude for so long; for all of his adult life, really, and most of his childhood.

Cal tried not to think too hard about all the different ways that might have affected him psychologically.

But still, he'd gotten used to a certain kind of peace; a stillness that came with being alone, with the knowledge that no one was relying on you but you. It was the times when he'd broken that commitment to his own peace, to his own solitude, that things had gone sideways.

That people had died.

"Cere," Cal said softly, his voice barely audible over the ever-present hum of the ship's engines. "Can I ask you something personal?"

Cere's eyes stayed on Cal's as she took a sip of her coffee. "Depends."

"Fair," Cal conceded. "I just . . ." He thought about the women in the echo, their feelings washing over him all over again, and he shivered. "Jedi aren't supposed to form attachments. Important rule."

"Important rule." Cere nodded but didn't add anything. She waited, giving Cal the space he needed to continue.

"I know that . . . it's usually meant in a romantic context." Cal could feel his cheeks getting red; it was so awkward to talk about these kinds of things with anyone, but especially with his mentor. "But wouldn't you say that we, here—everyone on board this ship—we've all formed connections?"

Cere's brows knit together over the rim of her cup. "I suppose?"

"We've traveled together for years. The longest I've—I've ever stayed with anyone since the Jedi Order fell. It would be disingenuous to say that I don't feel love in my heart for you." Cal studied his nail beds carefully as he spoke. "That I don't love Greez, or—or Merrin. And I know that you love this crew, too. I know you would lay down your life for us. You nearly have."

He heard the clink of Cere's teacup on the hard metal of the table and looked up at her. "How is that not an attachment? How does that not put us in danger? How does that not open us up to the dark side of the Force?"

Cere sighed, and Cal saw something behind her eyes that he wasn't sure he was ready to examine too closely. "I don't know."

It wasn't the answer Cal was expecting. And it wasn't one he'd often heard out of his master's mouth.

"Really?"

"Really," Cere said with a small shrug. "Because you're right. And you've seen what happens because of it; you know that I touched the dark side when we fought Vader. That I've had to stop myself from doing it again, from doing whatever it takes to keep this crew safe."

"I know," Cal said hastily. "I didn't mean to—"

"It's okay." Cere put up a hand to stop his backtracking. "And maybe this makes me a poor teacher. But I don't know how to not care. And I don't know if the galaxy is worth saving if there aren't people in it that you care about saving it for."

"So where does that leave us?" Cal wondered.

"Trying our best?" Cere suggested, half jokingly. "What brings this up, Cal?" she asked gently. He got the feeling she thought she already knew.

He could guarantee that she didn't. And he wanted to tell her— wanted Cere to know what he'd seen in his vision, even if it meant admitting he'd gone through Merrin's cabin, through Fret's things.

But when he thought about those feelings—that intimate moment—

he just felt like it would be a betrayal of an even broader magnitude to publicize Fret's pain and her past. And he still trusted Merrin's gut.

He probably always would.

And so he didn't say anything. Instead he asked:

"Why else did you want to go to Murkhana?"

Cere, too, didn't answer. And the two of them fell back into companionable silence.

Just a little more tense than before.

CHAPTER 8

"Murkhana approach, kids, get your pants on." Greez's voice crackled through the *Mantis*'s comms, jolting Cal awake with a start. He'd fallen asleep at the table in the kitchen, bent forward, jacket as a pillow, not intending to nap but drained after his psychometry. It didn't happen often, but when an echo was as powerful emotionally as the one he'd just experienced, there was nothing to do but be unconscious about it for a while. He would have preferred his cot, but Merrin had been locked in the engine room for hours as Greez had driven them toward Murkhana; she must have been having real luck with her powers, because the green fire around the door was as bright as ever.

Well, good for her.

"Crew call." Cere's voice was just a moment behind Greez's on the speakers, summoning everyone to the map room for a pre-mission brief. Cal sat up and shuffled his hand through his hair—he really needed a cut, it was getting out of control on the top. He blinked the last of the sleep out of his eyes in time to see Cere bounding up from the crew quarters, BD-1 clinging firmly to the back of her shirt. When the little droid saw Cal, he *brr-eep*ed and lit up, jumping down off Cere to scuttle over to his favorite person—if Cal did say so himself—and hopping up onto the bench to give him a nuzzle.

"Hey, little guy." Cal smiled, patting the droid on his little head. "Feeling better?"

As BD trilled in the affirmative, Cere added, "All repaired. Better than new, even."

"You took a couple of real good hits on that Brood rock, huh?" Cal asked BD with pride. He knew his droid could withstand way worse, and had. BD hopped from leg to leg, beeping about his bravery.

Out of his periphery, Cal heard when the green fire disappeared from around the engine room door with a *whoosh*, like the air being sucked out into a vacuum. A second later, a noticeably disheveled Merrin walked around the corner from the engine room into the galley; she must have been woken up unceremoniously from a nap by Greez's voice like he had, Cal reckoned. Her hair was out of its usual severe updo, mussed around her face in tangles; her eyes bleary. As she exited the room, she stumbled for a moment, her legs seeming a little unsteady. She was wearing a short red top Cal rarely saw her in. A dark-gray bruise bloomed out of her neckline, fresh; she must have taken a hard hit on the Brood base like BD. Cal made a note to get her some balm for it later.

"Yes, I'm here," Merrin said, less poetic than usual. Her voice cracked on the first syllable, still shaking itself out of sleep. "I just have to—"

Cal ducked his face away to hide his smile as Merrin launched herself toward the refresher; she moved so gracefully all the time, especially when she was terrifying, but even when she wasn't. He could barely remember what the *Mantis* was like without her on board; the thought of it was like a distant memory, leached of color.

"We made it already?"

Cal's eyes snapped back up to the galley entry, which was not empty, like he would have expected it to be after Merrin's unceremonious exit, but was instead filled with Fret's broad-shouldered shirtless purple form. Her chest was smooth all the way down to her black shorts, surprisingly similar to Cal's own, except for the color. She leaned against the doorframe with an eyebrow lifted and a wide grin that rivaled Greez's own damn smile, cocky like she owned the place.

And she must have been coming out of the engine room, right after Merrin.

"Right, crew brief," Cal said quickly, jumping to his feet. BD *breep*ed in surprise, startled away from his place close to Cal's lap.

Fret's brows twitched together, just for a fraction of a second. "If I'm going to be right there with you, I should know the full picture of what's going on. I'll be the fool putting us all in danger otherwise, and I really don't want to be that guy. I'm here to help. I want to help."

Ugh, thought Cal. Annoying that she was right. And he couldn't figure out *why* it was so annoying.

"Fine," Cal said, walking down toward the common room and the holomap at its center. "But don't be surprised if things move faster than you're used to with the Imperials."

A big hand clapped down on Cal's shoulder from behind and he turned with a start, looking directly into Fret's round, friendly face, expression open and for all the world just looking happy to be included.

"Thanks, boss," she said with a grin. "Promise I'm a team player."

Cal wanted to distrust her so much. He'd argued with Greez about why that shouldn't be the case, but it just bloomed up in his stomach anyway, a traitorous roiling that, as Fret just said, threatened to put his crew—his family—in danger if he didn't get it under control. Cal knew something about Fret that Merrin likely didn't, and he didn't feel he had the right to share it. That alone made him sick. But there was something else in the depths of him, a sour note that discordantly rang out with the desire to just open the air lock at the nearest port and chuck this gal out of it as far as the Force would take her.

So why'd she have to be so damn likable?

Cal rested both his hands on the edge of the holotable. "Greez, ETA?"

"Few minutes to atmo," came the quick response from the cockpit. The *Mantis*'s lighting flipped off to account for approaching a planet in its daylight hours to save power. Cal gestured over the map, calling up the visual of Murkhana in all of its gory glory.

"It was beautiful, once, you know," said Fret, watching. She looked serious, for once. "A real tourist attraction, black beaches, huge oceans, real amazing coral reefs; I saw holos of what it looked like before the Republic bombed the life out of it from orbit during the Clone Wars. Burned the Separatists out of their hiding places, and took everything else with them."

"Total eco-collapse," agreed Cere, settling down on the bench. "All that's left now is acid rain, quicksand, and murky, stagnant pools that breed nothing but more toxic gas."

"You got it," said Fret. "What's left of Murkhana City is now one of the galaxy's best-known black markets. Whole economy's run by smugglers and crime lords, the only people still bringing goods in and out of the atmo to folks who still try to live there. I know it—Empire's still got a limited presence there." She used her fingers to zoom in on the planet map, bringing up a massive facility just outside of Murkhana City, surrounded by a large stone curtain wall to keep people out—or in.

"The compound houses a garrison, a prison, and they've got an ambassador in there, too. That's where we're headed. But the locals hate the Empire as you do—should help us out."

Cal nodded. They were going to have no trouble infiltrating the place. No one would pay them any attention coming in or going out, and certainly no one on Murkhana was going to stop them from messing with the Empire's toys. It really couldn't have been better circumstances for the crew of the *Stinger Mantis*. He should have been overjoyed about it, really.

Cal stared hard at the glowing hologram of Murkhana as Merrin rushed back into the room, her hair back in its usual state, and he tried not to notice that she studiously kept her eyes off Fret and sat as far away from her as she could, on the end of the opposite couch next to Cere.

That frustrating half smile was back on Fret's face.

"All right. Plan is: same as we always do," said Cere from the bench. Cal zoomed in on Murkhana City, to the docks and the compound, the area they were going to need to focus on the most in the search for the schematics. "Tonight, recon. Tomorrow, in and out."

"Wait, wait," Fret threw up a hand. "Help the new kid out here. What's 'same as we always do,' exactly?"

"We split it up into parts," Cal explained, keeping his voice patient. "Tonight, recon. That's Cere and Merrin; they'll scope the place out, figure out what our best course of action is."

"You'll come into play here, both before and after," Cere added, to Fret. "With your knowledge of how the Imperials work, what we should know about their guard postings, rotations, entrances. We'll take anything you've got."

"I've got the codes," said Fret, with a grin. "I can get you inside that curtain wall without having to break down a single door. And I've got the outfit to prove it. I can walk right up and get you in, no problem."

"Helpful already," said Merrin, with a small smile.

Cal had to stop himself from rolling his eyes. "Right, huge. Great."

"After that, we execute on our tried-and-tested infiltration strategy," said Cere. "Greez and I were able to access maps of the facility, and found what we need to get ourselves in and out without getting caught." Cere swiped a hand over the holomap, bringing up a rotating image of the garrison's interior. "It's heavily guarded, as the prison area holds some of the galaxy's worst criminals, but that's nothing new for us. Once Fret lets us in the front door, Merrin, you take this entrance through the roof, here, and make sure it's clear for our exit."

Merrin sighed. "Always Cal in the line of fire, and always me sneaking in another way."

"Well, sure." Cal tilted his head. "I'm the target. The worst heat's gotta be on me. You're less likely to be hurt that way."

Merrin was looking at him like he was missing the point. Maybe he was.

"And Fret?" she asked.

"She'll come with you, in case of any interior codes," Cere confirmed. "Cal, you'll head for the service vents."

"Always into the basements," Cal teased. "No wonder I'm so pale."

Cere shook her head with a wry smile. She pulled the map down, revealing what lay under the garrison: miles of tunnels, most of which looked like they were half crumbling. This place likely hadn't undergone maintenance in years. "Several floors belowground, I've managed to locate the main electrical room that services the entire facility. That's where you'll head, if you can make your way around all this wreckage."

"Don't I always?"

Cere nodded. "And I've been doing some research with Greez on the prison portion of the garrison. I think this mission should be even more interesting than usual, in fact."

Fret looked at her, quizzically. "What's that supposed to mean?"

From the cockpit, they heard a laugh. "Oh, c'mon—we're not gonna ruin the surprise *now,* are we?"

Fret looked put out. Cal liked it.

"That's the same as we always do," said Cal. He wasn't surprised by Cere's plan; it was, as she said, their standard operating procedure. They'd have no trouble with it; they rarely did.

"Once again, just gonna throw this out there," came a shout back from the cockpit. "Should we be doing this at all? Kinda feels like a bad plan. Still time to turn around. That's all I'm sayin'. But what do I know? I'm just the most experienced and best looking of the group."

Fret frowned. "What does being good looking have—"

Greez cut her off with another shout. "Anyway, atmo in three, two—"

The *Mantis* shook as the ship breached Murkhana's gloomy atmosphere, and for a moment the whole ship went dark as the acidic clouds broke over the cockpit's glass. There was silence in the room for a moment, and Cal watched the people he loved illuminated solely by the glow of the holotable.

Greez focused hard on the controls, the best pilot in the skies, who cared for this ship like it was his own family, and maybe it was; family he'd protect at all costs, even if it meant running and running.

Cere, so deep in her own thoughts Cal worried, for one of the first times since they'd met, that he couldn't follow her where she was going; not through words, and not through the Force. She looked impenetrable, her own fortress, clouded.

Merrin, staring across the table, lost in a memory; in two different memories, her face shifting from ruined to wrecked in ways that Cal thought he should be able to understand, but found himself again lost and lacking.

And then there was Fret—staring right at Cal.

With a stutter, the backup lights flicked back on. Greez had forgotten there was no sun on Murkhana, no matter the time of day.

Things here were always shrouded in the dark.

Merrin had always been able to see well at night.

The streets near the Imperial facility on Murkhana were nearly empty at this late hour, everyone back in whatever passed for homes on this wasted rock. Laid out flat along the top of a closed market stall, Merrin watched two stormtroopers idle outside the massive prison gate, occasionally chatting with each other, obviously unworried and under-alert. Fools. Beside Merrin, Cere was adjusting her macrobinoculars, trying to find the right balance between focus and night vision.

A Nightsister's eyes were more accustomed to darkness; Dathomir was a dark planet, by its very nature, bathed in Domir's crimson glow, the planet's red sun. Merrin, like all her sisters, like her home, had been forged under the dim light of a red dwarf–type star—the smallest and most common type of star in the galaxy, and yet still regarded as an oddity among the many sentient species Merrin had met since leaving home.

Merrin shifted her gaze skyward. Murkhana's single dim star had set hours ago, and its moon only reflected what little light the small sun had to offer. So different from the sun on Merrin's home planet. Domir lit Dathomir's sky like a wound, splitting the clouds and, sanguine, soaking the planet. They were nearly twins, their orbits close by necessity, Dathomir reaching out for all the light it was able to get and drinking it in greedily. Solar-type stars burned through their hydrogen quickly, but red dwarves persisted for eternity. Nightsisters were patient, like Domir, quiet; they burned long and slow, need simmering in their veins alongside their magick. Merrin thought of her planet and her sun like binary stars, circling each other, each creating the other. Dathomir and Domir were so deeply interconnected, the light of its sun giving the planet its personality and the planet itself giving meaning to its sun. Merrin had come of age stained in it; even the light that reflected off Dathomir's four moons was bloody.

That was how Merrin liked it. She preferred to live in the shadows; faces had more depth, secrets could be hidden, quiet spaces were easier to find.

"For such a small facility, there's certainly no shortage of troopers here," Cere said matter-of-factly, bringing Merrin's focus back to the gate. She was right; they'd been watching the same spot for more than an hour, and four different sets of guards had come and gone during that short time. Whatever was being held in there, Merrin knew, the Empire was taking no chances when it came to its protection.

"Okay." Merrin shrugged. "Are we worrying about that? I didn't think we worried about that." More stormtroopers now meant fewer stormtroopers in the galaxy overall later. That was how it always worked when the *Mantis* showed up.

Cere breathed a noncommittal huff out of her nose, somewhere between a laugh and an agreement, and shifted, looking around to ensure nothing else in the area had changed. Merrin appreciated the Jedi's commitment to being forever alert, but really—nothing was changing. If Murkhana had nightlife, it certainly wasn't happening here. Stormtroopers weren't exactly known for their party atmosphere.

But still, Merrin had been glad that Cere had asked for her specifically to help on this reconnaissance mission. They always worked well together, striking a fine balance between impulse and patience that was necessary during moments like this. Cal and Greez remained on the *Mantis,* refining their plans for the extraction. Fret was back there, too—though Merrin wasn't sure if she'd be asked to participate. Thinking of Fret made Merrin's mouth go dry, her heart start to beat faster, and she had to stop for a moment to remind herself not to get distracted. They had work to do. For Fret. For them.

"I cannot get these things to focus right," Cere muttered in frustration, messing with the macrobinoculars again. "Everything is so dim."

Merrin shook her head. Other species were obsessed with the light.

They lived in blindingly lit homes, squinting against it, roasting under it like animals in an oven. They rebelled against the idea of darkness, feared it, did everything within their power to burn it out of their lives. Merrin had watched Cal's skin freckle under the light of glaring solar suns, his hair wilt, his pores sweat—but still he would turn his face up to it with tight-shut eyes and a grateful smile and drink it in like water. For others, the light was a fixation, a necessity. For those forged under the light of a solar star, they'd built their meaning around it. They needed the light, fought for it, died without it, withering away in darkness; their bodies starved for the chemical reactions set off by light, their bones crumbling into nothing without it, crawling blindly through the dark. Most beings were obsessed with light.

And Jedi, especially.

But Merrin was no Jedi. And she preferred to work in the dark.

"There," she said to Cere, pointing straight ahead. "I see it."

Cere squinted ahead in the darkness, night-vision binoculars pressed up tightly against her eyes. "Where?"

"*There*," Merrin repeated more emphatically, knowing that it wouldn't really help at all, but at a loss for how better to explain. She gestured with her hand again, this time with real gusto. She had to admit that Jedi were simply so useless sometimes, even if she loved two of them.

"Ohhh," Cere breathed, something clicking in her mind. Merrin and Cere had scouted enough missions together over the years that it really didn't take more than that for the two of them to communicate. She might not have had the same kind of connection to the Force that Cere and Cal did, but she and Cere had developed their own kind of quiet communication, their own secret language that the two of them spoke without knowing or meaning to. Cal got too itchy on reconnaissance, and BD was not, by nature, a quiet droid; Merrin and Cere were best suited for the task. And they executed it very well.

The compound itself was as it had looked on the aerial holomap back on the *Mantis*: a large stone-walled prison, surrounded by an expanse of courtyard. Outside of it all, a round, very tall curtain wall made of stone, with only one point of entry: a huge gate, guarded and secured by an entry code. The prison itself was massive, cut into the rock below; Merrin was surprised that Fret had called this a minimal presence.

Minimal to the Imperials, she supposed.

But what Merrin had spotted was a gap in the already lax security surrounding the Imperial compound in Murkhana City. It had the usual nonsense, the basic things the *Mantis* crew had bypassed a hundred times during their expeditions against the Empire: high walls, studded with sensors, patrolled by armed sentries.

But it was going to be easier than ever for them this time. Because this time, they had a stormtrooper of their own. And what Merrin was pointing to were the compound's literal front doors.

"Fret's codes drop security, we walk in during guard rotation," Cere said, reading Merrin's mind not through magick, but through experience. "I like it. Clean."

"Harder once we're inside." Merrin narrowed her eyes into the darkness, the moonlight blanching the color out of everything to the same shades as Merrin's own skin. Moonlight was always so much kinder than sunlight; she loved a mission at night. "Impossible to tell what's going on in there."

Cere nodded, lowering her binoculars. "We'll have to execute on our usual plan once you're inside." Merrin knew what she meant, of course: split the party. Cal and BD-1 in from below; Merrin as death from above. Cere on hacking and comms; Greez on the quick getaway sticks. Usually, everyone had a partner but Merrin, BD and Cal being an inseparable duo and Cere and Greez often operating in tandem.

But Merrin wouldn't be alone this time.

She liked the idea of that more than she wanted to admit to herself in the blanched light of the moon, bright enough for her to see the whole world lit up like new.

"Time to head back," said Cere, tucking away her specs. She'd brought a surprisingly large pack for a quick recon mission; she looked like she had an entire rifle case latched to her back. Merrin watched Cere double-check that her blaster was holstered securely on her waist; there was no telling who you were going to run into on a planet like this, at this time of night.

Not that they had anything to be afraid of. Merrin and Cere were two of the most elusive wanted people in the galaxy, hardened criminals in the eyes of the Empire. They'd survived worse than a crime-riddled rock and they'd do so again.

Still, tonight wasn't the night to pick a fight they didn't need. Out and back in again; recon and report. They had more important things to worry about than some drunken soldier looking to feel important by beating on someone smaller than him.

Not that Merrin would have minded the outlet for her excess energy. Of which she had lots, at the moment.

But now was not the time to focus on that, not the time to focus on violets covered in morning dew—not while they needed their minds on the job, their concentration on staying concealed in the shadows as they headed back into the city, darting between low buildings, alley to alley, making their way back toward the *Mantis*.

Murkhana City wasn't much of a city anymore, decimated by air strikes and the years of disastrous climate that followed. Acid rain had eaten away at its once grand buildings, spiraling into the sky, now crumbling into dust. Between ruined buildings was the detritus of war, the husks of Republic and Separatist war machines now indistinguishable from one another, both littering the ground of this planet they'd destroyed in their fight for power.

A flash of shiny white, a fragment—Merrin squeezed her eyes shut. It was not him. Grievous was gone, and would never return.

But Murkhana reminded her too much of Dathomir for her own sanity. It was too much, to stand on the ruined ground of a planet caught up in a war that didn't belong to it. She wanted nothing to do with it, and frankly, she wanted out of here as quickly as possible, so she wasn't going to argue with Cere. The two women moved as quickly as they could without compromising their own safety, back to where Greez had the ship waiting for them, at the city's remaining spaceport. One had virtually sunk into the sorry excuse for what was once Murkhana's ocean, now a torrential toxic sludge. The other had survived marginally better, built into a hillside and protected from the worst of the rains, but Merrin wouldn't charitably call it functional. It had no operational guidance system; Customs was so far into the city proper that no one who landed on the planet even had to bother with it. The *Mantis* was docked there, for the moment, taking full advantage of Murkhana's well-known policy of keeping your mouth shut about things that simply were not your problem.

Merrin and Cere were about halfway back, ducking and dodging in the darkness between bombed-out buildings and fallen land units, when Cere cleared her throat.

"So . . ." came Cere's quiet voice from the shadows behind Merrin. "You and Fret."

Clearly, Cere was not aware enough of the rules of Murkhana.

That or, more likely, she just didn't care.

"Me and Fret," Merrin responded in kind, equally as vague. If Cere wasn't going to be more direct, neither was she. Merrin's hand reached up to feel the gold teeth around her neck, shrouded in the dark fabric of her hood. They were as sharp as they were the day she got them, the necklace pressed into her hands.

Sharp and bloody.

Cere hummed quietly in response. Together they rushed around a corner, and then behind Merrin came Cere's voice again: "Your fire's back."

Merrin stopped around the side of the building and Cere avoided bumping into her back; it was dark, but Merrin assumed the Force warned Cere when Merrin stopped moving, made it easier for the two of them to communicate if Merrin saw something dangerous coming in the dark. Between Merrin's eyes and Cere's spirit, there was really no surprising them.

Cere, on the other hand, had very much just surprised Merrin.

"It was never *gone*," Merrin responded slowly. She turned her head to the side, just enough to see Cere watching her out of the corner of her eyes.

"I know that," Cere responded carefully. "But I know you better. I've seen you struggle lately. I don't . . ." She paused for a second. Merrin watched her face as she searched for the right words, gave her the space to figure them out. "I can't understand exactly what you went through.

On Dathomir. But I can sympathize. I think, probably, better than most people. And I can only imagine how hard that's made things for you."

Merrin swallowed. Cere was right, of course; no one but another Nightsister could ever truly understand how Merrin felt, what she'd been through, the way she had to dig into her soul to find the magickal itch in her palms and the despair when it never came. She'd been alone for so long, it would have been easier to remain that way in her heart. But she also knew that Cere had suffered, had lost the people she loved, had remade her life from scratch.

And most of all, that Cere was her friend.

"I know," Merrin said quietly. "I know you know."

Merrin picked out the hint of a smile on Cere's face in the darkness. "So if there's something about Fret that helps you heal that hurt, even for a minute, even a little . . . I think it's a very, very good thing."

Against her own better judgment, Merrin felt herself blush. Unwilling to risk Cere seeing and making fun of her for the rest of her natural days, even in the unlikely dark, she pressed on.

"Hang on," said Cere. "Let's turn this way instead."

Merrin frowned. It wasn't the way they'd come from, getting out here . . . but Cere had feelings about these things sometimes, and Merrin knew better than to question them. She made the opposite turn, away from the *Mantis,* and followed behind Cere now, letting the Jedi take the lead.

"So what is it about her, do you think?" Cere threw back behind her shoulder.

The blush in her cheeks heated and Merrin knew her chalky-white skin was tinged green. She was grateful to be behind Cere, to be hidden in shadow on top of that. She cleared her throat as she considered Cere's question.

"Come on, give me something. I like to see you so happy." Cere's eye roll was almost audible in her voice.

"It's . . ." Merrin paused for a second to collect her thoughts, her mind brought back to violets and sticky sweet dew, to smirks and snarls, to cold bunks and heated words. "She has—" Merrin stopped, embarrassed. "Very nice hands."

Cere burst out laughing and had to hush herself when she remembered where they were. "I bet she does."

"But it's more than *just* that!" Merrin continued, not wanting Cere to misunderstand. "It's . . . there is something about her, to me, that feels—I don't know how to say it. Like I'm drawn to her in a way I can't entirely understand. Like I had lost this part of myself, and she is showing me the way back to it." Merrin took a breath. "She's allowed me to feel things about Dathomir that I hadn't allowed myself to feel since I came aboard. Anger. Frustration. She is angry about her losses, too, and I am able to absorb those feelings for her, make them feel okay to voice. Like I absorb her light, and she does mine. Like . . ."

Red eyes and red skies. "Like binary stars."

Cere stopped, hidden in the shadow of a building, a massive fallen AT-TE in front of them. Merrin watched Cere nod, even though she wasn't certain that she'd made much sense. Cere seemed to understand all the same. She turned to Merrin, even though Merrin knew she couldn't see her face. "The Jedi believe in energy, in balance," said Cere, "the great Force in the world that unites us all. But in my time, I've come to see that some of us are tied together more tightly by the galaxy than others. A tether between hearts, if you'll permit me being a bit of a sap about it. I feel a real connection between the two of you. And I see how you both feed each other through it."

Cere paused. "She needs you, too, I think. Right now."

Merrin couldn't hold back her smile. "And you don't think that's . . . odd? We just met. She is a stranger to me—to us."

"And we're a Jedi and a daughter of Dathomir, fast friends," Cere laughed, and Merrin couldn't help laughing with her.

When they'd stopped, Cere added with seriousness: "We are all bound and connected by the Force. There's nothing unusual about two beings who had not previously met forming a strong connection, falling in love at first sight, even. That's the beauty of our galaxy. It's what makes everything we do worthwhile.

"I need to stop in here," she added, coming up behind the fallen and gutted AT-TE. It was bolted together, repaired from parts, and looked like someone lived inside.

"Here?" asked Merrin, confused. "We have to get back to the *Mantis*—"

And then Cere was ripping off the corrugated panels in one go with the Force, uncaring about anyone who might hear or see.

"Cere!" Merrin hissed in shock and warning. Inside the dilapidated war machine sat a singular person, a small Sugi, armored and helmeted, surrounded by their wares: weaponry of all kinds, in the Sugi custom. Without so much as a greeting, Cere walked straight to the back of the AT-TE, propelled by something Merrin couldn't feel but knew was there, ignoring the stuttering protests of the Sugi.

Regaining her senses after the initial shock of the moment, Merrin threw her hands up at the Sugi threateningly. "Not a move, and not a word."

The Sugi nodded. They were no fool.

Sensing they wouldn't be a threat, Merrin turned her attention back to Cere. She was shuffling through objects at the back of the shop— looking for a weapon? Something to help them break into the compound?

So Merrin was shocked when Cere stood back up to her full height holding not a blaster, not a laser sword—but what looked suspiciously like . . . a crown?

Merrin hadn't really thought of Cere as the tiara type, but she had no doubt she could pull it off. Still . . .

"This Circlet rightfully belongs to the Jedi." Cere's voice was quiet and intense, a viper ready to strike but not revealing its fangs. *Ah.* She didn't elaborate, as Merrin thought she might—nor did she stalk off into the night with the Circlet in her hands and the threat of violence in her wake.

Instead Merrin watched as Cere shrugged the pack off her back, slid it to the ground, and unzipped it. There was no rifle inside, no powerful weapon; instead there was an instrument, a mandolin. Not the seven-string hallikset Merrin had seen Cere play before, but rather a smaller instrument.

Her first stringed instrument. The one on which she'd learned to play as a Padawan. The one Cere had told Merrin that she'd rescued from the ashes of her former life, and which reminded her every day of where she came from, and what she was fighting for.

And she was trading it away for this crown. Why?

The Sugi looked at the instrument; at Cere. Nodded. Acceptable; they would have people who dealt in such rare treasures on Murkhana that they could trade with, Merrin knew; the same was true in most of these backwater planets. They would get their money's worth for it, more than a dusty crown they obviously didn't know what to do with, judging by how far it was buried in the back of their collection.

Cere was already stalking out of the arms dealer's makeshift den, crown clutched in one of her hands. Merrin gave the Sugi a last threatening glance before she followed after her friend.

"We can talk about it later," Cere said, preempting anything Merrin had been about to say.

But Merrin hadn't been about to say anything. As they rushed, practiced, between buildings back to the *Mantis,* Merrin felt the weight of the necklace against her clavicle, felt it bounce under her hood against her skin when she moved. She felt it sharp and dangerous, cold and a constant reminder of her first kiss; of trust, and what it had come to. Of love, and how it could . . . hurt.

End.

There is a power, in objects, in their stories, and Merrin knew it. Felt hands that had touched this necklace before hers; knew the feel of it in her palm. Knew the person who had crafted it, healing herself while making it.

Merrin knew the power of objects with history. And she knew Cere would tell her about what her plans were for this one when she was ready.

"You have got to tell me what in the galaxy this is." Cal had turned the tiara-looking thing over and over in his hands, wondering at the shape of it almost as much as he wondered at the power he could feel radiating off it. Not that it was a weapon, or read through the Force like anything he could throw through the air like a magic boomerang, slicing stormtroopers in half; more like it was imbued with the Force so deeply that it seeped out of its metallic pores like sweat.

Cal had been worried; Merrin and Cere never took this long on recon missions, especially not on ones that should have gone so easily, given all of Fret's advanced information. He hadn't heard from them—that, at least, was typical, keeping comms quiet to avoid potential detection—but *something* after the third hour out would have been nice. And then they'd come back with no apologies but with a crown?

Cal was trying not to be upset about it. But he wasn't exactly succeeding.

"It's a circlet," came Cere's reply.

Not helpful, Cere. "Yeah, I'm getting that much," Cal muttered. Cere's eyes were fiery with the success of her mission—a mission that nobody else, for the record, knew she was on, Cal thought with some bitterness and more than a little confusion.

They'd been gearing up in the engine room for their infiltration; Merrin and Cere had gotten back so late the rest of the ship had already been asleep. When Cal woke up, he found himself thinking about Merrin and Fret in her neat cabin together, marred by Fret's mess; kept thinking about Fret so much taller and wider than Merrin, purple arms wrapped around chalky-white back, the bruise on Merrin's collarbone, green fire around the door. Knowing that Fret was in love with someone else, and that Merrin probably had no idea.

He'd felt sick to his stomach. Probably hadn't eaten well yesterday; it had been a bit of a day.

Merrin could do what she wanted. Fret was, despite the pit in Cal's stomach, pretty damn nice, so far, and hadn't gotten any of them killed, which went a long way in his books these days. She was nice to BD. And Force knew that Merrin had been in such good spirits since Fret had come on board, looked lit up in a way he hadn't thought she was able to be again, maybe, after what had happened to her.

Which was a good thing. Those were all definitely good things. Objectively good things.

So why was he downright conflicted about it?

Still, he didn't have the time to dwell on that right now. The sick feeling in his stomach had intensified when he joined the crew for their morning meal and learned that Cere had put their entire mission—their entire family!—at risk by making some random grab for, what, a piece of jewelry? A Jedi heirloom with no real use?

That didn't seem like the Cere whom Cal knew, the Jedi Master who had taught him to put the safety of those he loved above all else. There was something else at play here, something she wasn't sharing.

Cal knew what happened when you didn't share your secrets with the people around you. Sometimes it was necessary, but sometimes—sometimes it got them killed.

Today was not the day he planned on getting killed.

"The Circlet of Saresh," Cere explained fervently, pulling on her gloves, "is an honored piece of Jedi history, crafted by a Jedi Knight and made to ensure that only servants of the light can use it. It is said to boost the wearer's connection to and abilities in the Force."

Cal squinted at it, setting it down on the worktable. "So you're thinking of adding a crown to your personal arsenal?"

Cere looked at him like he'd grown a second head. "I'm not going to wear it, Cal."

"Then what's the point of it?" This got more confusing by the second. "Why'd you pull such a risky move for something you're not even going to use?"

Pausing halfway through pulling on her vest, Cere sighed. "Cal, listen to me. You are a highly motivated person. It comes from within you. That's admirable, incredibly so. But not everyone is quite the same way. There are people who can't fight for a thing unless they have a symbol; people who can't look forward without first being able to look back. If we don't preserve Jedi history, how will we learn from the past?"

"I don't understand." Cal shook his head. "If we're not going to use it while we fight, why even have it?"

Cere's smile was wry, almost wistful. "People need something to look at and say, *There have been those who have come before. There will be those who will come again. And maybe that's me.*"

Cal thought it must be nice to have that kind of choice.

"Fine," he said. It would do him no good to argue with Cere about this, not right now, not on their way out the door. But it wasn't going to be the last time he brought it up. Not by a long shot. "Just be honest with me next time, okay? Family doesn't keep secrets."

She was silent as she finished gearing up.

Fret stuck her head into the engine room, hair scruffy as ever, smirk firmly in place. "Inquisitor chrono's ticking. We ready to go here, kids?"

"That's my line," Greez grumbled as he passed by.

"Born ready," said Cal, wishing, in this moment, anyway, that were less true than it was.

Cal was hiding in plain sight, pressed up against the wall separating the garrison's compound from the rest of the city, BD-1 on his back on watch. Cere and Merrin had done their job well, as he'd known they would: They'd found the time in which guards were rotating, briefly leaving the front gate untended. He watched as a stormtrooper approached, knowing it was Fret, able to see the little swagger in her bearing that Cal had become familiar with. He was skeptical—wouldn't the Imperials have changed their designations and codes once they'd realized Fret had abandoned ship?—but also knew the size of the Empire, how slow they were to move, how that had benefited the stealthy, speedy *Mantis* crew on nearly every occasion in the last couple of years.

So he leaned and waited as Fret approached the gate, approached him pressed up against the wall next to it, waiting for—

"Time. Open it now," came Cere's crackled voice over comms. She was back in the *Mantis,* strapped in next to Greez, running comms, slicing, and operations from a distance, the stuff she did best. "And Fret: Don't get fancy."

Pretty rich from Cere, after she'd risked this whole thing for her weird new fixation on museum curation, or whatever was going on with her.

And now it was just him and BD, like it almost always was out in the field, hoping against hope that this went as smoothly as it promised to, knowing that, given their history, it probably wouldn't.

At least Merrin would think it was more fun, that way. Small victories.

As Fret entered the code directly next to Cal at the great barrier, pretending not to see him, he felt the wall behind him shift. The movement was negligible, nothing that would alert troopers on break. The gate shifted just enough to allow humanoid-sized figures through, and Cal watched Fret slip from one side to the other, leaving it open behind her.

Heat at his back; a sigh of displaced air. "She did good," said Merrin.

Merrin had appeared behind him. BD beeped quietly on Cal's back; with enough time and effort, he probably could have also opened the gate. It wasn't *that* big a deal.

Cal fought a smile; he knew how hard compound security was to break, but he wouldn't have put it past his little droid anyway. He passed through the open barrier after Fret, knowing Merrin would be right on his heels, trusting her to shut it behind her.

They were through; guards were still rotating. None the wiser.

Maybe this would be smooth, after all. He *was* owed a good day.

Cal let Fret lead the way, keeping close to the interior of the curtain wall, scoping out the area. He paused to let Merrin pass him so that he could protect their backs, bring up the rear. The courtyard, mostly just dirt, splayed out in front of them concentrically, and on the other side of it the many buildings that made up the garrison compound— including the prison, with no clear method of entry or exit.

Not for a normal person, anyway. But Cal and Merrin were executing their normal plan of attack: Merrin from above, Cal from below. Cal had his eyes open for a grate; Merrin would approach from the roof. This was their first time seeing inside the compound properly, so they would be playing it a bit fast and loose from here, but they had a general plan, and it was no harder than missions they'd pulled off before. They were going to be fine.

He saw Merrin watching Fret's walk again.

"Wait." Cere's voice came through comms again. "I'm in the system and—this isn't right. We shouldn't have been able to get in."

Cal saw Fret's gait falter just slightly in front him. "Say again, Cere?"

"The entry codes, they were changed—" Cere stopped for a moment; Cal knew she was double-checking her work. "This morning. The keylogs were all updated this morning."

Now Fret attempted to speed up.

But Cal was faster. Cal was *always* faster.

In seconds he had Fret pushed up against the curtain wall, ignoring Merrin's choked protest, his forearm across the Imperial's throat.

"How." He didn't have to say more than that; his face said the rest of it for him. Cal couldn't see Fret's face under the helmet, but it wasn't difficult to imagine what was under there: a defiant smirk, a raised brow, cheeks ruddy purple with flush, hair a sweaty mess. Red eyes flashing a warning.

He wasn't playing into that. Not anymore.

Guess he had no reason to be mad at himself anymore. Greez had been right, after all.

He should have known. After what he saw with Irei, in the Echo . . . he should have known.

Wanting to see the best in people was going to get him killed one day—or worse, get someone he cared about killed. He hated that. He hated that it might be bad to try to see the good in people. That the optimist approach was that flawed.

But here he was again. And he didn't know what to do with that information.

Right now, the answer was threaten a traitorous Imperial about it.

"You heard Cere. How?" he repeated. He trusted that he didn't have to tell her not to make him repeat himself again, but just to be sure, he shoved his arm deeper into the soft fabric that separated the shiny white plates at her throat.

The filtering unit on her voice rendered it almost unrecognizable. "Because . . ."

Fret paused. Cal didn't like that pause.

"Because I never actually left the Empire."

Before Cal could read, Merrin interjected. "It's okay, Cal. Just let Fret explain."

Cal liked that even less.

CHAPTER 9

Several Nights Earlier

"Do you think we could just . . . never leave?" Merrin said with a sigh, infuriated at the tremulous note in her voice.

Fret shifted next to her on the narrow cot, adjusting the arm she had wrapped around Merrin so that it rested more comfortably under Merrin's head. Merrin buried her face into the other girl's burly biceps, hoping it would appropriately mask the green tinge her cheeks couldn't seem to shake. They'd managed to pass the time on the way to Murkhana shockingly quickly; Merrin knew that Greez would be signaling their arrival soon, and there was nothing she wanted to do less than get dressed and leave the engine room, this little sanctuary she'd created with Fret over the last few hours. Touching Fret, being with her, felt *green*—like the lush, foreign planets Merrin had visited over the last few years. Like the woods, like unfolding; blooming flowers, wet leaves, and tree cover. Like a home she'd never known.

"We could," Fret said with an aura of deep contemplation, her other hand behind her head. "We could just stay right here and never come out again. Of course—" She paused for dramatic effect. "—that *does* mean I'd eventually have to eat you."

Merrin couldn't help herself; she burst out laughing, shoving at Fret's bare stomach with her other hand, earning a playful shove in return that landed her on her back, her head back on Fret's biceps. The ceiling in the engine room was all gray pipe, but it suddenly had a very romantic tinge to it. She thought that she might be a big fan of pipes, actually, that they looked quite nice all tangled up in the ceiling together, that they had kind of an air of sweetness, actually.

Oh, no, Merrin thought, twisting her mouth up in frustrated acceptance. *I am in it. Bad.*

She suddenly wanted to know everything about Fret. Wanted to tell Fret everything about herself. They had, as Merrin knew they would, talked at length during Fret's first few days on the ship, about their shared trauma; their losses, the things they missed about their homes, the lives they were mourning that they would never, ever get back. About their resentment and frustration at their situations, so different from the way Cere and Cal talked about these things—with an air of fated resignation. With a calm sense of serenity and sadness.

Not Fret. Fret was *angry.*

And she let Merrin be angry, too.

Merrin hadn't realized how much she'd needed to be angry until she had started to talk all of this through with Fret. She felt like the poison from her wounds, each time she was able to experience fury with Fret, bled its way out, bit by bit.

Though Merrin still knew so little about Fret, they had shared enough, and bonded enough over their pain, that Merrin felt more than ever that she had made the right decision in allowing her on board.

But Merrin wanted there to be even less between them than there was right now. Wanted to crawl right into the divot in Fret's collarbones and curl up there, burying herself in the heat and warmth. She felt like she was going to overflow with it, and with the fire surging up from her belly and into her hands and her head and her heart. Her entire body was pulsing with it.

She couldn't handle it, couldn't keep herself apart from the other girl for a second longer. Languidly, she flipped herself over, her front pressing against Fret's, feeling the way their thighs connected, their bellies, their chests. Their bodies slotted together like a puzzle, tangled in each other on the small cot. Merrin looked down at her and felt what she could only describe in the moment as a mixture of awe and hunger.

"You are so handsome," she said without thinking, and then her lips were on Fret's.

"You make me feel, just . . ." Merrin mumbled into Fret's lips. "Alive. Again."

Merrin pulled away, trailed her mouth down Fret's jaw, her neck, clawed her hands into Fret's sides, exalted when she heard the sound that escaped Fret's lips, her head tilted back into the cot. Fret buried her hands in Merrin's hair, long since loose from her ponytail, and sighed.

"I can't believe anyone would take for granted the opportunity to tell you all the ways you're beautiful, all the parts of you that are just absolutely delicious," Fret said without opening her eyes, her hands tugging gently at Merrin's hair. "Someone should have been writing sonnets to your rib cage."

There it was again; green heat in her cheeks. Merrin nipped at the hair that trailed down her stomach, trying to hide her emotions under something easier, lighter. "You are quite the charmer."

Fret opened her eyes, smiled down at Merrin, biting into her bottom lip.

And then the smile started to fade.

"Merrin," Fret said suddenly in her surprisingly lyrical voice, sitting up on her elbows slowly. She sounded the way that sliding over her felt: soft and sweet and just a little dangerous. The promise of more.

Fret paused, like she couldn't quite get the words out. Merrin just waited; didn't want to frighten her off before she had the chance to trust her.

"Tell me something about yourself?" Fret finished. It wasn't what Merrin had expected.

Merrin knit her brows together, worrying at the skin of her bottom lip with her teeth. There was so much to tell; it was sometimes hard to know where to start. Especially since she'd never really found anyone she wanted to tell things to, anyway. Or hadn't other than Cal.

"I had a pet," Merrin offered, thinking back to the best creature she had ever known. "On Dathomir. Bramble lynx start out small, not a lot of people know that. But they are very cute, if you raise them right. Rip anything apart for you and protect you under all circumstances. Very good at murders."

Merrin watched with affection as Fret's nose scrunched up the way it did when she found something funny. "You little freak."

"Thank you," Merrin conceded with a smile, accepting the compliment for what it was. "Her name was Teeno. She liked being scratched under the chin and had a fondness for nydak blood. And after the Separatists attacked . . ." She swallowed. It never got any easier. "I never saw her again." She shook her head. "Did you have something similar, as a child?"

The cot shifted under their combined weight as Fret rolled onto her side. In an easy movement, she scooped Merrin up into her strong arms, pulling the shorter girl in against her chest. Merrin inhaled the scent of Fret's skin, grave thorn and ahrisa and sweat. Her own arms snaked around Fret's chest, forcing the other girl to lift up slightly so Merrin could slide her hand between her and the cot. She felt the breath leave her own chest as Fret squeezed and squeezed.

"You've been through so much." Fret's lips were on Merrin's hair, the words reverberating through the spots where their bodies connected, everywhere at once. Merrin noticed she'd deflected away from her question. "I'm so sorry. It's so much for someone to hold. So I'm going to be here to hold you."

Merrin squeezed her eyes shut; they suddenly stung. She found herself wishing more than ever that they never had to leave; or if they did have to escape their little bubble, that at the very least . . .

"You could stay." Merrin traced the words with her lips into Fret's soft, smooth skin, over the same dusky-purple freckles that covered her face, over the old scars that wrapped around her chest. "After the mission to Murkhana. We have room on the *Mantis,* we could use your knowledge—"

"I think the whole crew would have to agree to that." Fret didn't let her finish.

"You were so brave to leave," Merrin said softly. "And you never feared me. Approaching me on that rock—even when I threatened you with death—"

"Hot."

"—demonstrated a courage, a boldness of spirit that I found so admirable. The nerve it took for you to do all that impressed me from the start. The crew will see that same bravery, too. I know they will."

"Oh, Merrin." Fret swallowed. She sounded, for some reason, dismayed. "There's something I have to tell you about me." Her words came out quick and quiet, different from how they'd been just a moment ago. Merrin sensed the nerves she'd seen just before from Fret and had to push down her own nerves in response. She simply nodded into Fret's embrace, waiting for the other woman to put her words together in a way that made sense, that made her feel okay.

"When I came aboard the *Mantis,* I told you that I wanted out. Got out, with you."

Merrin immediately hated where this was going.

"There's something else you need to know." Fret pushed Merrin gently off her to one side, and Merrin felt her insides grow cold. The fire that was racing through her veins a moment earlier was racing to be extinguished, ice water dousing the heat. She didn't trust easily; she wasn't made a fool of easily.

If Fret was about to tell her something that would compromise her and her team . . .

Fret made Merrin feel alive, but if that were the case, Merrin would be the only one leaving this room alive.

"My job, in the Empire . . ." Fret sighed, hesitating. The two lay together, face-to-face, and Merrin was fine with it, because from this position it would be incredibly easy to hook her feet together behind Fret's back and snap her pretty, strong neck before she even knew what was happening to her.

But for now, Merrin just placed her hands on Fret's shoulders. She cursed her body for still reacting to Fret's. The fire might have receded in fear, but the rest of Fret's effect on her was still very, very evident.

"I told you I had been an analyst. Trained to be one my entire life.

Outer Rim troop deployments are my specialty—knowing who to send where and when and for how long; when to pull people out; when to put more in." She looked away for a moment. "The Empire almost always puts more in."

Merrin touched her hand to Fret's cheek, bringing their eyes back together. Gentle, caring, and one step closer to her neck. "Tell me, Fret."

The taller woman closed her eyes, slumped backward a bit, tilted her chin down. Had the good grace to look ashamed when she said, "Leaving the Empire is hard. It's so, so hard, Merrin. Which is why . . . I never did it."

Merrin's hand drifted back over Fret's shoulder. There it was.

The thing Merrin had been waiting to hear, this whole time.

The betrayal.

She felt the fire flare up.

"But you have to let me explain," Fret said, eyes open again, trained hard on Merrin's. "Because it's not what you think."

Merrin smelled the smoke before she saw the curls of it, but to the other woman's credit, Fret did not flinch from the heat radiating off Merrin's touch, or the way the tips of her fingers dug into her flesh.

"I'm not closely watched, not like someone more important would be." Fret spoke quickly but firmly. "They think I'm on a data-collecting mission to the Outer Rim. Took me ages to orchestrate. They expect me back. But I knew that the information and systems I had access to could help us get our hands on the Shroud. I couldn't risk losing that access, not when I was so close to finally finding it. To finally putting things right for—for me."

"I thought your *goal* was to escape the Imperials," Merrin said, attempting to keep her voice calm and hear Fret out. Something wasn't adding up. "Are you telling me the Shroud was always your real goal here? The real reason you came to us?"

"No." Fret shook her head. She paused for a moment. "Yes? I don't know. Both? Can both be the answer?"

Merrin swallowed hard. "Are you telling me it is?" She didn't know how to feel about any of this; it was too angering, too confusing.

Fret suddenly reached up, putting both her hands on Merrin's cheeks, gripping her face firmly. She brought her face close to Merrin's, whispering, desperate.

"It's all conflated. I'm sorry. I'm sorry I'm not easier to understand; that I'm not an easier person to be with at all. But I've always planned to leave the Empire, in the end. *Always.* You have to believe me."

Merrin stared hard into those red eyes, her twin stars. She wanted to believe Fret. Had no reason not to.

So why did something feel so wrong?

Now

Cal had Fret up against the prison wall, had demanded an explanation out of her right there, but they'd run out of time; shift change was up, Inquisitors were coming, and they were having to deal with the fact that they were lying to one another on top of it? It was too much. He'd wanted to hear the explanation, give Merrin the benefit of the doubt, but they didn't have time to do it in the courtyard and still execute the mission; they'd had to do it on the go.

Well, the other choice would have been to get caught attempting to slaughter a prison's worth of stormtroopers head-on, but Cal was frustrated, not foolish.

Not today, anyway.

So he'd let Fret go, taken the pressure off her neck, and watched Merrin disappear to run the two of them to the prison roof to execute the next part of the infiltration.

But he was starting to wonder—*very much wonder*, in fact—if this was all part of an elaborate trap Fret had set for them, walking them right into the hands of the Inquisitors.

So now, after finding an exhaust port in the courtyard, Cal was prowling through the prison's underground tunnels, listening to Merrin and Fret's shared explanation of what Fret had told her in the engine room, days ago.

"And you didn't tell us sooner?" Cal demanded, incredulous. He was sliding down a shockingly steep slope in the guts of the Imperial prison, a maintenance shaft it was clear no one had maintained in years. Cere had uploaded a map of the prison and its underground tunnel system to BD-1's memory bank, and Cal was following it as closely as he could, given that the whole thing had seemingly come to ruin in the time since the map was created. Cal was trying to concentrate—this kind of thing took a lot of concentration, dodging live electrical cylinders that happened to be in the dead center of the path, using the Force to shove collapsed metal beams out of his way before they impaled him, avoiding perilous falling debris—and he really needed to be present for it.

Unfortunately, he was decidedly *not* present. He was very much wrapped up in the fact that Merrin—*their* Merrin—had known a potentially life-threatening piece of information and had kept it from the rest of the crew.

Because of a hot purple lady with a mullet.

Cal knew that was being ungenerous. But *still*.

"This is why I did *not* want to tell you! I knew you would not take it well! She had done nothing to make us suspect her!" Merrin's voice came back crisp and vindicated over comms. She was elsewhere in the prison, flitting around from place to place taking out guards and stormtroopers that might cause them problems later in the mission. Cal knew it was one of her favorite jobs, sneaking up on Imperials and crushing them before they even had a chance to react. He got it. He understood her.

Or at least he thought he did.

Maybe he actually didn't at all.

"How can we be sure she isn't lying about everything?" Cal asked through clenched teeth. "How can *you*?"

"I am *right here*," came Fret's voice through comms, also a fierce whisper. "I'm telling you, this is real, and we have to stay on track—"

"I can't!" Merrin's admission cut Fret off mid-sentence, surprising Cal. "I can't. I am not foolish, Cal, I can tell something isn't right!"

"Then why—?"

"Did I always act the way you expected me to when I first came aboard the *Mantis*?" Merrin demanded fiercely. "Was I not scarred by Dathomir? By Malicos? Did I not make strange choices, treat people badly?"

Cal squinted at an upcoming blockage; slid around it. "That was different."

"Different how!" Fret said incredulously. "Wait, Merrin, do you not trust me?"

"I don't know!" Merrin's voice was more emotional than Cal was used to hearing it. "I don't know. Why didn't you trust *me* enough to tell me from the start?"

There was a pause; Cal leapt over a crack, swinging by a hanging broken cable to get back on track. "I'm not used to having anyone to trust, inside the Empire." Fret's voice was quiet. "Maybe it was a mistake, not telling you. But I am the way the Imperials made me. It might take me a long, long time not to be."

"This is what I am saying, Cal!" Merrin whispered hotly into comms. "I made the decision to see how things played out on the mission!"

BD-1 booped on Cal's back, bringing him back into the moment just in time to push up off his slide into the air and launch himself forward—but he had been too distracted to notice that the ground beneath him was falling away fast, and the only thing left in the maintenance shaft below was a pool of water that Cal hoped was deep enough to catch him safely as he plummeted.

"Cal, the electrical room is coming up." Cere's voice on comms interrupted the discussion. She sounded a little . . . awkward, bringing focus back to the mission. "Do you have the jammer?"

"Yep," Cal responded as best he could while still in midair.

"What does that mean?" Fret interjected, still fishing for any details about the plan.

Greez huffed. "Please. Now I'm even *less* inclined to spoil the surprise for you. Just do your part, *stormtrooper,* and we'll do the rest."

Cal hit the water with a splash, enjoying the silence of submersion for just a moment before kicking his feet and resurfacing. He could feel BD-1 shake himself out on his back. He glanced ahead; the way was blocked by more crumbling walls. This place really needed looking after. The only way forward, as usual, was down.

Cal fumbled in his pocket for his rebreather, but he had to get one more response in before he couldn't. "You don't get to decide what's important information for the crew or not, Merrin. That's not how this works." He decided to ignore the fact that he had also been holding information about Fret back from the crew. But that had been different; that had been personal. This—this was important.

"She still uses her Imperial information; how is that different from my still using magick through the dark side? You have to be reasonable," Merrin insisted in Cal's ear as he shoved the breathing apparatus into his mouth with more anger than he probably should have, jarring his teeth. With a huff, he resubmerged himself, knowing BD would probably hate it but realize that it was necessary and put up with it anyway, like the good droid he was.

Cal did not have to be reasonable. He didn't have to do anything, in fact, because he was pretty sick of giving people the benefit of the doubt and having it bite him in the ass. First there was that Gungan on Abafar, and that couldn't have gone worse; Cal couldn't even bring himself to think about the Twi'lek from that one bar on Chandar's Folly (aptly named). All he wanted to do was dismantle the Empire and rescue as many folks lost to their cruelty along the way as possible. Why did people being abjectly awful have to ruin that so damn often?

And then he'd gone, conflicted, to the maintenance shafts to do his part. Because his part was and would always involve taking on the unknowns for his team, and this mission had so, so many unknowns—Qeris, the Shroud, the Inquisitors, Fret—and didn't Merrin appreciate how *dangerous* this job was?

"She just wanted to retain access to their codes." Merrin was still talking through comms, even as Cal was swimming through water full of—he really didn't want to consider what, actually. Especially while Merrin was having an actual good time killing soldiers and probably making out with her hot purple mullet lady.

Why did he keep having thoughts like that? He was better than that.

It must have been the lack of sleep, or the stress. He hated seeing the worst and pettiest parts of himself come out, especially in moments like this, where teamwork was more important than ever.

Merrin continued, "They change on a rotating system, she knew she wouldn't be any good to a resistance force without them, it made the most sense to appear as though she was still on a mission to the Outer Rim. Using her codes again further ensures that the Empire thinks she's still on active duty, makes it look like she hasn't disappeared. It all makes sense!"

It was very convenient that Merrin was having this discussion with him while his mouth was stuffed full of rebreather and the only way he could respond would be to die.

It seemed unlikely Merrin knew he was actually swimming at the moment, but still. Very convenient.

It didn't matter; Cal had given Fret the opportunity to be honest with them when she first came aboard, and she hadn't been. That was that.

But *beyond that,* it was Merrin. It was Merrin! Putting the well-being of her own crew, the people who loved her—like family, obviously, but—Merrin, prioritizing the well-being of the people who *loved* her less than the well-being of someone she had just met? Making decisions on behalf of the entire team? Deciding what would possibly put them in danger and what wouldn't?

Cal couldn't even comprehend it.

He kicked off a rock and swam around meters of sheet metal, working his way toward the grating he knew would be ahead from Cere's digital map scouting. And, okay, it wasn't that he couldn't *comprehend* it; he had to admit to himself that he'd made similar calls in the past, when it came to sharing information with the crew. But that was in cases where he knew it would hurt them, or would just lead to an argument, or trouble. It was for their own protection.

But this? This was just selfish.

"I have to say I did not expect the silent treatment from you, Cal," came Merrin's voice. "I thought you were better than that."

Cal reached the grating and watched gratefully as BD clambered off his shoulder, using his white-hot cutter to sear through the metal that was blocking the one access point Cal needed to make it to his next destination. Squeezing through the narrow vent beyond, he finally found a vertical chute and was able to come up for air, ditching the rebreather.

"I was underwater," he said as soon as he had the lung capacity for it. BD bleeped on his back in support.

"I understand this feels emotionally drowning," Merrin said, sympathy in her voice. "But—"

"I mean I was *swimming*," Cal cut in before she could get any further. "And now I'm about to get on with this plan before we actually end up dead on this mission, so can we just save it till we're back on the *Mantis* with these schematics in hand?"

Cal took the silence as an affirmative.

He shimmied up the half-submerged vent shaft and crawled through another until he found himself right where he needed to be: the prison's electrical room. It was as shabby as the rest of the facility, but clear that someone made at least semi-frequent visits to make sure all the wires and breakers that supplied electricity to the prison cells were functional and effective.

Unfortunately for them, if Fret had pulled through on her part of the stormtrooper-incapacitating bargain, they would not be making their rounds today.

BD-1 hopped off Cal's back and raced to the nearest input while Cal examined the crawl space in front of him: mostly a tangled mess of wires, repeatedly and hastily repaired over years of geothermal and war-torn instability on Murkhana, but still something recognizably like an electric control center.

It happened, sometimes. Tough line of work, this.

"Cere," Cal said, momentarily opening a private channel solely between himself and his fellow Jedi Knight. "Fret's lying. No time to explain how I know, but I do. The one person who could have actually gotten her to leave the Empire—Irei—couldn't manage it. I can't imagine why things would have changed now. It's possible she never plans to leave. We have to be prepared for that."

"All right." Cere's voice came through clipped and clear. "We had suspicions. We will be on alert. Everyone has their trackers on; Greez can see Fret's location at all times on the holomap. He'll keep an eye on her. But even if there's a high, high chance this is all a trap—if there's a one percent chance that this is on the level, Cal, we have to continue. The Shroud would be too powerful in the Empire's hands."

Cal huffed a breath. "I know you're right. Is it okay that I don't like it that you're right?" He pulled out the jammer Cere had given him before the mission and waited for the signal from BD before hooking it into a now exposed portion of live wire, miraculously managing to keep himself from being electrocuted.

Cere gave a short, terse laugh. "It is."

Cal nodded to himself as the jammer activated, and switched his comms back to public. "You're patched in, Cere."

There was a pause, and then: "We're a go."

Which, actually, Cere hadn't even really needed to say, because in the same moment, from the other side of the wall, Cal heard a blaring siren and an almost deafeningly loud *clank* reverberating through the whole building, followed by a roar that could only have come from a hundred or so hardened criminals and Imperial enemies realizing they'd been granted a chance at freedom all at the same time.

Cere had unlocked every prison cell in the building, and they had just created a major distraction. Maybe even started a riot.

Exactly as they planned.

The stormtrooper's neck made a very satisfying sound under the cold fire of Merrin's magick. It was hard for Merrin to believe that, days ago, she'd still been struggling to find her blaze.

Now she drew upon it so easily, it was nearly all-consuming.

Merrin activated her comms. "Fret, confirm your location?"

"Coming to meet you now."

Merrin smiled. It felt good, having a partner in the field, not being left to her own devices for once. It made her feel grounded; like someone was watching her back in the same way Greez and Cere watched each other's, the way Cal and his strange but cute little droid did.

Yes, Cal was upset with her for keeping Fret's secret to herself, but really it was no one's business but Fret's, and she hadn't wanted to betray the other woman's trust, not so early into her freedom from the Empire, from people who had done nothing but lie and cheat Fret her entire life. It wouldn't have been fair. Merrin had flown with the *Mantis* long enough to know what would put the crew in danger and what wouldn't; knew *very* well that Cal made similar decisions about knowledge sharing all the time. So why should this have been any different?

Merrin stepped over the stormtrooper's rapidly cooling corpse and felt her chest expand as she saw Fret come bounding down the hallway to her, a crushed white helmet still in one of her hands. She dropped it in time to scoop an arm around Merrin's waist to drag her into a somewhat-safe hiding spot to wait for Cal. Merrin felt a traitorous ache in her chest about the way those arms felt, strong and secure around her, holding her in place in the midst of all this chaos. She knew she should be more suspicious of Fret, should stop her feelings from getting in the way of her logic. But there was something about the security Merrin felt with Fret's broad body warm against her back, coupled with the rage and pain they'd shared with each other over the last few days; the knowing that she wasn't alone, and that she didn't have to handle everything herself . . .

She liked it. Probably more than she should have.

The sounds of the prison roared around them as Merrin and Fret tucked themselves into a notch in the wall near the corner they knew that Cal would be coming around when he finally made his way to them. As Fret pulled Merrin into her front to keep her hidden from sight, Merrin heard yells of fury, screams of fear; blaster shots and the slam of electric batons; guards barking orders and (former) prisoners shouting their own back. It was a cacophony.

As if sharing the thought, Fret burst out into nearly hysterical-sounding laughter. Merrin looked up at the woman's face, crinkled up into a massive grin at the circumstance, and couldn't help herself; she was laughing right along with her, had to turn back around to catch enough breath to keep herself upright.

"So the big surprise plan was 'prison break'?" Fret's breath was hot in

Merrin's ear as she huffed out the last of her laughter. "You folks don't really do anything by half measures, huh?"

Merrin grinned, even though she knew Fret couldn't see it. "We do, sometimes, like to cause a little chaos."

Fret's arm tightened around Merrin's stomach, squeezing her in close. "You're real cute when you're chaotic." Merrin bit at the top of Fret's arm playfully in response.

"I think we might actually be able to grab these plans," Fret whispered between dying laughs, close enough for Merrin to hear her over the chaos without raising her voice, wiping away her own tears before reaching for the corners of Merrin's eyes next. "You're all nuts, do you know that? You guys pull this kind of thing all the time? You're nuts."

Merrin twisted around again. The admiration and awe in Fret's voice were matched by the look in her eyes. Merrin met them with the same kind of fervor.

Raising herself up onto her toes, Merrin slid her hands from where they rested on Fret's chest up to her shoulders, over her neck, into her hair, threading her fingers through the curls at the base of her neck. She pressed herself fully into Fret's front, though even on her toes she wasn't quite at eye level with the other woman, still had to tilt her head back to get on a level with her. She watched the last of the hysteria drain from Fret's expression, replaced by heat and need.

Fret's hands squeezed Merrin's waist. "Wild."

Merrin raised an eyebrow. "You would know."

And then, against her better judgment, her lips were on Fret's, and Fret's hands were snaked around her waist, and she felt the heat she could see in Fret's face everywhere: in her insistent tongue and her teasing fingers and the growls she made between kisses.

Behind her eyes, Merrin saw green. Grave thorns and fire.

Cal skidded around the corner, nearly crashing into Merrin and Fret as BD screeched a proximity warning on his back. Merrin jumped back from Fret just in time to save the two of them from colliding with the Jedi, and also probably a little bit to save herself the embarrassment of Cal having to see her kissing Fret in the middle of a mission.

"Time to go!" Cal shouted above the din, appearing not to have noticed the compromising situation he had nearly rushed into. Merrin didn't think too hard about why that relieved her.

"I have the location of the schematics." Cere's voice crackled over comms. "But . . . it doesn't make any sense. The records here, they say the Shroud plans are in a cellblock, close to your location. But why would they keep a datacard in a cell?"

"Why do the Imperials do anything?" Merrin asked, letting Cal lead the way, guided by the holomap, but this time she didn't bother to flash in and out of view. She didn't feel the need to disappear. Instead she grabbed Fret by the hand and pulled her on, and on, down the halls, avoiding the riot and the guards and the stormtroopers. And Fret was next to her the whole time, hand still hot in hers, fiery eyes everywhere at once but somehow also always on Merrin, and she felt the fire in her veins burning a path through her mind.

She hadn't felt this clear in years.

"This is the block." Cal threw up a hand to stop the women before they could go any farther. He pushed open a door, revealing a long hallway lined with cells on both sides. For all that it held something of such great import, this block was unremarkable, conspicuous in its sameness to all the others. It didn't feel special.

But it was. It had to be, for all of this to be worthwhile.

Cere's voice cracked over comms. "Cal, I've got—"

"Hang on, Cere," Cal cut her off with a whisper. "I need to go quiet for a minute."

Cal stalked down the cellblock with purpose and Merrin let him go, past open door after open door, abandoned cell after abandoned cell, and Merrin realized too late a flaw in their plan: What if someone had grabbed the schematics from their cell—strange enough already—when the riots started and had absconded with them before they'd arrived?

Merrin thought of the way Fret, who obviously had some kind of personal stake in this mission, would look disappointed, and it made her feral. She would burn this place to the ground to find the schematics, kill every stormtrooper in the place single-handedly, if it meant preventing that look on Fret's face.

She thought she probably should have been more afraid of the fervor with which she felt this, but instead . . .

She just felt powerful with it.

"Wait, what?" Cal's voice came from the end of the hall. Merrin frowned and looked at Fret; wordlessly, they decided the best call was to follow.

"Cal, I really—"

"Cere, not now!" Cal cut in again. This wasn't the moment for a status update.

As they approached the final cell, what had Cal so confused quickly became apparent: Far from being abandoned, or holding only a small datacard, the last cell was very much occupied. The door was wide open, the occupant more than free to escape, but they hadn't. They simply stood there, clutching absolutely nothing at all in their hands, staring through the wide-open door. They were tall and lithe and graceful, even in the way they stood, and they looked, for lack of a better term on Merrin's part, like a very pretty lizard.

That was when Merrin realized Fret had let go of her hand.

"Irei," breathed Fret.

The lizard-person behind bars swallowed. "Chell."

"Cal!" Cere's voice was demanding this time. She wasn't going to be shut down again.

"It's the Inquisitors," she continued. "They're here."

CHAPTER 10

Okay, Cal thought, *so the schematics come attached to a person. Fine.* Not the kind of mission-altering issue that they would usually make a big deal over. The *Mantis* crew loved a person in dire circumstances. They'd made a whole reputation out of rescuing people just like that from worse situations than this. And this was far from the worst kind of issue they'd come across in their time on the run. This was nothing. Amateur hour. Not worth the data to write home about.

Certainly nothing compared with the fact that *Inquisitors were in orbit and they had to move now.*

Except this person—*this person* was the Nikto from Cal's echo. The one Fret—Chellwinark Frethylrin, Cal remembered, the nickname *Chell* clicked into place—had turned down, however many years in her past that had been. The one she wouldn't leave the Empire for.

Irei.

And now she was right here, in front of them, apparently the key to their whole mission.

There was a second, only a moment, where Cal felt utterly and completely convinced that he had been right: that Fret had been playing them, had pulled the rug out from under them, and was condemning them to death. But all it took was one look at Fret's face, equal parts devastated and elated at once (a contradiction Cal didn't know if he'd seen, previously, on a person), to know that three things were true:

First, whatever truths Fret had been concealing, she had not been expecting this.

Second, Irei had not been expecting this.

Third, they were both having a real hard time about it.

But as swiftly as Cal had noticed the expression on Fret's face, his eyes were back where they usually were: focused right in on Merrin's. Her expression was confusion, betrayal—hurt. Mostly confusion, but Cal knew her well enough to see the other things in her gaze, too, as her eyes flipped back and forth between Fret and Irei, taking in what Cal knew to be a fraught reunion in silence.

He hated to see her hurt. In any situation.

But especially—*especially*, for some reason—this one.

"Impossible," Fret breathed. "You're not real. You're—a hologram."

Irei laughed, her clawed fingers wrapped around the bars of her cell, despite the wide-open door, hanging on as if for dear life. "You think the Empire can make holograms this good? Please."

Cal watched Merrin watch as Fret launched herself forward at the bars, stopping herself just before she came into contact with them, dropping her hands centimeters from Irei's. "You can't be."

Irei didn't move her gaze from Fret's face. "I can. I am."

"Fret." Merrin spoke in a small voice Cal almost didn't recognize. "How do you know this woman? What is she doing here?"

"She's . . ." Fret took a deep breath. "She's the inventor of the Shroud. And she's dead."

Cal felt a lot of things about Fret—most of them, in the moment, pretty bad—and he was even seeing red about Merrin's betrayal, a feeling he tried very hard to manage in himself because of his connection to the Force, but he was still just a person, and it was sometimes unavoidable. But right then, watching the expression on Merrin's face as Fret didn't even bother to tear her eyes away from Irei to answer—right then, his heart broke for her.

Just a little.

"Not dead," Irei corrected, still from inside her cell. "Not a hologram. Very much alive."

"Fret," Merrin was more insistent now. "What do you need us to do?"

Even in the midst of her pain, Merrin was thinking about Fret. She was like that; always thinking about the people she cared about most, doing anything to keep them safe. Cal stepped forward to—he didn't even know what. He wanted to grab Merrin in a tight embrace, squeeze, tell her it was going to be okay, that they would figure all of this out like they always did, because that was what family did.

Instead he just grasped her by the shoulder and tightened his fingers enough for her to know that he was there, that she wasn't alone. Her posture relaxed, ever so slightly, and right then, for Cal—that was enough.

Fret finally, finally turned her head to look at Merrin, and Cal saw tears in her eyes, barely hanging on. "We need to get her out."

"No," Irei interjected forcefully. "I'm not leaving this cell."

Great. This was just what Cal needed right now. An obstinate inventor.

"No problem," Cal said wryly, only half joking, really. "All we need are the schematics, so if you could just hand those on over, we'll be—"

"New friends, Chell?" Irei interrupted, directing her dry question to Fret, who was back to being transfixed by the Nikto woman.

Fret half shrugged, blinking back her tears. "Thought you'd like them better than my old ones."

At this, Irei nodded. "I really do. That's not saying much."

"Cal Kestis. And Beedee-Wun." He decided to just get things moving here, himself, if Fret—current Imperial analyst Fret—was going to continue to be a complete mess about her not-dead girlfriend. What did she even mean by that?

Whatever, not the time.

"Merrin," she said from beside him, a hard and discordant note. Her voice sounded the way it did when Cal first picked her up on Dathomir: mistrustful and curt. Cal felt furious about it, to know she'd been forced back to that place. "Nightsister of Dathomir."

Though he knew it was unlikely Irei knew *exactly* what those words meant, Cal saw the fear creep into Irei's face, ever so slightly, and he felt his chest expand.

Atta girl.

"We're—" Cal paused. He never quite knew how to describe what it was the *Mantis* crew *did,* exactly. *Anti-Imperial insurgents* felt too organized. *Revolutionaries* sounded too grandiose. *Anarchists* wasn't right; they didn't mess with the Empire to sow chaos. *Rebellious Knights of Good* was maybe the best possible descriptor for them, but when Cal thought about the way their little ragtag crew looked to outsiders— scruffy Greez, terrifying Merrin, baby-faced Cal (to his own chagrin), stoic Cere, and little BD-1—well.

It seemed a bit much.

"We're working against the Empire," Cal landed on, aware that every second they spent talking was another that the Inquisitors had to get closer to them. "Fret—Chell, here, led us to someone who believes the Shroud could be a powerful tool if used against the Empire. But more so, he believes that in the Empire's hands, it could mean the end of people like us. Rebels. For good."

"Lar," Irei surmised with a nod. "Chell, I'm surprised he even let you in the door."

Cal watched Fret's eyes go hard for a moment. "Yeah, well," she said, a hint of bitterness in her voice, "I've been busy since you've been dead."

Irei had the good sense to look at the floor on that one.

"Well, Qeris Lar is right," Irei agreed, looking back up to glance at Cal. "The Shroud is too dangerous to end up in the hands of the Empire. I won't let it."

"Glad we're on the same page." Cal stepped forward toward the cell— and was confused when Irei took a step back.

"Oh, Cal Kestis," she said, slowly shaking her head. "I really don't think we are at all."

Fret started to rush into the cell—but she was stopped, suddenly, by the ground shaking under all of them, and an explosion from somewhere else in the prison rocking the very foundation itself. Fret grabbed the cell bars to stay upright. A prison already neglected was becoming more and more unstable with every passing instant here, and if they waited around much longer with Irei, they were all going to be dust under a collapsed prison or at the hands of a Purge Trooper within minutes.

When the shaking stopped, the four of them all looked at one another. The first person to make a move would be the one to determine how the next part of this went, Cal knew.

And he knew it had to be him.

In the not-so-far distance, a door slammed open; the noise of the riot came rushing back into the cellblock, bringing Cal back to the present and out of this bizarre reunion that, frankly, just did not matter that much right now, in the grand scheme of things. They had a job to do, and Cal got the job done. No matter what.

So that was just about enough of this. Time was ticking; whatever was going on here, it would have to wait until they were back aboard the *Mantis*. They were on a time crunch, here, and the chrono was running.

"O-kay," Cal said, loudly clearing his throat to interrupt the moment. "We're gonna talk about this later, but Irei—we really gotta get you out of here. Well, the Shroud schematics. But I have to assume now that you're keeping those hidden."

Irei dragged her eyes away from Fret, turning her head to look at Cal with those eyes that reminded Cal so much of the echo he'd been a part of that he found, for a second, it was hard to remember which reality he was in. "Yes. The Shroud stays in my hands."

"And I'm assuming that's also what you told the Empire," Cal surmised. Fret was standing stock-still holding the bars, Merrin's face a wreck looking at her. "Why didn't they just kill you?"

"I told them they would only be able to create the thing with my help. That the schematics only exist in my head. That I *am* the schematics." Against all odds, Irei actually laughed. "I was being honest, actually. Which is why you can't let them near me."

The Nikto was speaking, but Merrin was having difficulty concentrating on her words.

It was hard to pay attention to the Nikto at all when Fret—*her* Fret, as she'd foolishly started to think of her, far too quickly—was clearly so affected by the woman's presence.

The two of them had history, that much was clear. And Merrin didn't like how much that scared her.

What was wrong with her? She knew better than to let people in like this, let them have access to the deepest parts of her. It took her years to even begin to dismantle her walls, piece by piece, for Cal and the rest of the *Mantis* crew. Why had she wanted to do it so quickly for Fret?

"Wanted" wasn't even the right word. It hadn't been conscious. It had just . . . happened. Fret was there, and then she was inside Merrin's head, and in her heart, and it had happened all at once.

And now, it was clear, another piece of Fret's heart was standing in front of them.

Fret hadn't said as much, but Merrin could see it on her face—and worse, could see it on Cal's. She'd wondered if the Jedi had gone rifling through Fret's things in search of one of his strange and uncanny visions, teleporting himself in his mind into someone else's, watching their life and feeling their feelings and riding uninvited through their memories and into their pasts. She should have known he would do it.

She just didn't expect him to have found a very pretty, very tall lizard-woman.

And apparently Fret didn't expect to find her here, either.

"Talk, but you're going to have to do it on the move," Cal said, interrupting Merrin's thoughts and nudging her toward the cellblock doors.

Irei was stubborn in her stance. "One thing, first. You have to promise me you won't let them take me. No matter what."

Merrin watched Cal's studied calm as he tried not to sigh too obviously. "We are not leaving you here under any circumstances. I understand you're scared, and you've lost hope, but we are going to get you to safety, and then we're going to figure out our next move. They are not going to take you. I will never let it come to that."

Irei considered it. Fret watched her like a big purple chirodactyl. She hadn't gotten too close to Irei yet, clear that she wasn't still completely convinced that she was real; that if she touched her, the Nikto would crumble to dust again beneath her fingers.

Irei looked at Fret, and Merrin recognized it. A look that said: *If you love me, you'll do what needs to be done.*

Fret stayed silent. Merrin didn't know her well enough to read the look on her face back.

Clearly, Merrin didn't know her at all.

Finally, Irei gave one quick nod. "Deal, Jedi." In response to Cal's immediate frown, Irei tilted her snout at the lightsaber swinging from its hilt on his waist. "You lead me toward safety, and we'll talk."

So they did.

As Irei adjusted her leather vest, Cal and BD led the way out of the cellblock. Merrin felt the loss of his hand on her shoulder more acutely than she'd anticipated; she hadn't even consciously realized it had been there, supporting her, until she felt the lack of it.

She missed it.

Merrin knew what her job would be here: to bring up the rear, keep watch on the ground team, ensure that nothing snuck up on them. There were few things worse than her in this wide galaxy; she wasn't afraid of being caught unawares.

But the stormtroopers always should be, around Merrin.

Irei followed right behind Cal, hopelessness and fear on her lips and in her posture. Barely a ghost of a step behind her rushed Fret. Merrin tried to catch her eye, needed to, *had* to know that she was okay, and that they were going to be okay—but she found no reassurance, no relief. Fret kept her eyes trained on Irei's heels as she rushed by.

A different kind of fire, this time. Not one born of love.

This time, anger.

She let the fire push her forward.

She had missed the fire, yes, but this—there was something here, an edge, that reminded her of the moments after Dathomir, alone on the red soil, screaming her agony to Domir.

Domir, who never screamed back.

"A right," Cere said over comms, keeping them on the right track as they exited the cellblock's long hallway. "Then your first left. I'm sending you toward a mess hall—if I'm reading this right, there's an emergency hatch onto the roof from there. We can get you away if you can just get yourselves outside."

They took the right, into another block, and then the left, out of another, and found themselves in a big open space—a reading room, once.

Now just a giant mass of bodies in combat, troopers versus prisoners: carnage.

The four of them entered the fray like they were diving headfirst into a violent storm: flashes of lightning in the form of electric batons, cracks of thunder in blasterfire, the crush of bodies like being buffeted by strong winds. It had truly been the perfect distraction, the ideal cover: The stormtroopers and guards were so busy with the escaping prisoners that they hardly looked twice at one other escapee and three people who might as well have been. Merrin would let Cal handle the brunt of the fight; it was her responsibility to catch the enemies he might miss and cut them off at the knees before they could get the jump on him or their precious cargo.

"Start talking!" Cal yelled over the cacophony, shoving Irei out of the line of a trooper's fire just in time to keep her from being hit directly in the chest. Fret stepped in front of her, her broad body acting as a shield for Irei moving forward; she wasn't about to allow the other woman to get herself killed any more than Cal was.

Merrin was on the fence.

"I'm an engineer, a tinkerer," Irei's voice projected itself through the din. "Found out I was Force-sensitive. Knew I'd have to be on the run for the rest of my life."

Cal's head swung around to look at Irei, behind him, for just a moment while he used the Force to push a group of rushing troopers into a cell and slam it shut behind them.

"So you invented the Shroud?" Cal pulled out his own blaster and began firing at the guards who'd gotten too close to Irei for comfort. Not that any of this was comfortable. "To hide?"

"No." Irei tried to shove past Fret, to little effect. The other woman was like a wall. "Not to hide myself. Not only."

"End of the room, next block!" Cere's voice cut through the din over comms. The group pressed themselves to the wall as best they could, sliding toward an exit that was mostly hidden behind the fray. They managed to pry the door open and rush through into an empty maintenance corridor, slamming the door behind them, long enough to take a breath.

"You wanted to take someone with you. Someone who was too scared to run. Who would have needed to be hidden."

Merrin saw Irei's eyes flash—then roll, a very strange gesture in someone with slitted pupils and triple eyelids. "Yes, Jedi. That is what I wanted."

But Cal couldn't mean . . .

But Fret's brows were knit, and she steadfastly refused to look at Cal, and it had to be, that *had* to be what was happening here, and oh, this was so much worse than Merrin had even anticipated it might be.

There was a tale told by elders on Dathomir about when Nightsisters were overwhelmed with emotion, when the only other choices in front of them would be to shut down or to run away. There was a downside to playing with fire: It rarely stayed under a person's control. Fire was wild and rabid and hungry, it knew no limits, and it would eat and eat and eat forever until it ran out of fuel.

When Merrin first left Dathomir aboard the *Mantis*, she worried that she would feel nothing. Without her sisters, without her planet, she was certain she would be empty. Deadened emotions meant no kindling, no spark. Instead, Merrin had been initially surprised to find the opposite. Spending time with the *Mantis* crew, especially Cal, her fire had burned on.

But it was not to last. As time went on, the longer she had been away from Dathomir—the more her anger had festered. Merrin had felt as though she were starving, the void inside her a vengeance that could never truly be sated. Her depression had led her to difficulty that only the spark of whatever her—she shuddered, but it was true—*love* for her crew had opened her up to receiving from Fret was able to reignite the soaked, rotten branches that had so recently encased her soul.

Finally, she had fueled her fire with the light of something new. Of something good, of something possible. Of hope.

Now, with what she was realizing about Irei, about Fret, about the two of them, about what Merrin had inadvertently gotten herself—and, far more embarrassingly, her *heart*, ugh—involved in, there was a rush of air; a backdraft. Oxygen rushing into a previously depleted environment, filling a void with so much fuel that it caused auto-ignition, spontaneous combustion, rapidly expanding and consuming in an instant.

She felt the ends of her hair catch fire first.

This was . . . this was Fret's *lover.*

As she felt smoke curl around the nape of her neck, there was a flash; the acrid smell of burning that wasn't coming from herself. Merrin realized too late that she'd been so engrossed in the conversation she'd forgotten her responsibilities, and watched in horror as Fret took a blaster bolt shot through the door behind them that would have otherwise hit Irei. It sizzled through her jerkin but didn't penetrate the underlayer, made to protect her from just such effects. It was enough of a shock to Merrin's system that she was able to get her emotions under control, stop the consumption before it got any further.

But it was still there, under the surface, biding its time. Pyrolysis.

"Stop trying to get yourself *killed*," Fret growled. So low, so threatening, Merrin could more feel it than hear it over the chaos.

"I'm not trying!" Irei snapped, the fear evident in her voice alongside concern for Fret. "They've attempted to pull this out of me while I've been in this garrison and haven't succeeded. But now they're flying in what seems like the big guns. And the Inquisitors are going to kill me anyway, as soon as they pull the Shroud out of my head against my will!" She stopped for a moment, and the panic became evident on her face. "I can't do this. I don't know if I can do this!"

"We're getting you *out of here*," Cal yelled, taking down two troopers with one deflected blaster bolt in a very impressive move that Merrin would have to remember to compliment him on later, if he wasn't still furious with her for being so wrong about Fret.

Which, apparently, she deserved.

"End of the hall, up the ladder!" Cere's voice pushed them onward, keeping them moving. "We're going to try to keep you hidden on the way to the mess!"

Merrin put one hand in front of the other on the ladder to the prison's next level, watched as Cal followed Cere's instructions and his map to push them through more doors, more back hallways, hearing the fight rage on around them.

"Were you ever going to tell us about this?" demanded Cal, shoving Fret and Irei between himself and Merrin to keep them safe.

"If you'd give me back my blaster, I'd be more useful!" Fret snapped back.

"I am *not* giving you a blaster!"

"I would have told you!" said Fret. "She was dead! Or, I *thought* she was dead!"

"I'm not dead!" said Irei. "And this is deeply complicated! You can't—"

With sufficient warning via comms from Cere, they shoved through a crumbling set of double doors out of the maintenance hall and into another cellblock, wider than the ones downstairs but just as full of raging bodies, Purge Troopers and stormtroopers outnumbering prisoners nearly five to one, jammed full, and Merrin thought, for a minute, this would be their end, and maybe that would be okay.

"You can't know how it feels—" Irei continued.

"I know how it feels!" Cal's shout was so loud it shocked the rest of the block, simultaneous with a push through the Force so powerful that the guards and troopers in the area weren't prepared, and it landed them on their backs.

The room was suddenly silent. Those who'd gone down weren't getting back up. The fight continued in other wings—but not here. Here, it was over.

"I know how it feels," Cal repeated, quieter this time, "to want to disappear so completely from the rest of the galaxy. To know how scared you are about . . ." He looked up to find Merrin already staring at him. "About protecting the people you care for from harm. About feeling so desperate and hopeless that you can't see through to any other possibilities. Or to a future."

Cal took a breath, and Merrin watched him bring himself under control. "Irei, you've made something that could mean no one ever has to be scared like that again." The sigh was from such a deep place in Cal's chest that it seemed to come from his very soul. He turned to hold Irei by the shoulders and looked up into her wide eyes.

He was so earnest. It was one of Merrin's favorite things about him, even though it made her sick to her stomach sometimes. So *wholesome.* Eugh.

"Please, Irei." It was Fret now slowly approaching and reaching out a hand. Merrin's stomach twisted into a knot as Fret finally, for the first time, touched Irei, grabbed her fingers, threaded hers between them. "The Jedi need you, the galaxy needs you. Just keep moving. Just keep moving, and don't get shot. We're going to keep you safe."

Fret didn't have to say the rest of it. It was obvious from the look in Irei's eyes that she already knew.

Merrin smelled smoke.

Irei stared into Fret's face, her eyes searching, as Cal and Merrin looked on. Despite the emotional devastation of the moment, and Merrin's own body trying to eat her alive as she watched, even she had to admit: There was something very humorous about having this conversation in the main hall of a prison wing surrounded by fallen stormtroopers blown onto their backs by an angry Jedi. Like they were the central petals of a very Dathomirian flower, even. It would have been kind of poetic, thought Merrin, if it hadn't made her want to set herself and everything she'd ever had the audacity to love on fire.

"I never meant for my idea to end up in the hands of the Imperials," Irei said softly, slow and deliberate. "When they found me, and realized what I'd made designs for, and what the Empire could use it for if it could be realized, I knew they'd take it from me to make something . . ." She couldn't even finish her sentence. She didn't have to; they all knew what would happen if the Empire got their hands on the Shroud, what was at stake here.

There just happened to be a little more at stake for Merrin than for everyone else. That was all.

Cal stepped forward, placing his hand on Irei's scaled forearm. "For whatever it's worth, I give you my word as a Jedi and as a protector of those who need it most that we will do everything within our power to keep you and your invention out of the hands of the Empire. I know I speak for my whole crew when I tell you we've laid down our lives in risk of less, and we would do it again. We exist to fight the Empire and to help those in need."

Merrin wasn't sure she liked the "we" in that sentence, as if they were still some sort of unit, but that was a problem for a later discussion.

Irei contemplated for only seconds, still staring into Fret's eyes, before she nodded. "All right, Jedi. But if it looks like they're going to take me—"

"They won't take you." Fret surprised them all by jumping in before Cal had the chance. "I know you'd never be able to live with yourself if the Shroud was being used by the Empire. We won't let them. We'll protect you and the people you love. I promise."

The skin around Irei's snout tightened. "I'll take his promises over yours."

Fret dropped the other girl's hand.

The heat around Merrin's ears faded, too.

"Merrin, a second?" Cal was walking over to put his arm around her shoulder and shepherd her away from Irei and Fret's ears, for a private moment in the dark of the room. Merrin watched Irei and Fret devolve into heated whispers before her sight line was blocked completely by Cal's ginger head.

"Are you with me?" he asked, not uncaringly, eyes searching her own. He was standing very close to her; Merrin wished he wouldn't right then. Just for the moment.

"Of course," she answered coolly. "I'm always with you."

"I know that." Cal's response was fast. "But I mean are you with me *right now*. Are you here? This is a lot; I need to know you're going to be able to keep it together long enough for us to get out of here."

Merrin's cheeks tinged green, remembering her earlier error in judgment. She hated being scolded by people she respected because she knew they were usually right. "I'm here," she reassured Cal. "I'm with you," she added, and she almost meant it.

"Good." Cal nodded, dropping his arm. "'Cause I'm about to say something you're not going to like, and I'm sorry for it." He took a breath. "I don't think Lar's equipped to handle what Irei's created; I don't know if he understands the full ramifications of what this thing could do in the wrong hands."

Merrin bit her bottom lip with her top teeth. She hated when he was right when it made her angry. "Me neither. We have to take her with us."

"I'm sorry but I think we have to take her with us—wait, what?" Cal cut himself off when he realized Merrin had just suggested the same thing. "Really?"

"Yes." Merrin nodded decisively, her body language hopefully portraying more confidence than she actually felt. "We can keep her safe from the Inquisitors for now, and talk through what to do with her with Greez and Cere. It's the only move."

Cal smiled his grateful little smile, the twist of his lips familiar and comforting under all that flaming hair. "Good. Okay. Ladies—!"

He turned to update Fret and Irei on the plan, but Merrin saw the problem in the very same moment that Cal did: The pair simply were no longer there.

Fret and Irei had run. And Merrin and Cal were left alone.

She'd been faced with a choice: Stay with Merrin, or leave with Irei. And she'd chosen Irei.

Merrin felt so much, in that moment, that it was almost like feeling nothing at all. Burned away to ash.

"Cal?" came a panicked voice over the comms. Cere. "We have a problem."

Merrin had rarely heard her sound so grim. "It's the Inquisitor himself. He's inside in the prison, approaching your position."

CHAPTER 11

"Back to the *Mantis*." Cal was decisive in the moment; there was nothing else to be done. Fret and Irei could be anywhere—could be in the hands of the Inquisitorius already—and they were in no position to take on Purge Troopers, let alone an Inquisitor, in their pursuit. Better to get back to Greez and Cere, and then reengage with a new plan about how to stop the Empire from using the most powerful weapon they'd ever had and that Cal and his crew had let fall directly into their hands.

Neat.

Cal was used to missions going sideways. It was, frankly, the way things went most of the time for the *Mantis* crew. No plan survives contact with the enemy, as they say, and that had been true for Cal nearly his entire adult life. The Empire was predictable, yes, but individuals were not, and Cal had learned that the hard way over and over and over again.

They'd known the Inquisitors were coming for the Shroud. They'd known they were on a tight time line. But it wasn't meant to be this tight.

And there was no planet on which Cal should have possibly imagined that an Inquisitor would come *personally* to collect schematics.

But now that he knew it was to collect *Irei*? The person who *was* the schematics? Now it made sense.

He didn't know what this meant for their promise to Qeris about delivering him the plans for the Shroud. About rescuing it from the Empire. If Irei was gone, were the plans for the Shroud just going to end up right back in the hands of the Imperials?

It was too dire to consider.

Merrin was already gone in a curl of fire and back again, standing by the exit to the cellblock, waiting for Cal to catch up with his little legs, jogging toward the door, much slower than magick, really unfair that the Force didn't let him do that. On the scale of useful abilities in that particular moment, "experience strangers' past traumas through their inanimate objects" fell slightly below Merrin's "magick death fire," Cal felt with chagrin.

An Inquisitor was here. And they were in serious, serious trouble.

Cal didn't have a death wish. As much as he itched to bring the Empire to their knees, his last face-to-face experience with an Inquisitor hadn't been exactly a cakewalk. If it hadn't been for a serendipitously well-timed rescue from Cere, Cal would never have survived his first encounter with the Ninth and Second Sisters on Bracca. They'd had him outgunned and outskilled; he hadn't had the tools in his Jedi arsenal to even put up a fight. And those had been in well-prepared-for circumstances; though he wished he could bring down the entire Inquisitorius, facing off against an unknown Inquisitor in the middle of a prison riot didn't make for ideal terms.

Cal moved to run straight out the cellblock door, but he was stopped by a touch to his arm, burning hot even through the fabric of his tunic. He stopped and turned to look at a Merrin that he hadn't seen since the day he'd fought her on Dathomir—the day they'd met.

"Cal," she said quietly, "if we find them . . . you leave Fret to me."

Cal knew the note in Merrin's voice. He'd heard it before. He hoped to all the stars in the sky that it was never trained against him again.

"You got it." Cal clapped his hand on top of Merrin's for reassurance and pulled it away just as quickly; it felt like she was burning through her own skin. That felt like it was . . . probably bad?

A question to ask her later.

Cal felt the weight of his lightsaber in his hand, considered one of previous times he'd used it against an Inquisitor.

At their final encounter in the Fortress Inquisitorius, Cal had finally felt able to bring the Second Sister, Trilla, to her knees in defeat—and even then, he knew, it wasn't due entirely to his superior prowess in battle. Cal had weaponized Trilla's emotional baggage against her, weakened her hate and thus her connection to the dark side of the Force by making her relive her trauma, her anger at Cere while they fought. He knew he'd needed the advantage; knew that his power alone might not have been enough to stop the Second Sister in her tracks. The Imperials had brainwashed Trilla so well; it was enough to make Cal almost see red, even though he knew he couldn't afford the risk that anger might open up in him.

Touching Trilla's lightsaber had been the key to her history; Cal's ability to travel through the echoes of the Force to a person's past had been the thing that had both saved Trilla in spirit and led to her death at the vengeful hands of Darth Vader. And even after all these years, after Trilla, after his face-off with Vader—after all the practice and training and missions and battles with the Brood and Purge Troopers and garden-variety bucketheads and bounty hunters and the thankfully once-in-a-lifetime Oggdo Bogdo—Cal still wasn't sure that he had it in him to beat an Inquisitor in face-to-face combat again.

Not without something to use against them. Not without a way to cheat.

Okay, maybe "cheat" was the wrong word. Not without an advantage.

Cal wasn't alone, he knew that. But he still hesitated to put his crew in unnecessary danger. He thought so often of Master Tapal; of Prauf, the one friend he'd dared to make after years of solitude, his best and first friend on Bracca, who'd ended up dead at the hands of the Inquisitors for daring to stand up for Cal. Was Merrin even in a headspace where she'd be able to face down an Inquisitor with him?

It was his fault the Inquisitors were after them all. He couldn't stand for it to be his fault if they died.

So if there was an Inquisitor here, right now, bearing down on this Imperial prison on Murkhana?

He was going to have to face them alone.

And honestly?

He was scared.

The second Cal and Merrin realized they were abandoned and about to be drowning in Purge Troopers, they heard the screams of the riot change from rage to fear. It was palpable in the air, wherever Inquisitors and their cadre went, Cal always knew, and not just because he was so attuned to the Force; there was something particularly terrifying about the Purge Troopers' red pauldrons and black lightsaber-resistant armor, their purple-flashing electrohammers, their eyes flashing through deep-red visors.

Kind of reminded Cal of Fret's eyes, come to think of it.

But wherever they went, terror followed, and it started to bleed through the walls of the prison almost immediately. He hoped any remaining prisoners would escape. Merrin turned to Cal with wide eyes, now twice betrayed by Fret, and Cal thought he had perhaps never seen Merrin so angry.

And was it possible that . . . the ends of her hair were smoking?

Cal really needed to start getting better sleep.

He watched Merrin's hands light up green—clearly her fire was back and better than ever—and Cal unhooked his lightsaber from his belt while BD-1 readjusted himself on his back. They all knew it was go time, and there were no more minutes to waste.

The flash of blue from Cal's lightsaber complemented the fire in Merrin's hands almost perfectly, and he relished the vibrating hum of the sword under his palm, the sound it made that almost drowned out the riot in the background when he concentrated on it. He took a second, just a second, to recenter himself in the Force, to make sure that he was connected to everything and nothing and all at once he felt the atoms in the floor, the heat under Merrin's skin, the fear from the prisoners, the clean and cruel desire from the troopers.

He was in. And it was time to go.

CHAPTER 12

Purge Troopers were far more satisfying to kill than typical stormtroopers, Merrin thought, as she watched green ichor flow from
her fingertips into the airholes of the trooper's helmet. She probably
shouldn't take so long on one death; getting back to the *Mantis,* at this
point, was about speed, and not style.

But she couldn't help herself as she watched the Purge Trooper drop
their electrobaton to claw at their face, relief blocked by their shiny
black helmet. Merrin felt her magick end the trooper from the inside
out, and she couldn't help a pleased raised eyebrow as they hit the
ground with a thud.

"Did I know you could do that?" Cal lunged forward next to her,
lightsaber flashing as it bounced a blaster bolt back at its shooter. He
sounded out of breath, but not struggling. Not yet.

Merrin shrugged. "I am full of secrets," she said with mock-
seriousness, wiggling her soot-tipped fingers at the Jedi while scanning
the room for her next target.

To her surprise, Cal actually laughed. "That much is *not* a secret,
Merrin."

Before she had a chance to respond, there was an electrostaff in her face.

Cursing, Merrin threw up a shield of green fire that was a beat too late; the tip of the staff, crackling with purple electricity, broke through. Still next to her, Cal pulled her back from the attack just in time.

Merrin could feel the air and energy around her shift as Cal raised his hand and *shoved* with all his might, attempting to push the trooper farther away from them both with the Force. Merrin heard the trooper curse; they swung their staff down and jammed it into the concrete at their feet, holding themselves in place and effectively resisting Cal's efforts.

They would die for that.

"I had him," Merrin hissed at Cal. She didn't need the assist. Didn't want it, not in this fight, and not today.

She was fine on her own. Just fine.

"I know." Cal gritted his teeth and dropped his left hand as BD-1 trilled a warning; Cal was away from her side in an instant, turning to deal with a rush of stormtroopers pouring in from another cellblock. It never seemed to end.

It had only seemed like seconds after Cere's call that things had really started to fall apart in the prison. Arguably, it had been seconds before: when Fret had chosen to leave Merrin in the lurch, alone on the floor in this forsaken prison, absconding with Irei to who knew where.

Merrin didn't know the whole story, there, but Fret had made a choice.

And it wasn't Merrin.

The Purge Trooper with the staff took Cal's moment of distraction to try to rush Merrin; she flooded the air between herself and the trooper with green mist, listening to them cough and drop to the ground, trying to get air.

Merrin took a moment to take stock. With Cere's help, they'd made it to the mess hall. They still had no idea where Fret had gone with Irei, and didn't have the time to find out. Cere had confirmed that Fret had removed her tracker; she wasn't showing up on Cal's map or Cere's. An Inquisitor's ship in orbit was serious, the Inquisitor in the prison more serious still. They'd attempted to steer clear of the Inquisitors entirely since their nearly fatal escape from the Fortress Inquisitorius years ago. Why invite trouble when enough of it followed you around the galaxy, anyway?

But when you were a Nightsister on the run with two fugitive Jedi, the Inquisitors were bound to find you eventually, no matter how many times you escaped into the depths of space where it seemed no one could follow. Greez was a master at keeping them hidden; he made it look easy, but Merrin knew how much work he put into keeping them safe.

And here they'd walked right into the kind of mess they tried so hard to avoid.

One apparently caused by someone she had been determined to trust. Strong hands, but apparently a stronger desire to screw Merrin over.

So Merrin and Cal had kept running, bypassing security doors left swinging open by Cere's riot-inducing security hack. They had hoped to make it out onto the roof and at least back to the courtyard before being confronted by landing parties of Purge Troopers, the Empire's elite troops that supported the Inquisitors.

But luck hadn't really been on their side today. Certainly not on Merrin's.

Inside the mess hall, the Purge Trooper raiding party had been waiting for them, already cutting down escaped prisoners in their bid to get their hands on Irei—and now, Merrin had to imagine, as a delightful bonus prize, Cal Kestis. Tables were turned over to be used as makeshift barriers, the prisoners using whatever they had at their disposal to still try to make it to an exit and take advantage of their own fortune, brought on by the *Mantis* crew. Stormtroopers exchanged shots back and forth with the prisoners, but some well-placed bolts seared through metal and flesh.

The mess hall had smelled more like cooked meat than Merrin thought it probably had since its inception.

The stormtroopers had looked up at Merrin and Cal's rushed entrance, shocked out of their rapid fire just long enough for both Merrin and Cal to send most of them to whatever awaited them on the other side of the dark stars, Cal with a crushing pull of the Force that slammed most of them headfirst into walls; Merrin following up with a wall of dark fire that incinerated enough of the soft tissue under their armor that it rendered them all—

Well. They died.

Merrin and Cal had just enough time to settle themselves behind one of the makeshift barricades before the first Purge Troopers broke through the security doors on the opposite side of the hall, five of them all at once, their batons and staffs and hammers crackling with energy made specifically to repel lightsabers. The guard tower in the center of the hall was dark; that, at least, was a small miracle. Merrin sent a silent thank-you to Cere, for that—the Jedi had clearly managed to reseal those doors once the guards inside had died so that no one could get back in. Merrin eyed the turret guns spaced evenly along the underside of the circular tower with immense gratitude that those, at least, were not currently trained on them.

Since Cal had taken down the baton-wielder while Merrin had suffocated the other staff-holder, buying enough time for the escapees to rush out, only three troopers were left now: the staff trooper blocking their path; another, attempting to use their hammer to bust down the entrance to the guard tower; and a commander, hiding behind the counter over which meals were typically served, protecting themselves from attack while preparing their own.

Merrin knew the commanders were deadliest from a distance. She would have to deal with them first.

"Your deaths will be meaningless," hissed the Purge Trooper from behind their staff.

Merrin couldn't help a smile. "Yes," she agreed easily. "They will be."

From beside her, she saw Cal give the smallest nod, but enough to let Merrin know he was on board with the plan. This was how they communicated on the field together, in battle, after years and countless fights: wordless, simple, fluid.

Merrin didn't need help.

But she found herself unbearably grateful for it, anyway.

She thought of Fret, and her grin turned wolfish. "They will be meaningless, but not today."

Everything happened in the space of an instant: Merrin broke off from Cal, dissolving the green mist and using her fire to disappear out of sight. By the time she'd reemerged on the counter above the commander, Cal was already engaged in fierce one-on-one combat with the staff trooper. Merrin didn't have the time to watch, but she knew Cal could handle himself.

So she turned her focus to the commander below her. They saw her the instant before she twisted her hands, her fire catching nothing but dead air as the commander rolled away with a speed Merrin didn't expect. The trooper was up on one knee with their blaster out and ready to fire, but Merrin had already disappeared and rushed away by the time the blaster bolt soared through what had been her chest just a millisecond earlier. She rerevealed herself directly behind the commander and had her hands on their arms to incapacitate them quickly, but Merrin heard something hit the floor with a *clink* and there wasn't enough time for her to register that it was a shock grenade before the floor around her had become electrified.

The shock flooded up Merrin's body from her feet to her head in a cresting wave, rendering her completely immobile, her muscles locked into place; she was completely unable to access her magick because of it. Furious through the cloud of pain, Merrin heard the commander laugh—actually *laugh*—as they stood and quickly backed off, preferring to fight from range, their armor protecting them from the electrical trap they'd just laid on the floor around them.

"You aren't even a Jedi," they said, the humor still in their voice, distorted by those ridiculous helmets. "What makes you think you stand a chance?"

Their blaster was out and raised again; Merrin watched with increasing rage as the commander fired off one, two, three bolts in a row and she had no direction in which to run, nowhere to go, no choice but to just stand there frozen in the pool of purple electricity—violet, like her skin now—and wait for the impact.

The first missed. The second just barely grazed her shoulder; the pain hit her an instant later, the speed of the hit and the searing heat of the shot bleeding through her body armor and radiating down her left arm.

The third bolt hit her square on her upper chest, or it should have.

The shock grenade's effects wore off, finally, and Merrin dropped to her knees, her palms slapping the cold mess hall floor hard. She looked down; the bolt had glanced off one of the metal teeth of her gold necklace. It was hot against her chest.

It wasn't personal before, but it was now.

She'd already been shot in the heart once today; Nightsisters knew that would have been more than enough.

If any of them had still been alive.

There were no words for the sound that came out of Merrin's mouth then; it was more of a roar than anything, a feral yell accompanied by the smell of smoke as the fury completely overtook her, hair singeing and skin peeling. She moved faster than she knew she could, the ichor in her veins taking over her thoughts almost entirely as she gave herself over to pure instinct.

She was there, and then she was not; she was there again behind the trooper and her fire was around their feet; gone again and back on their other side, fire around their wrists; gone again and then back in front of them, fire immolating their helmet right off their head, curdling up and away from their face, that blank face so many of these troopers shared, eyes more lifeless than most of the droids Merrin had met, programmed and without original thought, barren and devoid of personality or person at all.

Poor soul.

To be put out of their misery would be a gift.

And Merrin was feeling generous.

"You're right," Merrin agreed, watching the commander struggle against the fiery restraints at their wrists and ankles. She leaned forward, close enough to their ear that they couldn't mistake what they heard; that they'd know who had killed them in the end, even if they didn't know exactly what it meant. "I'm not a Jedi. I am much, much worse."

The fire raced up the commander's arms, wrapped itself prettily around their neck, and squeezed.

She watched them struggle; she waited long enough to let the fire go off their wrists, letting them scrabble at their throat, attempting to claw the ichor away so they could breathe. She watched with great interest as she released their feet, twisting one of her hands so that the Purge Trooper was lifted into the air by the fire around their neck, just enough so that she could see their feet kick desperately at the air as their lungs burned and begged for oxygen.

They wouldn't get it.

They went limp too quickly for Merrin's taste. With a flick of her wrist, she sent them flying directly into the Purge Trooper with the electrohammer, now locked in combat with Cal, who had already, it seemed, dispatched the staff trooper. The commander's deadweight slammed into the hammer-wielding trooper, sending them both flying. Another flick of the wrist; the fire around the commander burned up the other trooper's eyes, flooding into their brain.

Both of them hit the floor with an echoing thud.

Merrin chuckled.

"Merrin," came a hushed whisper. It was Cal. He sounded . . .

She blinked, and the world came rushing back to her all at once.

The floor in the mess hall was absolutely littered with bodies: Purge Troopers, prison guards, stormtroopers, prisoners. It was a garden of death, makeshift paths carved between bodies and blasters. The lights were too bright, fluorescent, and Merrin had to squint away from them suddenly. And at the center of it all, looking at her like he'd never seen her before, was Cal, sweaty and breathing heavily—the fight had taken a toll on him, too—lightsaber in one hand and stim in the other, BD on his back as ever. He didn't take his eyes off Merrin as he injected himself with the stim.

She waited for his judgment.

This would be the moment, then, when the Good Jedi Cal Kestis realized who he had been traveling with; *what* he had been traveling with. That the Nightsisters of Dathomir were a different beast than what he was accustomed to; that they could make their own choices, yes, decide what side they fought on, sure. But that at their core, at the very heart of Merrin and of everyone who had been like her—of her family, her blood family, bound by ritual and ichor—there was darkness.

Dathomir was bathed in red light, and so was Merrin.

Cal opened his mouth; Merrin put up her shields, the ones around her heart she had so foolishly dropped.

And then the sound of boot falls drowned out everything else.

They came rushing in through every door, all at once: Purge Troopers and stormtroopers, too many to count, clogging the open security doors and slipping between bodies. They were outnumbered by masses; there would be no escape from here, not for Merrin and Cal. Not against this many, not all at once. They were good, but they weren't immortal.

Not yet, anyway.

Cal's eyes went wide, and whatever he had been about to say was stolen off his lips.

She knew what he was asking.

To go back to the ship, and protect Greez and Cere.

To leave him here. Leave him here to die.

The Purge Troopers flooded into the room and Merrin shook her head. That wasn't how this was going to end.

If Cal was going to think she was a monster, well—she'd give him a real show about it, then. Just to be sure.

And Merrin wasn't going to die here. Not on this cursed planet. Not for Irei.

And certainly not for Fret.

Cal's lightsaber flashed up; there were only so many bolts he could deflect at once, and the distance between himself and the surrounding troopers was closing with every moment.

There was no instinct this time; this was all choice. Merrin dug deep, looked inside herself, found her well of fire. Found the ichor at her core, and knew what the only answer was.

She didn't have the seeing glass she would need for a full and true Chant of Resurrection. It might only last a few moments, but she could still try.

Merrin inhaled and closed her eyes and dove deep, deeper than she had in months. She felt everything ignite: her body, her breath, the room itself. A spell like this held so much history and power; once she started it, there was no going back. Green mist burst forth from Merrin's hands, great masses of it, rolling across the floor like an unnatural morning mist. It engulfed everything in its tracks at a speed so fast it was barely visible; a foot of verdant cloud cover that was not there and then, suddenly, was. The brightest thing in the room. A shock.

The troopers had frozen in fear; the air in the room, during the chant, would do that to a person. A lesser person.

Merrin took a deep breath, and with everything she had left in her, cried the final words of the spell, like a kind of prayer to her home, functional or not: "*Rise and avenge Dathomir!*"

And then some prisoners among the garden of bodies at their feet bloomed to life.

Merrin felt them all at once, bursts in her mind like flowers opening to the sun, half-life returning to them, each body the mist touched that was without a current inhabitant. Merrin controlled them all, and yet controlled none of them; she was all of them, but she was herself. She was frozen to the spot, focused entirely on ensuring the spell did what it needed to do for long enough that both she and Cal could escape this place once and for all.

The small group of fallen prisoners—including a couple of Aqualish and a pair of Duros—rose from the lush fog with groans and moans that Merrin imagined would haunt their enemies until their dying breath. So, for about the next three minutes.

Cal didn't waste a second, once he saw what was happening; he got to work cutting down the distracted and terrified troopers, now on the defensive against both a Jedi and the reanimated dead. Cal had witnessed Merrin use this spell only once before, on Dathomir, before she'd joined the *Mantis* crew, back when she was using the chant to attack Cal himself. She hadn't dared use it again since then; and then more recently she hadn't been able to, her connection to Dathomir and her fire dampened enough that there was simply no chance she could perform so powerful a spell.

How much things had changed in such a short time.

Around Merrin, she felt the battle more than she saw it. The undead prisoners cut down stormtroopers with ease, without the fear of death to slow them down, used their force to drop trooper after trooper to the ground. Merrin tended the plot in her mind, watered her blooms, trimmed dying leaves and supported sagging stems, sustaining her small garden with every death. She felt Cal in the midst of it all, lightsaber flashing, picking up the slack where her burgeoning, budding corpses couldn't, ensuring none survived.

When the room was finally silent, Merrin closed her fists. The mist vanished; the corpses fell. The garden wilted; dead matter would feed its next iteration. The way things were meant to be.

Cal looked at her, and Merrin couldn't place the expression on his face.

And that, more than anything, broke her heart.

"Go," Cal said, and it was all Merrin had to hear before turning and shrouding herself from the world once more, preparing to dash out of the room.

But in the moment before she was gone, racing back toward the *Mantis* to protect Greez and Cere, Merrin heard something: a new voice, a strange one. A threat. A gleeful threat.

"*Jedi.*"

And then: a flash of fiery, bloody red.

The Inquisitor was walking into the room before Cal had time to watch Merrin fully disappear. He had been in awe of her power, of the way she was able to call on her heritage, her magick, to protect the people who mattered most to her in the times when things were most dire. He wished he'd had a chance to tell her. But her green mist was already gone, and the bodies were back to just being bodies—which, too bad, Cal thought, he really could have used some undead support at this exact moment, but better for the rest of his family to be safe than to risk them here, with an Inquisitor.

Cal had let his lightsaber go dark, and he kept it that way. He didn't want the Inquisitor to know he was threatened too soon.

He wasn't someone Cal knew, wasn't an Inquisitor he'd had the displeasure of meeting before. "*Jedi,*" he spat, full of contempt and a little too much excitement for Cal's taste.

"What gave it away?" Cal asked, taking a few steps backward for every step the Inquisitor took forward.

Cal took him in as he stalked into the room, scoping out his competition for any sign of weakness—or anything, really, that he might be able to use in the inevitable ensuing combat. The Inquisitor was tall and his black armor and uniform were as imposing as they were meant to be, with wide shoulder pauldrons that made him look broader than he actually was.

"Nice hat," said Cal. It looked like someone had taken the top off an R2 unit, spray-painted it black, and placed it delicately on this guy's head. Nearly as wide as his fake shoulders, the helmet was domed on top, flat on the underside, and extended in a full oval. "Keep you dry on those real rainy planets?"

"I'm afraid," the Inquisitor said calmly, "that your words cannot annoy me any more than your existence does."

"Big talk from a guy who looks like he's got headlights," Cal said, nodding toward the four bright red lights shining from the front of the Inquisitor's chest piece. The Empire always did love those over-the-top touches. "And no mask? I think you might want to take some advice from your friends on that one. Got a face made for comms."

"I don't care for jokes," came the Inquisitor's low voice. As the Inquisitor stepped closer, Cal became more certain he'd never seen someone of his species before; a rarity, for someone as well traveled through the galaxy as Cal had become. His skin was a sallow gray-green, his upward-tilted eyes so light minty in color—pupils included—that they nearly blended with the whites of his eyeballs entirely. His wide, flat nose flared out over his long mouth, set in a grimace that seemed permanent. A strong chin looked like it could take somebody's eye out if he wasn't careful.

The Inquisitor adjusted his grip on his double-bladed red lightsaber, both sides connected at the center by a circular hilt with a crossbar. Cal had seen what those double-bladed lightsabers could do, knew that an

Inquisitor could make the blades spin around the circular hilt like the galaxy's deadliest ceiling fan, and had heard that some could even use it to make themselves fly. Though the lightsaber's blades were smaller—the whole thing together was hardly longer than Cal's lightsaber with one blade active—the Inquisitors knew how to use them with alarming precision, the shorter blades allowing them better control and a more intense offensive combat style.

Cal's eyes darted around the room; he wanted to make sure he was putting himself with his back to an exit as quickly as possible before this got ugly. "What number are you, then? Lucky thirteen?"

The Inquisitor didn't so much as crack a smile. Tough crowd. "I am the Fifth Brother."

Cal lined himself up with one of the doors, hoping it was the right choice. "You got a name?"

"Not anymore."

Fighting the urge to roll his eyes—all of these Inquisitors were so *dramatic*—Cal flipped his lightsaber hilt from hand to hand, testing the weight, watching the Fifth Brother's eyes to see if he was watching his movements, too. "Okay, Fifth Brother. But you did, once. I was just wondering what—"

"I am aware of what happened with the Second Sister," the Fifth Brother cut in. "You will not find the same cracks in me, Jedi. I have chosen to be here."

Cal settled his lightsaber into his dominant hand, weighing it—weighing his opponent. "Yeah? You a real loves-to-hunt-down-the-innocent kind of guy?"

The Inquisitor's mouth settled into a thin line. "You use humor to deflect from your nerves. And I know what you are nervous about, because it's true. You would have done well with us, Cal Kestis. I can smell it on you."

Cal froze, and felt BD shiver on his back. He had dreamed, once, about having turned to the dark side; being made an Inquisitor.

Liking it.

But it wasn't real. It was merely his own fear manifesting in his mind. That's what the dark side did to you, after all. Made you doubt. Made you nervous. Made you question everything you believed in, whether you wanted to or not.

It was called the dark side for a reason.

Cal would never turn to the dark side. He could have, after Order 66. He could have turned himself in at any time. But he didn't. He didn't, and he never would, and it was that choice that mattered, and he would keep making it every single day.

He ignited his lightsaber, and the fiery light flowed through his hand into the blade.

BD trilled fierce encouragement, and the sound brought Cal's focus back into the moment. Five was trying to get into his head; Cal wasn't going to let him.

He couldn't afford to.

"That's sweet," Cal said, trying to keep his voice easy. "You this nice to all the Jedi you're trying to kill, or am I just special?"

"You are not special." The Fifth Brother hadn't stopped walking forward, not for a second. Cal was backed almost all the way into the door now, and his only two options were to stand and fight or to run.

If he ran, he was going to lead the Inquisitor right back to the *Mantis*, and to the people he had sworn to protect. And they deserved a fighting chance to escape.

Cal was going to do everything within his power to give it to them.

He smiled, grim and determined. "That's where you're wrong."

Both Cal and the Fifth Brother leapt into the air at the same time, their connections to the Force lending their jumps impossible height. Their lightsabers clashed in midair, the reverberating cymbal-crash enough to repel both men backward. Cal used his free hand to grab onto a fissure in one of the concrete walls, hanging high enough off the ground to still maintain the advantage in height. He kept his eyes on the Fifth Brother as the Inquisitor landed in front of the guard tower with both legs bent, one end of his dual-bladed lightsaber slamming into the floor in front of him.

"Merrin, status?" Cal muttered into his comms quickly.

"Back at the ship, starting engines," Merrin replied in an instant. "But there's an issue—"

Before he could hear any more, the Fifth Brother was back in the air, lightsaber raised above his head, poised to swing it down onto Cal from above. He had to concentrate; his crew could figure out the issues on their end on their own.

They had to.

Cal narrowed his eyes and, with his lightsaber still clenched in his hand, gestured to try to wrench the Inquisitor's weapon out of his grip using the Force. Cal was shocked when he felt the equivalent of a hand-slap through the Force, knocking his attempt away with ease and disdain. But it was enough of a distraction to have sent the Fifth Brother off course, slamming his blade into the wall directly next to Cal instead of through his skull. The wall crumbled down around both of them, and Cal slid to the floor, careful to keep his eyes on his opponent's lightsaber the whole way down.

As soon as Cal's boots hit the floor, he was on the defensive. The Fifth Brother didn't have a particularly graceful fighting style—as far as Cal could tell, there wasn't a whole lot of technique going on here, and he seemed clumsy on his feet. But what he did have was pure, brute force.

The Fifth Brother slammed his lightsaber down in overhead chops that would have cleaved a less careful Jedi in two over and over and over again. He drove Cal back and back and back across the room, bullying him into parry after parry, block after block. Cal's arms were sore almost immediately, the pressure of the Inquisitor's attack so intense that Cal had to use all his strength to keep the red lightsaber away from his chest.

Cal's foot caught on a corpse, and in an instant he was tumbling backward to the floor, watching the Fifth Brother's triumphant face as he lifted his blade for what he clearly believed would be the last time, planning on pinning Cal to the ground just like this, burning a hole clean through his chest and into the concrete, leaving him here forever to rot next to Purge Troopers and bucketheads—

But the Fifth Brother underestimated Cal. Inquisitors usually did.

He was rolling away by the time the red blade hit the ground, and Cal rocked back onto his palms before launching himself back up onto his feet, giving himself an extra boost with the Force. The Fifth Brother was big and imposing and his swings were strong—but those swings were wide, and left huge openings for an agile and clever opponent.

Luckily, Cal was both agile and clever, in the right moments. And he was feeling like this was going to be one of those moments. Most important, he had finally created some distance from his opponent to take advantage of his opponent's lack of technique.

"Stay *still*—" the Fifth Brother growled, swinging around to find Cal already gone from where he'd leapt to his feet. But Cal was already in the air, overhead, swinging his own lightsaber down, the Fifth Brother's upward vision blocked by the visor on his ridiculous helmet, and it was a matter of seconds before Cal's lightsaber made contact with the top of his head and—

Glanced off, sending Cal skidding sideways and tumbling onto the ground. So *that's* what the helmet was for, thought Cal. Lightsaber-resistant.

Still looked pretty silly, though.

Then again, Cal knew he'd worn a pink poncho for a while there, so. He supposed he was the last person in a position to judge someone's fashion sense in battle.

Cal regrouped, but knew he was on the right track. If the Fifth Brother was going to be aggressive and clumsy, Cal would be smart and patient. He would wait for the right moment, and then he would find his opening and strike.

Back and forth it went like this, for how long Cal could barely keep track. The Fifth Brother would charge and charge, Cal would block and dodge, and when the moment was right, he would get a hit in wherever he could. A nick on his armor; a slice on his hand; a mark on his cheek. There was only so long someone could keep up an attack as forceful as the Inquisitor's; eventually, the body would wear down, and Cal would wear him down.

But Cal was wearing down, too. He lost track of how many stims he caught from BD-1, worried about running out, about how many times he risked defeat to wipe sweat out of his eyes. He was bolstered by knowing that the more time he wasted, the more likely it was that the *Mantis* was in deep space, far away from here. But it was a cold comfort, ultimately, and there was only so much he could do with that before it stopped being useful.

There, finally: Cal saw his ultimate opening. The Fifth Brother stumbled into the side of the guard tower; Cal lunged. His lightsaber found the space between armor and flesh under the spot where the Inquisitor's arm met his chest, moved smooth like butter to try to slice him open—

But he wasn't fast enough. It was too late. Before he knew it, the Fifth Brother had pushed off the tower, and Cal was on his back; the Inquisitor was over him. He'd bought himself as much time as he could, but as he'd always known, he wasn't ready to face down another Inquisitor one-on-one. He just didn't have it in him.

"You should have joined us when you had the chance, Cal Kestis." The Fifth Brother kept his sword close to Cal's throat, close enough that he could feel its heat almost searing his skin, blisters rising in its proximity. He was afraid that if he swallowed, it would be enough to burn his Adam's apple clean through. He barely dared breathe, let alone respond.

And what was there to say, really? He had been beaten. Cal Kestis, on his back, defeated at the hands of a pugnacious, brutish Inquisitor. It was humiliating; it was the worst death Cal could possibly have imagined, on a planet far from home, so far from his goal of fighting the Empire that he might never even register as a footnote in the historical logs. Would people even know that he had broken into the Fortress Inquisitorius and nearly brought the place to its knees? Would anyone even remember?

Did he even make a dent?

"I would never," Cal hissed, careful to keep his chest still, wincing through the blistering heat, "ever join you. *Ever.*"

The Fifth Brother nodded solemnly, bringing the tip of his lightsaber to rest gently on Cal's shoulder, slowly burning its way through the armor there, the residual heat causing Cal to bite through his lip in order to avoid screaming from the burning pain.

"I know," he said, almost sadly. "You wouldn't. You're too much of a Jedi."

He moved his lightsaber up toward Cal's cheek, and Cal squeezed his eyes shut. He would rather have it be quick and easy. But he knew the longer he kept the Fifth Brother talking, the longer his family would have to get away.

So he would keep him talking.

"What's that supposed to mean?"

Cal heard the Fifth Brother sigh. "You called me killer of innocents. And how innocent are you, Cal Kestis?"

Cal winced away from the lightsaber's heat. "The same as you, I'd imagine."

"And what have the Jedi done for you, hmm? What has your life been like?"

Cal swallowed. "One of my own making."

"And yet even so," the Fifth Brother said, satisfaction in his voice, "only one of us has control over our destiny. And unfortunately for you . . ." The lightsaber crept closer to Cal's eyes. "Well. You know who's in control here. But you tried your best."

Cal held his breath. He knew his end would come for him like this. He always had.

He'd just hoped it wouldn't have been quite so soon.

And the harder he squeezed his eyes shut, the more the red light of Five's lightsaber appeared to be green. Comforting. Cal let the green fire rush behind his eyes, surround him, and waited for the end to come.

"One mistake." A voice rang out from above, one Cal was both intensely relieved and incredibly frustrated to hear. "You forgot that a Padawan is never far from his master."

And then Cere Junda came crashing down onto the Fifth Brother's back, taking advantage of his lack of overhead vision.

CHAPTER 13

There was a moment, just a moment, when Cere was grasping the Inquisitor from behind, hands around his throat, trying to keep him off balance long enough for Cal to get up off the damn ground and get back into the fight, when she thought: *Ah. This is it. This is what the life of a great Jedi Master has come to.*

Swinging around on the back of some poor, brainwashed kid who deserved better and got far, far worse.

Just like all the stories of heroic Jedi during the High Republic always promised.

The Inquisitor roared and tore Cere from his back, tossing her into the air with the ease that only came with the Force, but she had expected it enough that Cere was able to land on her feet. The distraction had worked well enough for Cal to roll up onto his knees and away from the tip of the Inquisitor's lightsaber. Cere barely had a moment to steady herself before the Inquisitor was charging at her full speed, double-bladed lightsaber spinning now in a vortex of bloody fury.

He was strong, but he was sloppy. Cere's connection to the energy around him and through him showed her his openings, his weaknesses, without him even knowing it. All she would have to do was use his own hubris to her advantage, let him think he had the upper hand, pull his guard down for an instant, and then take her hit.

She didn't have to use brute strength to beat him.

Still, she thought. It might put him in his place.

Planting her feet one in front of the other for the most solid stance, Cere pulled out and ignited her lightsaber with one hand while raising the other and holding it out, palm-first, toward her rushing opponent. She watched the blades of his lightsaber forming a perfect circle of light, too fast to individuate the sides of the weapon, narrowed her eyes—and *held.*

Reaching out through the Force was second nature to Cere at this point in her life. It was as much one of her senses as sight or smell, a constant input and output from her energetic body that pulsed into the world around her, flowed through her mind, seeped out of her pores. She let her mind roll out through her palm, across the rapidly closing space between herself and the Inquisitor, into his lightsaber, and all at once time slowed.

Her nerves felt electrified as she rushed down each side of the sword, its blazing atoms searing her brain, and she willed it, just enough, not too much to get her into trouble, to *hold.*

She knew what Cal would see, from where he was getting back on his feet. He would see the Inquisitor slow like he was hitting a wall of water, his feet betraying his own orders to continue their forward motion. He would see the red lightsaber and its circular threat halt, frozen mid-spin, returning to its less dangerous form. He would watch the Inquisitor sweat as he tried to push back through the Force, to regain control over himself and over his lightsaber, and he would see the dawning fear on the Inquisitor's face as he realized he was outmatched.

Cere had faced down Darth Vader himself and lived. She had come the closest any living soul ever had to ending the Sith's reign of terror over the galaxy. She was possibly the most powerful remaining Jedi in existence.

And she wasn't going to let this punk forget it.

She felt the pushback through the Force, the Inquisitor's attempt at ruining her control, and bit down on her bottom lip. There was a way to end him through the Force, just like this, and it would be so easy. It would be an assured victory. To flow up from his lightsaber over his arms, to spill over his shoulders and creep around his neck before he even became suspicious, before he was even able to notice. All she'd have to do was curl her fingers into a claw as she squeezed the Force around his neck. She would watch the light drain from his eyes and she would know that the *Mantis* crew would be safe, that the future of the Jedi Order would be one step closer to assured.

Connecting to that energy—to the dark side—that was how she'd held out for so long against Vader.

She knew it, and Vader had, too.

But that was a slippery slope to nowhere good, and Cere didn't have to go there ever again. Not against someone who pulsed back at her through the Force with raw emotion, all rage and spite and lack of control.

And, of course, one of the ways the dark side lied to you was by trying to convince you it was the only way. For in truth, it was Cere connecting to the light again that had allowed her to defeat Vader in that moment, after all.

She could feel that the Fifth Brother was getting ready to break. But she would use the light to break him first.

With a yell, Cere dropped her hand and the control over the Inquisitor's lightsaber and movement and flung herself toward him, launching herself forward with her blue blade. It took him too long to realize he'd been freed; he wasn't ready for her when she came at him in a flurry of swipes that put him on the defensive. With each clash of their weapons, Cere hit again and again, matching his style almost exactly, knowing that it would disconcert him and keep him off balance to see his own technique mimicked back at him, and more effectively.

"Want to finish this together?" Cal was beside her, lightsaber out and up at the ready, and the Inquisitor's eyes were wide at the challenge of two Jedi at once, both bearing down on him with a ferocity he clearly hadn't been expecting when he showed up to take down Cal on his own.

The Inquisitor was clearly infuriated by this development; all his energy was now focused on the fight at hand. He barely managed to dodge a swing from Cal's blade without going reeling into Cere's, and she knew they had him.

If they kept on like this, they could destroy him.

But Cere knew that wasn't always the way. She had to try.

Just as with Trilla, she had to try.

Using the same energy she had a moment ago, Cere threw up her other hand as she blocked an attack with her lightsaber—but this time, she stopped Cal and his lightsaber in their tracks.

The Inquisitor paused in surprise as Cal, too, gurgled his shock from next to her, the only sound he could manage while frozen.

"This isn't the only way," Cere said through gritted teeth, holding back his weapon with hers, arms straining in the effort of it. "You can leave them. Come back to the light. It isn't too late."

The Fifth Brother paused, for just a moment. Cere watched a shadow pass over his eyes, reflected in the red light of his blade.

And then he laughed, breaking away from Cere's lightsaber, lunging backward, and swinging madly toward Cal.

Cere dropped her hold on Cal just quickly enough for him to throw up his sword in defense, which infuriated the Inquisitor no end. With a *snap*, the Fifth Brother disconnected the two sides of his lightsaber, wielding one in each hand. Cere focused on his right while Cal bore down on him from the left. The Inquisitor was strong, but it was two against one, and Cere could still manipulate some of his movements through the Force, could still anticipate his next move before he made it. Together, Cere and Cal pushed forward, keeping the pressure on the Fifth Brother, meeting and matching each one of his blows with one of their own. He was outmatched and overpowered but his stamina was endless; he met each of their hits with one of his, both of his hands moving at lightning speed, rarely reaching for the Force, relying purely on his skill with the blade to try to keep them on the defensive.

The question, the wondering, even for a split second, was a distraction Cere couldn't afford. The Fifth Brother saw his moment through the sweat dripping into Cere's eyes and he took it, lunging forward with both swords as Cal rebounded from a parry, and Cere was just too slow by just a fraction of a second, and one of his red lightsabers burned into her shoulder before she could spin away.

It was the worst thing that could have happened in that moment. Cal looked over in shock, worried about Cere—he *was* too attached, would always protect his allies over everyone else at all costs, even if his ally told him to do otherwise. It was always going to be an issue with him, but it was also what made him so good, and Cere wasn't ever really sure what to do with that, how to handle it, and right now it looked like it would be his own downfall. The Inquisitor threw out a hand, shoving Cal back off his feet and up into the air, slamming him into the ceiling with so much speed that Cere winced when she heard the concrete crack under the force of it.

She had to make a split-second decision as Cal, unconscious from the hit, came tumbling back to the ground, and there was no choice at all, not really, even though she knew she would be leaving herself vulnerable. Cere pulled her focus back from the Inquisitor just long enough to cushion Cal's fall with the Force, to catch him and place him gently on solid ground.

It was enough of an opening for the Fifth Brother to regain control over the situation, just as Cere knew it would be.

And there would only be one way out.

Cere had less than a second before the Fifth Brother's lightsaber was slicing up toward her abdomen with every intention of cutting her in two straight up the middle, ruthless and unstoppable.

For anyone who wasn't Cere.

Reaching deep into the Force had a feeling to it, a rush that Cere knew would be addicting if she gave in to it one too many times, if she let that channel stay open longer than was absolutely necessary. It felt like triumph and glee, spice and starfire skee, like there was something telling her she was meant to feel this way and wasn't everything better like this and didn't she want to stay here forever, couldn't she just live in this right here and never leave?

That's what it felt like.

There was a time when Cere would have reached out to the dark side of the Force in a moment like this. Had done so, first to attempt to save Trilla, then to save Cal from Vader. But she knew better than to go there again. Would *never* go there again.

Cere saw Cal hit the ceiling, watched the twitch of the Inquisitor's lightsaber as it changed course to gut her, and all she felt—all she allowed herself to feel—was empathy.

Empathy for Cal, and for everything he'd lost. For this poor Inquisitor, and for the Knight of Good he was supposed to be. For herself, and the way she'd had to run from everything and everyone in this damn galaxy for her entire life, if only to save it. But most of all, empathy for even the Sith; for the people who would misunderstand and misuse their galaxy-given purpose to destroy balance in the Force, to bend it to their will alone, all for the glory of power and empire and personal gain. That seemed so very lonely.

Cere let her empathy flow through her, and the Fifth Brother's lightsaber shattered wide into its component parts.

Not like an explosion, nothing so uncontrolled. It was more like an unmaking, an unraveling, each piece of the lightsaber separating itself from the next, spiraling outward into a little galaxy itself, orbiting the now exposed kyber crystal at its core.

Cere looked up into the Fifth Brother's shocked eyes as the tiny pieces of what was once his lightsaber clattered to the floor.

She saw awe in his eyes, and in that moment—all Cere wanted was to see *more.*

She could help this man.

She could help them all.

Neither Cere nor Cal was responding to Greez's calls over comms from the *Mantis,* and that was never, ever good.

It really wasn't that long ago, Greez thought, that he'd been telling this crew, this idiot crew that he loved so damn much, that they should just walk. Actually, forget walking; they should run toward the exit, is what he'd been saying. Get out while the getting was good! Walk away with what they had, which wasn't much of anything, really, but did include a few real nice plants, the knowledge that they'd saved a lot more people than they'd screwed, and they'd adopted a bogling, too. That was pretty good, at the end of the day. More than most people could say for themselves.

He really thought he'd had the best possible idea.

But did any of those idiots listen? No, of course not. They barged into danger headfirst like they always did in the name of good energy, or whatever the Force was, and now he was on a hell planet in the middle of nowhere with Inquisitors and *nobody was answering his damn calls.*

"Merrin!" Greez shouted, rushing out of the cockpit. "Where in blazes are they?"

Greez had never seen Merrin look so lost, not even her first day on the *Mantis.* Back then, she had looked more determined than anything.

Now? Now she looked like she barely knew where she was, let alone what was going on.

That really didn't bode well.

"I don't know," Merrin said, pacing around the map table and shaking her head. "I was supposed to come back to protect you both, but she was adamant about going back for Cal, and what was I going to do, tell her no? Of course she was going to go get him. I never should have left him there—"

"Hey." Greez grabbed ahold of one of her arms, stopping her frantic movements. The last thing he needed was a panicked witch on his ship on top of everything else. "C'mon. You were doing what was right for the team. We just gotta figure out which right thing is next."

Merrin's eyes came back into focus as she looked down at Greez. He watched her collect herself, piece by piece, before taking a deep breath. "You're right."

Greez shrugged, trying not to look too self-satisfied. "I usually am."

Greez had moved the *Mantis* into the courtyard of the garrison, as close to the mess hall's roof access as he could get it without putting a giant neon COME GET US RIGHT HERE, INQUISITOR! sign on the sail, ramp down and waiting for the rest of their crew. He knew the storm-trooper and her schematics-that-turned-out-to-be-a-person were long gone, which was just as well, since they were the whole reason he was in this position now anyway, so they just needed Cal and Cere back on board so they could vamoose.

Peering out the side of the ramp, the grounds outside the prison looked surprisingly quiet. No one was going to be rushing him, Greez would've been willing to bet, and even if they were, he had as many blasters as he did arms. He could look out for the *Mantis* on his own for a couple of minutes while Merrin magicked herself out and back again with Cere and the kid.

Merrin shook her head, as if reading his mind as plain as day. "Absolutely not. I am not leaving you here alone."

"Merrin, geez." Greez sighed. "I can take care of myself. What kind of a pilot would I be if I couldn't watch my own ship for a couple of minutes? Get out there and get back—it'll take longer to argue about it than it will to just—"

"Medbay!" The shout came from outside the *Mantis,* just loud enough to cut Greez off. He swung his head back around in surprise, and there, limping herself away from the prison with a big ol' lizard across her shoulders—a Nikto for sure—was the stormtrooper herself. Most of her plating had been blown off or singed beyond recognition; the lizard was smoking from a couple of holes that she probably wasn't supposed to have (not that Greez was an expert on lizard-lady anatomy or anything).

Merrin was out of the ship before Greez could even fully process what was going on, watching the explosion of green fire appear next to the stormtrooper and then just as quickly disappear. He heard the crackle behind him before he saw it, turning around just in time to see Merrin rematerialize with the stormtrooper's biceps in a death grip, the Nikto still on her back.

The second her feet were on solid ground, the stormtrooper fell to her knees. Greez rushed forward, helping Merrin to relieve the woman of her Nikto-shaped burden. This close, Greez could see all of the Nikto's injuries in gory detail—blaster wounds and burns from electro-weapons scattered across her dry, scaly skin.

"Please," whispered the stormtrooper. "You have to have something—"

"No." Greez's mind raced, trying to figure out what they could do for the Nikto, but coming up blank. "No, we don't have a medbay; we have some basic supplies, but—"

"I can do it." Merrin was already standing, fire gathering around her hands. It spilled onto the floor, around the Nikto's body, and the fire surrounded her without burning her, lifting her into the air like she was on an invisible stretcher. "But, Fret—I'm going to need help."

The stormtrooper looked up at Merrin through tear-filled eyes, and Greez thought he'd never seen someone look like they were seeing a god before, but that's what he was seeing in those red eyes right now. Like Merrin was her savior, and she would do anything for her, would worship on her knees for her until the end of time if she was able to do this one thing, if she was able to help where no one else could.

And then the three of them were gone through the door to the engine room, and it was sealed with that telltale line of green fire, and ah, *kriff*.

Greez let out what he felt must have been the longest sigh of his life.

And then he grabbed his blasters and a holomap HUD, and he ran as fast as he could down the *Mantis* ramp.

When Merrin and Fret had rushed her into the engine room, Irei had been in a dire state. Merrin had never had a gift for healing; though it was something some Nightsisters were capable of using their skills for, it had simply never been Merrin's calling. She had always been better at taking life than giving it. But Merrin wasn't going to let the woman die, not someone so important to Fret, no matter how she felt about her in the moment, which was real growth for Merrin, she thought. Fret and Merrin had swept all the tools and clutter off the engine room's repair bench and used it as a makeshift gurney for Irei's body, her long legs hanging off the end. She was far too large for Cal's tiny cot.

Fret was ready with whatever Merrin needed—hydration, a comforting touch, words of support—as Merrin started what would pass in these dire circumstances for medical aid. They would have to use the ship's lackluster supplies, but she could at least soothe Irei's pain and ensure she didn't wake up during the worst of it. Merrin worried, briefly, that she wouldn't be able to find her fire at the worst possible time—but no, it was still there, waiting for her, though it still felt different than it once had, and different even from a few days ago when she had first met Fret, when it had first come roaring back to her. It was settling into something new, something entirely her own. Something disconnected from anyone else, and even—though it scared her to think about it—disconnected, in a way, from Dathomir.

But that was a worry for another time.

Green mist gathered around Merrin's upturned palms, flooded across the engine room floor, surrounding Irei's prone body on the bench. In Merrin's mind, it was different from taking a life, always different. Far easier to extinguish than to soothe, always, no matter the circumstance, and the same applied to her powers. When she had to kill, when she could send her fire trickling down an enemy's throat or wrap it gently around their neck or use it to burn them up in place or tear them limb from limb, there was something quick and instinctual about it. It didn't take thought or even patience, really; to destroy was the work of an instant, a slight pressure with her mind that sent her magick deep into its stated purpose. And she could tell that her fire liked it.

Wanted it.

Soothing was not like that. Bringing comfort felt antithetical to the fire, contradictory to its will. Fire was consuming and destructive; it was not mending or curative, medicinal or remedial. It wanted to eat and it was never, ever sated. To soothe, it had to be molded into something opposite itself; usually, the Water of Life helped with this, the potions and formulas the Nightsisters would rely on to create the proper environment for healing. All Merrin had to rely on here was her willpower, her ability to wrap her mind around the fire and force it to calm and alleviate and lull. And, while she did that, there was so much to fix.

Merrin didn't know how Irei had gotten so badly injured, and Fret was hesitant to say—Merrin imagined it was the guilt of failing to better protect her. She imagined Fret would have had a hard time handling her by herself.

Still, the two of them had run off. Had they stayed with Merrin and Cal, they might have been protected. What was their plan? And why did they come back to the *Mantis* after all?

Had they just stayed put, Irei might have stayed whole.

Instead they ran. And now they were all in this horrible position.

And Merrin still didn't know what Irei truly was to Fret, or vice versa.

It had been . . . a very long day.

By this time Merrin had finished her work on Irei, had managed to use her magick mostly to calm her and numb her pain while she and Fret worked on her with the *Mantis*'s meager medical supplies. The woman would likely need more proper medical attention soon, but for now she slept and her breathing appeared stable. Merrin was drenched in sweat, shaking, and collapsed almost immediately into Fret's waiting arms as Irei fell back to the bench. Merrin noticed belatedly that Fret's face was covered in tears, but she was just whispering words of comfort and praise to Merrin, and she was too exhausted by her own efforts to question it any further. She had no idea how much time had passed; all she knew was that she heard the rattle of the *Mantis*'s ramp far too soon after that for her to have any of her strength back.

Her well was dry, and her fire needed time to recover.

The thing about being small and kind of weird lookin' to most of the galaxy, Greez had come to learn, was that it was real easy to put yourself in places where other species just didn't really want to bother to see you. As Greez followed the pings on his map toward Cere and Cal's location, he kept mostly to the shadows and the service corridors of the prison, turning when he heard the signs of battle, rushing away from anything that seemed dangerous or like it would put him in the face of imminent dying.

But even when he managed to cross paths with stormtroopers, they barely gave him a second glance—at this point, nobody was looking for somebody who looked like him. They probably mistook him for an escaped prisoner, and at this point, those poor suckers were the last thing on anybody's mind in here. The Imperials were tasked with either finding the Nikto or killing the Jedi.

A panicked and scurrying Latero in a leather jacket? Not exactly high on the priority list.

Still, Greez wasn't exactly a planetside kinda guy. He liked to be the getaway driver; that was his whole shtick. He wasn't allergic to danger or anything quite as pitiful as that; piloting the *Mantis* was, a lot of the time, way more dangerous than whatever the kids got up to on the shore, what with all the space lasers and the asteroids and just generally the fact that space wanted to kill you all the time in every way. But he preferred to be where he excelled, and that was behind the controls of his sweet little space yacht, with big ol' walls between him and the faces of the people who were trying to kill him.

It was just easier that way, he found, to forget what he was really doing. When he was behind the controls, things made sense. There was a pattern to it. Practice and patience.

On the ground, in a battle environment, everything was chaotic in a way he sometimes had trouble keeping up with. There wasn't a lot surprising going on in here, at least—some troopers to avoid, but overall pretty straightforward by this point in the fight. Still, like all ground missions, there were all these people and sounds and shouting and blaster shots and it just wasn't really made for a little guy with, apparently, more limbs than sense.

But here he was, because there wasn't anybody else gonna save his idiot crew tonight. There was just him.

And he wasn't gonna leave anybody behind. That's just not what good pilots did.

His map pinged; he was close to their location now. Looked like they were still in the mess. How they hadn't managed to move outta there this whole time, Greez couldn't figure out, but he was glad, at least, their trackers were all functioning properly and he was able to get a read on them at all. He wasn't far now; a couple more corners, dodging down a few out-of-the-way hallways to avoid the sound of stompin' white boots, and—

When Greez rounded the corner into the mess hall, he realized he'd been wrong, actually. There were some things on this mission that could still surprise him.

And he immediately wished he hadn't seen 'em.

He took in the scene in front of him as quickly as he could. Cal was down and out on the ground, wedged between two overturned tables, BD-1 frantically nudging at him trying to get him to wake up. He looked like he'd been smacked around pretty bad, judging by the bruising Greez could see on his face; definitely not the kid's best moment.

But that, somehow, was not the worst thing going on in the room.

Cere was in here, like the tracker said, which was good; but she was not alone. She had a whole Inquisitor backed up against another door, her lightsaber against his throat, illuminating his pale-gray face under just the dumbest helmet Greez had ever had the displeasure of seeing. Where the Inquisitor's lightsaber had gone, Greez had no idea—he couldn't even spot the thing discarded elsewhere in the room.

Which all sounded good, in theory. If Cere hadn't looked the way that she did.

Greez had been flying with Cere for years now. Whole years, longer than he'd ever flown with anyone else in his whole damn life. She was the most caring person Greez had ever known, caring to a fault, really, and he felt fiercely protective of her, would drive her to the ends of this stupid galaxy for her cause and had, because he loved her like she was family, dammit, and family did things for one another that they didn't want to do. (See: right now.) He'd seen Cere elated; crushed; joyous; in pain. He'd seen her cry, and he'd seen her laugh so hard she wept again. He thought he'd seen pretty much every iteration of Cere Junda there was to see. That's just what happened when you lived on a tiny yacht in the middle of empty space. You really saw it all.

But he'd never, *not once,* seen Cere look like this.

He couldn't hear what she was saying to the Inquisitor—her voice was too low, she was talking calmly to the guy. But her face; her face was the single scariest thing Greez had ever seen.

Not because it was filled with rage, like Greez might have expected if Cere had gone all dark side on them again. Cere wasn't doing that anymore; she'd promised them. But instead, because she looked absolutely *desperate*—desperate to get this degenerate waste of space to listen to her, to turn him, to give him the chance nobody else had.

This damn crew. When were they going to learn that reaching out their hand to every bad guy in the galaxy was gonna end with them losing it?

He must have made a sound—he didn't realize he'd done it, but he must have, a gasp or some kind of cry or even, probably, a curse—because Cere said loudly, without turning around:

"Not now, Greez!"

The Inquisitor moved to grab at Cere's lightsaber hilt; she swung her off-hand up and used the Force to shove him back against the door. "Please," she said, clearer now, to the Inquisitor. He tried to move for the door behind him—but he wasn't fast enough. Cere swung back around and with a grasping of her fist, wrapped the Inquisitor in the metal of the door, ripping it from its frame to surround him, trapping him into place.

"I don't want to hurt you!" Cere snapped. "Just talk to me. Please. We can help you. We might be the *only* people who can help you."

Greez shook his head. They didn't have time for this. He knew she was in it, deep, wanted to save this kid so bad; but there were some things just couldn't be saved. If he could just get through to her, now that the Inquisitor was incapacitated, he might be able to get things back in order so they could get out of here as quickly as possible.

"Cere, c'mon," Greez said, stepping toward her. He would drag her out of here if he had to, her and Cal both, like those people who lifted whole spaceships off their pets with pure adrenaline. "He's stuck there. We can try to get through to him next time, but we gotta go."

Cere swung around, that desperate look still in her eyes. Greez knew what was up, knew she was painting Trilla's face onto this guy's head. He couldn't let her lose herself there.

"Listen, I know you wanna save everybody," Greez said, stepping forward again. "But we gotta move, okay? Cal needs saving, too, Cere. Merrin needs you. I need you. Got it?"

Greez took another step forward; he could touch her now, if he wanted to, wrap her up in a big four-armed hug and make her feel better about all the ways this galaxy was messed up. Looking up at her, the lines were smoothing from her face; she looked over at Cal.

"Okay," Cere breathed. "But next time—"

"You've failed," came a voice from behind Cere. She spun at the same time Greez moved to look—and they'd forgotten about the Inquisitor, who in that moment used pure brute strength to rip the metal cage from his body. With all his might, he *shoved* at Cere, sending her flying into a wall across the room, her back making a startling cracking noise as she hit it. With his other hand, he *pulled,* and Cere's lightsaber went soaring into his hand.

Greez had only a second to react. He didn't need the Force to know what was about to happen; it was clear as day. Cere, unwilling to do what had to be done in the moment, wasn't going to make it there in time—she was sliding down the wall, reaching out a hand to try, futilely, to regain her weapon. Greez knew he had to keep Cere from the guilt of what was about to happen; he owed her that much and more, especially since she'd just been trying to do the right thing, even if it ended up being very, very much the wrong thing.

Greez had been there. He knew what it was like, and he wasn't about to let Cere pay for it afterward.

She didn't let it happen to him. He wouldn't let it happen to her.

So, without thinking, Greez ran forward, taking advantage of his small stature and speed, slid around the Inquisitor, and launched himself in front of Cal's prone body as the Inquisitor spun and brought Cere's lightsaber swinging down.

And Greez started to scream.

CHAPTER 14

"Greez—?" Merrin came rushing out of the engine room as soon as she heard the clattering of the ramp, the green fire evaporating, anticipating Greez rushing back up with Cere and Cal hot on his tail, protecting him from any stray blasterfire that might try to follow them out of the prison. They'd managed to stabilize Irei before things had gotten too dire; but still, she was exhausted, and the sooner they got off this awful planet the better.

Which was why she really, really wanted the clatter on the ramp to be Greez running back with the only two Jedi she'd ever liked in the galaxy.

When Merrin exited the engine room, she was nearly relieved.

Nearly.

It *was* Greez. But not all of him.

Cere and Cal each had one of Greez's lower arms over their shoulders, hoisting him up the ramp as quickly as they could, given that Greez was out cold. Understandable, because Greez very clearly only had three of his four arms.

"Fret!" Merrin yelled back into the engine room. "Fly us out of here!"

Merrin rushed into the galley, and Fret burst out of the engine room behind her, no questions asked, sprinting toward the cockpit at the pan-icked note in Merrin's voice. Without speaking, Merrin slid her shoul-der into Cere's place to support Greez's body as Cere slammed the button to raise the ramp and rushed into the copilot's seat. Fret was al-ready initiating the launch sequence, the *Mantis* shaking itself to life as it rose above Murkhana's soil.

Glancing over at Cal as they made their way toward the couches around the holotable, Merrin saw how badly bruised his face was, how shaken up he looked, off balance. He caught her eye for just a second, and she knew that his worry was reflected in her face.

This crew had been through a lot together. But these were some of the worst injuries they'd suffered by far.

"Seats!" came the order through ship comms, Fret's commanding so-prano crackling through the speakers over Merrin's head. She and Cal worked in tandem to get the unconscious Greez strapped into a seat so as not to further damage him on a bumpy takeoff, and as soon as Mer-rin was buckled in next to him, she immediately began examining Greez's injury.

His top right arm was sheared off just above the elbow, a clean cut, clearly made by a lightsaber—nothing else, Merrin knew, cauterized so quickly and evenly. It's what made the lightsaber such a mean weapon; your opponent wouldn't bleed out, no matter how many times you hit them. Their wounds immediately sealed themselves, which meant you could, hypothetically, injure them over and over and over again, until they were begging you for mercy.

At which point you could simply slice them in half.

Or you could wait for them to try to heal, and start all over again.

She'd never had the urge to wield one herself, but Merrin *did* have to appreciate the lightsaber simply for its creativity in prolonging some-one's death.

Merrin looked up at Fret on the *Mantis* controls—a competent pilot in her own right, after all those years flying herself around the galaxy on research and reconnaissance for the Empire—and watched her struggle to operate Greez's complex system of levers and switches, designed spe-cifically for a Latero with four arms and a too-high caf tolerance.

She looked back at Greez's wound with a frown. Merrin knew what it was to operate missing a part of yourself that you once considered a key component, something you couldn't live without because you'd never had to consider living without it. Why would you? What were the odds that you would ever lose it?

When Merrin had struggled with the connection to her magick, she'd felt, sometimes, pain where it once lived in her chest, a twinge or an ache, an itch she couldn't scratch. That connection was dwindling, she'd thought, muted, too far from Dathomir and too removed from her dead sisters to ever replenish fully.

But she had gotten it back. It looked different now than it did before, felt different, came from a different place, slightly, in her soul and in her body. But it was there. It did what she needed it to do. She was different. Merrin was different. And she was better for it.

Greez would survive. He would do better than survive; he would thrive. Things would be different, and he would be different. The *Mantis* would be different. But it would be fine.

The hardest part would be getting there. And the only way out, Merrin knew, was through.

She reached out for one of Greez's uninjured arms and grasped his wrist, looking into eyes blurred with shock.

"You are going to be okay, Greez," Merrin said firmly, trying to push through his haze. "You have enough people here to hold the rest of your hands through it all. I promise you this."

Greez looked at her through shock-clouded eyes and nodded.

"Did we get 'em?" Greez mumbled, as the ship shook its way into space.

"We got 'em, Greez," Cal said, his voice overly reassuring. Merrin looked at Cal with curiosity; Cal just shook his head. Now wasn't the moment for whatever had really happened. Merrin would have to be content to wait.

"Get us into hyperspace," Cere said, voice clipped and strained.

"I'm trying my best," Fret said through gritted teeth. "Most of my flight experience comes from my little analyst solo ride, and that doesn't have a four-armed setup."

"I know, sorry." Cere held up one of her hands. "I'm just—"

"They're both going to be okay," said Fret, clearly trying to convince herself as much as anyone else as she struggled with the *Mantis*'s controls. "They're strong—Irei and Greez. Maybe the strongest ones on this damn ship."

"Punch it." Cere cut her off the second they were clear of atmo, and Fret wasted no time in sending the ship soaring out of Murkhana's range.

Merrin felt the familiar jerk in the ship and the unsettled feeling in her skull that meant they'd entered hyperspace; Fret and Cere had successfully maneuvered them away from the Inquisitor's ship in orbit over Murkhana, allowing them to escape into the unknown dark once again down a path that couldn't be followed, at least not for the moment. The ship was plunged into quiet and darkness once again, the overhead lights buzzing to life in a low hum.

Merrin watched Cere unclip herself from the copilot's seat, leaving the ship in Fret's control. She walked back toward Merrin and Cal and gently unbuckled Greez from his seat, lifting him over her shoulder.

"I'm going to see what I can do," she said without looking at either of them directly. "You two look after yourselves."

And then she walked Greez back into the bunks in silence, stewarding him into the bowels of the ship for treatment, BD-1 racing after them with stims ready.

The *Mantis* had given them all so much. It had given Merrin a home when all that had been left of hers was an empty shell. Given her a family, when the one she'd been born to had been so cruelly ripped from existence for no reason at all. It had given her a purpose when she'd felt like she might never have one again. Given her Cere and Greez and even that strange little droid. Given her Cal.

But it had taken so much from each one of them, too. It had taken Cal and Cere's Order. It had taken her away from the only home she'd ever known and unmoored her from her own past, her own sense of identity. It had taken her to Fret, who may have belonged to someone else all along, even if she hadn't known it when she met Merrin, wrenching her from happiness when it looked to be so close within reach. It had taken such a toll, to be constantly on the run.

And now it had taken Greez's arm.

Though she supposed that wasn't fair. It would have been the Inquisitor who did that. The *Mantis* wasn't to blame.

Still.

"Is there anything you can do? Your magick . . . ?" Cal was asking in a worried voice. It was hard for Merrin not to stare at Cal's bruised face, his torn-up shirt, and his bloodied hair, matting itself to his head. No one had come out of this in good shape, none of them.

Merrin shook her head slowly. "No. There isn't anything I can do for Greez right now. I had to . . ." She looked down at her lap with a sigh. "Fret brought Irei back. She was dying. It took everything I had to—" She turned her gaze up, hoping to catch Cal's, hoping he would understand. "I am no healer, Cal. You know this. It took everything I had, and after the reanimation spell I was already weak. I didn't realize . . ."

Cal was already nodding but she saw him wince through the pain of moving his neck like that just a little too soon. "It's okay, Merrin. I understand. And we kept the Shroud from the Empire. You did the right thing."

She hoped Cal was right. Because she honestly wasn't that certain about it herself.

And Merrin couldn't wait any longer. She had to know; there was too much tension in the ship for her not to. So she turned to Cal, ignoring the stricken look on his bruised face, and asked:

"Cal . . . what happened?"

Cal shook his head slowly. "I don't know."

It had been a very long night on the *Mantis,* the longest one Cere could remember.

When she'd righted herself from her hard hit against the mess hall wall, Cere had watched her own lightsaber slice through Greez's arm; had used the Inquisitor's momentary surprise to call the weapon back with the Force just in time to save Cal from the same grisly fate, if not much, much worse. She'd screamed, wrenching every piece of metal in the room into a cage that sealed the Inquisitor in long enough for her to get Greez and Cal to their feet and out the hatch in the roof, back to the courtyard where the *Mantis* had been waiting.

And then Cere had disappeared into the bowels of the ship with Greez on her back, feeling the weight of what she'd done, the responsibility.

Cere laid Greez down on his cot, left to find whatever bacta they had on the ship, and tried to find the strength to be sympathetic toward herself, tried to find kindness—she knew how strong and easy the lure of the dark side could be, knew it *too* intimately—but it was hard to reach sympathy while feeling absolutely *furious* with herself.

She knew better. She *knew* better.

Or did she, Cere wondered, as she returned to pull the burned jacket off Greez's back, revealing the cauterized injury to his arm. Cere had admitted to herself—even, once, to Cal—that she'd felt this inside her since Trilla, the desire to help rather than harm even when it wasn't wise.

She had found her way into the darkness after learning of Trilla's transformation into the Second Sister, escaping before the Sith could imprison her indefinitely, too. She'd done it again to save the *Mantis* crew from Darth Vader himself, when he otherwise would have killed them all.

Vader had said she would have made a good Inquisitor herself, and now Cere could see it, too; saw it in the way it was so easy, so *quick* to flood her mind, to warp her thoughts, and to overtake her emotions. That was the peril and the possibility of the dark side, always: so much power, but also so much power over *you*. It whispered things in your mind, your deepest fears, your darkest secrets; it told you things that you tried so hard not to believe, and made them convincing and real. It would do anything to get its claws into the soft tissue of your brain and *hold* itself there, shadows curling around the neurons, squeezing until you were gone and all that was left was the dark side, the darkness.

No balance, no light. It would choke it all out, and leave only itself.

She hated that she could sense that in Cal, too. The same predilection toward the darkness. He was motivated so much by spite, by vengeance toward the Empire, and that was a slippery slope that even Cal couldn't slide down with skill. She hated knowing that was in him, too, waiting for him to be weak enough for it to strike. And more than anything, she hated that Cal would have now seen that part of himself that he feared so much being made flesh. Given his own master's face and voice.

Hurting the people she loved because of it.

So she had vowed never, ever to do it again.

But in turning away from the darkness, had she gone too far in the other direction? Had she been so desperate to fix the mistakes she'd made with Trilla—something that could never be fixed, not now, not really—that she would put her own crew at risk?

She knew turning to the dark side was inexcusable. But she'd never expected to experience these kinds of consequences for abstaining from the fight altogether. Why shouldn't she have tried to save that Inquisitor when all their other options—Cal included—were lying done and dusted in the dirt?

If she was being honest with herself, completely honest in the dark and quiet hours, Cere was tiring of the fight. Skirmishes with the Empire would never have the lasting impact that Cere wanted to make on the galaxy, on what was left of the Jedi. There were times when she didn't even know if she was the right person to lead the *Mantis* crew anymore; her heart was moving slowly but surely in another direction, in one that wasn't in alignment with Cal's, as much as it hurt her to admit. She wanted to build a legacy, to build a foundation on which the next generation of fighters could grow strong and sure.

But there had been consequences to that want this time, Cere thought, as she slowly rubbed bacta into Greez's wound, knowing it wasn't enough and would never be enough. Cere hadn't been willing to act, and it had cost her. She wasn't committed enough to their purpose, and she'd put the people she'd sworn to protect in danger.

So Cere had taken Greez away and tried to fix her mistake, and she couldn't, of course, because there was no arm to reattach, and Cere had no magic, and the Force simply didn't work like that for them. The best she could do was clean the wound, wrap it, make sure that Greez was comfortable, and prepare to deliver him the news and an explanation when he woke up.

Merrin, weak and shaky after her efforts to keep Irei alive, had needed food and rest, but even so she was still right there to help Cal with his own wounds. In the galley, in the quiet of hyperspace, she helped him strip off his ruined shirt, his shredded pants, examining the skin below with the practiced eye of someone who had done this many times; she had helped him recover from so many injuries in the past. And yet Merrin noticed Cal still blushed a bit under her gaze.

Merrin took out the medpac from its spot above the galley sink, doused two cloths in disinfectant, and handed one to Cal before she began going over the cuts and scrapes on his back.

"Fair's fair. You wanna tell me what's going on with Fret?" Cal said, quietly enough that the woman in question couldn't hear him from the cockpit.

"I would love to," Merrin answered from behind him, the cloth making deft strokes over his exposed back, "but we haven't exactly had a moment to talk about it ourselves."

Cal hummed in interest. "So you really didn't know."

"No." She went over a cut a little more harshly than she needed to, and Cal winced. "I really did not."

Merrin's breath caught in her throat. She hadn't spoken a word to Fret after she'd gotten them into hyperspace. Since then, whenever she wasn't flying the ship, Fret had stayed vigil next to Irei's prone form on the workbench, holding one of her clawed hands, watching the slow rise and fall of the other woman's breath.

Merrin didn't know if Fret prayed. Frankly, she had to admit to herself that she knew almost nothing about her, aside from the shared trauma that had bonded them so quickly. That the feelings she'd had for this woman almost immediately were purely cosmic, not based on logic or knowledge but rather on gut instinct and chemistry and connection. It felt, to Merrin, like she'd been waiting for Fret, though she hadn't known it. The moment that Merrin's fire had been lost to her, the galaxy had delivered her the spark that would rekindle it. The kind of person that Merrin almost felt she had known before, even though it didn't make sense, if there had been a before at all.

But still, Merrin knew almost nothing about Fret. She obviously hadn't known about Irei.

She imagined, though, that if there was a higher power to which Fret had dedicated herself, Fret had been praying to her this past day.

Merrin would not pay attention to the pull that had on her heart; would ignore it at all costs.

She couldn't afford to listen to it now, not when it was already hurting so badly. That would only lead to more trouble.

She didn't know if she could look into Fret's eyes. Refused to think about how she had wanted to slay armies and kill men for the chance to see them crinkle up at the corners in a smile before they'd gone to Murkhana, before everything had gone wrong.

This was what happened when you let yourself care about someone, thought Merrin. You experienced their pain as your own. Foolish.

But Merrin's heart still ached all over again.

"I didn't know about Irei," Merrin repeated over Cal's cuts. "But you did."

Cal swallowed; Merrin imagined this was worse than the pain from the bacta.

"I didn't know her connection to the Shroud. And I still don't know what that means we do about Qeris," said Cal, deflecting from the real question for a moment. "But about Fret and Irei . . . I did. I went into your bunk and I—"

"I guessed that, too," Merrin cut in, pushing particularly hard into a scrape. "I thought you might have. I know you look after us. But Cal . . . you should have told me."

"I didn't put it together," he admitted, hissing when she hit a big cut. "Didn't realize until they were together, face-to-face. But it doesn't matter. I should have told you what I saw anyway. And I'm sorry."

Merrin sighed over his back, watching his shoulder blades move as he breathed. "It feels like all we're doing lately is hurting each other and apologizing for it. Why do you think that is?"

She knew Cal didn't have a good answer for that. And Merrin wasn't particularly looking for one.

They lapsed into silence together while working over Cal's wounds; she wouldn't have called it a comfortable silence, but more of a truce. It was enough for now.

Once Merrin had finished with his back, she took him by the shoulders and gently turned him to face her, her hands much softer than the stern expression she knew she wore on her face. She raised her cloth up to his face, moved in closer, and started to scrub the blood off his forehead. Her mouth was right over his nose; she could smell Cal after a fight, dirt and sweat mixed with his usual scent, leather and oil.

"The ship is very quiet right now," Merrin exhaled, moving the cloth down to Cal's own lips, cleaning a gash down the center of his bottom lip. Her other hand still rested on his shoulder. Cal's own were balled into fists at his side. "It's not going to stay that way."

"No," Cal agreed with a sigh. "It's not." He paused, taking a moment to gaze at her, and Merrin braced herself.

"You went real far, there, earlier. Worried me."

There it was. The thing Merrin had been waiting for. She stopped herself from pulling away and running, her urge, and instead stayed very still. She didn't want to scare him further.

"You're right." She nodded. "It was too far. And it scares me, sometimes, that I go there. I think—" she paused and gathered herself. "I think it's why I have been struggling with my magick."

She saw Cal exhale, his chest dropping. His gaze softened in the familiar way Merrin often noticed when he was talking to her. "Okay. Although, raising the dead *was* pretty helpful."

Just like Cal, to crack a joke at a time like this.

Merrin couldn't look at Cal right now, either, staring directly at his lips instead. Her voice was low enough that she knew it would be hard for Cal to hear, even this close. "Are we going to be okay?"

Cal sucked in a breath when Merrin pressed too hard on his cut. He reached up quickly and grabbed her hand by the wrist, gently but firmly, enough to drag her eyes up to his, finally.

"We," Cal said, not taking his eyes off hers, "are always going to be okay. Okay?"

He squeezed her wrist in reassurance.

"Okay," Merrin breathed. "Okay."

She went back to cleaning his face, and Cal put his fists back at his side.

Merrin very much wanted to believe him.

CHAPTER 15

Cal and the crew had been aboard the ship a full day and a full night since Cere had disappeared into its bowels with Greez, since Irei had been resting in the engine room, and things were tense. Nothing important had been said, everyone had stayed mostly separated, and it had been silent.

But Cal knew, as well as the rest of them, that it had been tense.

Which was why he was thrilled when he finally, on the second day, heard:

"Don't everybody get up at once," a gravelly voice said from the entrance to the crew bunks. Cal swung around from sitting over his caf, disrupting BD on his lap, to watch as Greez made his way, slowly, into the galley.

"Let me help," Merrin hurried over, offering Greez a hand as he struggled with his balance entering the galley. His movement was slow and unsteady, as if he were moving through mud.

"Don't!" Greez flung up a hand to stop Merrin before she could touch him. "Don't you dare."

Merrin stepped back, and Cal watched her school her features to keep the hurt off her face. Greez wore his usual outfit, but he looked entirely different: shirtless, his leather jacket resting over his shoulders, the sleeves hanging limply at his sides. He couldn't see it, but Cal knew that hiding under the bulk of his jacket, one of Greez's arms now ended just above the elbow, the stump wrapped in medical-grade gauze.

But it was mostly in his face that Cal noticed the difference. Greez was always on the wrong side of grumpy; it was part of his charm. But he'd never seen Greez look like this. He looked more green than gray, his cheeks sagged, the lines on his forehead were deeper. And beyond that, he looked . . .

Cal had seen that kind of expression before, usually when he was in trouble with his masters. It was the kind of face worn by someone who was so, so deeply disappointed and furious with the people they trusted that they couldn't form any kind of emotion at all.

Blank. Blank, and terrifying.

"Where is she." It was more of a demand than a question out of Greez, and everyone else on the ship looked up with fear and shame the moment they heard Greez enter the *Mantis*'s kitchen.

"Here," said Cere, walking up to the galley from where she'd been resting on a bench in the common room. "Greez, I—"

Greez was already shaking his head. "Not you." Cal watched Cere's brow crease. "The stormtrooper."

"I have a name." Fret came storming out of the engine room, and Cal thought her face was in shambles; it was clear she'd been crying, a strange thing to see on a face typically so tough.

Greez was in Fret's space before anyone on the crew had a chance to stop it. "You think that matters to me?" he demanded, shoving a finger as close as he could get it into the tall Keshiri's face. "You left me and my crew to die, and now you're back on board like nothing happened? Because I got news for you, stormtrooper." Greez shrugged the shoulder under which only one arm now protruded. "Something happened."

Fret's eyes widened as she took in Greez's injury, but she stayed on the defensive. "If you're trying to put the blame on me for that and not the *Imperials*—"

Cal saw Greez's eyes get fiery and knew he had to step in. This couldn't go on. Cal moved forward, touching Greez gently on the other shoulder, keeping him from making any mistakes he might regret.

"He's right," Cal said to Fret, softer than Greez, but not by much. It's not that Greez was wrong; he just didn't want the two coming to blows about it. "You disappeared with your friend. She's hurt; we're not in the habit of leaving people to die. But you'd better be able to explain yourself." Cal ticked off her sins on his fingers as he spoke. "You lied—or at the very least omitted the truth, that there was the possibility that the Shroud was a person, and not merely a datapad or plans. You lied—or, again, conveniently omitted—that you had a *deeply* personal connection to the Shroud and the person who created it. You absolutely lied to us about leaving the Empire. And then you abandoned us as an Inquisitor was bearing down on our location."

Cal stared at her, hard and pointed. "So you'd better be able to explain. Or we're dropping the both of you at the nearest rest stop and not looking back."

"You really want to blame me for what happened?" Fret said, hurt in her voice. "You really think things would have gone differently if I'd stuck around with the walking target back there?" She tipped her head in the direction of the engine room. "There wasn't a thing I could have done that would have made things better if I'd kept her close to you two. The Inquisitor would have had his hands on her, or she'd be dead. Either way, we'd be worse off."

"Easy for you to say." Greez shrugged Cal's hand off his shoulder and turned away, moving on unsteady legs down the steps and toward the common room's semicircular couches.

"Fret." Cal sighed. "You gotta tell us what's going on. What's *really* going on. It's the only way we're going to be able to help you."

"*If* we can help you," added Cere. With a sigh of her own, she moved to follow Greez to the common room. Neither of them were looking at each other, either.

"Fat chance," Greez muttered from his seat, keeping his eyes on the floor.

Merrin wouldn't meet Fret's looks; Cal wouldn't meet Merrin's; Greez and Cere were acting like the other didn't exist. BD-1 was hiding somewhere, probably with the bogling; they both knew better than to be around the crew when the energy in the air was this rancid.

"Fine." Fret moved toward the holotable room, too, and Cal watched Merrin follow a step behind her.

"Then talk," Merrin spat with more venom than Cal thought to hear out of her as she picked the seat directly across from Cere. All of them were equally spread around the map room's couches, none of them getting too close to the others, and all of them keeping their gazes trained on the relative inoffensiveness of the holotable as it glowed in the center of the room.

"Talk," Merrin repeated. Cal saw she had finally dragged her eyes from the map over to Fret's. The pain in Merrin was clearly back, or hadn't gone away, and Cal still hated to see it; would do everything within his power to fix it. "Talk, or get off my ship for good."

"I thought she was dead," Fret started, staring down at her hands, and Cal watched her worry at the skin around her nails. Merrin did that sometimes, too. "We met when I was training to be an analyst; Irei was apprenticing at her parents' droid repair shop in town. I . . ." Cal watched Fret's eyes flick over to Merrin for just a moment, and then back down to her hands. One of her fingers was bleeding; she'd picked a hangnail too deep. "I fell in love with her. We fell in love."

Out of the corner of his eye, Cal saw Merrin stiffen.

"We had to keep it a secret, obviously; as a trainee, free time was limited, and we were discouraged from fraternizing, with each other or with people on the outside. Took away from the focus on the work," Fret continued.

Cal was studying both Fret and Merrin closely as the woman talked. Fret took a moment to suck at her finger; Merrin studied the floor. She paused, a faraway look clouding her face.

Cal knew it well. It was the memory of learning that the things you thought were good, the people you thought you knew and could trust, were actually less worthy and less worthwhile than you ever could have imagined.

"But then . . . Irei admitted she was Force-sensitive—not enough to be trained, but enough to stand out." Fret let that hang in the air for a moment, let it settle into the cracks and crevices of the map room, into Cal's head and his thoughts. That changed everything.

That explained everything.

"Through her eyes, her fear—I saw everything the Empire truly was." Fret swallowed, back in the moment. "She helped me see that the Empire wasn't what I'd been told it was; what I saw from the data streams I combed through each day; how it was hurting people. How I would be hurting people when I joined them. She showed me what it meant to be part of the broader galaxy; that what individuals do matters. That I mattered."

She sighed, the kind of deep sigh of regret Cal also knew intimately. "She spent a year working on a way to stay hidden from the Empire. Irei was—is," she corrected herself, after a moment, "a genius with mechanics. She was always wasted on wrecked droids in her parents' shop. I knew that if anyone would have been capable of doing it, if anyone could have found a way, it would be her. I didn't know she'd finished it; I didn't think she wanted to, sometimes. She was too scared. But I guess she did it after all." Fret paused. "The Shroud. A good name for it. I knew she could do it."

From across the table, Cere nodded. She knew what it was to believe in the potential of people, even when they were scared.

Cal knew that well, too.

"She asked me to leave, to run away with her," Fret continued. "She didn't want me involved with them; she was willing to hide us for as long as it took to keep us safe, until they stopped looking."

"So why didn't you?" Merrin's voice was cold, curt. It was like an ice pick to Cal's heart.

Fret looked wrecked, like she'd spent so much of her life avoiding thinking about this moment and was now so imminently confronted with it that she had no choice but to dredge up all the feelings she'd spent years and years avoiding.

Cal knew that feeling, too.

"I was scared," Fret answered, her voice barely above a whisper. "The consequences for deserters to their posts are . . . dire. And," she continued, sighing, "I was foolish. I thought I could change things from the inside, use my position within the Empire to warn people or keep them safe, somehow . . ." She shook her head, clearly frustrated by her past self. "The Empire was all I ever knew. To learn that they were—what they were—"

She paused. "I thought I would do Irei more harm than good on the run with her. I thought that, from the inside, from a position of privilege, I could more effectively keep her safe. I stayed, and I convinced her to stay, too. I thought I was doing the right thing for her; for both of us. I thought I was being *selfless.*" She spat the last word out like it was poison. "Irei didn't think that. She thought I was choosing the Empire over her. And I don't blame her now. I get it. It was only a matter of time before they discovered her," she said, voice low. "I'd stopped going to see her, but they found her anyway. Burned the whole shop to the ground. Everything her parents had built, everything she had . . . I thought they'd taken her. Or killed her. I knew it was the end. And I—" Cal saw the tears in Fret's eyes now. "It was my fault. I put her in danger. I put her at risk."

"How?" Cal asked. "Just by being in love with her?"

"No." Fret shook her head. "No. Once I found out about Irei's— condition—I started manipulating Imperial records. Her parents worked for the local Imperial garrison, repairing droids, fixing electronics; they were in contact with the local troopers and officers all the time. Their names were all over Imperial records and reports. She was constantly terrified to be found out. Anytime she popped up in any kind of routine surveillance, I would alter a name, swap out a picture record, delete a security holo. Little things; things I didn't think anyone would notice. I thought if she didn't exist at all in Imperial records that she would never be found out. Especially once she went on the run."

"They still found her, though," said Cere.

Fret bit her lip. "This was three years ago; I'm twenty-one now, but I was still really just a kid. Not as good at this stuff as I am now. I messed up. Ended up drawing attention to her. Nobody knew it was me who'd been manipulating her records, but . . . they still found her because of me."

She took a deep breath; steadied herself. "And so it was my fault," she said. "My fault that she died."

"But she'd escaped," Cal offered after a pause, seeing that Fret clearly needed someone to help her go on.

"I don't know how." A tear fell out of Fret's eye onto her bloodied finger; the combination of blood and tears pooled and hit the *Mantis*'s floor. "I still don't know how. I still can't believe she's alive. She's—"

Fret stopped to wipe her eye frustratedly, like she hated that her body was acting without her consent to produce tears. "That's what changed me. That's why I committed to leaving. It took her death for me to see my foolish mistake. I spent my entire career as an Imperial trying to figure out ways to help others. I found a way to run counter-intel, sifting through data streams, intercepting comms for illegal activity. Doing what I wanted to do for Irei, but right. When I started to hear murmurs on the channels about something called the Shroud, it led me to Qeris's doorstep. He was the one who gave me the rest of the information I needed, the one who told me that the schematics did exist, that Irei had finished them, and that he could point me toward them. I assumed they were on a datacard. And then I spent an age and a small fortune figuring out how to get myself to Irei's life's work. To save the last and only part of her that I could. To get myself out."

"Which, for the record, you didn't," Greez said snidely.

Fret's head snapped up to look at Greez, at that. "I had to stay active, had to stay aboveboard. I knew that after what had happened with Irei, if I was caught out of line, even by a single step, I'd be investigated and— disappeared. I had to appear to be the perfect Imperial, until the right moment."

Fret looked like she didn't know whether to be desperate, hurt, or furious. "That's not when I heard about the *Mantis*. Heard about all of you." She flushed. "It was Qeris. He also gave me the information I had about the *Mantis*. I—lied about that, too. To butter you up a bit, admittedly. You're not that well known among the Imperials, I'm afraid. You're not a beacon of hope to people on the inside. But . . ." Fret took a deep breath. "But you were to me. Once I learned about you, that's what you became to me. So it wasn't completely a lie. So I put myself in your path, tracked your movements, made sure I knew where you'd be and when, and made sure I was going to be there, too. I knew you'd take me to safety."

She sighed. "But I also knew that I wouldn't be any use to you if all my access codes were months out of date, and if I couldn't continue to track troop movement across the galaxy. The only way—the *only* way— I was ever going to be able to help Qeris help you get the Shroud schematics was to retain my access to the compound on Murkhana. Those codes change every few hours. I was always going to leave *after*."

"Ohhhh." Greez nodded, the sarcasm dripping off every syllable like acid. "You were going to leave *after* you put our ship and entire crew in danger for possibly weeks at a time while we went off to find your dead girlfriend's little pet project that maybe never existed at all? Is that it? You calculated the odds in your mind, and this crew—this crew that was, as you said, *your only chance at getting out*—was an acceptable expenditure to you?"

"No—"

"It was okay," Greez continued, undeterred, "that in the meantime, your *continued access,* for all we knew, could have led the Imperials straight to our ship? You don't think access goes both ways? Are you really that foolish?"

"*No,*" Fret said, louder this time, stopping Greez's tirade before he could start it up again. "No. I knew how to make sure they weren't going to follow me. I wasn't going to make the same mistakes I did with Irei. I wasn't that important; I did stats work on the Outer Rim. No one was going to be looking for me. I wasn't due back to report for another month. I was checking in under an assumed location bouncing off several different locator beacons. I had a long time to plan this; I wasn't going to mess this up for me or for you. For any of us."

She took a deep breath. "Qeris told me stories of the *Mantis* crew. Of Cal Kestis. Of—" The purple on her face deepened for a moment, and Cal noted with pleasure that at least she had the decency to feel some shame. "Of the witch. No one else was going to pick up a stranger on the edge of space—an Imperial, no less—and give them the benefit of the doubt. I would never have put you in danger."

"And yet here I am, short an *entire arm!*" Greez slammed himself back down into his seat, his lower arms crossed, refusing to look at anyone.

Cal had to admit, he had a point. As much as he sympathized with Fret and Irei—especially Irei—they had acted completely irresponsibly, put his crew in danger more than once, withheld sensitive information . . .

And hurt Merrin.

Still. Cal had experienced a fragment of this story in his echo, had felt the way that Fret felt about Irei, had known the despair and the desire, the all-encompassing love and the mind-boggling fear. He had been in Fret's shoes, literally, and had experienced her emotions, her thoughts, the way it felt when she kissed Irei; and, so much worse, the way it felt to turn her down.

He knew Fret was telling the truth. He had been there.

And as much as they weren't family—not like the *Mantis* crew—as far as Cal was concerned, any Force-sensitive on the run from the Empire deserved a shot. Deserved the best shot that he could give them.

What was the point of fighting the Empire if everyone they were trying to save ended up dead by their hands first?

Fret was leaking properly, now, tears spilling over her cheeks unbidden, and Cal knew he had to say something because no one else on this ship was going to, not anyone but him.

"They were never going to stop looking, Fret." Cal could feel the weight of his words like the weight he felt on his chest just thinking about what Irei had been through; what she was going to continue to go through, for the rest of her life, because of something she couldn't help, didn't ask for, maybe didn't even want. "You would have been on the run with her forever. You would never have been safe, not for a second. I understand that you made the decisions you did based on fear. Fear can have a powerful impact. But . . ." Cal looked at her with as much sympathy as he could get to pour out of his eyes, to show her that he understood. "You're on the run now anyway. Both of you. What are we going to do about it?"

"Oh, absolutely not." Greez was standing almost instantly. "Did you miss the part of this where these two star-crossed suckers nearly cost us everything?" He pointed at his arm. "I told you all to stop taking these idiotic missions before we ended up dead, and look at us. *Look at my frickin' arm, Cal!*"

"From the way I understood it"—Fret jerked her head toward Cere—"that was *her* fault."

"You don't understand a thing," snapped Cere.

"Doesn't she?" Greez rounded on Cere now, fierce hurt shining clear through his face. "Because when I walked into the room with that Inquisitor, *Jedi,* it sure looked like you weren't gonna make the moves you needed to make were it not for me and my former arm. Or are you really gonna tell me it's not your fault, that you were just trying to save everyone? Even *him*? No matter the cost?"

"You did *what*?" Cal couldn't believe what he was hearing; he refused to believe it. Cere wouldn't. She knew better. She would never. "Cere, tell me he doesn't know what he's talking about."

Cere wouldn't meet his eyes, and that's when Cal knew that Greez, somehow, wasn't lying.

"Cere," Cal said slowly. "Is this really true?"

She looked up, and Cal saw in her face that it was.

"I can't believe this." Cal dropped his head into his hands. "You're the reason this happened? To Greez?"

"No," Greez said firmly. "The *Inquisitor* is the reason this happened to me."

"No, *Fret* is the reason this happened to Greez," Merrin snapped, finally breaking her long silence. "I cannot believe you would blame this on Cere when everything she did was to save *you,* after *you* sent me away for *no* reason, when I should have been there, I should have had your back. *Fret* is the one who ran off with her—*girlfriend.*" Merrin struggled even to get the word out, Cal could hear it. "With two extra bodies in the room, we could have defeated anyone."

"Two extra—?" Fret laughed in disbelief. "Did you miss the part where Irei is not exactly a master on the battlefield. She's an *engineer.* She needed to be taken to safety. Otherwise, that would have left us without the Shroud *and* a person down!"

"Oh, and that's why you did it?" Merrin turned on her, finally looking the other woman dead in the eye. "Merely out of the kindness of your heart for all the poor little Jedi in the galaxy? For the *Shroud*? Not because you'd found your—"

"Yes!" Fret shouted. "Yes, of *course* because I had found *my dead girl-friend, Merrin,* you *have* to understand—"

"Safe to say I don't understand *anything*," Merrin spat. "I really thought I did. And I do *not*."

"We have to finish the mission," Fret said sharply. "We have to take Irei back to Qeris to keep her safe—"

"Whoa, we promised Qeris we would get the schematics away from the Empire. We had yet to decide whether we'd *actually* deliver them to him," said Cere. "And do we really think handing over a *person* is the same thing as—"

"We don't have to do anything you say, stormtrooper," interrupted Greez. "We have to hide our asses as quickly as possible before Brother Dearest back there catches up to us and roasts us all on a spit, your sweet lizard-lady included, and drop you off at the first breathable-air planet we find."

"We can't just abandon them," said Cere.

Cal shook his head. "Is that you talking?" He knew he was going to regret what he said next in anger before he said it, but he couldn't stop himself anyway; it was too late. "Or is that your guilt about Trilla?"

"I take responsibility for Greez's loss," offered Cere. "I never meant for any of this—"

"No, of course you didn't," Greez drawled. "All we ever mean is to throw ourselves in front of the Empire like the galaxy's tiniest wrecking ball and hope that we somehow miraculously come out of it unscathed every single time. And that's not going to happen! It's gonna get worse! We're all tired, and we've been on the run for *years,* and where's it *got* us—?"

"One step closer to defeating the Imperials!" Cal couldn't believe what he was hearing. "That's the whole point of us. That's why we're here." Cal was still caught up on the fact that he had been pretty certain— for years, in fact—that even if they all had other ideas about *how* to go about it, at the end of the day they were all on board the *Mantis* for the same reason, the same ultimate purpose.

There was only ever one ultimate purpose. There was only one reason, as far as Cal had been able to see, that he had been put into this messy, beautiful galaxy.

And that was to make sure no one ever had to suffer like he had, ever again.

"No." Cere was shaking her head. "Cal, you know that's not true. We're here to establish a future for the Jedi. That's the answer. It's the only way. Greez is right: We're too small to make a real dent—"

"No, we're here for the *Shroud*," Fret insisted. "That's our *mission*—"

"That's all well and good for you"—Merrin cut Cere off without standing on ceremony—"but I'm not here for any of those reasons. I'm here to put a very specific dent in the Empire, the one I can never put in the Separatists. A dent in the shape of every dead Nightsister. And this ridiculous nonsense has thrown us so far off that path, I hardly know what I'm doing here."

"Well, I sure as hell don't know what *I'm* doing here anymore," snapped Greez.

"I can't believe this," Cere said incredulously. "We're never going to be able to help the other targets of the Empire in the galaxy if we can't even help this *one*—"

"How are we all not here to bring down the Empire?" Cal demanded.

"Stop! Enough!" A soft, sibilant voice from the back of the galley: Irei was up, holding on to the engine room doorframe with what looked like all the strength she had. Fret was up in the space of a moment, hustling herself to wedge a shoulder under Irei's tall frame to help keep her upright. She walked the Nikto woman down to the benches by the holotable while everyone watched, shocked out of their argument for just long enough that it seemed ridiculous to start it up again.

"Enough, please," Irei said softly. "I'm sorry to have brought such trouble to your crew, when I owe you so much. I'm sorry to say, too, that the Empire will still be coming after me, and the Shroud, for as long as I draw breath—but it sounds like I'm not alone in that predicament here, am I?"

Cal shook his head. "Unfortunately for all of us, you're in the best possible company."

"She's right." Cere stood, an air of finality in her voice. "And Greez is right. We have to hide, we have to get Greez medical help, and we're in no position to be making decisions right now." She turned to her pilot. "Can you fly?"

"Of course I can fly." Greez rolled his eyes—but Cal could see the questioning in his own eyes. His setup was made for four arms. Fret at the console hadn't exactly been smooth sailing. *Could* he fly?

"Okay," Cere said, nodding. "Then navigate to these coordinates. We're going to need to lie low. And we're all going to need to get our heads on straight before we decide what we're going to do next."

And as much as Cal appreciated the order—it was the same thing he would have suggested, if he'd had a couple more minutes to clear out his head—he couldn't help but wonder: What *was* going to be next for the crew? That he couldn't yet answer that question worried him, but he knew he would find an answer.

CHAPTER 16

Just hours after everything had gone wrong, the *Mantis* arrived on Zimara. As Greez brought the ship shaking into atmo, Cal noted how surprisingly close they had been to Cere's latest find for a brief respite. They'd found a few places, over the years, where they could be relatively certain they wouldn't be followed when they needed to catch their breath after a particularly risky mission, or just one that had gone sideways, but never for longer than a night or two at the most. It was too risky. Staying on the move was exhausting; sometimes it was better to find your way into a nydak den and lie low until you could be certain—more certain, at least—that the eyes of the galaxy had decided to move on.

Zimara was a smallish moon on the Outer Rim, a village backwater populated mostly by settlers who had escaped one dangerous life or another in the Core Worlds and wanted to remain off the Empire's sensors. They didn't look too closely at ships that came or went, and that suited the needs of the *Mantis* just fine. This place in particular was so far on the edge of inhabited space that few people thought to look out here for anyone of import—and it was just large enough that no one noticed comings and goings with much interest. Perfect.

As the *Mantis* came in to land, Cal watched Greez from his vantage point on the nearby couch. He felt strangely calm, in the moment, not letting himself think about what had just happened until they were safely off the ship and he was alone. He'd stayed in the room where they'd all argued, while everyone else had scattered: Fret and Irei back to the engine room, Merrin into the galley, Greez and Cere into the cockpit. The ship had been eerily silent, save for BD-1's occasional beeps at the bogling, who answered with muted grumbles. It seemed even the smallest occupants aboard knew that something wasn't quite right.

That was made even more clear by the ship's bumpy landing, practically unheard of for Greez. But Cal could tell he was and had been struggling; he'd seen the frustration in Greez's movements as he kept trying to reach out with his missing arm for controls that were no longer within his grasp. Cere would pick up his slack from the copilot's chair, making sure to always be there to hit buttons and pull levers that Greez couldn't, but it wasn't the same as when Greez was in total control.

Cal thought of the way it must have felt recently for Merrin, to reach for something that had been such an intrinsic part of her, and come up dry. Something that had made up so much of her identity for her entire life. How it had felt for him to try to reach for the Force after suppressing his abilities for so long, after the trauma and pain that using them had caused him and everyone he loved. How it felt to lose connection to that thing, to have to find a new way to it; to have to learn what it meant to be a Nightsister without planet or power, to be a Jedi without an Order.

He watched Greez reach futilely for a lever, and he knew what the next few years were going to look like for the pilot.

And Cal hated it.

"Forty-eight hours," said Cere, gearing up as the rest of the crew filtered their way back toward the ramp, kitted out in their own gear for overnight stays. "You have forty-eight hours to get your heads on straight. And when that's up, and I mean to the minute, every single one of you better be back on this ramp so we can figure out what's next. Understood?"

Cal watched Fret and Irei nod as Fret fitted a belt around her waist. Greez was obviously in a hurry to get off the ship, but Merrin just looked—scared.

She looked like she genuinely wasn't certain if everyone was going to be back on that ramp in forty-eight hours, or if they were going to lose people for good.

Or maybe, Cal thought, he was just projecting. Because there was a part of him—a big part—that wondered the exact same thing.

That, if everyone else on board was so singularly focused on their own wants and needs, and if they weren't going to continue to align with his own, well . . . Cal wondered if they had any reason, really, to come back here at all.

As Cal forced himself to drag his eyes away from Merrin, to walk down the ramp, he took a deep breath in and remembered what he'd read about Zimara on the way here.

It was the closest moon to the system's nearest star, tidally locked, which meant one side of the planet was consistently in day and the other in night. Most of the inhabitants lived on the night side, where it stayed relatively cool, and worked on the day side, where they could cultivate crops and harvest solar power with ease. The acrid burn of the air as it hit Cal's throat reminded him of Bracca; though there weren't any scrapyards, something about the barren, cracked land, the persistent sun, and even the deadly potential of staying for too long on the light side of the planet was enough to make Cal feel a kind of nostalgia.

He blinked, and the planet's parched air dried the tears right out of his eyes.

As the *Mantis* crew hit the bottom of the ramp on the planet's dark side, landing just meters away from the borderline between night and day, the crew all, for the most part, went their separate ways. Cere told them she'd be settling in at what passed for the local library, as was her favorite thing to do on rest days wherever they were, searching for any lost piece of information on the Jedi; Fret and Irei moved to follow her into the village, needing continued medical services for Irei. Merrin strode off toward the merchant square without so much as a backward glance. Greez walked straight toward the light-side border.

Cal took a moment, once his feet hit gritty dirt, to decide where he needed to be at that moment. Forty-eight hours; not exactly a lifetime, but not a short time, either. He needed somewhere he could feel safe and comfortable; somewhere he could really think, without distraction.

After a few more breaths, he headed off for some solitary reflection.

Cal walked through the market square on the planet's scorching light side, letting the heat build up his own hot temper, in disbelief about what this mission had come to. The more he'd walked, the more his pain had turned to frustration. He at least took some cold comfort in knowing that everyone else on the *Mantis* crew was having as miserable a time as he was; no one looked happy when they left the ship, and with good reason.

It seemed like Cal had, somehow, been completely mistaken about his crew this entire time. Go figure. He'd thought they were all on the same page—that they were family, and they all were on his team—but, Cal supposed, he'd thought wrong.

It seemed none of them were there for the same reasons. And Cal wasn't sure what that might mean, or if they truly weren't aligned in their goals.

Cal wandered around the square looking at absolutely nothing, trying to keep his frustration as fully in check as he could. He was entirely on his own. Greez had refused help from anyone, wanting his own alone time, but had assured them all he'd be finding a medical center. But Cal wasn't so certain and suggested to BD-1 that it was a bad idea for Greez to be alone just then. So BD had scuttled off after their Latero friend. Cal knew how it felt to be in the lowest of low times; the last thing he wanted was for Greez to end up in whatever passed for this village's casino, spiraling into a dark place himself. BD would keep an eye on Greez. Even though Greez couldn't understand the droid, Greez and BD had always had a good relationship, after they'd gotten to know each other. Cal knew Greez found the little droid's presence very comforting—most people did, with the exception of Merrin, who was mostly neutral about him, in her own weird and kind of scary way, even though he sometimes thought he sensed something more. And BD knew that Cal would be all right on his own, once he'd calmed down.

And he *was* going to calm down. He was just—so frustrated.

So frustrated, and so, so scared.

On his third lap around the market stalls, he started to orient himself in the space in an attempt to center his focus, to keep himself away from any dangerous paths in his mind that he wasn't prepared to go down at this moment or ever. He breathed in the searingly hot air, feeling it burn at his nostrils. That brought to him the sharp, vinegared aroma of the nancili being cooked up in various tucked-away corners of the market. It was Zimara's most common dish, made of something bitter and delicious they grew on the light side of the planet. It was a bit spicy for Cal's taste, but he managed.

Finally, he set himself up with a repair shop that looked trustworthy, using their workbench to tool away at his rebreather for a bit, making sure it was in good working order after Murkhana. It had been damaged, slightly, in the fight with the Inquisitor; he needed a moment to fix it. This was something that always brought Cal peace; even, sometimes, in the middle of a mission, if he was able to find the time and space for it. There was something about the finicky nature of the process of fixing and upgrading his gear—the way in which he had to be so careful about what he removed and how he replaced it, so as to keep it in perfect balance, just as he tried to be with the Force. It steadied him; grounded him. Gave him time to empty his mind, and to think about absolutely nothing but the task at hand.

It was always useful, and this day, this time, was no exception.

When Cal had finished with his rebreather, he had a fully functional, smoothly operating tool, and a weary mind. He needed rest and meditation; he was always better after a good sleep.

Tomorrow would be a new day. And then—then he would deal with all this. But tonight?

Tonight, he just needed to close his eyes and pretend none of it was happening at all.

By the time Cal had found his way to a small hotel, rented a room, and set himself up on the tiny straw mattress in the corner, he was exhausted. It was impossible, really, for him to tell if it was evening here yet, or anywhere close to the time when he could reasonably call it bedtime, but that was one of the perils of living as a nomad; you made your own time, often, and hoped that the rest of the galaxy would keep up with it.

Or at the very least, your own crew.

Before sleep, Cal leaned back against the wall, crossed his legs, and placed his hands gently over his knees. He took a deep breath and felt himself fall into the dark, deep void that was the Force, sliding gently into a meditative state that would help heal his mind and prepare him for both battle and rest in a way that he couldn't find anywhere else. As he swam through the deep waters of the energy of the universe, he heard a voice in his mind, unbidden, but still welcome:

Do not make hasty decisions based only on your emotions, it said. It was Jaro Tapal, his first master.

And even in death, he was still frustratingly right.

When Cal woke up in his little straw bed, he wasn't alone in his room. He felt it through the air, first, the way he could feel the wind on leaves and the breath of flowers when they were ready to unfurl in the morning light—not that there was morning light here. But he knew, as he was pulled out of sleep, could sense it, that he was being watched.

He sat bolt-upright in bed, one hand already on the lightsaber under his pillow, when he realized he recognized the energy, would know the smell of that particular vine anywhere, and relaxed when he saw he was right: It was Cere. She was seated on the concrete floor against the opposite wall, arms crossed over her chest. She looked like she hadn't slept in days; maybe she hadn't, Cal realized.

"Are you going to be mad at me, or can we talk?" Cere asked, knowing that once Cal was up, he was up. That always annoyed Merrin, the galaxy's least-morning person, but it's just always how Cal had been. Probably all those years on the run.

Dark.

"I'm not mad at you." Cal leaned back on his palms. "Okay, I'm a little bit mad at you. But that doesn't mean we can't also talk."

Cere nodded curtly. "You and I have to get ourselves in order or the rest of the crew won't be able to. They follow our lead. We have to be the adults here."

"Funny, I always kind of thought there were no adults on the *Mantis*," Cal said wryly.

Cere cracked a smile. "You might not be wrong about that. But we have to at least act like it today. We can't be breaking down like that. It's going to jeopardize our whole mission."

And there was the crux of it, right out of the gate. "And what's that, Cere? Really. What *is* our mission?"

Cere blinked at Cal, those big watery brown eyes staring right into his soul, right through him. "It seems we're not going to agree on this, no matter what the next words out of my mouth are, because I know they're not going to be what you want to hear."

"Try me," Cal said, shrugging.

Cere sighed. "All right. Our mission is . . . to guarantee that the wisdom of the Jedi lives on. To establish a . . ." Cal watched her struggle for the right word for a second. "A *legacy*," she landed on with a firm nod. "There has to be meaning to what the Jedi believed and taught, even if there aren't Jedi to pass that wisdom on to. It's valuable knowledge about life and the nature of the galaxy, and it shouldn't disappear just because its stewards are no more. And it might help the people who take up this fight after us, and there has to be a safe haven out there, not just for our rest stops, but for people like us all the time. For people like Irei."

Cal looked away. She was right: He didn't agree, even though he saw the sense in her words. They weren't there yet.

"What's the point of setting something up for the future if we haven't even managed to make a dent in the Empire yet?" Cal asked. "What future are you even setting up for?"

"It's the future, Cal, but it's also *now*. People need symbols," she said softly. "We aren't always going to be around to be the thing that inspires hope in people like Fret, people caught up in something they want to escape. I don't know that this Circlet I found is the answer." She sighed. "I don't know that it has to be. But it's . . . it feels like the first step. The first step to building something that people can look at—that people who need help, and hope, can look at—and say, *This is a thing that exists. It has existed, and will continue to exist. It can help me. And I want to chase after it.*"

Cal nodded, still looking at the ground. He heard her, even if their priorities were not the same. But he knew that fighting was only half the battle.

The other half was having something to fight *for*.

"You know this is no kind of real life, Cal," Cere implored gently. "Look at how it chafes even at Greez, and he's the least homebody kind of guy I've ever met. You saw how the idea of a life on the run tore Fret and Irei apart, eventually. There are kids out there, right now, Cal, kids like you were, like—" She nearly stopped herself, and Cal could hear her push herself to keep going. "Like Trilla was. They're going to grow up knowing that they're never safe, just like you did. Don't you want to put an end to that?"

"Of *course* I do!" Cal couldn't stand to listen anymore, not without a proper response. "Of *course* I do, Cere, don't you think that's what this is all about? Is that really what the *Mantis* crew is supposed to be doing with our limited time here? We don't even know if there are going to *be* Jedi in the future. Are we going to teach everyone about the lessons of the Jedi? You and me alone? Are we the new Jedi Council?" Cal shook his head. "You know as well as I do that the only long-term solution is eliminating the Empire once and for all. Everything else is an excuse, a joke."

Cere raised an eyebrow. "I'm sorry; do you think us taking down the Empire on our own is *less* funny than us setting up an entire Jedi legacy on our own? Are both of those not equally ridiculous? Why is your huge, impossible thing more legitimate than mine? And I'm not even suggesting we *do* that, by the way. Master Yoda, I am not."

"I don't know how we do it," Cal said with a sigh. "But I don't know how we do anything else, either."

"What have we been doing these last few years, Cal?" Cere pulled her legs up, wrapping her arms around her knees. "Even the big jobs we've taken, the ones that were really supposed to make a dent, have barely left a scratch on the Empire's hull. We're four people. Greez is right: If we're not smarter about this, we're all going to get killed. And then there's going to be *no one* left to fight."

"So, what." Cal frowned. "You're worried about wisdom for people in the future. I'm worried about survival for people *now*. That's why we destroyed the holocron, Cere. To avoid exposing those kids to this kind of life." He ran a hand through his hair, frustrated. "We're a *weapon*, Cere. *I'm* a weapon. Point me in a direction, let me go, I'll do damage. But building something?" He shook his head. "I don't know how to do that. I've never had to."

Cere rested her chin on her knees, and Cal thought that he had never seen her look quite so impossibly small before. She looked . . . sad. And she looked halfway to defeated. He hated seeing her like that.

But he imagined he might just look exactly the same.

"I'm mostly worried about *you*," Cere admitted, her voice quiet. "Your dogged determination to topple the Empire stops you from seeing the good we've been doing in the moment. Even these small things, they've all helped, even if we can't keep doing this forever. Single-minded obsession is dangerous, for a Jedi. Even good intentions can lead to a dark path."

Cal swallowed. He didn't want to hear that.

But he knew he had to.

"I know you're scared," Cere said. "I am, too. I don't know how to do it, either," said Cere. "And I know you're right: There's no good solution. Not to any of this. And I don't think we're going to solve it today."

Cal nodded, slowly, while Cere rested her forehead on her knees. He knew she was right. This wasn't the moment. And it certainly wouldn't be the last time they had this discussion.

They had a lot of work in front of them, and a lot of decisions to make. So starting with the biggest one? Didn't make a lot of sense.

"You knew about Fret and Irei, and you didn't say anything to the crew," Cere asked softly. "Why is that?"

Cal sighed. "It didn't feel like my story to tell. Don't we all have secrets in our heart?"

Cere didn't answer; she just looked down. It was too close to their earlier conversation about attachments, and that had no solid answers, either, Cal knew. So much about this was complicated.

So much about people was complicated.

"The Fifth Brother," Cal asked instead, in return. "You could have done what you did to Vader. Could have gone to the dark side to eliminate him once and for all. Why didn't you?"

Cere gave a wry smile. "Cal. You know why."

"Tell me anyway."

The older woman took a breath. "The dark side of the Force, your potential connection to it," Cere responded after a moment, "is not something to turn on and off like a faucet. It's not a switch you flick when you need it. It's the first step on a road you often can't get off once you start down it. It was successful when I used it against Vader, but it was the wrong thing to do. Jedi can't judge everything based on success. We must judge our actions on whether they were right, and in service of the light."

Cal sighed. "Thank you. It's hard to remember that, sometimes. When things are bad."

"I know," Cere said with a nod. "It helps me to say it out loud, too."

"You know what Master Jaro used to tell me," said Cal to the top of Cere's head. She grunted: *Maybe.* "Whenever I was overwhelmed in a lesson, or had too much on my plate, or couldn't keep my work straight, he would see me start to kind of melt down about it, you know? Get so—so overprogrammed I'd just shut down. Not a great coping mechanism, admittedly, but there you go."

Cere looked up; she wasn't sure where Cal was going with this. Cal hoped to the stars it made as much sense to her as it did to him.

"He'd assigned me this incredibly large, tedious task—asked me to catalog every single part of a lightsaber, including sketching them out, detailing their use, how they could break, how to fix them. I don't know if you know how many parts are in a lightsaber—" Cere laughed; of course she did. "Right." Cal laughed, too. "It's a lot. And of course, I left it to the night before I had to get it back to him. Real Padawan move."

Cere raised an eyebrow. "So what happened?"

"I told him," Cal said with a hint of disbelief; he still couldn't believe he'd been so brazen and disrespectful, honestly. "I came to him that night and I told him I hadn't done it, and I didn't know how I was going to get it done by morning. And you know what he told me?"

Cere tilted her head, waiting.

" 'One piece at a time.' " Cal laughed, remembering the advice. "Just one piece at a time. And he was right. Sometimes you just gotta focus on the very next piece."

"So did you?" Cere asked.

Cal frowned. "Did I what?"

"Did you finish it on time?"

"Oh." Cal laughed, shaking his head. "Absolutely not. But I tried. And I learned a good lesson out of it. I wish I could say that's what Master Jaro had really valued about the situation, but no. He really gave it to me."

"Oh, I *bet*," laughed Cere.

Cal exhaled sharply, letting some of the stress of the last day leave his body. "So that's what we're gonna do," he said as firmly as he dared. "Piece by piece. And the first piece is what we do with Irei and Fret. The rest of it, we worry about later. But we don't hide it from each other. Okay?"

Cere nodded. "Piece by piece."

And Cal hoped on his master's memory that he was doing the right thing.

But there was something still bothering him about what she'd said; what she'd tried not to say. "Cere, hey."

She looked up; she always knew when Cal had something important to say, to get off his chest. "You know I'm not going to end up like Trilla. Right?" When she didn't move or say anything, just stared at him, Cal prodded again: "Right?"

"Sure," Cere said, but Cal knew her. She didn't sound certain at all. "Sure."

Merrin had been looking to get away from distractions, and yet distraction found her, before long, as it tended to. It had been a full day since Merrin had left the *Mantis,* and she hadn't seen anyone from the crew. She'd taken a room at the sulfur baths, apparently one of Zimara's best features, and something that Dathomir certainly lacked; Merrin supposed there were *some* benefits to having seen more of the galaxy than she ever would have otherwise.

At that thought, Merrin waited for the telltale pull in her stomach, the tug at her heart, the shame boiling up in her mind. She waited but . . . nothing happened. Nothing at all.

Funny; she used to immediately feel guilty for having such thoughts, like she should never allow herself to feel even remotely grateful for the things that had happened to her as a consequence of the death of her people.

But as she sat in the yellow, vaporous waters, the steam relaxing her muscles and opening her lungs, she found she just couldn't muster that feeling anymore. She didn't have it in her to muster much of anything.

Was it possible, Merrin wondered, to hurt so much for so long that you simply no longer felt at all?

She didn't know, yet, if she was meant to return to the *Mantis.* She could reach her fire again, could access her power—in a new way, certainly, but it was still access. What need did she have for the *Mantis,* if they weren't aligned in their goals? Did she really need them? She could simply throw herself headfirst at the people who had hurt her, and hurt them back, over and over again.

Sure, it might get her killed.

But she would take so many of them with her, it wouldn't matter. And she would have served her purpose.

She would finally be able to avenge her sisters. And then . . . then, she could rest.

She wiggled her fingers on the surface of the opaque water in the rocky hot spring she'd been soaking in for the last few hours, alone with her thoughts, as she usually preferred to be. For as long as she could remember, that was how she'd found it easiest to think. Submerged, floating, drifting, no other people to cloud her mind or her opinions. She was fine on her own. She had never needed anyone, not in that way.

And yet here in the pools, today . . . she felt nothing. And strangely, her head was equally empty. She found herself almost . . . ugh, *yearning* for someone to talk to, to bounce ideas off.

Not just *someone,* if she was being honest with herself. Not just Greez, or Cere, as much as she cared for them.

No. Today, this time?

She just wanted Fret.

So Merrin had sunk down further in the water, submerged up to her nose, her knees poking out above the surface, and closed her eyes. And there she sat, and sat, and sat. Until she heard:

"Want a little company, weirdo?"

Merrin found it hard to believe she'd already started hallucinating after just one day of solitude, but she supposed anything was possible. Still, when she cracked an eye open, she was a little bit surprised to see, actually *see* Fret standing next to her in all her frustrating glory: shirt off, towel under one arm, trunks slung low on her waist, her broad shoulders and the soft roll of her stomach on full display, her half smile more genuine than usual.

Merrin gestured to the round pool next to hers without saying anything, then closed her eyes again. She knew she wanted to talk to Fret; so, so badly. But she just had no idea what to say.

So she would let Fret do the hard work. She was the one who'd showed up, after all.

Merrin heard the splash as Fret dropped herself as gracefully as Fret ever did anything into the water, yelping softly at the heat in a way that made a smile tug at the corners of Merrin's lips unbidden. Annoying.

After a few seconds of silence broken up only by Fret's sighs and splashes as she settled into the pool, she said: "Okay if we talk?"

Okay if we talk.

Merrin sighed and opened her eyes, feeling like they were weighed down by bricks. She kept her eyes trained on the sky as she said: "Okay. Where's Irei?"

"She wanted some time to rest after her medical treatment, so she's spending the day in town at a nice inn," Fret said, voice neutral. "And frankly, I told her that I needed to come talk to you. I told her about . . . us. She knows how important it is, that I come and . . ." Fret trailed off. It seemed like neither one of them really knew why Fret was there.

Still, she could hear as Fret shifted in the water, turning to face Merrin, resting her arm on the rim of the small pool and her chin on her forearm. "Irei and I . . ." She sighed. "It started a long time ago. I care about her. I'll probably always care about her, in some way. I'm sorry if that's not what you want to hear, and I'm sorry that this has . . ." Fret shook her head sadly. "Complicated things. With us."

Merrin took a second to digest what she'd just heard, to process. And then she dropped her gaze to Fret, too, needing to look at her head-on, to see the answers to her questions in her face as well as hear them in her voice.

"I didn't know." Fret lifted her head so she could stare Merrin right in the eyes. "You have to believe me. I had no idea. Merrin . . ." Fret swallowed around a lump of pain in her throat. "She was dead. She'd been dead for . . . years. If I had known, I would have told you. I would never have—" She took a deep breath, collecting herself. "I would never have deceived you like that, and I never wanted to hurt you. I know I did, but you have to believe me. I would never put you in a position where you were . . . consenting to something with me that you didn't realize you were. I would never, ever do that."

Merrin looked into Fret's eyes, those red embers that lit up her insides, still, despite everything, and she knew that the other woman was telling the truth.

"I don't begrudge you the way you feel about her," Merrin said with all the kindness she could muster out of her numb heart. "I am genuinely glad for you. I am just . . . surprised. I wasn't expecting—I don't know what I was expecting. Just not that."

"Yeah," Fret said, running a wet hand through her shaggy hair. "Me neither, my fiery gal. Me neither."

"Are you okay?" Merrin asked, surprising even herself for a moment.

Fret looked as caught off guard as Merrin felt. "Me? I—I don't know.

I honestly don't know. What do you do when you end up haunted like this?"

Merrin laughed. "Well, we have some very pretty ghosts on Dathomir. Very good kissers."

"You're kidding," Fret demanded.

Merrin just shrugged, letting the smile finally overtake her lips. "Am I?"

Fret narrowed her eyes and there was that smirk again, the one that drove Merrin wild. "I hate that I'm just as convinced you're telling the truth as I am that you're lying. Either is just as likely."

After they'd both let themselves laugh about it for a moment, Merrin took a deep breath. She had to ask; she had to know. It was the last big thing hanging in the air between them.

She shifted in the bath, trying to figure out if it was her body that was uncomfortable, or just the situation. "Did you love her?" asked Merrin. It was hard to maintain eye contact, but she did it even still.

Fret didn't hesitate. "Yes."

With a nod, Merrin asked the real question: "And do you still . . . love her?"

It took Fret a moment this time, then Fret nodded. "Yes."

The answer was what Merrin had expected. Fret's face was serious, as serious as Merrin had ever seen it in the time they'd known each other. "Yes, I do. I think, on some level, I probably always will. But Merrin—" Fret pushed back against the edge, freeing her arms, reaching across the wide chasm between their two pools, desperate to close the distance that seemed to somehow be widening by the second. "That doesn't change how I feel about you. Not at all. Not for a second."

Merrin let Fret grab her hands, wind their fingers together; watched as the muscles in her shoulder flexed, her eyes grew soft and pleading, and her hair ruffled in the arid breeze. Even Fret's touch, light as it was, from as distant as it came, was still enough to set Merrin's heart racing; even seeing Fret, just like this, had been enough, if Merrin was being honest. She couldn't help the way she felt about her.

And she so, so did not want to.

"Fret." Merrin heard her voice, and it sounded so strange to her, so foreign—strangled, emotional to a fault. "You have brought me back to myself in a way I did not think was possible, again. On Dathomir, my magick came to me so easily. It was the source of my powers. But once I was out in the galaxy, I had to be my own spark, and I think—" Merrin shook her head. "After a while, I lost sight of myself. Of the core of who I am. Meeting you, getting to know you, seeing myself through your eyes, I've felt like . . . I'm starting to find myself, a little, again. To know that there are things out in the universe I can find and have for myself, that have nothing to do with my past. That make up the core of me, piece by piece. Things beyond just the *Mantis*. Things beyond just the anger that I've guided myself by. I feel like, somehow, I have known you for—so long. So much longer than I have. When I feel you, through—through my magick . . ." Merrin squeezed Fret's hands; a desperate, longing motion out of her own control. "I cannot unsee what I see there, cannot unfeel it. I cannot take it back. I don't want to."

"Merrin—" There was a great crash of water onto the dirt as Fret got out of her pool so quickly she nearly tripped, her hands still in Merrin's, pulling herself over toward Merrin as quickly as she could, displacing more water onto the ground as she sank into Merrin's pool, leaving both of them more exposed, their skin chilled even in the warm desert air. Fret settled herself in, coming to rest on her knees, sitting between Merrin's legs, the steam from the water curling around both of them as if it were trying to embrace them before they were able to embrace each other, a futile task.

The way they had come into each other's lives was fated; cosmic. Fret had allowed her to be angry—more than that she had understood that anger when no one else had. Had unlocked the thing inside her that had so recently seized up with vengeance. She and Fret, they were like binary stars.

But binary stars orbited for eons before colliding, and sometimes they never collided at all.

There was no easy way to say the next part. So Merrin just had to say it.

"But, Fret—more than that, right now." Merrin let the words spill out of her mouth like the water splashed out of the pool as she leaned forward, needing to be closer to Fret, needing her to feel how much she meant it. She felt her cheeks turning green, hot under her skin, embarrassed at the way she was allowing herself to feel, to be so vulnerable in front of someone like this. It made her trip over her words, made her hands shake in Fret's. "I need time. To myself. To figure out what is next, for me. For this crew. Does that make sense?"

"Are you sure that's it?" Fret asked hesitantly. "I see what you and Cal have. And that's okay. I'm happy for you if it is."

Merrin's brows knit. Cal? He didn't. He couldn't.

. . . Did he?

She shook her head to clear it. Fret was seeing things. "Cal is like that with everyone. Always putting himself in the line of fire so that no one else gets hurt. He's the same with everyone he cares about. It's not unique to me."

Fret smiled, and Merrin wasn't convinced that *she* was convinced, but now was not the moment to worry further about that. "Okay," said Fret. "It would be good for me, too, to figure out what is left between me and Irei. So we should . . . be friends?"

"I'd like that very much. Yes."

Merrin nodded, swallowing hard as Fret's body surrounded hers in a great and all-encompassing hug.

She knew that it had to be this way, for her sake and everyone's. But it didn't make it any easier.

Doing the right thing, Merrin knew, was far more often scary than it was easy.

"Kiss me one last time? Before we do this difficult and right thing?" Merrin asked.

Fret was nodding now, too, moving closer so slowly it was nearly torturous. "Yes." She pressed a light kiss to Merrin's exposed shoulder, breathing "yes" again as she moved to her clavicle, her neck, behind her ear, a "yes" between each kiss, a promise, a prayer.

And then Fret's weight was on top of her, and their lips were together one last time.

When Cere walked back toward the *Mantis* outside of the village the next morning, she wasn't sure what—or whom—she was going to find waiting for her. They'd parked on the planet's dark side, the only way to keep the *Mantis* from becoming a boiling oven in their absence, but she was afraid that she would find only shadows waiting for her. Shadows and an empty ship.

When she'd left two days earlier, she'd known the crew had needed time to cool down. Cal, for all his pigheadedness sometimes, had shared good wisdom: They really had needed to handle this piece by piece, and trying to solve everyone's simultaneous existential crises while they had two more Imperial fugitives on board than usual was not in anyone's best interest. The best they could do was reapproach the current situation when saner heads prevailed.

But if she was being honest with herself, she wasn't sure if saner heads really existed aboard the *Mantis* even on the best of days. They were, after all, some of the most wanted criminals in the galaxy, and spent their days poking at the hornet's nest over and over again, betting that they'd live to do it the next day, too. That wasn't particularly sane behavior.

But it was their normal. And that was, at least, what Cere hoped they could all return to. Even if just for long enough to get Irei off her damn ship.

She wasn't surprised to find Cal waiting for her in the shadow of the *Mantis*'s fin, with BD-1 at his back; after their talk yesterday, she knew Cal was committed to finishing their current job. That, and really—Cal had nowhere else to go, and Cere knew it. The *Mantis* was both his mission and his life, the crew his family. He would have been back here no matter what.

And no matter the risk to himself.

But Greez, Merrin, and the other two—them, Cere was less certain about. As she inclined her head toward Cal in greeting, she could see the same doubt reflected in his face. Were they going to be alone in this? Or would they be greeted by anyone else, with a smile or without?

The waiting was the hardest part. Cere had said to the minute, but it was hard to tell time on a planet that had none.

Surprising them both, Irei was first, and alone. Cere squinted, watching her stride from the light side of the planet into the dark, her long, loping steps closing the distance between them quickly. She was expecting Fret to be with her; when Irei appeared alone, Cere wondered if the two of them had agreed to part ways for the rest of their journey. She wasn't sure what was going on between the two of them, exactly, but she could imagine that it was as complicated as the rest of their lives.

And that was fairly complicated.

Irei joined them in silence, leaning up against the ship's hull, nodding at Cere and Cal by way of acknowledgment, looking for all the world perfectly at ease.

Then Cere watched her chew one of her claws to the quick as they continued to wait.

It was Cal who noticed them first; he almost launched himself off the side of the ship, and Cere saw him stop to collect himself for a moment before he made a fool of himself. It was Merrin—and not as Cere would have expected her, materializing from nothing in a burst of green flames. Instead she approached the relatively normal way, if anything in their lives was normal: walking up from a distance, her chalky-white skin stark in the darkness, trailing Fret behind her, Fret's hand dwarfing Merrin's as she allowed herself to be towed.

"Sorry we're late," Merrin offered once they were close enough.

"Are we?" Fret had a teasing eyebrow up. "It's, like, five minutes after we were supposed to be here. Is that really late?"

"You are so ridiculous," Irei said with affection, shaking her head. It was what they all needed to break the tension; everyone chuckled a little, Cal lowered the ramp, they all got on board making small talk about their last forty-eight hours.

And no one mentioned that Greez was nowhere in sight.

They waited on the *Mantis* another ten minutes, another fifteen, while Cere and Fret ran preflight checks and Merrin heard all about Cal's upgrades to his lightsaber (which, honestly, even Cere found a little tedious; Merrin was being very kind).

The checks were done; the small talk had run dry. It was time.

And Cere had never felt more guilty in her entire life. She had done this; she was the one who had driven Greez away. It was her fault he had lost his arm; her fault that she hadn't united the crew under one common goal sooner. She was supposed to be their leader.

She was failing.

"Prepare for takeoff," Cere said, hitting comms so that she knew the rest of the ship would hear her. "Hit the—"

"Where the hell do you think you're goin' with my ship?"

Cere swung around from her seat and couldn't believe her eyes: there, a full half hour late, was Greez, striding up the ramp. Someone in town had altered his jacket; his empty sleeve had been tailored to swoop around his arm as it was now.

He looked hurt. He looked older, too.

But he looked good.

A relieved laugh escaped Cere as Fret slid out of the copilot's seat and Cere jumped out of the pilot's seat to rush over to Greez and envelop him in the biggest hug she'd ever given him. She was beaten there by seconds by Merrin and Cal.

"Okay, okay, sheesh," Greez grumbled, halfheartedly attempting to push them all off, but not really trying. When Cere pulled back, she could see the tears in his eyes. "We gonna figure out the plan, or not?"

CHAPTER 17

"Oh, it's just *awful*," Greez gasped dramatically, grasping his injured arm, rocking back and forth. "It's the most pain a guy can be in! I'm tellin' ya!"

The crew was sitting around the kitchen with food and drink, still parked on Zimara, but back together and willing to figure this stuff out. Greez was perched on the galley counter, playing his arm up for laughs, wanting the crew to know he was okay but still wanting them to feel just, like, *real* bad about it also, at the same time. They'd been so concerned once he got back on board that he'd gotten medical help, and he had—the best Zimara could do.

He'd be on the hunt for a real good mechanical prosthetic after this. But for now, he was gonna play it up. Oh, yeah. He was gonna play the lost-arm guilt card for a long, long time.

But in all honesty, had he almost not come back to the *Mantis*? For sure. He didn't have a death wish, and as much as he didn't *really* blame Cere for his arm, he was still *short an arm* and sure hadn't had the time or energy to process any of that quite yet. Piloting the ship—his baby— felt wrong. His body felt wrong. *He* felt wrong.

Every time he reached for something—nothing. Every time he moved—nothing. It felt like a gap, a blank space where there used to be texture and feeling and life. It was like learning how to walk again, to breathe again, something so natural, using four arms, that he'd never even considered what it would mean to use three. Had never had to consider what it might do to the way he operated as a pilot if he was short one of the core components of his skill set.

Greez didn't want to think about what it meant that he found himself losing his marbles every time he thought about participating in any kind of dangerous mission again, every time he even considered staring a threat in the face. It made him sweat and it made him shake and his vision started to black out and that just wasn't gonna do, it wasn't gonna stand, not with the kind of job Greez had, not with this life he'd chosen to lead. Greez Dritus didn't freak out.

So he knew it was gonna be a long time before he started to feel right again. But also that there was only one place he was gonna be able to do all that.

And only one group of people he felt like he could even begin to talk to about it.

So what was he gonna do, not come back?

Of course he was gonna come back.

It was his dang ship, after all. And these freaks were gonna get themselves *all* killed without him.

Still, he was gonna be playing the arm card quite a bit.

"So, what're we gonna do here, kids?" Greez asked after he'd finished his theatrics and reassured everyone that he was okay; far more okay than he actually felt, but whatever.

"Irei has to be our first priority," Cere said with authority as they all sat around the galley. Greez had to give Cere credit: The cool-down really was what they'd all needed, and his overnight in the med lab had given him the breather and alone time he'd needed to really focus in on himself, on putting on the face that would allow him to keep moving forward the way he needed to right now. There was a part of Greez that realized this was all just an elaborate bandage; that the problems they'd fought about were still swirling around through the ship's air processors, and that things were probably going to come up in a bad way again real soon.

But for now, they had the stormtrooper and the stormtrooper's time-bomb wife on board, so it made sense to deal with that first.

"We're not just gonna take you back to Qeris Lar," Cal reassured her from where he leaned up against the counter. "We're not going to treat you like a special delivery. You get to choose the move here. This is your invention, and your life."

Irei nodded thoughtfully from her spot at the galley table, seated across from Merrin and Fret. Irei had one hand on top of Fret's on the table; Fret's other hand was on Merrin's thigh, under it.

"Thank you, Cal," Irei said serenely. "I had been working on the Shroud for so long, for something that would help me, and help Fret, but I couldn't create it alone. Through—certain pipelines—I heard about Qeris Lar, and knew he would have the ability to get me the materials I needed."

Irei shook her head. "But in doing so, I had to divulge more than I wanted to about the Shroud to him. It was the only way. I've never fully trusted Qeris Lar, but he was necessary when it came to the Shroud—he was one of the only people who could help me access the mirkanite that I needed for the prototype, and he'd dedicated his life to working in opposition to the Imperials. But," she added fiercely, "I never intended to work with Qeris in the long term. I always wanted to use the Shroud to disappear off Qeris's sensors, literally and figuratively, the second it was done. I never wanted to give him the tech, and I fear that going back to him now will simply mean trading one prison for another."

Now, Greez wasn't an I-told-you-so kinda guy—oh, why was he kidding himself. He was *absolutely* an I-told-you-so kinda guy.

"No kiddin'," Greez drawled. "Big bird, untrustworthy? Who coulda called that?"

Irei nodded, unfazed by Greez's sarcasm. "I want to believe he's trustworthy. I do."

Greez wasn't new; he heard a real *but* comin' in there.

"But," continued Irei, "I think we really do have to be prepared for all possible circumstances."

Merrin burst out laughing. "Oh," said Merrin, "we are almost *never* prepared for all possible circumstances."

Greez held back his own laugh as he watched Irei's head swivel around on her long neck, watching the entire crew nod somberly in agreement.

"And yet we're still here," Cere said with what was supposed to be a reassuring smile, but to Irei probably looked just like pure menace.

"I didn't want to go to him to find the Shroud—to find you." Fret was looking down into her cup of caf. "I knew I shouldn't have. But he was the only one with a lead to what I thought was the last part of you."

Irei smiled at Fret from across the table. "So we both went to him in times of need when we didn't want to."

"But Fret's right—you both are," said Cere. "We can't just drop you two off anywhere we want now. The Imperials are after you, sure, but Qeris is *definitely* going to be after you both, too. And he's far more dangerous."

"Agreed," said Cal around a mouthful of Bespin Bar. "The more people you have to run from, the harder it is. So if you have to run, let's at least get you away from Qeris clean."

"Kid's right," Greez agreed, snatching the remainder of the bar out of his hand and taking a bite. "Blech, needs salt. Qeris is the harder one to get away from; he's got money on his side, and he could buy the same people that would help you. And he seems to know a whole hell of a lot about *us*. We gotta deal with him. Big ol' spindly jerk."

"But what do we do?" asked Merrin. "He seems to have every advantage at his fingertips. And though we didn't make a specific promise, he's expecting us to deliver the Shroud."

"Precisely. So we give him what he wants," said Cere, matter-of-factly.

"We can't," argued Irei. "I can't make the Shroud. It's still theoretical. Plus, we don't have the materials to try."

Cere nodded. "Exactly. We're going to give him a fake. No one's seen a working prototype; he'd never know it. And by the time he realizes it, we're going to be long, long gone."

"Y'know, stormtrooper," Greez said, looking up at Fret's big purple grin, "guy's probably just gonna kill you the second you walk in that door."

"Funny," said Fret, looking at the big pile of cybernetic ship scrap still sitting in the corner of the galley. "I was thinking that exact same thing."

And as the plan began forming around all of them at the same time, Greez started to smile.

This was why he'd come back. This, right here.

"All right," said Greez, hopping down off the counter. "Keep talkin', but I'm gonna let Qeris know we are on our way."

And so, after their Big Chat back on the ship, they'd headed for Hosnian Prime, jumping through hyperspace here and there to make sure they weren't followed from their moon. Cal and Irei spent a couple of days huddled over Cal's workbench; Merrin and Fret worked furiously to build Fret new armor out of the junk pile; BD and the bogling worked on just bein' cute and stuff, runnin' around the ship.

And Greez stared at his big pile of junk from the Haxion Brood asteroid with a smile. He knew it was gonna come in handy.

He told 'em so.

This time, when they got to Hosnian Prime, Greez hadn't even bothered to land out of sight. He'd just rolled right on up to that eyesore skytower, parked the dang thing on a floating landing pad, and slammed the ramp down practically right into Qeris Lar's living room, as far as he was concerned. They didn't have time to mess around anymore. They were armed, and they were ready.

Well, Greez was a little less armed than he could have been.

If he didn't laugh about it, he was gonna start crying about it, so. He was gonna be like this, with himself, for now.

"Noticed a lot of Brood ships in orbit on the way in here," Greez said, watching his scans as the crew prepped to exit the *Mantis*. "Not betting they're some sort of good-guy Haxion Grood we've never heard of. Any chance that's a coincidence?"

Cere just laughed.

"We need to worry about it?" asked Cal.

"Nah," Greez said, waving him off. "You let me and Cere worry about that."

Cal frowned at him; Greez saw his eyes flick to his injured arm. "You sure?"

Greez smiled. "Never been more sure in my life."

And so Greez and Cere watched Merrin, Cal, Fret, and Irei disembark, as prepared as they were ever going to be, and raised the ramp behind them.

With the clang of the ramp back in place, Cere looked over at Greez. "You think everything's going to go okay?"

Greez looked back at Cere. He nodded, slowly.

"Oh, yeah," he said. "For sure. I mean, when's the last time something went wrong?"

And then they both laughed all the way to the cockpit, and Greez prepared to take them into low orbit, missing levers a few times and cursing about it, trying not to dwell too hard on it, not right now, leaving the rest of the crew to execute on their part of the plan.

Cal had been repairing his lightsaber, which had taken some dings in his fight against the Inquisitor, and preparing for landing when he heard his name come quietly from the engine room doorway.

"Is now a good time?" Merrin asked.

"Good a time as ever," said Cal, strapping his lightsaber back onto his belt. "You okay?"

Merrin looked like she wasn't quite sure what she wanted to say; unusual for her, Cal knew. It must be something important. He gestured to the cot, and they both sat next to each other on the edge, their hands not quite touching, but close enough to be reassuring.

"While we're in Chikua City," said Merrin carefully, after a pause. "Whatever happens in Qeris's tower—do not ask me—if things go *bad*, don't ask me to leave. Not this time."

Cal frowned. "I only ever do that to protect you. It's my job—"

Merrin didn't let him finish, waving his words away. "I want to protect people, too. This is my crew, too. And you do not have to sacrifice yourself for us."

Cal stared at Merrin, trying to fully engage with what she was saying while still not entirely agreeing. It was his job, whether she liked it or not.

"It's not that I don't think you're capable, Merrin," Cal explained. Or tried his best to. "I know what you can do. But I would never, ever forgive myself if something happened to you out there that I could have prevented."

"And do you think I would feel differently if something happened to you?" Merrin demanded. "Promise me, Cal."

"Merrin." He sighed. He didn't want to make her a promise he wasn't entirely certain he could, or would, keep. "You don't have to prove anything to me," he landed on instead. "I know you. I know who you are, and I see you. And we are in this together. Okay?"

Cal knew Merrin was no fool. By the intensity of her gaze, he could tell she understood he had very clearly not made the promise she had asked for.

But she nodded anyway. "Good enough. For now."

Cal placed one of his hands over hers, and felt the heat of her skin, and hoped she felt the warm comfort of his, too. "For now."

They sat in comfortable silence and listened to the hum of the *Mantis* engine until it was time to leave.

The *Mantis* holotable was generally a bit of a one-trick pony; Greez knew they used it mostly for displaying planetary maps and, well, not much else. But Fret had been right about Irei: She really was some kind of mechanical engineering genius, because she'd been able to rig the thing up to show Greez and Cere exactly what was going on in Qeris's cloud-lounge in live action, projected from little cams that the crew had affixed to their outfits, and to the top of BD's head, like a tiny little BD-hat.

Even Greez thought it looked pretty cute, for an espionage device.

"She lives!" They heard Qeris's whistly voice pipe through the speakers on the holotable as his tall figure wavered through the air in front of them, graceful despite the scanning lines distorting his image. For all his pretense, he didn't actually sound that surprised.

"He knew," Cere said. Greez hummed in agreement.

The holotable reconstructed the scene as accurately as it could from the perspective of the cams: Cal and Merrin entering the room together, followed closely by Fret and Irei, passing the guards at the door, walking toward Qeris's open arms.

"Please, sit, sit." Qeris gestured to the little cloud-couch seating area they'd been grouped around last time, and the crew took their places accordingly. As Qeris spoke, he had beverages brought out for all of them.

It was difficult to tell through the static, but Greez was fairly certain Cal and co. were only pretending to drink theirs. Smart kids.

"Irei, you have the schematics for the Shroud with you, then?" asked Qeris. "They're not, say, back on the *Mantis,* for instance? They are safe?"

"I have better than that," Irei confirmed. "I built a prototype myself."

And with that, she pulled out a disk, no bigger than her own palm, that Qeris would think contained so much power it could bring down the very galaxy as Greez and everyone else knew it.

He'd been pretty surprised that Irei had been able to pull it off in the days it had taken them to fly back to Hosnian Prime; she'd been bent over Cal's workbench every day for hours. Cal and Greez together had collected so much stuff on their travels for repairs and upgrades that the *Mantis* was just swimming in materials, and the one bit they were missing—well, Greez had known a guy who'd known a guy who'd gotten it to them in no time flat.

When it was finished, it was the most anticlimactic moment of Greez's entire life, little disk-lookin' thing the size of a medium-sized hand.

He had to admit, it was a pretty good goof. Qeris was definitely gonna fall for it.

Greez felt the space where his arm was supposed to be, and hoped the whole plan was going to pay off.

"Beautiful," breathed the Omwati, apparently feeling as awed about it as Greez expected him to. "May I?"

Irei closed her palm around the disk. "I wanted you to see that I could produce; that it was real. And I thank you for helping free me from that place. But Qeris, I have to ask: Can you guarantee my safety? And Fret's?

With your resources, I know you can keep us safe from the Empire for as long as is necessary."

"Of course," Qeris murmured.

Greez reached for the bowl he'd put down on the couch between him and Cere full of their favorite salty snack, little fluffy crunchy things that he made sure to pay extra for in the best flavors, and tossed one into his mouth, chomping away at it while they listened in.

"This is it for sure," said Cere.

"Oh, I dunno," Greez mused. "I think he's gonna draw it out, mess with them a little. Guys like this love that kind of drama."

Greez watched Cal and Merrin's heads whip around to the sound of something off cam.

"Something wrong with your doors?" asked Fret.

"Just trying to keep you safe," demurred Qeris. "We're talking about very sensitive subjects. When plotting against the Empire, you can't be too careful. I don't want anyone walking in who shouldn't be."

"Naturally," said Merrin. Greez knew that tone in her voice and grinned as he chomped away on another kernel.

"Your safety, and Fret's, however, were not part of the original deal," Qeris said. Cere nudged Greez. "We will need to . . . renegotiate."

"We figured," Fret said drily, settling back into her chair.

"You will leave the Shroud plans here, with me, along with the prototype, and come work for me, helping to improve and ultimately manufacture the Shroud," suggested Qeris, too casually. "Do that, and I will ensure you're kept from the Empire for as long as need be."

"That's not going to happen," said Cal. "We've gotten the tech away from the Empire. But it's too dangerous to develop. And, all due respect, we didn't free Irei from one prison just to condemn her to another. Those plans, and Irei, stay with us."

"Hmm," mused Qeris. "That's a real shame. Especially for you, Frethylrin; I'm sure the Imperials will love to know that I can give them the whereabouts of an Imperial asset on the run."

"Wow." Fret drew the word out into several syllables. "I always knew you were a real me, myself, and I kinda guy, Qeris, but it usually isn't this obviously at the expense of others. What happened?"

Qeris let out a long, elaborate sigh that had Greez rolling his eyes back into his skull. "Perhaps you simply did not know me as well as you thought. Are you certain you don't want to reconsider my offer? It really is in everyone's best interest here."

"Now," said Greez, pointing at the holo. "Watch."

"We will not be changing our minds," confirmed Merrin. She was looking straight at Qeris this time.

"A real shame," breathed Qeris.

And then the holofeed exploded into static.

CHAPTER 18

This was not the plan, Cal thought in a bit of panic.

The plan was give Qeris the fake Shroud, then get the heck out. They were supposed to be gone by now.

The plan was not: *We may have to kill Qeris.*

And yet here they were.

It happened so quickly that even Cal, with all his deep connection to the Force, didn't have time to react before it happened.

Qeris had been vaguely threatening them with a good time.

Then suddenly he had a weapon out—the tiniest blaster pistol Cal had ever seen—and had shot Fret directly in the chest.

Whatever that tiny blaster was, it packed a *real* punch, because one second they were all sitting around Qeris's cloud-table, and the next Fret had been blown halfway across the room onto her back, a smoking hole in the front of her leather jacket.

Merrin, Irei, and Cal were all on their feet within an instant, like a well-oiled machine: Irei running straight to Fret with BD in tow, his stims at the ready, Merrin setting her palms alight, and Cal rushing at Qeris while unholstering his lightsaber. But Qeris was hollow-boned, so light and fast, the tricky little traitor, and he was out of Cal's reach before he could even get his blade ignited.

"Did that armor you made out of Greez's junk pile work?" Irei called out, rushing to Fret's side.

"Yes!" said Merrin. And then, so quiet that Cal could barely hear it, with realization: "Oh, please. Please. It has to."

And that's when Cal, too, realized that the elevator doors hadn't, in fact, sealed themselves shut earlier; the elevators had actually just been summoned to another floor, to pick up new cargo.

With a soft *ding!* that Cal hadn't attended to before, the elevator doors slid back open, disgorging a heap of warriors armed to the teeth, all with their weapons trained directly on Cal and Merrin.

Cal stared for a moment and all at once he recognized those ugly outfits: Haxion Brood. Obviously. They were, as always, just the *worst*.

Then he realized, suddenly, some of these warriors resembled the security guards Cal had seen when they first met Qeris. In fact, they were exactly the same guards. Yet another thing Greez had been right about. Cal smiled thinking of how much Greez would say "I told you so" after they survived all of this.

Qeris wasn't shooting; he was simply watching the scene play out with interest, overconfident in his own plans. Cal took the free moment to look over at Merrin, confirm that the plan was still the plan, even as things were unraveling.

He didn't have to.

What Cal saw when he looked at Merrin was—beautiful and terrifying, all at the same time.

He knew, in principle, that Nightsisters used magick they gained from the Force, and that it was mostly siphoned through the dark side. It was why so many Jedi found the very idea of the Nightsisters challenging at best and repulsive at worst: They were harnessing energy in a way that was antithetical to what the Jedi believed in.

Cal knew, in principle. But it had been a very, very long time since he'd seen it in practice.

And he'd never seen it quite like this.

Her face perfectly still, perfectly calm; if you didn't know Merrin as well as Cal did, you would probably be tempted to say she looked undisturbed and unbothered.

But Cal did know her. And what Cal saw on her face was a mask of pure rage, uncontaminated holy terror, the kind of thing that made the Nightsisters the stuff of the galaxy's nightmares, the villains in stories and the creatures in the shadows. Her hair smoked at the edges; curls of smoke poured from her nail beds, her tear ducts, the corners of her mouth. Considered, cold, calculated. And worry that Qeris had just killed Fret had ignited Merrin's very core, set her magick ablaze.

And she was going to make every single person in that room pay.

"Don't tell me to leave this time, Cal," Merrin reminded him. "Because I won't."

Merrin disappeared out of sight and reappeared in front of the elevator as Cal watched; she moved so quickly and so efficiently that Cal only had to watch her for a second more as she used her fire to consume three bounty hunters instantly, and then turn her aim on the rest of them.

Okay, so Merrin would handle the Brood. Got it.

Cal turned back to Qeris, who now had his tiny blaster pointed right at Cal's chest. Cal had to stop himself from rolling his eyes (what, was he going to just shoot at him? How disappointing!) and instead asked:

"Was this the plan all along, then? Blackmail us for the Shroud or kill us? But end up with it one way or another?"

Qeris's hand was shaking; he had to put his other one onto his weapon to hold it steady. "I've been watching galactic politics for years," he said, his voice less confident than it had been moments ago as, behind Cal, Merrin continued her single-handed reign of terror against every new batch of Brood that came pouring out of the elevators. "I've seen what happens to people—and to planets—who resist the Empire."

Cal took a step forward and watched with pleasure as Qeris took a step back. "So, safer for you to just play along? What happened to the free market? Competition? I thought siding with the Empire was bad for business."

"It was," agreed Qeris. Cal heard a droid shriek behind him. "But being dead is worse for business. The galaxy's changed, Kestis. People who work with the Imperials are profiting and benefiting. So I had to pivot."

"Pivot," Cal repeated with disdain, taking another step forward. He was attempting to back Qeris into a wall, but it seemed like this infernal place hardly had any. He'd just keep him talking, for now, while Merrin did her work.

"What brought Irei to me originally is that the Shroud requires mirkanite to operate," Qeris continued with a shrug. "A very rare mineral. Only a few mines in the entire galaxy. Incredibly dangerous to mine; even a fraction of a gram can be incredibly explosive if exposed to an open flame. Only a brave few are willing to own mines like that. And once the Empire has the schematics and begins producing the Shroud en masse, they're going to require . . . a *lot* of mirkanite."

"And you own all the mines there are to own?" Cal shifted the grip on his lightsaber, watching the way Qeris's eyes shifted to his blade.

Maybe Merrin wasn't *always* wrong about playing with her food. Cal was starting to see the appeal.

Qeris tilted his head in acknowledgment. "Most of them. Enough that, if the tech is as impressive as it sounds, I am about to become one of the wealthiest men in the galaxy. Who knows," he said wistfully, "maybe the Imperials will appoint me to take over Alderaan from that fool queen and her even more foolish husband."

Cal shook his head in disbelief. "Wow," he said, swinging his lightsaber in slow circles next to him, "you've really got this all figured out. Just had to get us out of the way first, huh?"

Qeris's eyes flicked back to behind Cal, where he knew Merrin was still on her Brood-murder spree. "I still have some tricks up my sleeve."

And then he rushed at Cal head-on, firing his blaster as he went.

He was so, so fast, thought Cal, as he managed to dodge a bolt and Qeris's attempted body slam almost simultaneously. The Omwati was so light that he faced almost no resistance as he moved and fired, flitting around like the birds he resembled, keeping Cal constantly on the move, so much so that he barely had time to set his feet and swing his lightsaber before he was forced to turn again and keep moving, or reposition his lightsaber to block more incoming shots from Qeris's blaster. Cal found himself getting dizzy before long; the man was keeping him busy, trying to tire him out, he knew, and the worst part was: It was working.

Cal shook the sweat out of his eyes, and Qeris took that moment to fire again, hoping Cal would be distracted long enough that he wouldn't be able to get his lightsaber up to deflect the bolt—but he was wrong, and Cal's blade swung up just in time, deflecting the bolt when it was a hair's breadth from his face.

Deflecting it straight back toward Qeris, who wasn't anticipating it.

The bolt hit Qeris in the arm, earning Cal a shriek—and then, in a burst of feathers and a flurry of motion, the Omwati fired up a jetpack on his back and soared away to safety, but also well out of range for his tiny blaster to be of any real danger.

Cal shook his head. Of course this rich jerk had a fancy jetpack. *Of course he did.*

Taking the moment for what it was, Cal slid behind a cloud-chair for a second to catch his breath, and activated his comms. "Are you catching all this?"

"We got him," Greez's voice came back instantly. "Recorded his audio. If he doesn't end up dead today, his little speech is going to end up on every vidscreen from here to the Outer Rim, and then some guerilla relying on Qeris for their survival is gonna make sure he ends up dead real quick. If he's gone full Imperial, the whole underworld is going to make sure he doesn't betray anyone else."

"Good." Cal breathed heavily, scoping out the scene. Merrin was finishing up with the latest reinforcements, more having continued to appear with every *ding!* of the elevator, green mist surrounding two Brood hunters up to their necks, their faces slowly turning purple with every passing moment while she looked on. Irei had pulled Fret's body into a shadowed part of the room under the clouds that passed for the room's ceiling, bent low over Fret's chest, half protecting her with her own body, and half doing whatever she could with BD, Cal imagined, to try to save her.

"How's it going up there?" Cal gulped out.

"There're a *lot* more of them than we thought there would be!" responded Cere, slightly out of breath. "We've been able to take five different Haxion Brood reinforcement ships out at the knees before they even hit atmo. It would have been a different scene in there had we not stayed aboard. Greez is pulling off some pretty fancy flying."

"Oh, shut up," Greez responded. "You're just buttering me up 'cause you feel bad about how you cut off my arm."

"I did *not* cut off your arm—!"

"You're only up here with me 'cause you're afraid to leave me alone—"

"And because I know Cal can handle some bounty hunters without a babysitter—"

The comms cut out, and Cal thanked Cere for presumably muting the conversation so he could think, glad that everything seemed to be okay back aboard the *Mantis,* more or less.

He felt a tap on his shoulder: BD, who had rushed back over with a green syringe. Cal nodded gratefully, injecting the stim, feeling himself knit back together as he crouched.

"You okay, buddy? Fret okay?" Cal breathed a sigh of relief as the cool liquid flooded his veins.

BD beeped back. He sounded unsure about Fret, but Cal knew the droid would do all he could to help her.

As BD rushed back over to Fret, Cal heard two muted thuds. Cal poked his head up from behind the couch, a bit revitalized, to watch Merrin's last two Brood hunters hit the floor, dead. She turned to look at him; their eyes caught, fury and empathy, hurt and worry.

Then they both turned to look at Fret.

But just as they'd both moved to stand, there was a flurry of wings, a flutter—and Qeris swooped down, floating in the air between the two of them, out of range of Cal's saber strikes.

"You've done much better than I anticipated you would," he said patronizingly. "Only one dead of four; not my best record. I've fired people for less."

Cal watched Qeris's eye bulge out of his head as he noticed that Merrin was stalking toward him at a slow, deliberate pace that made her look more frightening than any giant spider he'd ever had the displeasure of seeing up close. Green flames glittered around her hands, and Cal knew that look in her eyes: She was going to take her time, and she was going to enjoy it.

He was out of lightsaber range, but Qeris had no idea what constituted Nightsister magick range.

"You're dead, Cal Kestis," the Omwati hissed. "And I'll have the Shroud. No matter what."

Cal leapt upward with a yell, slicing with his lightsaber, but by the time he got there Qeris was already on his way into the sky, high enough that Cal couldn't follow. Coward.

Cal let out a groan of frustration as he slammed the floor with his lightsaber blade, hitting nothing but air on the way down. Merrin gripped him by the shoulder.

"Are you okay?"

"Yeah," Cal answered, looking her face over for any obvious signs of injury. "Are you—?"

"Yes. But Fret—she's not getting up, I think the armor didn't work, Cal, I'm afraid she's—"

"*Cal!*" He heard the frightened shout and spun around. It was Irei, screaming at him from across the room. "*Are your comms working?*"

Cal checked his comms, but heard nothing but dull empty static. Cere hadn't muted the conversation after all.

"The *Mantis* isn't responding," Irei yelled. "And it sounds like someone set up some sort of jamming tech—"

Ding.

The elevator doors slid open once again. And at the same time, he heard:

"Cal Kestis. Are you ready to lose, one last time?"

Fret was likely dead. Irei was panicked. Cal was looking exhausted.

And Merrin was more deadly furious than she had ever been in her life.

She watched the elevator doors slide open, watched the Fifth Brother stalk from its depths with his wide-brimmed helmet and pallid gray face and lightsaber glowing and all Merrin could see was the red of Fret's eyes in the color of his blade, staring at her, taunting her, screaming at her.

She was going to kill him, and then she was going to kill Qeris. And she was going to make him apologize before she choked the life out of his lungs for good.

"Did you think the Empire did not have a tracking device on its precious cargo?" the Inquisitor asked, gazing over at Irei, who was frozen with fear. Merrin glanced back to Cal, face contorted in anguish. He was probably blaming himself. They hadn't thought to check Irei in the chaos that was the aftermath of Murkhana. Foolish. But the error wasn't Cal's alone, the whole crew shared it. Merrin hoped he understood that.

The Inquisitor had fixed his gaze back onto Cal, seemingly ignoring everyone else in the room. "Try as you might, you cannot escape the destiny the Force has set out for you. And you will *not* deny me mine." the Fifth Brother said, lazily spinning his double-bladed lightsaber in a circle. He walked right past Merrin and she moved to raise her hand, to burn him to the ground on the spot, and she found herself frozen in place, completely unable to move—

He was using the Force on her. Pure, unbridled, not like what Merrin used to access her magick, but something much deeper, something far more sinister.

And she had to stand there and watch, horrified, as he approached Cal like a cat stalking his prey.

"What are you doing here? Who are you? You'll not deny me my prize!" Qeris screeched and swooped down toward the elevator on his jetpack.

Merrin watched the Inquisitor sigh, not bothering to take his eyes off Cal. Reaching back with one hand, Merrin saw Qeris jerk back and forth in midair as he was seized by the Inquisitor through the Force. The Omwati hung there in stasis for a moment, then all at once, was pulled forward at great speed, headed straight for the Inquisitor and his red blade.

Qeris let out one more scream, then was silenced. With a flick of his arm, the Inquisitor casually sent the body of the man toward the corner of the room, landing with a heavy thud, near Irei and Fret.

And then the Fifth Brother ran at Cal with a roar, his blade spinning full force, and Cal prepared to dodge the attack.

Merrin stayed frozen as Cal and the Fifth Brother traded blow after blow, the Inquisitor trying to keep Cal on the defensive, aggressively coming at him over and over, while Cal kept up with him at all times. Their blades flashed against each other faster, and faster, until the two weapons were a whirl of color that Merrin could barely track. The two of them were moving closer and closer to Fret and Irei without noticing. Merrin struggled and still, *still* couldn't move against her invisible constraints.

Cal attempted to disengage for a moment, to find his footing and regain his breath, shoving himself backward out of the Inquisitor's range. And then she had to watch as the Inquisitor pulled the same trick on Cal, and froze him to the spot in a moment when Cal had tried to use a stim to regain his strength.

But the concentration it took for the Fifth Brother to shift his focus in the Force to Cal was all Merrin needed to break free. In the same instant that the Fifth Brother brought his lightsaber screaming down over Cal's head, Merrin was able to wrench a hand free, slicing out with her magick, her fire in easy reach now, for the worst of reasons, to shift the Inquisitor's blade just enough off course that it only grazed Cal's arm, instead of cleaving him in two. He was silent; the stasis stopped him from crying out.

But it was the work of a second for the Fifth Brother to realize what had happened and come swinging back upward again.

Merrin reacted without thinking: She disappeared out of sight, ran and lunged, burned back into view, right in front of Cal, right between the Inquisitor's blade and her Jedi's face, and she held up her hands covered in green fire, and she caught the blade between her palms.

The Inquisitor's eyes widened as he registered what was happening: the Nightsister holding the red blade between hands covered in green fire, their combined light shining bright yellow across her face. She pushed back, as hard as she could, and felt the lightsaber shift back toward its wielder, just enough to scare him; just enough to propel her on.

The Fifth Brother narrowed his eyes at her, and behind them, Merrin thought she saw something like admiration. "I sense your strength," he said, and his words burned through the air between them.

"I get it," Merrin shoved out through gritted teeth, "from my family."

And then Cal screamed as the statis wore off and he registered the cauterized pain tearing down the length of his arm; and Merrin, brought back into the moment, screamed as the pure, searing heat of the lightsaber burned through to her palms and the strength of the Fifth Brother's arms made her own muscles scream as she pushed back. Then Cal's hands were on her waist, shoving her to the side, pushing her to the ground next to Fret's body, still protected by Irei's large form, and Cal almost dodged the downfall of the Fifth Brother's lightsaber, but not quite, and Merrin felt him land next to her, his lightsaber arm useless at his side, the muscles burned through, and her hands ruined and her power draining and she thought:

This is it. This is where we're all going to die.

Just like all my sisters.

I wasn't strong enough. I came all this way—all this way from Dathomir, into the galaxy, to avenge them, and this is how I'm going to die.

And then she saw the false Shroud next to Irei, and she had an idea.

Cal had been frozen, infuriatingly still, when Merrin had burned into place in front of him, putting her body between him and the Fifth Brother, risking her life for his.

That was his job, not hers. And there had been nothing he could do about it.

He watched the Inquisitor's blade come down, the way Merrin had incredibly, beautifully, unnervingly pushed it back with her bare hands, saving them both from destruction, and Cal had promised himself: *Never again.*

He wouldn't let her put herself in danger like that for him ever again.

And he would do everything he could, right now, to get her and the rest of his crew out of this building alive.

Everything.

And then, as Merrin pushed back, illuminated by the combination of her magick and the Inquisitor's blade, Cal felt the hold on him dissipate, replaced by a white-hot heat from his injury, and he heard more than felt himself scream at the sudden influx of pain. But there was no time to think about himself: Merrin.

Merrin was the only thing he could see, and the only thing he could think about.

Wrenching himself forward and ignoring the scream in his injured lightsaber arm, Cal flung his arms around Merrin's waist and *yanked,* pulling them both down to the ground next to Fret and Irei, feeling the downward swing of the Fifth Brother's lightsaber as it singed through his pant leg, his flesh centimeters out of reach. He reached out a hand and with the Force sent a sudden burst of energy toward the Fifth Brother, driving the Inquisitor back several meters.

And then he saw Merrin's eyes flash to the Shroud.

He knew what Irei had really made. Not the Shroud at all, but a small detonator, rigged to blow the moment Qeris attempted to use it.

But small. Too small to really hurt anyone. Just a sparkler, Irei had said, meant to convince Qeris that the prototype was a dud.

But looking at it now that's not what Cal had in mind for it. Not at all.

Merrin seemed to realize what Cal was going to attempt at the same moment Cal did, and with his good hand he snapped up the disk before she could, ignoring the Inquisitor's cold laughter in the background as he once again approached the beaten, broken pile that the two of them made in the cloudy corner of this sky-bright room with patience, knowing he'd won; knowing they were beaten.

As Cal closed his hands around the Shroud Merrin suddenly kicked her leg out, sending the disk skidding across the room.

"Do not do something foolish, Cal," she hissed, rolling onto her side. "Do not get yourself killed for us." She was starting to smoke.

Cal rolled out of the way as the Inquisitor's blade came down again. "You get everyone else out and let me deal with this! It's the only move!"

Merrin was already up on her feet and streaking toward the disk. "And then what? You blow yourself up with him?"

Cal shoved himself back to his feet with his one good arm. He briefly feinted as if trying to swing his lightsaber, then kicked out his leg, knocking the Fifth Brother off balance as the Inquisitor had prepared to block a saber swing that would never come. "I don't know!" he called to Merrin. "It's my only plan! It keeps everyone else safe!" He was off across the room after her.

"You can't run from me!" roared the Inquisitor, getting back onto his feet.

"Shut up!" Cal and Merrin both yelled at the same time.

Merrin was almost to the disk. Cal reached out with his injured arm, barely functioning, and used the Force to grab the disk a second before she could, and Merrin screamed. A green flare shot out from her body like a wave. Cal winced, expecting it to hurt, or burn—but it didn't. It swept past him and surrounded the Fifth Brother. For a moment, the Inquisitor was trapped in a cyclone of pure, green fire. Cal knew a spell this powerful wouldn't last long—they had to talk fast.

And when Cal turned back to meet Merrin's gaze, her eyes were glowing a bright, unnatural green.

"Do not tell me to leave, Cal," she said firmly. "We are part of a team. You have to let me help you. You have to trust me. And you have to *let* me."

"No." Cal shook his head emphatically, refusing to listen to what she was saying. "No, I won't. Every time someone puts their life on the line for me, they get hurt—or they die. I'm not letting that happen to you. I can't. I *won't*."

Merrin pushed her hair back off her face. Cal knew how it always irritated her. "If you don't let me help—all of us, help—we are *all* going to die. Us, and eventually every Force-sensitive in the galaxy, and everyone who would ever stand up against the Imperials from now until the end of time."

Cal was still shaking his head; he felt ruined.

Because she was right.

He couldn't think of another way. And she was right.

"I know," he whispered, just barely audible over the sound of the Inquisitor screaming in rage as he sought to break through the flames. "I know, I just—I can't do it, Merrin. I can't lose you."

Merrin stepped forward, into Cal's space, and took his hands into hers, so cold where hers were burning hot. She brought his hands slowly up to her mouth, and placed a light kiss on the back of each of his hands, first one, then the other, keeping her eyes trained on his.

Cal saw something in her eyes he wasn't ready for.

"Fearing to lose those you care about is natural. But, if you really care for me, Cal Kestis," she said, her lips still on his hands, "you will understand that you can't do this all on your own. And you do not have to."

She took a deep breath and lifted her face to stare into his. "Together, Cal?"

Cal could tell Merrin knew his answer by the way she looked at him.

"Together," he said, just as the cyclone of fire around the Inquisitor finally collapsed.

Merrin shoved Cal away, watched him make a break for Irei, clutching the Shroud in his hands. Merrin turned to face the Inquisitor, who was stalking toward her with determination. He had ignored her earlier, but now she had earned his attention and his rage.

Good. She would keep him busy, while Cal executed his plan.

She squeezed her eyes shut, found she could access all of her fire again, finally, all of her magick. Merrin went to a safe place in her mind's eye. Dathomir, of course, one of the rivers before they'd all run dry. Red sky, red dirt, illuminating her from the inside.

For a moment, she felt as though she were really back there, the power from the planet infusing her with new strength, the bodies of her fallen sisters propping her up, demanding vengeance, proud of Merrin and who she had become. The Water of Life, rushing through and around her, the magick from the planet's core swirling through her own.

She let it flow through her and over her, and she felt truly a Nightsister once again.

She thought of her fallen sisters, the ones who had fought until their last breaths, who'd had their futures stolen. But it wasn't about revenge.

She thought of Fret, a violet smirk; red eyes that saw to her core and sparked the fire that had reignited all of this. But it wasn't about rage or anger.

She thought of the *Mantis* crew. The closest thing to a family she had, maybe that she'd ever had. Cere, her clever and kind older sister. Greez, his easy laugh and his fierce, undeniable kind of love. Cal. Cal, who had given her his hand when he didn't have to; had brought her into this new life with a trust she'd never expected to know. Cal, with his soft smile and his quiet wisdom. But it wasn't about pain or suffering.

It was about rebirth. About a reset. About moving forward and on. She would do them all proud.

As she opened her eyes, one spell came to Merrin's mind right away, one that felt right.

The reanimation spell. She felt it come fast and easy into her mind. She turned to Qeris's still form and concentrated.

Merrin saw Qeris's broken body jerk itself back to life, and Merrin watched the Inquisitor falter at the sight.

Two to one. Merrin liked those odds.

"Your move, Cal," she whispered, as she and her corpse rushed at the Inquisitor head-on.

Cal knew Merrin was up to something intense behind him as he raced across the room, Shroud in hand, and tried not to worry that he had just condemned her to death at the hands of the Fifth Brother. *Together,* he reminded himself. He slid to a halt right next to Irei, still hunched over Fret's body, and grabbed her by the shoulder, pulling her back. Her eyes looked wrecked.

"I can't help her, Cal, I don't know how—"

There was no time. They were all dead if she couldn't help.

"Irei, I need you to focus for a moment." He shoved the Shroud into her hands. "Can you make this small explosive into a big explosive?"

"What?" Irei was having trouble wrapping her mind around Cal's panicked ask.

"Big bomb. Can you do that?"

Cal watched the gears click into place behind Irei's eyes as she glanced at the Shroud, then him. "Yes. Give it to me."

She was tearing pieces off it before it was entirely out of Cal's hands.

"Is that going to blow the entire room up?" he asked.

Irei ignored the question, "Beedee, I need one of those stimpacks," she said, calling to the droid.

BD-1 hopped over from where he had been checking on Fret and popped a stim into Irei's hand.

"Thanks, Beedee. You see Qeris's blaster over there? Could you grab it for me?"

Before Cal could repeat his question, BD let out a delighted trill and dashed over to the tiny blaster and pushed it within Irei's reach with a few pulses from his thruster. The small droid then moved closer to watch the Nikto work, beeping and warbling with interest. Cal was always impressed at how joyous BD-1 could be, even in the middle of danger.

"Irei, did you hear me?" Cal repeated. At any other time Cal would be asking Irei a dozen questions about her tinkering and tweaking, but they didn't have time for that. Behind him, he heard Merrin and the Inquisitor trading barbs as they clashed again and again. He also heard another sound, a strange almost wet thud followed by the Inquisitor's renewed promise to end Merrin. He was about to turn around when Irei finally replied.

"You said you wanted a big bomb, right?"

"Well, yes, but . . ."

"Just give me as much time as you can. And when the time comes, direct the blast with the Force, or something. Or we *might* all blow up."

Cal shook his head. "Right. So just winging it, then."

"Fret told me that was what you were all best at!" Irei shouted after him, as Cal rushed back off toward Merrin and the Inquisitor, BD-1 back in his favored position on Cal's shoulders. She wasn't exactly wrong.

"Sure you wouldn't be safer back there with Irei and Fret, buddy? This is going to be dangerous," he asked the droid as they crossed the room. He'd barely asked the question before BD-1 replied with a series of short deep trills in a tone the droid only used when he really wanted Cal to pay attention. Cal sometimes referred to it as BD-1's "serious beeps." It was also a message he had shared with Cal enough times that its meaning was crystal clear.

Where you go, I go.

Cal smiled and turned his attention to the battle ahead of him. Merrin was alive; Cal was more relieved than he thought it was possible to feel. But so too was the Fifth Brother. What Cal hadn't expected to see was a third player.

"Where did he come from?" Cal shouted to Merrin, gesturing to Qeris's animated corpse as he launched his lightsaber directly at the Inquisitor's back. The Fifth Brother managed to spin and shove it back toward Cal with the Force, who caught it again with ease.

"Well, he was just laying around. I thought we could use the help," Merrin shouted back.

"Irei needs more time, so let's do what we do best," Cal said, dodging back to avoid a lunge from the Fifth Brother, his red lightsaber nearly skewering Cal.

"Wing it?" asked Merrin, as she directed the reanimated Qeris back toward the Fifth Brother to give Cal a moment to recover.

Cal couldn't help but laugh. "I was going to say work as a team, but yeah . . . let's wing it."

It was Merrin and Cal, one in front of the Fifth Brother and one behind, trading spells and sabers and the Force back and forth while Qeris's reanimated corpse kept the Inquisitor distracted from the side. They moved too fast; they were too in tune with each other, and the Inquisitor didn't have time to catch his breath or catch up. A well-timed stim from BD; a devastating spell from Merrin; a slice with Cal's lightsaber. Once, the Inquisitor's lightsaber managed to catch Cal across the nose—he knew he would have another scar there, later. He knew Merrin wouldn't be without injury, too. But while Irei worked, they managed to keep the Inquisitor off balance; they might not have been winning, but they were holding their own.

But Cal knew it couldn't last. He could feel himself tiring; knew BD was nearly out of stims, and the reanimated Qeris was starting to falter, a clear sign that Merrin's own concentration and magick had started to flag. He couldn't let himself panic, not now, but he was desperately close to wondering if his plan really had been a dud after all when he heard—

"Kestis!" Irei called from across the room. "Ready!"

Cal looked at Merrin, who was already nodding. She would keep the Inquisitor occupied, one last time.

Cal had to hope she could do it.

He knew she could.

Without a moment's hesitation, Cal raced back toward Irei, who had the modified Shroud extended toward him. He scooped it out of her hands, turned back—and realized too late the flaw in their plan. Merrin was too close to the Inquisitor, and with her concentration waning, she couldn't make enough space between them for him to throw the Shroud without risking her life in the process, and he wouldn't, he couldn't—

He remembered Merrin's face.

Promise me.

He looked down at the Shroud, took a deep breath, and used the Force to levitate the device above his hands.

And he threw it, guiding and pushing it with the Force, aiming directly at the Inquisitor, with all his might.

At the last moment, Cal watched as the Inquisitor tore his attention away from Merrin and spun his lightsaber to deflect the object hurtling toward him. Then there was a great booming sound that caused Cal's ears to pop, and then the whole room came crumbling down around him.

CHAPTER 19

Cal didn't expect his eyes to open again at all, frankly.

So when they did, he wasn't sure what he would see.

The explosion had shaken the entire building, and he was still injured from the fight. He knew he had to open his eyes to see what was waiting for him on the other side of the rubble that surrounded him.

But he just . . . didn't want to.

The first thing he heard was the crackle of a radio; a comms system active, though his wasn't. He could hear Cere's voice coming through at a yell: "Come in, ground team, do you copy? Do you copy?"

He groaned in response, hoping that, whoever's comms those were, they would pick it up, and Cere would understand.

Then Cal felt several rapid taps on his shoulder.

"Yeah, buddy, I'm still here. You okay?"

BD-1 warbled in the affirmative.

Gathering his strength, he cracked one eye open, bleary, then the other; he was still on Qeris's sky room floor. Haxion Brood littered the ground, and Cal remembered Merrin's single-handed attempt to anni-

hilate the Brood from existence as they stepped from the elevator, one
by one—

And then it all came rushing back to Cal in a flash: the Inquisitor, his
arm, Fret—Merrin.

Cal struggled to push himself up with his one good arm, and the first
thing he saw was Irei, her leathery body laid out next to him, still breathing. "Cal?" she asked softly, her voice sounding burned to a crisp.

Under Irei lay Fret—poor Fret, hit by Qeris's blaster, down from the
start; Fret, whom Irei had tried to save, had protected from everything
in that room to the last, using her own body as a shield just as Cal had
thrown the Shroud.

When you care about someone, you have to accept that they would
lay their own life down for yours as soon as you would for theirs.

Cal shifted, desperate, wrenching himself to the other side, looking
out across the room, ignoring the scream in his arm when he did so—
and breathed a sigh of relief.

Merrin. She was still there, still in one piece. And there was no sign
of the Inquisitor.

Good.

Cal couldn't tell if Merrin was breathing. He didn't know if he could
stand to know.

Ding!

Cal closed his eyes for a second in defeat; he truly didn't know if he
had it in him to defeat even one more Brood hunter coming up the elevator.

This day—it had taken everything out of him. He had nothing left.

If some droid called T1L-D4 wanted to punch him in the throat, he
was going to have to let it.

But when the elevator doors slid open, it wasn't the Haxion Brood
waiting to throat-punch him—it was Cere and Greez, in all their glory,
rushing their way into the room to care for the rest of their family.

"What the hell happened to you guys?" Greez slid to his knees next
to Cal, touching him gently on the arm. "You tryin' to end up like me?
I know I'm a fashion plate, but c'mon, kid—"

"Greez—" Cal tried to cut him off, but he was on a roll.

"You shoulda seen me up there." Greez continued his ramble, helping Cal to an upright position while Irei sat up, too. "We were fightin' off Brood ships left and right, crashin' 'em into each other, it was wild, and me with only three arms, and—"

"Merrin," Cal rasped out. "You have to check on Merrin."

And that's when Cere noticed Merrin and rushed to her collapsed form.

"Merrin, wake up," Cere said as she knelt down next to her friend. "I know you're in there. You must be in there. Please," she whispered. "Wake up."

Merrin didn't move. Cal looked away.

"Ugh," came a voice from Cal's other side. "Somebody kill that guy?"

Cal turned as fast as he could with Greez for leverage—and there, sitting up from under Irei, was Fret, gingerly pushing herself up onto an elbow while she rubbed her chest with her other hand.

"Oh, thank the skies," breathed Irei, swooping down to embrace Fret in the strongest hug Cal had ever seen.

Fret huffed a laugh, pushing the other woman off her. "Careful, ouch, it's tender," she said, opening the front flap of her leather jacket.

And there, under it, just the way they'd hoped it would work, was the armor that they had fashioned from the scrap Greez had stolen from the Haxion Brood base, way back from before all this had started—from the planetoid where they'd found Fret in the first place.

It had been a worthwhile pickup after all. It had saved her life.

Yet another thing he'd have to tell Greez he was right about. Just as soon as he was feeling better.

"Told ya so." Greez nudged Cal in the side with his elbow. Greez always did love a good *I told you so.*

Fret looked around with a frown. "Where's—?"

She spotted Merrin on the ground, still unmoving, and, without speaking, Irei helped Fret shift herself over across the room to Merrin, just as Greez helped Cal pick his way there through the bodies, too.

Fret knelt down next to Merrin as Cal looked down on her from above, upside down over Merrin's face. Fret used one of her hands to stroke her cheek, her hair, to trace her lips. Cal felt as though he was intruding on something, but he also couldn't look away; he needed to know, had to know if Merrin was still in there, if Fret could pull her out.

"Hey, weirdo," Fret whispered. "It's not fair if the rest of us get to stay. So you better get back here."

She leaned forward, and she pressed a soft kiss to Merrin's forehead. "That's an order."

And Merrin gasped a breath.

Cal didn't realize he'd been holding his own until it happened. It was the same moment he felt the tears on his cheeks.

She had made it.

She had done it.

His wonderful, unnerving, terrifying Nightsister; his unlikeliest of allies. His Merrin.

Cal smiled, the relief so strong through his body he didn't know where to put it all, and he threw himself forward onto Merrin in the strongest hug he could manage. Her body was so warm and so very *alive*.

Then everyone else crowded around Merrin at the same time, checking her vitals, making sure she was okay, finding injuries, asking her questions, and it took Cere pushing them all back to get them to give her some air, some space. Merrin said that the last she'd seen the Inquisitor, he'd been burned up and blasted through a tower window. She said she was going to be okay. And she suggested they all get back to the *Mantis* to regroup, together.

It was the best idea Cal had ever heard.

"What are you going to do?" Merrin reached out to try to touch Fret's wound, but Fret batted her hand out of the way. They were seated on the cot in the engine room again, one of their favorite spots to be on the ship, the buzz of the hyperdrive nearly drowning out their conversation as they sat with their legs crossed, knees touching, patching each other up. Irei sat on the floor at their feet, repairing Fret's leather jacket. Even as friends, they were still comfortably touchy with each other, and Merrin thought that was very nice, if unusual.

"Hey, this is *my* time to take care of *you*," Fret chastised, continuing to dab at one of Merrin's wounds with bacta.

"I'm not very good at that," Merrin admitted. "Letting myself be taken care of."

Fret snorted. "You don't say."

Merrin swatted her on the arm; Fret stuck her tongue out.

Merrin didn't want to ask, but she had to.

"When are you leaving? Where are you going?" Merrin hardly managed to get it out.

Fret paused. She set the bacta and cloth on the floor next to the cot, and Irei shuffled them over next to her. "Greez is going to drop us back on Zimara," Fret answered. "Cere says the tracker on Irei the Inquisitor used to find us is taken care of now, but Greez wants to make a few pit stops through hyperspace to throw anyone who happens to be following us off our trail. We're going to—" She sighed; paused.

"We'll have to go into hiding, for a while," Irei picked up from where Fret left off. "For a long while. But we can figure it out from there. I have the technical know-how; Fret has a network. Cere's making sure our communications are untraceable and monitoring Imperial channels— they think we all died in that explosion. We're going to be okay."

Merrin nodded, trying her best to keep the emotion out of her eyes and knowing that she was failing. "It's not going to be the same on the *Mantis*."

"We have an offer for you," said Irei. "And I want you to know it comes from both of us, most sincerely." She placed her hands on the floor and stood up, gathering up the jacket and her supplies. "You should talk about it with Fret, but I want you to know, with all my heart, it comes from us both."

Merrin nodded, looking up at Irei with affection and respect. "Thank you."

Once Irei had left the engine room, shutting the door behind her, Merrin looked at Fret and waited.

"Did you . . ." Fret stopped. "And are you still happy? On the *Mantis*?"

"Happy is hard for me to quantify," said Merrin, not wanting to give her a real answer; not knowing if she could. "But . . . Yes, I think I am."

Fret inhaled and looked at her, considering.

"You could . . ." Fret paused, before looking down into Merrin's eyes. "You could come with us. There's a place for you, with us. If you want it."

Merrin smiled; she was genuinely touched by the offer, and for a minute—just for a second—she was almost tempted to take it. "Irei would really be okay with that?"

Fret sighed and looked away, down at her lap. "Irei and I . . ." She shook her head; Merrin knew the way Fret looked when she was trying to collect her thoughts and not misspeak. "Irei came into my life when I needed her to; she showed me that I could be more than what the Empire wanted me to be, and that I could get myself out of that—that half-life, that dreadful life—if I just had the strength. And I got her out of that prison, with your help. We were there for each other when we were supposed to be. But . . ."

She sighed. "I'll always love Irei," Fret said, looking back at Merrin. "She'll always love me. But . . . not like that. Not anymore."

Merrin should have been more shocked to hear that than she was, but she had seen it in the way they interacted; in the way that it was different from what she would have expected. "What happened?"

Fret exhaled heavily. "A lot of things. A lot of life. I'm a different person than I was back then. You know how it is. But also . . ."

Merrin raised an eyebrow at Fret's dramatic pause. "Also . . . ?"

Fret leaned forward conspiratorially. "I met this girl."

And they both laughed.

But Merrin's home was here, on the *Mantis*. It always had been, since the day she'd left Dathomir. Things had become tenuous for a moment, difficult. But Merrin wanted to see them through. Needed to.

"I can't," Merrin said, after a pause. "I don't know my purpose, not yet. But I know I do not want to run, to start over, to create a new identity. You helped me to see that vengeance cannot last forever, and that bleeding out my anger—being able to be true and honest about it—was the way to come back to myself. And I will always be grateful for that, and for you. But I'm not ready to give up what I have here. I need to figure out who I am. And I can't do that pretending to be someone else."

She smiled. "So I'm staying. I *want* to stay."

"What *are* you gonna do?" Fret asked, holding Merrin's hand gently in her own, staring down at it.

Merrin shrugged, looking at the way Fret's fingers dwarfed her own. "I don't know," Merrin admitted. "But I know I'm done hiding."

Fret nodded. "I understand. And I'm proud of you. I'm so, so proud of you."

Merrin leaned forward, bumping her shoulder against Fret's. "I'm proud of you, too."

"I hope to see you again someday."

"I hope so, too."

"You better bring that dressy outfit I like."

Merrin laughed; the two of them went back to their work.

"We're going to have to talk about it eventually," said Cal, sitting next to Cere as they waited for Merrin, Fret, and Irei to emerge from below with the women's things. BD and the bogling were chasing each other around the holotable, playing some new game they'd invented that only BD understood the rules to, but they both enjoyed. Greez puttered around the common areas, watering his plants. They'd landed back on Zimara, and they would be seeing Fret and Irei off before the morning. It wasn't safe to stay much longer.

Whenever "morning" meant on a moon with no sunrise and no sunset.

"Yeah," said Greez. "You wanna talk about it now?"

"A little," Cal admitted with a shrug. It had been on his mind since they left Murkhana, of course, like he assumed it had been on everyone else's. "For years, we've been chasing all these things that we keep assuming are going to be the magic solution that brings it all down. Gambling on it. The thing that defeats the Empire, that safeguards the Jedi wisdom, whatever we're trying to do: the holocron, defeating the Brood, even finding the Shroud, I mean, Irei. But . . . that's just not it. That's not it at all."

"It's not," agreed Cere, watching BD chase the bogling. "It's getting up every day, and making the choice to survive. And it's about surrounding yourself with people who are going to help you do that."

"And sometimes people who chop off your arm," Greez added somberly. Cere rolled her eyes dramatically with a snort.

Cal appreciated that they could joke about it. But as someone who had been through a lot of trauma and a lot of pain in his life, he knew the other shoe would be dropping for Greez sometime very soon. There was only so much time you could spend masking your hurt with humor.

And he was worried about that day.

He worried about that day as much as he worried about the day Cere realized she wanted to put down roots for the Jedi more than she wanted to tear down the Empire, and as much as he worried that Merrin would realize, now that she was done looking backward, that her destiny waited for her to find it out in the wild reaches of space, and not on the *Mantis*.

But there were only so many things Cal could worry about at once.

"Do you think they're gonna be okay?" Greez asked, and Cal knew he was referring to Fret and Irei, because Greez couldn't be referring to the crew.

Only one of those questions had a real answer.

"I do," said Cere, with sincere confidence. "They're going to be two more seeds that grow the revolution, the fight against the Empire. And we're going to need all the help we can get."

"We'll be there for you when you need us," said Irei, claws clattering her way into the galley, laden down with supplies they'd collected over the past few days after Hosnian Prime.

Merrin and Fret followed her out of the crew quarters, hands clasped, holding more packs on their hips. "We'll be able to contact you? If we need to?" Fret asked.

"You better believe it," said Greez. "Irei rigged up a whole thing connected to the holotable. You better call; Cere hasn't shut up about how excited she is to see something that's not planets on that table for once. Made her whole year."

"He's right about that," Cere agreed, taking some of the supplies from Fret, her chest wound still fresh enough that she needed assistance with these things. "It does get a little repetitive."

"You know," said Irei, "I already owe you all so much; but for the Shroud, too. It actually took building a fake one for me to realize that a real one just isn't possible. The technology isn't there yet."

"Too smart for your own good," Fret said, bumping into her with her hip. "Gotta wait for the tech to catch up to *you*."

Irei laughed; Cal thought it was a particularly musical sound.

They made the rounds, saying their goodbyes; Cal was thrilled to feel how small and fragile it felt to be in Irei's tall embrace, her scaly skin delightful under his fingers. And he was even more surprised by how tender he felt about Fret when she brought him into a big, strong hug, slapping him on the back a few times for good measure. The happiness and the fire she brought to Merrin. Cal actually thought . . . he might genuinely have grown to like Fret, after all.

Cal moved to pull back, but Fret held fast. She brought her mouth to his ear, and, quiet enough that no one else aboard could hear, she said:

"I know she can take care of herself, but—."

Cal pulled back; he looked Fret straight in the eyes, and clasped his hands onto her shoulders.

He nodded. He knew what she was trying to say, and there was nothing he took more seriously in the galaxy than that.

Fret clapped him on the shoulders back, and then she was gone, Merrin absconding into the back of the galley for a moment; for their last moment.

As Merrin and Fret shared one last tearful goodbye out of sight, Irei leaned down to give BD-1 one last pat on the head, and she left a few things for the crew, things they'd picked up at resupply stops as gifts, or that they'd made in their time aboard: Fret's favorite kind of caf; Irei's schematics for a bunch of ship repairs and upgrades; a new plant for Greez's terrariums; a little toy for the bogling; and a brilliant new blaster for Cere that she'd souped up to her own specifications.

She really was good at what she did.

Merrin walked back toward the ramp, this time a few steps behind Fret. She stopped next to Cal, and he felt Merrin reach out to take his hand.

Cal and the crew watched Fret and Irei walk off onto the sunless side of the moon.

"We're never going to see them again," Merrin said.

"Probably not," agreed Cal. "But you stayed."

"I did." Merrin nodded. "The elders always said foolishness runs in my family."

She was looking at him sidelong, with the kind of wry smirk she reserved just for moments like this. And Cal knew what she meant, deep down, even if she was no good at saying it.

He always did.

He squeezed her hand; she squeezed back.

They were going to be okay. For now, they were going to be okay.

And all they could ever do is be okay for now. One day at a time.

Piece by piece.

Cal Kestis and the crew of the *Mantis* will return in
Star Wars Jedi: Survivor.

ACKNOWLEDGMENTS

Creating a book takes a village, and never is that more true than during the creation of a book with this many moving pieces, depending on the hard work of just as many people. This was a big one, and I'm so, so happy we made it.

The biggest and brightest thank-you, as ever, goes to my amazing agent, Maria Vicente. We've come up together since the start, and it's been a wild and incredible adventure these last nine (Nine! What happened!) years. I'm so glad I get to call you my friend and DnD squad-mate, too. Thanks for always knowing what's going on (in both my work life and in DnD).

"Thank you" does not seem to be a large or broad enough sentiment for what I need to express to my editor at Random House Worlds, Tom Hoeler. Tom was the person who saw this book coming and sought me out for it, knowing how I felt about the characters, and I'm so grateful. But beyond that, Tom was endlessly patient, kind, incisive, clever, and collaborative, the best co-conspirator a writer could ask for. This book simply would not exist in any way if not for his dedication and support, and I am going to be sending him flowers for a long time about it. I'm going to miss our 2:00 A.M. editing chats, sincerely. (It's okay if you won't, Tom. I understand.) *[editor's note: I will miss them.]*

Thank you to the entire team at Random House Worlds, including Elizabeth Schaefer, Lydia Estrada, Gabriella Muñoz, Lauren Ealy, Ashleigh Heaton, Eliana Seochand, Nancy Delia, and Erich Schoeneweiss. Your work is so appreciated and makes this book so much better. Thanks also to Anthrox Studios for this incredible cover; I can't believe the same people who draw my favorite Apex Legends drew my book cover. Still geeking out about it.

There would be no Cal, Merrin, Cere, BD-1, or Greez without the brilliant Jedi team at Respawn Entertainment. I'm so grateful to have gotten to play with their characters and appreciate all of the trust and direction the team gave me along the way.

Thank you especially to Blair Brown, who acted as my in-house support system while I wrote this book (both literally and figuratively). Our soup sessions were saviors, and you'll always be my family. Especially big thanks to our little dog Eevee, who looks like a sad Porg and absolutely rules.

Thank you to Michael Siglain, Jennifer Heddle, Jennifer Pooley, the wonderful Lucasfilm Games team, and the amazing Story Group at Lucasfilm, especially Kelsey Sharpe, who were stellar in their shepherding of this project. I love to play in this sandbox so much, and it will never stop feeling surreal that I get to. Thank you for letting me.

Huge thanks to just every synthwave artist and the creators of the Lo-Fi *Star Wars* playlists on Spotify. Also shout-out to every editor I blew off during the very intense writing and editing of this book; thank you for not firing me. I promise I'm going to send that thing in soon. For sure.

I am one of the lucky people in this world who have amazing, supportive, loving parents, who never fail to show up for me in every way, and I am so grateful for them. My parents saw *A New Hope* over twenty times in theaters in the 1970s and did not hesitate to pass that fanaticism down to me. Thanks for pulling me out of school in the sixth grade to see *The Phantom Menace* in the middle of the day and cementing my lifelong *Star Wars* fandom. Mom and Dad, you held my hand through every draft, through all the emotions and the difficulties, and I really don't have words for how appreciative I am. Love you.

I think I probably would have simply perished due to overwhelming emotion and stress and *everything* during the writing of this book were it not for Adrienne Chu and Matthew Gilbert (and their sweet kitties, Bucky and Fia). Thank you for listening to all of my voice notes and playing videogames in silence next to me for hours at a time. You're my family, too, and I'm so glad we found one another.

And, perhaps most important of all, my endless gratitude to Shannon Watters, because of whom I almost didn't finish this book; but without whom, I couldn't have. You gave me poetry and planets while I wrote, and I'll never forget it.

ABOUT THE AUTHOR

SAM MAGGS is a bestselling writer of books, comics, and videogames, including *Marvel Action: Captain Marvel*, *The Unstoppable Wasp: Built on Hope*, *Tell No Tales*, and Marvel's *Spider-Man*. You can usually find her as host at comic conventions and for geeky networks like the Nerdist. A Canadian in Los Angeles, she misses Coffee Crisp and bagged milk.

sammaggs.com
Facebook.com/SamMaggsSays
Twitter: @SamMaggs
Instagram: @sammaggs

ABOUT THE TYPE

This book was set in Minion, a 1990 Adobe Originals typeface by Robert Slimbach (b. 1956). Minion is inspired by classical, old-style typefaces of the late Renaissance, a period of elegant, beautiful, and highly readable type designs. Created primarily for text setting, Minion combines the aesthetic and functional qualities that make text type highly readable with the versatility of digital technology.

STAR WARS
THE HIGH REPUBLIC

Centuries before the Skywalker saga,
a new adventure begins…

Now a
New York Times
Bestselling
Series!

Books, Comics, Ebooks, and Audiobooks Available Now!

Visit StarWars.com/TheHighRepublic for the latest news